"In **ALIENS!**, Dann and Dozois have assembled a top-notch lineup, notable for the wide variety exhibited in their choices. Gaughan's illustrations add greatly to the overall effect. For any reader of the science-fiction field this book is a treat!"

—F. M. Busby, author of *The Demu Trilogy*

"The best collection on this subject by far. Dann and Dozois catch the breadth and depth of the alien theme in SF. The stories are telling and mind-expanding. A superior anthology."

—Gregory Benford, author of *In the Ocean of Night*

ALIENS!

Edited by Gardner R. Dozois
and Jack M. Dann

PUBLISHED BY POCKET BOOKS NEW YORK

Another *Original* publication of POCKET BOOKS

POCKET BOOKS, a Simon & Schuster division of
GULF & WESTERN CORPORATION
1230 Avenue of the Americas, New York, N.Y. 10020

ISBN: 0-671-83155-0

First Pocket Books printing April, 1980

10 9 8 7 6 5 4 3 2 1

POCKET and colophon are trademarks of Simon & Schuster.

Printed in the U.S.A.

Acknowledgments

"Assimilating Our Culture" copyright © 1977 by *Cosmos*. Reprinted by permission of Larry Niven and Robert P. Mills, Ltd. Literary Agency.

"Grammar Lesson" copyright © 1977 by *Cosmos*. Reprinted by permission of Larry Niven and Robert P. Mills, Ltd. Literary Agency.

"The Subject Is Closed" copyright © 1977 by *Cosmos*. Reprinted by permission of Larry Niven and Robert P. Mills, Ltd. Literary Agency.

"The Schumann Computer" copyright © 1979 by *Destinies*. Reprinted by permission of Larry Niven and Robert P. Mills, Ltd. Literary Agency.

"We Purchased People" copyright © by Frederik Pohl. Reprinted by permission of Frederik Pohl.

"Guesting Time" copyright © 1965, 1970 by R. A. Lafferty. Reprinted by permission of R. A. Lafferty and Virginia Kidd.

"And I Awoke and Found Me Here on the Cold Hill's Side" copyright © 1972, 1978 by James Tiptree, Jr. Reprinted by permission of James Tiptree, Jr. and Robert P. Mills, Ltd. Literary Agency.

"Angel's Egg" copyright © 1951 by World Editions Inc. Reprinted by permission of Edgar Pangborn and Robert P. Mills, Ltd. Literary Agency.

"Oh, To Be A Blobel!" reprinted by permission of Philip K. Dick and Scott Meredith Literary Agency, Inc.

"Be Merry" copyright © 1966 by Galaxy Publishing Company. Reprinted by permission of Algis Budrys.

"Pattern" reprinted by permission of Fredric Brown and Scott Meredith Literary Agency, Inc.

"An Honorable Death" reprinted by permission of Gordon R. Dickson.

"The Reality Trip" copyright © 1970 by Universal Publishing & Distributing Corp. Reprinted by permission of Robert Silverberg.

"Rule Golden" reprinted by permission of Damon Knight.

v

Contents

Foreword

People have always been fascinated by the Alien: the Stranger, the remorseless and unknowable Other whose motivations, thoughts, and actions we can never fully understand.

For uncountable centuries, the Other was supernatural—gods, ghosts, demons, elves, vampires, night-gangers, the dark and inscrutable face of the Other dimly visible behind whatever mask it wore. At best, the Other was one of the people who lived around the curve of the river or across the sea, the people who lived over the hill and far away—the people who walked around with their heads on upside down, or who painted themselves blue, or who paved their streets with gold.

Today, science and rationalism have combined to shrink the globe and dwindle Faerie—in a world filled with McDonald's and superhighways, there is no place left for the Other now to dwell: except for deep space, on other worlds. As the twentieth century advances, the Other has increasingly become the Alien, the creature from another world, taking over the psychological/archetypical/literary function once served by pixie, gnome, and grue—or, for that matter, by the natives in Kipling's Indian stories (Kipling "used" British India, in a literary sense, in almost exactly the same way later writers would "use" planets of a distant star, and their outré inhabitants) or the lost races of Merritt and Haggard.

There is more interest in the Alien today than ever before, as indicated by the periodic outbreaks of UFO hysteria—so intense and perfervid as to be almost religious—and by the enormous success of movies like *Star Wars* and *Close Encounters of the Third Kind*, to say nothing of the cult status of *Star Trek*. And yet, in spite of all the ink spilled and all the film footage shot during the last thirty years, the general public has barely scratched the surface when it comes to considering the actual consequences, for good and evil, of contact with alien civilizations.

But science-fiction writers have been considering that topic in depth now for close to a hundred years, ever since H. G. Wells wrote *War of the Worlds*—and long before the first "flying saucer" was sighted in 1947.

There have been literally thousands of SF stories dealing with human contact with alien beings, and over the years SF writers have developed a depth of sophistication and explored a range of possibilities far beyond anything yet seen on the screen, dreamed up imaginative and highly ingenious scenarios that far transcend the limited either/or dualism (*either* the aliens are benevolent sky-saints who will solve all our problems for us, *or* they are malevolent, in which case they eat us) that still hampers the minds of many UFO enthusiasts.

The stories in this book deal with a far greater range of options than that, exploring many facets of alien encounter, proving that humans and aliens can interact with one another over a wide spectrum beyond what we see in the movies. Sometimes they are benevolent space brothers, sometimes sinister monsters, sometimes they love us, or collect us, or keep us as pets, or teach us, or learn from us; sometimes they don't care about us at all—sometimes they don't even notice us, brushing us aside like insects. Sometimes they are greeted peacefully, sometimes with gunfire and atomic missiles. Sometimes the aliens are already here, among us, unseen—and perhaps they have always been here. Sometimes alien and human can interact, merge, form partnerships and strike bargains, dicker, learn to love each other, perhaps even have sex with each other; sometimes contact only serves to demonstrate to either side how ineffably different and remote, how untouchable, how unfathomable, is the mind of the other. The contact can be parasitic, benign, destructive, symbiotic, absurd, solemn, uproariously funny, irredeemably sad; it can instruct and uplift us or cast us disastrously down, but it must always affect us, change us, alter our perceptions of ourselves and the universe.

Of all literary forms, SF is perhaps the best suited to give us this kind of knowledge and perspective, to let us know what an encounter with otherness would be like; and just as a distorting funhouse mirror can sometimes present the clearest picture of a man, so it may be that we see ourselves most plain and most instructively when we look into the face of the Alien.

This anthology, we hope, provides such a mirror.

ALIENS!

Four Vignettes

BY LARRY NIVEN

*One of the most popular scenes in the enormously success-
ful movie* Star Wars *took place, like the series of inter-
connected Larry Niven vignettes that follow, in a spacer
bar—a dim-lit, rundown Rick's Café of some far-future
Casablanca where dozens of bizarre creatures from as
many worlds gather to drink, intrigue, argue, philosophize,
hunt for work on the big interstellar liners, and, occasionally, hunt each other as well. The popularity of the* Star
Wars *bar scene is a good indication of the way the attitude
of the general public toward aliens has changed in recent
years. Before this, when a movie character met an alien,
either he shot the alien or the alien ate him; the closest to
friendly contact they'd ever come was when the alien would
shanghai the movie character and give him an ultimatum
to deliver to the UN—at least they were talking to each
other. Now it seems that the movie audience is finally
willing to accept the option of everyone letting his hair—
or feathers or scales or tendrils—down and just having a
drink with his fellows instead, certainly a less strenuous
alternative.*

*Within SF, of course, spacer bars are nothing new—
Leigh Brackett's and C. L. Moore's were shadowy places
frequented by sinister Venusian princesses and Byronic
Martian swordsmen; the incomparable Jack Vance created
dozens of them, from unbelievably sumptuous pleasure
palaces to the bleak Smade's Tavern, where you mind
your own business if you don't want to get pitched into
the sea; and in* Babel-17 *and* Nova *Samuel R. Delany described some very hip ones that catered to customers so
full of flash and freakiness that they might even have*

1

trouble getting into Studio 54. There is a special ambiance, however, to Larry Niven's spacer bar, the Draco Tavern— almost alone among his peers, he goes beyond the clash and clamor, the assassinations and assignations, to relate what all those strange alien creatures (humans included) actually talk about when they belly (or whatever) up to the bar. And the implications of that talk—the different perspectives engendered, the unexpected moral dilemmas explored, the sudden insights into what had seemed totally outré and bizarre, the ordinary things and attitudes seen suddenly through alien eyes—are fascinating.

Larry Niven is no stranger to the task of showing his readers the view through alien eyes. His Known Space series is notable for the lush variety of alien races who in- habit it—the cowardly Puppeteers, the fiercely intractable Kzinti, the handless, telepathic Grogs—and for the com- plex interactions between them. His novel Ringworld—part of the Known Space series, describing the discovery of an immense, ring-shaped artificial world, perhaps SF's ultimate alien artifact—won him both the Nebula and the Hugo awards; he has subsequently gone on to win four more Hugo Awards. His other books include Protector, A World Out of Time, Tales of Known Space, World of Ptavvs, Neutron Star, A Gift from Earth, and All the Myriad Ways. His latest books are Convergent Series, a collection, and Ringworld Engineers, the sequel to Ringworld.

1

Assimilating Our Culture, That's What They're Doing

I was putting glasses in the dishwasher when some chirps walked in with three glig in tow. You didn't see many glig in the Draco Tavern. They were gray and compact beings, proportioned like a human linebacker, much shorter than the chirpsithtra. They wore furs against Earth's cold, fur patterned in three tones of green, quite pretty.

It was the first time I'd seen the Silent Stranger react to anything.

He was sitting alone at the bar, as usual. He was forty or so, burly and fit, with thick black hair on his head and his arms. He'd been coming in once or twice a week for at least a year. He never talked to anyone, except me, and then only to order; he'd drink alone, and leave at the end of the night in a precarious rolling walk. Normal enough for the average bar, but not for the Draco.

I have to keep facilities for a score of aliens. Liquors for humans, sparkers for chirps, flavored absolute alcohol for

3

thtopar, sponge cake soaked in cyanide solution—and I keep a damn close watch on that—lumps of what I've been calling green kryptonite, and there's never been a roseyfin in here to call for it. My customers don't tend to be loud, but the sound of half a dozen species in conversation is beyond imagination, doubled or tripled because they're all using translating widgets. I need some pretty esoteric sound-proofing.

All of which makes the Draco expensive to run. I charge twenty bucks a drink, ten for sparkers, and so forth. Why would anyone come in here to drink in privacy? I'd wondered about the Silent Stranger.

Then three glig came in, and the Silent Stranger turned his chair away from the bar, but not before I saw his face.

Gail was already on her way to the big table where the glig and the chirps were taking seats, so that was okay. I left the dishwasher half filled. I leaned across the bar and spoke close to the Silent Stranger's ear.

"It's almost surprising how few fights we get in here."

He didn't seem to know I was there.

I said, "I've only seen six in thirty-two years. Even then, nobody got badly hurt. Except once. Some nut, human, tried to shoot a chirp, and a thtopar had to crack his skull. Of course the thtopar didn't know how hard to hit him. I sometimes wish I'd gotten there faster."

He turned just enough to look me in the eye. I said, "I saw your face. I don't know what you've got against the glig, but if you think you're ready to kill them, I think I'm ready to stop you. Have a drink on the house instead."

He said, "The correct name is gligstith(click)optok."

"That's pretty good. I never get the click right."

"It should be good. I was on the first embassy ship to Gligstith(click)tcharf." Bitterly, "There won't be any fight. I can't even punch a glig in the face without making the evening news. It'd all come out."

Gail came back with orders: sparkers for the chirps, and the gligs wanted bull shots, consommé and vodka, with no ice and no flavorings. They were sitting in the high chairs that bring a human face to the level of a chirp's, and their strange hands were waving wildly. I filled the orders with half an eye on the Stranger, who watched me with a brooding look, and I got back to him as soon as I could.

He asked, "Ever wonder why there wasn't any second embassy to Gligstith(click)tcharf?"

"Not especially."

"Why not?"

I shrugged. For two million years there wasn't anything in the universe but us and the gods. Then came the chirps. Then *bang*, a dozen others, and news of thousands more. We're learning so much from the chirps themselves, and of course there's culture shock.

He said, "You know what we brought back. The gligs sold us some advanced medical and agricultural techniques, including templates for the equipment. The chirps couldn't have done that for us. They aren't DNA-based. Why didn't we go back for more?"

"You tell me."

He seemed to brace himself. "I will, then. You serve them in here, you should know about them. Build yourself a drink, on me."

I built two scotch-and-sodas. I asked, "Did you say *sold?* What did we pay them? That didn't make the news."

"It better not. Hell, where do I start? . . . The first thing they did when we landed, they gave us a full medical checkup. Very professional. Blood samples, throat scrapings, little nicks in our ears, deep-radar for our innards. We didn't object. Why should we? The gligs are DNA-based. We could have been carrying bacteria that could live off them.

"Then we did the tourist bit. I was having the time of my life! I'd never been farther than the Moon. To be in an alien star system, exploring their cities, oh, man! We were all having a ball. We made speeches. We asked about other races. The chirps may claim to own the galaxy, but they don't know everything. There are places they can't go except in special suits, because they grew up around red dwarf stars."

"I know."

"The glig sun is hotter than Sol. We did most of our traveling at night. We went through museums, with cameras following us. Public conferences. We recorded the one on art forms; maybe you saw it."

"Yeah."

"Months of that. Then they wanted us to record a permission for reproduction rights. For that they would pay us a royalty, and sell us certain things on credit against the royalties." He gulped hard at his drink. "You've seen all of that. The medical deep-radar that does what an X-ray does without giving you cancer, and the cloning techniques to grow organ transplants, and the cornucopia plant, and all the rest. And of course we were all for giving them their permission right away.

"Except, do you remember Bill Hersey? He was a reporter and a novelist before he joined the expedition. He wanted details. Exactly what rights did the glig want? Would they be selling permissions to other species? Were there groups like libraries or institutes for the blind that got them free? And they told us. They didn't have anything to hide."

His eyes went to the glig, and mine followed his. They looked ready for another round. The most human thing about the glig was their hands, and their hands were disconcerting. Their palms were very short and their fingers were long, with an extra joint. As if a torturer had cut a human palm between the finger bones, almost to the wrist. Those hands grabbed the attention . . . but tonight I could see nothing but the wide mouths and the shark's array of teeth. Maybe I'd already guessed.

"Clones," said the Silent Stranger. "They took clones from our tissue samples. The glig grow clones from almost a hundred DNA-based life forms. They wanted us for their dinner tables, not to mention their classes in exobiology. You know, they couldn't see why we were so upset."

"I don't see why you signed."

"Well, they weren't growing actual human beings. They wanted to grow livers and muscle tissue and marrow without the bones . . . you know, meat. Even a f-f-f—" He had the shakes. A long pull at his scotch-and-soda stopped that, and he said, "Even a full suckling roast would be grown headless. But the bottom line was that if we didn't give our permissions, there would be pirate editions, and we wouldn't get any royalties. Anyway, we signed. Bill Hersey hanged himself after we came home."

I couldn't think of anything to say, so I built us two more drinks, strong, on the house. Looking back on it, that was my best answer anyway. We touched glasses and drank deep, and he said, "It's a whole new slant on the War of the Worlds. The man-eating monsters are civilized, they're cordial, they're perfect hosts. Nobody gets slaughtered, and think what they're saving on transportation costs! And ten thousand glig carved me up for dinner tonight. The UN made about half a cent per."

Gail was back. Aliens don't upset her, but she was badly upset. She kept her voice down. "The glig would like to try other kinds of meat broth. I don't know if they're kidding or not. They said they wanted—they wanted—"

"They'll take Campbell's," I told her, "and like it."

2

Grammar Lesson

It was the most casual of remarks. It happened because one of my chirpsithtra customers shifted her chair as I was setting the sparker on her table. When I tried to walk away something tugged at my pants leg.

"The leg of your chair has pinned my pants," I told her in Lottl.

She and her two companions chittered at each other. Chirpsithtra laughter. She moved the chair. I walked away, somewhat miffed, wondering what had made her laugh at me.

She stopped me when next I had occasion to pass her table. "Your pardon for my rudeness. You used intrinsic 'your' and 'my,' instead of extrinsic. As if your pants are part of you and my chair a part of me. I was taken by surprise."

"I've been studying Lottl for almost thirty years," I answered, "but I don't claim I've mastered it yet. After all, it is an alien language. There are peculiar variations even between human languages."

"We have noticed. 'Pravda' means 'official truth.' 'Pueblo' means 'village, considered as a population.' And all of your languages seem to use one possessive for all purposes. My arm, my husband, my mother," she said, using the intrinsic "my" for her arm, the "my" of property for her husband, and the "my" of relationship for her mother.

"I always get those mixed up," I admitted. "Why, for instance, the possessive for your husband? Never mind," I said hastily, before she could get angry. There was some big secret about the chirpsithtra males. You learned not to ask. "I don't see the difference as being that important."

"It was important once," she said. "There is a tale we teach every immature chirpsithtra . . ."

By human standards, and by the chirpsithtra standards of the time, it was a mighty empire. Today the chirpsithtra rule the habitable worlds of every red dwarf star in the galaxy—or so they claim. Then, their empire was a short segment of one curving arm of the galactic whirlpool. But it had never been larger.

The chirpsithtra homeworld had circled a red dwarf sun. Such stars are as numerous as all other stars put together. The chirpsithtra worlds numbered in the tens of thousands, yet they were not enough. The empire expanded outward and inward. Finally—it was inevitable—it met another empire.

"The knowledge that thinking beings come in many shapes, this knowledge was new to us," said my customer. Her face was immobile, built like a voodoo mask scaled down. No hope of reading expression there. But she spoke depreciatingly. "The ilawn were short and broad, with lumpy gray skins. Their hands were clumsy, their noses long and mobile and dexterous. We found them unpleasantly homely. Perhaps they thought the same of us."

So there was war from the start, a war in which six worlds and many fleets of spacecraft died before ever the ilawn and the chirpsithtra tried to talk to each other.

Communication was the work of computer programmers of both species. The diplomats got into it later. The problem was simple and basic.

The ilawn wanted to keep expanding. The chirpsithtra were in the way.

Both species had evolved for red dwarf sunlight. They used worlds of about one terrestrial mass, a little colder, with oxygen atmospheres.

"A war of extermination seemed likely," said the chirpsithtra. She brushed her thumbs along the contacts of the sparker, once and again. Her speech slowed, became more precise. "We made offers, of course. A vacant region to be established between the two empires; each could expand along the opposite border. This would have favored the ilawn, as they were nearer the star-crowded galactic core. They would not agree. When they were sure that we would not vacate *their* worlds . . ." She used the intrinsic possessive, and paused to be sure I'd seen the point. "They broke off communication. They resumed their attacks.

"It became our task to learn more of the ilawn. It was difficult. We could hardly send disguised spies!" Her companions chittered at that. She said, "We learned ilawn physiology from captured warriors. We learned depressing things. The ilawn bred faster than we did; their empire included thrice the volume of ours. Beyond that the prisoners would not give information. We did our best to make them comfortable, in the hope that someday there would be a prisoner exchange. That was how we learned the ilawn secret.

"Rick Schumann, do you know that we evolved on a one-face world?"

"I don't know the term," I said.

"And you have spoken Lottl for thirty years!" Her companions chittered. "But you will appreciate that the worlds we need huddle close to their small, cool suns. Else they would not be warm enough to hold liquid water. So close are they that tidal forces generally stop their rotation, so that they always turn one face to the sun, as your moon faces Earth."

"I'd think that all the water would freeze across the night side. The air too."

"No, there is circulation. Hot winds rise on the day side and blow to the night side, and cool, and sink, and the cold winds blow across the surface back to the day side. On the surface a hurricane blows always toward the noon pole."

"I think I get the picture. You wouldn't need a compass on a one-face world. The wind always points in the same direction."

"Half true. There are local variations. But there are couplet worlds too. Around a red dwarf sun the planetary system tends to cluster close. Often enough, world-sized bodies orbit one another. For tidal reasons they face each other; they do not face the sun. Five percent of habitable worlds are found in couplets."

"The ilawn came from one of those?"

"You are alert. Yes. Our ilawn prisoners were most uncomfortable until we shut their air conditioning almost off. They wanted darkness to sleep, and the same temperatures all the time. The conclusion was clear. We found that the worlds they had attacked in the earlier stages of the war were couplet worlds."

"That seems simple enough."

"One would think so. The couplet worlds are not that desirable to us. We find their weather dull, insipid. There is a way to make the weather more interesting on a couplet world, but we were willing to give them freely.

"But the ilawn fought on. They would not communicate. We could not tolerate their attacks on our ships and on our other worlds." She took another jolt of current. "Ssss . . . We needed a way to bring them to the conference arena."

"What did you do?"

"We began a program of evacuating couplet worlds wherever the ilawn ships came near."

I leaned back in my chair: a high chair, built to bring my face to the height of a chirpsithtra face. "I must be confused. That sounds like total surrender."

"A language problem," she said. "I have said that the planetary system clusters close around a red dwarf star. There are usually asteroids of assorted sizes. Do your scientists know of the results of a cubic mile of asteroid being dropped into a planetary ocean?"

I'd read an article on the subject once. "They think it could cause another ice age."

"Yes. Megatons of water evaporated, falling elsewhere. Storms of a force foreign to your quiet world. Glaciers in unstable configurations, causing more weather. The effects last for a thousand years. We did this to every couplet world we could locate. The ilawn took some two dozen worlds from us, and tried to live on them. Then they took steps to arrange a further conference."

"You were lucky," I said. By the odds, the ilawn should have evolved on the more common one-face worlds. Or should they? The couplets sounded more hospitable to life.

"We were lucky," the chirpsithtra agreed, "that time. We were lucky in our language. Suppose we had used the same word for *my* head, *my* credit cards, *my* sister? Chirpsithtra might have been unable to evacuate their homes, as a human may die defending his home"—she used the intrinsic possessive—"*his* home from a burglar."

Closing time. Half a dozen chirpsithtra wobbled out, drunk on current and looking unstable by reason of their height. The last few humans waved and left. As I moved to lock the door I found myself smiling all across my face.

Now what was I so flippin' happy about?

It took me an hour to figure it out.

I like the chirpsithtra. I trust them. But, considering the power they control, I don't mind finding another reason why they will never want to conquer the Earth.

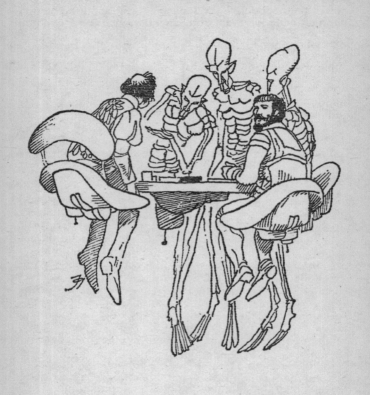

3

The Subject Is Closed

We get astronauts in the Draco Tavern. We get workers from Mount Forel Spaceport, and some administrators, and some newsmen. We get chirpsithtra; I keep sparkers to get them drunk and chairs to fit their tall, spindly frames. Once in a while we get other aliens.

But we don't get many priests.

So I noticed him when he came in. He was young and round and harmless-looking. His expression was a model of its kind: open, willing to be friendly, not nervous, but very alert. He stared a bit at two bulbous aliens in space-suits who had come in with a chirpsithtra guide.

I watched him invite himself to join a trio of chirp-sithtra. They seemed willing to have him. They like human company. He even had the foresight to snag one of the high chairs I spread around, high enough to bring a human face to chirpsithtra level.

Someone must have briefed him, I decided. He'd know better than to do anything gauche. So I forgot him for a while.

An hour later he was at the bar, alone. He ordered a beer and waited until I'd brought it. He said, "You're Rick Schumann, aren't you? The owner?"

"That's right. And you?"

"Father David Hopkins." He hesitated, then blurted, "Do you trust the chirpsithtra?" He had trouble with the word.

I said, "Depends on what you mean. They don't steal the salt shakers. And they've got half a dozen reasons for not wanting to conquer the Earth."

He waved that aside. Larger things occupied his mind. "Do you believe the stories they tell? That they rule the galaxy? That they're aeons old?"

"I've never decided. At least they tell entertaining stories. At most . . . You didn't call a chirpsithtra a liar, did you?"

"No, of course not." He drank deeply of his beer. I was turning away when he said, "They said they know all about life after death."

"Ye Gods. I've been talking to chirpsithtra for twenty years, but that's a new one. Who raised the subject?"

"Oh, one of them asked me about the, uh, uniform. It just came up naturally." When I didn't say anything, he added, "Most religious leaders seem to be just ignoring the chirpsithtra. And the other intelligent beings too. I want to *know*. Do they have souls?"

"Do they?"

"He didn't say."

"She," I told him. "All chirpsithtra are female."

He nodded, not as if he cared much. "I started to tell her about my order. But when I started talking about Jesus, and about salvation, she told me rather firmly that the chirpsithtra know all they want to know on the subject of life after death."

"So then you asked——"

"No, sir, I did not. I came over here to decide whether I'm afraid to ask."

I gave him points for that. "And are you?" When he didn't answer, I said, "It's like this. I can stop her at any time you like. I know how to apologize gracefully."

Only one of the three spoke English, though the others listened as if they understood it.

"I don't know," she said.

That was clearly the answer Hopkins wanted. "I must have misunderstood," he said, and he started to slip down from his high chair.

"I told you that we know as much as we want to know on the subject," said the alien. "Once there were those who knew more. They tried to teach us. Now we try to discourage religious experiments."

Hopkins slid back into his chair. "What were they? Chirpsithtra saints?"

"No. The Sheegupt were carbon-water-oxygen life, like you and me, but they developed around the hot F-type suns in the galactic core. When our own empire had expanded near enough to the core, they came to us as missionaries. We rejected their pantheistic religion. They went away angry. It was some thousands of years before we met again.

"By then our settled regions were in contact, and had even interpenetrated to some extent. Why not? We could not use the same planets. We learned that their erstwhile religion had broken into variant sects and was now stagnant, giving way to what you would call agnosticism. I believe the implication is that the agnostic does not know the nature of God, and does not believe you do either?"

I looked at Hopkins, who said, "Close enough."

"We established a trade in knowledge and in other things. Their skill at educational toys exceeded ours. Some of our foods were dietetic to them; they had taste but could not be metabolized. We mixed well. If my tale seems sketchy or superficial, it is because I never learned it in great detail. Some details were deliberately lost.

"Over a thousand years of contact, the Sheegupt took the next step beyond agnosticism. They experimented. Some of their research was no different from your own psychological research, though of course they reached different conclusions. Some involved advanced philosophies: attempts to extrapolate God from his artwork, so to speak. There were attempts to extrapolate other universes from altered laws of physics, and to contact the extrapolated universes. There were attempts to contact the dead. The Sheegupt kept us informed of the progress of their work. They were born missionaries, even when their religion was temporarily in abeyance."

Hopkins was fascinated. He would hardly be shocked at attempts to investigate God. After all, it's an old game.

"We heard, from the Sheegupt outpost worlds, that the scientifically advanced worlds in the galactic core had made some kind of breakthrough. Then we started losing contact with the Sheegupt," said the chirpsithtra. "Trade ships found no shuttles to meet them. We sent investigating teams. They found Sheegupt worlds entirely depopulated. The inhabitants had made machinery for the purpose of suicide, generally a combination of electrocution terminals and conveyor belts. Some Sheegupt had used knives on themselves, or walked off buildings, but most had queued up at the suicide machines, as if in no particular hurry."

I said, "Sounds like they learned something, all right. But what?"

"Their latest approach, according to our records, was to

extrapolate rational models of a life after death, then attempt contact. But they may have gone on to something else. We do not know."

Hopkins shook his head. "They could have found out there wasn't a life after death. No, they couldn't, could they? If they didn't find anything, it might be they were only using the wrong model." -

I said, "Try it the other way around. There is a Heaven, and it's wonderful, and everyone goes there. Or there is a Hell, and it gets more unpleasant the older you are when you die."

"Be cautious in your guesses. You may find the right answer," said the chirpsithtra. "The Sheegupt made no attempt to hide their secret. It must have been an easy answer, capable of reaching even simple minds, and capable of proof. We know this because many of our investigating teams sought death in groups. Even millennia later, there was suicide among those who probed through old records, expecting no more than a fascinating puzzle in ancient history. The records were finally destroyed."

After I closed up for the night, I found Hopkins waiting for me outside.

"I've decided you were right," he said earnestly. "They must have found out there's a Heaven and it's easy to get in. That's the only thing that could make that many people *want* to be dead. Isn't it?"

But I saw that he was wringing his hands without knowing it. He wasn't sure. He wasn't sure of anything.

I told him, "I think you tried to preach at the chirpsithtra. I don't doubt you were polite about it, but that's what I think happened. And they closed the subject on you."

He thought it over, then nodded jerkily. "I guess they made their point. What would I know about chirpsithtra souls?"

"Yeah. But they spin a good yarn, don't they?"

4

Cruel and Unusual

Chirpsithtra do not vary among themselves. They stand eleven feet tall and weigh one hundred and twenty pounds. Their skins are salmon pink, with exoskeletal plates over vital areas. They look alike even to me, and I've known more chirpsithtra than most astronauts. I'd have thought that all humans would look alike to them.

But a chirpsithtra astronaut recognized me across two hundred yards of the landing field at Mount Forel Spaceport. She called with the volume on her translator turned high. "Rick Schumann! Why have you closed the Draco Tavern?"

I'd closed the place a month ago, for lack of customers. Police didn't want chirpsithtra wandering their streets, for fear of riots, and my human customers had stopped coming because the Draco was a chirpsithtra place. A month ago I'd thought I would never want to see a chirpsithtra again. Twenty-two years of knowing the fragile-looking aliens hadn't prepared me for three days of watching television.

But the bad taste had died, and my days had turned dull, and my skill at the Lottl speech was growing rusty. I veered toward the alien, and called ahead of me in Lottl: "This is a temporary measure, until the death of Ktashisnif may grow small in many memories."

We met on the wide, flat expanse of the blast pit. "Come, join me in my ship," said the chirpsithtra. "My meals-maker has a program for whiskey. What is this matter of Ktashisnif? I thought that was over and done with."

She had programmed her ship's kitchen for whiskey. I was bemused. The chirpsithtra claim to have ruled the galaxy for untold generations. If they extended such a courtesy to every thinking organism they knew of, they'd need . . . . how many programs? Hundreds of millions?

Of course it wasn't very good whiskey. And the air in the cabin was cold. And the walls and floor and ceiling were covered with green goo. And . . . what the hell. The alien brought me a dry pillow to ward my ass from the slimy green air-plant, and I drank bad whiskey and felt pretty good.

"What is this matter of Ktashisnif?" she asked me. "A decision was rendered. Sentence was executed. What more need be done?"

"A lot of very vocal people think it was the wrong decision," I told her. "They also think the United Nations shouldn't have turned the kidnappers over to the chirpsithtra."

"How could they not? The crime was committed against a chirpsithtra, Diplomat-by-Choice Ktashisnif. Three humans named Shrenk and one named Jackson did menace Ktashisnif here at Mount Forel Spaceport, did show her missile-firing weapons and did threaten to punch holes in her if she did not come with them. The humans did take her by airplane to New York City, where they concealed her while demanding money of the Port Authority for her return. None of this was denied by their lawyer nor by the criminals themselves."

"I remember." The week following the kidnapping had been hairy enough. Nobody knew the chirpsithtra well enough to be quite sure what they might do to Earth in reprisal. "I don't think the first chirpsithtra landing itself made bigger news," I said.

"That seems unreasonable. I think humans may lack a sense of proportion."

"Could be. We wondered if you'd pay off the ransom."

"In honor, we could not. Nor could we have allowed the United Nations to pay that price, if such had been possible, which it was not. Where would the United Nations find a million svith in chirpsithtra trade markers?" The alien caressed two metal contacts with the long thumb of each hand. Sparks leapt, and she made a hissing sound. "Ssss . . . We wander from the subject. What quarrel could any sentient being have with our decision? It is not denied that Diplomat-by-Choice Ktashisnif died in the hands of the"— she used the human word—"kidnappers."

"No."

"Three days in agony, then death, a direct result of the actions of Jackson and the three Shrenks. They sought to hide in the swarming humanity of New York City. Ktashisnif was allergic to human beings, and the kidnappers had no allergy serum for her. These things are true."

"True enough. But our courts wouldn't have charged them with murder by slow torture." In fact, a good lawyer might have gotten them off by arguing that a chirpsithtra wasn't human before the law. I didn't say so. I said, "Jackson and the Shrenk brothers probably didn't know about chirpsithtra allergies."

"There are no accidents during the commission of a crime. Be reasonable. Next you will say that one who kills the wrong victim during an attempt at murder may claim that the death was an accident, that she should be set free to try again."

"I am reasonable. All I want is for all of this to blow over so that I can open the Draco Tavern again." I sipped at the whiskey. "But there's no point in that until I can get some customers again. I wish you'd let the bastards plead guilty to a lesser sentence. For that matter, I wish you hadn't invited reporters in to witness the executions."

She was disturbed now. "But such was your right, by ancient custom! Rick Schumann, are you not reassured to know that we did not inflict more pain on the criminals than they inflicted on Ktashisnif?"

For three days the world had watched while chirpsithtra executioners smothered four men slowly to death. In some

nations it had even been televised. "It was terrible public-
ity. Don't you see, we don't *do* things like that. We've got
laws against cruel and unusual punishment."

"How do you deal with cruel and unusual crimes?"

I shrugged.

"Cruel and unusual crimes require cruel and unusual
punishment. You humans lack a sense of proportion, Rick
Schumann. Drink more whiskey?"

She brushed her thumbs across the contacts and made a
hissing sound. I drank more whiskey. Maybe it would improve my sense of proportion. It was going to be a long
time before I opened the Draco Tavern again.

We Purchased People

BY FREDERIK POHL

Frederik Pohl broke into the professional SF world in 1939 as the nineteen-year-old editor of two SF magazines (Astonishing Stories *and* Super Science Stories), *and ever since has been one of the genre's major shaping forces, as writer, editor, agent, and anthologist.*

On the editorial side of the slate, Pohl founded SF's first continuing original anthology series (the famous Star *series, which lasted from 1953 to 1960), was the editor of the Galaxy group of magazines from 1960 to 1969 (during which time he won three consecutive Best Professional Magazine Hugos for* Worlds of If, *Galaxy's sister magazine), and served until recently as consulting SF editor for Bantam.*

As a writer, Pohl first came to prominence with a series of novels written in collaboration with the late C. M. Kornbluth, including The Space Merchants *(one of the most famous SF novels of the fifties),* Gladiator-at-Law, *and* Search the Sky. *Perhaps the best of the Pohl-Kornbluth collaborations, though, and one of the best novels ever written about alien contact, was* Wolfbane, *a marvelously bizarre work, years ahead of its time conceptually, in which the abducted citizens of a conquered Earth are forced to act as plug-in component parts in an organic alien computer. Pohl's first writing Hugo—won in 1973—was also for a Pohl-Kornbluth collaboration, a short story called "The Meeting," completed by Pohl from an incomplete Kornbluth draft after Kornbluth's death. Subsequently, Pohl went on to win the Nebula Award for his novel* Man Plus, *and both the Nebula and the Hugo awards for his brilliant novel* Gateway *(another fine alien-contact novel, in which the discovery of an ancient alien space station, abandoned for aeons, may give us the freedom of the universe—if we can discover how to use it and survive). Pohl's other books include* Slave Ship, The Gold at the Starbow's End, A Plague of Pythons, The Best of Frederik Pohl, *and* Critical Mass, *a collection of short pieces done in collaboration with Kornbluth. His latest books are* The Way the Future Was, *an autobiography, and* Jem, *a novel.*

In the horrifying love story that follows, Pohl writes of a very cool, modern, cerebral form of alien contact: the aliens stay at home and deal with us by remote control, by proxy, only their voices—and their knowledge—whispering between the stars. But knowledge is power—and money—and Pohl's alien entrepreneurs need not bother to leave their distant home to, in effect, take over the Earth; they buy it, piecemeal, everything from Van Goghs to harpsichords, and we, of course, sell them everything we have—including ourselves.

On the third of March the purchased person named Wayne
Golden took part in trade talks in Washington as the
representative of the dominant race of the Groombridge
star. What he had to offer was the license of the basic
patents on a device to convert nuclear power plant waste
products into fuel cells. It was a good item, with a ready
market. Since half of Idaho was already bubbling with
radioactive wastes, the Americans were anxious to buy,
and he sold for a credit of $100 million. On the following
day he flew to Spain. He was allowed to sleep all the way,
stretched out across two seats in the first-class section of
the Concorde, with the fastenings of a safety belt gouging
into his side. On the fifth of the month he used up part of
the trade credit in the purchase of fifteen Picasso oils-on-
canvas, the videotape of a flamenco performance and a
fifteenth-century harpsichord, gilt with carved legs. He
arranged for them to be preserved, crated, and shipped in
bond to Orlando, Florida, after which the items would be
launched from Cape Kennedy on a voyage through space
that would take more than twelve thousand years. The
Groombridgians were not in a hurry and thought big. The
Saturn V booster rocket cost $11 million in itself. It did

25

not matter. There was plenty of money left in the Groom-bridge credit balance. On the fifth of the month Golden returned to the United States, made a close connection at Logan Airport in Boston, and arrived early at his home kennel in Chicago. He was then given eighty-five minutes of freedom.

I knew exactly what to do with my eighty-five minutes. I always know. See, when you're working for the people who own you you don't have any choice about what you do, but up to a point you can think pretty much whatever you like. That thing you get in your head only controls you. It doesn't change you, or anyway I don't think it does. (Would I know if I were changed?)

My owners never lie to me. Never. I don't think they know what a lie is. If I ever needed anything to prove that they weren't human, that would be plenty, even if I didn't know they lived 86 zillion miles away, near some star that I can't even see. They don't tell me much, but they don't lie.

Not ever lying, that makes you wonder what they're like. I don't mean physically. I looked that up in the library once, when I had a couple of hours of free time. I don't remember where, maybe in Paris at the Bibliothèque Nationale, anyway I couldn't read what the language in the books said. But I saw the photographs and the holograms. I remember the physical appearance of my owners, all right. Jesus. The Altairians look kind of like spiders, and the Sirians are a little bit like crabs. But those folks from the Groombridge star, boy, they're something else. I felt bad about it for a long time, knowing I'd been sold to something that looked as much like a cluster of maggots on an open wound as anything else I'd ever seen. On the other hand, they're all those miles away, and all I ever have to do with them is receive their fast-radio commands and do what they tell me. No touching or anything. So what does it matter what they look like?

But what kind of freaky creature is it that never says anything that is not objectively the truth, never changes its mind, never makes a promise that it doesn't keep? They aren't machines, I know, but maybe they think I'm kind of a machine. You wouldn't bother to lie to a machine, would you? You wouldn't make it any promises. You wouldn't do it any favors, either, and they never do me any. They don't tell me that I can have eighty-five minutes off because I've done something they like, or because they want to sweeten me up because they want something from me. Everything considered, that's silly. What could they want? It isn't as if I had any choice. Ever. So they don't lie, or threaten, or bribe, or reward.

But for some reason they sometimes give me minutes or hours or days off, and this time I had eighty-five minutes. I started using it right away, the way I always do. The first thing was to check at the kennel location desk to see where Carolyn was. The locator clerk—he isn't owned, he works for a salary and treats us like shit—knows me by now. "Oh, hell, Wayne, boy," he said with that imitation sympathy and lying friendliness that makes me want to kill him, "you just missed the lady friend. Saw her, let's see, Wednesday, was it? But she's gone." "Where to?" I asked him. He pushed around the cards on the locator board for a while, he knows I don't have very much time ever so he uses it up for me, and said: "Nope, not on my board at all. Say, I wonder. Was she with that bunch that went to Peking? Or was that the other little fat broad with the big boobs?" I didn't stop to kill him. If she wasn't on the board she wasn't in eighty-five-minute transportation range, so my eighty-five minutes—seventy-nine minutes—wasn't going to get me near her.

I went to the men's room, jerked off quickly, and went out into the miserable biting March Chicago wind to use up my seventy-nine minutes. Seventy-one minutes. There's a nice Mexican kind of restaurant near the kennel, a couple of blocks away past Ohio. They know me there. They don't care who I am. Maybe the brass plate in my head doesn't bother them because they think it's great that the people from the other stars are doing such nice things for the world, or maybe it's because I tip big. (What else do I have to do with the money I get?) I stuck my head in, whistled at Terry, the bartender, and said: "The usual. I'll be back in ten minutes." Then I walked up to Michigan and bought a clean shirt and changed into it, leaving the smelly old one. Sixty-six minutes. In the drugstore on the corner I picked up a couple of porno paperbacks and stuck them in my pockets, bought some cigarettes, leaned over and kissed the hand of the cashier, who was slim and fair-complexioned and smelled good, left her startled behind me, and got back to the restaurant just as Alicia, the waitress, was putting the gazpacho and two bottles of beer on my table. Fifty-nine minutes. I settled down to enjoy my time. I smoked, and I ate, and I drank the beer, smoking between bites, drinking between puffs. You really look forward to something like that when you're working, and not your own boss. I don't mean they don't let us eat when we're working. Of course they do, but we don't have any choice about what we eat or where we eat it. Pump fuel into the machine, keep it running. So I finished the guacamole and sent Alicia back for more of it when she brought the chocolate cake and American coffee, and ate the cake and the guacamole in alternate forkfuls. Eighteen minutes.

If I had had a little more time I would have jerked off again, but I didn't, so I paid the bill, tipped everybody, and left the restaurant. I got to the block where the kennel was with maybe two minutes to spare. Along the curb a slim woman in a fur jacket and pants suit was walking her Scottie away from me. I went up behind her and said, "I'll give you fifty dollars for a kiss." She turned around. She was all of sixty years old, but not bad, really, so I kissed her and gave her the fifty dollars. Zero minutes, and I just made it into the kennel when I felt the tingling in my forehead and my owners took over again.

In the next seven days of March Wayne Golden visited Karachi, Srinagar, and Butte, Montana, on the business of the Groombridgians. He completed thirty-two assigned tasks. Quite unexpectedly he was then given 1,000 minutes of freedom.

That time I was in, I think it was Pocatello, Idaho, or some place like that. I had to send a TWX to the faggy locator clerk in Chicago to ask about Carolyn. He took his time answering, as I knew he would. I walked around a little bit, waiting to hear. Everybody was very cheerful, smiling as they walked around through the dusty, sprinkly snow that was coming down, even smiling at me as though they didn't care that I was purchased, as they could plainly see from the golden oval of metal across my forehead that my owners use to tell me what to do. Then the message came back from Chicago: "Sorry, Wayne baby, but Carolyn isn't on my board. If you find her give her one for me."

Well. All right. I have plenty of spending money, so I checked into a hotel. The bellboy brought me a fifth of

Scotch and plenty of ice, fast, because he knew why I was in a hurry and that I would tip for speed. When I asked about hookers he offered anything I liked. I told him white, slim, beautiful asses. That's what I first noticed about Carolyn. It's special for me. The little girl I did in New Brunswick, what was her name—Rachel—she was only nine years old, but she had an ass on her you wouldn't believe.

I showered and put on clean clothes. The owners don't really give you enough time for that sort of thing. A lot of the time I smell. A lot of times I've almost wet my pants because they didn't let me go when I needed to. Once or twice I just couldn't help myself, held out as long as I could and, boy, you feel lousy when that happens. The worst was when I was covering some kind of a symposium in Russia, a place with a name like Akademgorodok. It was supposed to be on nuclear explosion processes. I don't know anything about that kind of stuff, and anyway I was a little mixed up because I thought that was one of the things the star people had done for us, worked out some way the different countries didn't have to have nuclear weapons and bombs and wars and so on any more. But that wasn't what they meant. It was explosions at the nucleus of the galaxy they meant. Astronomical stuff. Just when a fellow named Eysenck was talking about how the FG prominence and the EMK prominence, whatever they were, were really part of an expanding pulse sphere, whatever that is, I crapped my pants. I knew I was going to. I'd tried to tell the Groombridge people about it. They wouldn't listen. Then the session redactor came down the aisle and shouted in my ear, as though my owners were deaf or stupid, that they would have to get me out of there, please, for reasons concerning the comfort and hygiene of the other participants. I thought they would be angry, because that meant they were going to miss some of this conference that they were interested in. They didn't do anything to me, though. I mean, as if there was anything they *could* do to me that would be any worse, or any different, from what they do to me all the time, and always will.

When I was all clean and in an open-necked shirt and chinos I turned on the TV and poured a mild drink. I didn't want to be still drunk when my thousand minutes were up. There was a special program on all the networks, something celebrating a treaty between the United Nations and

a couple of the star people, Sirians and Capellans it seemed
to be. Everybody was very happy about it, because it seemed
that now the Earth had bought some agricultural and
chemical information, and pretty soon there would be more
food than we could eat. How much we owed to the star
people, the secretary general of the UN was saying, in
Brazilian-accented English. We could look forward to their
wise guidance to help Earth survive its multitudinous crises
and problems, and we should all be very happy.

But I wasn't happy, not even with a glass of John Begg
and the hooker on her way up, because what I really wanted
was Carolyn.

Carolyn was a purchased person, like me. I had seen her
a couple of dozen times, all in all. Not usually when either
of us was on freedom. Almost never when both of us were.
It was sort of like falling in love by postcard, except that
now and then we were physically close, even touching. And
once or twice we had been briefly not only together, but
out from under control. We had had about eight minutes
once in Bucharest, after coming back from the big hydro-
power plant at the Iron Gate. That was the record, so far.
Outside of that it was just that we passed, able to see each
other but not to do anything about it, in the course of our
duties. Or that one of us was free and found the other.
When that happened the one of us that was free could talk,
and even touch the other one, in any way that didn't interfere with what the other was doing. The one that was
working couldn't do anything active, but could hear, or
feel. We were both totally careful to avoid interfering with
actual work. I don't know what would have happened if
we had interfered. Maybe nothing? We didn't want to take
that chance, though sometimes it was a temptation I could
almost not resist. There was a time when I was free and I
found Carolyn, working but not doing anything active,
just standing there, at TWA Gate 51 at the St. Louis airport. She was waiting for someone to arrive. I really wanted
to kiss her. I talked to her. I patted her, you know, holding
my trenchcoat over my arm so that the people passing by
wouldn't notice anything, or at least wouldn't notice anything much. I told her things I wanted her to hear. But
what I wanted was to kiss her, and I was afraid to. Kissing
her on the mouth would have meant putting my head in
front of her eyes. I didn't think I wanted to chance that.
It might have meant she wouldn't see the person she was

there to see. Who turned out to be a Ghanaian police officer arriving to discuss the sale of some political prisoners
to the Groombridgians. I was there when he came down
the ramp, but I couldn't stay to see if she would by any
chance be free after completing the negotiations with him,
because then my own time ran out.

But I had had three hours that time, being right near
her. It felt very sad and very strange, and I wouldn't have
given it up for anything in the world. I knew she could
hear and feel everything, even if she couldn't respond. Even
when the owners are running you, there's a little personal
part of you that stays alive. I talked to that part of her. I
told her how much I wished we could kiss, and go to bed,
and be with each other. Oh, hell. I even told her I loved
her and wanted to marry her, although we both know
perfectly well there's not ever going to be any chance of
that ever. We don't get pensioned off or retired; we're
owned.

Anyway, I stayed there with her as long as I could. I
paid for it later. Balls that felt as though I'd been stomped,
the insides of my undershorts wet and chilly. And there
wasn't any way in the world for me to do anything about
it, not even by masturbating, until my next free time. That
turned out to be three weeks later. In Switzerland, for
God's sake. Out of season. With nobody in the hotel except the waiters and bellboys and a couple of old ladies
who looked at the gold oval in my forehead as though it
smelled bad.

It is a terrible but cherished thing to love without hope.

I pretended there was hope, always. Every bit of freedom I got, I tried to find her. They keep pretty careful
tabs on us, all two or three hundred thousand of us purchased persons, working for whichever crazy bunch of
creepy crawlers or gassy ghosts happens to have bought
us to be their remote-access facilities on the planet they
themselves cannot ever visit. Carolyn and I were owned
by the same bunch, which had its good side and its bad
side. The good side was that there was a chance that some
day we would be free for quite a long while at the same
time. It happened. I don't know why. Shifts change on the
Groombridge planet, or they have a holiday or something.
But every once in a while there would be a whole day,
maybe a week, when none of the Groombridge people

would be doing anything at all, and all of us would be free at once.

The bad side was that they hardly ever needed to have more than one of us in one place. So Carolyn and I didn't run into each other a lot. And the times when I was free for a pretty good period it took most of that to find her, and by the time I did she was like half a world away. No way of getting there and back in time for duty. I did so much want to fuck her, but we had never made it that far and maybe never would. I never even got a chance to ask her what she had been sentenced for in the first place. I really didn't know her at all, except enough to love her.

When the bellboy turned up with my girl I was comfortably buzzed, with my feet up and the Rangers on the TV. She didn't look like a hooker, particularly. She was wearing hiphuggers cut below the navel, bigger breasted than I cared about but with that beautiful curve of waist and back into hips that I like. Her name was Nikki. The bellboy took my money, took five for himself, passed the rest to her, and disappeared, grinning. What's so funny about it? He knew what I was, because the plate in my head told him, but he had to think it was funny.

"Do you want me to take my clothes off?" She had a pretty, breathless little voice, long red hair, and a sweet, broad, friendly face. "Go ahead," I said. She slipped off the sandals. Her feet were clean, a little ridged where the straps went. Stepped out of the hiphuggers and folded them across the back of Conrad Hilton's standard armchair, took off the blouse and folded it, ducked out of the medallion and draped it over the blouse, down to red lace bra and red bikini panties. Then she turned back the bedclothes, got in, sat up, snapped off the bra, snuggled down, kicked the panties out of the side of the bed, and pulled the covers over her. "Any time, honey," she said. But I didn't lay her. I didn't even get in the bed with her, not under the covers; I drank some more of the Scotch, and that and fatigue put me out, and when I woke up it was daylight, and she had cleaned out my wallet. Seventy-one minutes left. I paid the bill with a check and persuaded them to give me carfare in change. Then I headed back for the kennel. All I got out of it was clean clothes and a hangover. I think I had scared her a little. Everybody knows how we purchased people came to be up for sale, and maybe they're not all the way sure that we won't do something bad again, because they don't know how reliably our owners keep us from ever doing anything they don't like. But I wished she hadn't stolen my money.

The overall strategies and objectives of the star people, particularly the people from the Groombridge star who were his own masters, were unclear to the purchased person named Wayne Golden. What they did was not hard to understand. All the world knew that the star people had established fast-radio contact with the people of Earth, and that in order to conduct their business on Earth they had purchased the bodies of certain convicted criminals, installing in them tachyon fast-radio transceivers. Why they did what they did was less easy to comprehend. Art objects they admired and purchased. Certain rare kinds of plants and flowers they purchased and had frozen at liquid-helium temperatures. Certain kinds of utilitarian objects they purchased. Every few months another rocket roared up from Merritt Island, just north of the Cape, and another cargo headed for the Groombridge star, on its twelve-thousand-year voyage. Others, to other stars, peopled by other races in the galactic confraternity, took shorter times—or longer—but none of the times was short enough for those star people who made the purchases to come to Earth to see what they had bought. The distances were too huge.

What they spent most of their money on was the rockets. And, of course, the people they purchased, into whom they had transplanted their tachyon transceivers. Each rocket cost at least $10 million. The going rate for a healthy male paranoid capable of three or more decades of useful work was in the hundreds of thousands of dollars, and they bought them by the dozen.

The other things they bought, all of them—the taped symphonies and early-dynasty *ushabti*, the flowering orchids, and the Van Goghs—cost only a fraction of 1 percent of what they spent on people and transportation. Of course, they had plenty of money to spend. Each star race sold off licensing rights on its own kinds of ·technology. All of them received trade credits from every government on Earth for their services in resolving disputes and preventing wars. Still, it seemed to Wayne Golden, to the extent that he was capable of judging the way his masters conducted their affairs, a pretty high-overhead way to run a business, although of course neither he nor any other purchased person was ever consulted on questions like that.

By late spring he had been on the move for many weeks without rest. He completed sixty-eight tasks, great and small. There was nothing in this period of eighty-seven days that was in any way remarkable except that on one day in May, while he was observing the riots on the Place de la Concorde from a window of the American embassy on behalf of his masters, the girl named Carolyn came into his room. She whispered in his ear, attempted unsuccessfully to masturbate him while the liaison attaché was out of the room, remained in all for some forty minutes, and then left, sobbing softly. He could not even turn his head to see her go. Then on the sixth of June the purchased person named Wayne Golden was returned to the Dallas kennel and given indefinite furlough, subject to recall at fifty minutes' notice.

Sweetest dear Jesus, nothing like that had ever happened to me before! It was like the warden coming into Death Row with the last-minute reprieve! I could hardly believe it.

But I took it, started moving at once. I got a fix on Carolyn's last reported whereabouts from the locator board and floated away from Dallas in a cloud of Panama Red, drinking champagne as fast as the hostesses could bring it to me, en route to Colorado.

But I didn't find Carolyn there.

I hunted her through the streets of Denver, and she was gone. By phone I learned she had been sent to Rantoul, Illinois. I was off. I checked at the Kansas City airport, where I was changing planes, and she was gone from Illinois already. Probably, they weren't sure, they thought, to the New York district. I put down the phone and jumped on a plane, rented a car at Newark, and drove down the Turnpike to the Garden State, checking every car I passed to see if it was the red Volvo they thought she might be driving, stopping at every other Howard Johnson's to ask if they'd seen a girl with short black hair, brown eyes and a tip-tilted nose and, oh, yes, the golden oval in her forehead.

I remembered it was in New Jersey that I first got into trouble. There was the nineteen-year-old movie cashier in Paramus, she was my first. I picked her up after the 1 A.M.

show. And I showed her. But she was really all wrong for me, much too old and much too worldly. I didn't like it much when she died.

After that I was scared for a while, and I watched the TV news every night, twice, at six and eleven, and never passed a newsstand without looking at all the headlines in the papers, until a couple of months had passed. Then I thought over what I really wanted very carefully. The girl had to be quite young and, well, you can't tell, but as much as I could be sure, a virgin. So I sat in a luncheonette in Perth Amboy for three whole days, watching the kids get out of the parochial school, before I found my second. It took a while. The first one that looked good turned out to be a bus kid, the second was a walker but her big sister from the high school walked with her. The third walked home alone. It was December, and the afternoons got pretty dark, and that Friday she walked but she didn't get home. I never molested any of them sexually, you know. I mean, in some ways I'm still kind of a virgin. That wasn't what I wanted, I just wanted to see them die. When they asked me at the pretrial hearing if I knew the difference between right and wrong I didn't know how to answer them. I knew what I did was wrong for them. But it wasn't wrong for me, it was what I wanted.

So, driving down the Parkway, feeling discouraged about Carolyn, I noticed where I was and cut over to Route 35 and doubled back. I drove right to the school, past it, and to the lumberyard where I did the little girl. I stopped and cut the motor, looking around. Happy day. Now it was a different time of year, and things looked a little different. They'd piled up a stack of two-by-twelves over the place where I'd done her. But in my mind's eye I could see it the way it had been then. Dark gray sky. Lights from the cars going past. I could hear the little buzzing feeling in her throat as she tried to scream under my fingers. Let's see. That was, oh, good heavens, nine years ago.

And if I hadn't done her she would have been twenty or so. Screwing all the boys. Probably on dope. Maybe knocked up or married. Looked at in a certain way, I saved her a lot of sordid miserable stuff, menstruating, letting the boys' hands and mouths on her, all that . . .

My head began hurting. That's one thing the plate in your head does, it doesn't let you get very deeply into the things you did in the old days, because it hurts too much.

So I started up the car and drove away, and pretty soon the hurting stopped.

I never think of Carolyn, you know, that way.

They never proved that little girl on me. The one they caught me for was the nurse in Long Branch, in the parking lot. And she was a mistake. She was so small, and she had a sweater over her uniform. I didn't know she was grown up until it was too late. I was very angry about that. In a way I didn't mind when they caught me, because I had been getting very careless. But I really hated that ward in Marlboro where they put me. Seven, Jesus, seven years. Up in the morning, and drink your pink medicine out of the little paper cup. Make your bed and do your job—mine was sweeping in the incontinent wards, and the smells and the sights would make you throw up.

After a while they let me watch TV and even read the papers, and when the Altair people made the first contact with Earth I was interested, and when they began buying criminally insane to be their proxies I wanted them to buy me. Anything, I wanted *anything* that would let me get out of that place, even if it meant I'd have to let them put a box in my head and never be able to live a normal life again.

But the Altair people wouldn't buy me. For some reason they only took blacks. Then the others began showing up on the fast radio, making their deals. And still none of them wanted me. The ones from Procyon liked young women, wouldn't ever buy a male. I think they have only one sex there, someone said. All these funnies are peculiar in one way or another. Metal, or gas, or blobby, or hardshelled and rattly. Whatever. And they all have funny habits, like if you belong to the Canopus bunch you can't ever eat fish.

I think they're disgusting, and I don't really know why the USA wanted to get involved with them in the first place. But the Chinese did, and the Russians did, and I guess we just couldn't stay out. I suppose it hasn't hurt much. There hasn't been a war, and there's a lot of ways in which they've helped clean things up for us. It hasn't hurt me, that's for sure. The Groombridge people came into the market pretty late, and most of the good healthy criminals were gone; they would buy anybody. They bought me. We're a hard-case lot, we Groombridgians, and I do wonder what Carolyn was in for.

I drove all the way down the coast, Asbury Park, Brielle, Atlantic City, all the way to Cape May, phoning back to check with the locator clerk, and never found her.

The one thing I did know was that all I was missing was the shell of her, because she was working. I could have had a kiss or a feel, no more. But I wanted to find her anyway. Just on the chance. How many times do you get an indefinite furlough? If I'd been able to find her, and stay with her, sooner or later, maybe, she would have been off too. Even if it were only for two hours. Even thirty minutes.

And then in broad daylight, just as I was checking into a motel near an army base, with the soldiers' girls lined up at the cashier's window so their boyfriends could get back for reveille, I got the call: Report to the Philadelphia kennel. Soonest.

By then I was giddy for sleep, but I drove that Hertz lump like a Maserati, because soonest means soonest. I dumped the car and signed in at the kennel, feeling my heart pounding and my mouth ragged from fatigue, and aching because I had blown what would have to be my best chance of really being with Carolyn. "What do they want?" I asked the locator clerk. "Go inside," he said, looking evilly amused. All locator clerks treat us the same, all over the world. "She'll tell you."

Not knowing who "she" was I opened the door and walked through, and there was Carolyn.

"Hello, Wayne," she said.

"Hello, Carolyn," I said.

I really did not have any idea of what to do at all. She didn't give me a cue. She just sat. It was at that point that it occurred to me to wonder at the fact that she wasn't wearing much, just a shortie nightgown with nothing under it. She was also sitting on a turned-down bed. Now, you would think that considering everything, especially the nature of most of my thinking about Carolyn, that I would have instantly accepted this as a personal gift from God to me of every boy's all-American dream. I didn't. It wasn't the fatigue, either. It was Carolyn. It was the expression on her face, which was neither inviting nor loving, was not even the judgment-reserving look of a girl at a singles bar. What it especially was not was happy.

"The thing is, Wayne," she said, "we're supposed to go to bed now. So take your clothes off, why don't you?"

Sometimes I can stand outside of myself and look at me and, even when it's something terrible or something sad, I can see it as funny; it was like that when I did the little girl in Edison Township, because her mother had sewed her into her school clothes. I was actually laughing when I said, "Carolyn, what's the matter?"

"Well," she said, "they want us to ball, Wayne. You know. The Groombridge people. They've got interested in what human beings do to each other and they want to kind of watch."

I started to ask why us, but I didn't have to; I could see where Carolyn and I had had a lot of that on our minds, and maybe our masters could get curious about it. I didn't exactly like it. No exactly; in fact in a way I kind of hated it, but it was so much better than nothing at all that I said, "Why, honey, that's great!"—almost meaning it; trying to talk her into it; moving in next to her and putting my arm around her. And then she said:

"Only we have to wait, Wayne. *They* want to do it. Not us."

"What do you mean, wait? Wait for what?" She shrugged under my arm. "You mean," I said, "that we have to be plugged in to them? Like they'll be doing it with our bodies?"

She leaned against me. "That's what they told me, Wayne. Any minute now, I guess."

I pushed her away. "Honey," I said, half crying, "all this time I've been wanting to—Jesus, Carolyn! I mean, it isn't just that I wanted to go to bed with you. I mean—"

"I'm sorry," she cried, big tears on her face.

"That's lousy!" I shouted. My head was pounding, I was so furious. "It isn't fair! I'm not going to stand for it. They don't have any *right!*"

But they did, of course, they had all the right in the world; they had bought us and paid for us, and so they owned us. I knew that. I just didn't want to accept it, even by admitting what I knew was so. The notion of screwing Carolyn flipped polarity; it wasn't what I desperately wanted, it was what I would have died to avoid, as long as it meant letting *them* paw her with my hands, kiss her with my mouth, flood her with my juices; it was like the worst kind of rape, worse than anything I had ever done, both of us raped at once. And then—

And then I felt that burning tingle in my forehead as they

took over. I couldn't even scream. I just had to sit there
inside my own head, no longer owning a muscle, while those
freaks who owned me did to Carolyn with my body all
manner of things, and I could not even cry.

After concluding the planned series of experimental procedures, which were duly recorded, the purchased person
known as Carolyn Schoerner was no longer salvageable.
Appropriate entries were made. The Probation and Out-
Service department of the Meadville Women's Reformatory
was notified that she had ceased to be alive. A purchasing
requisition was initiated for a replacement, and her account was terminated.

The purchased person known as Wayne Golden was
assigned to usual duties, at which he functioned normally
while under control. It was discovered that when control
was withdrawn he became destructive, both to others and
to himself. The conjecture has been advanced that that
sexual behavior which had been established as his norm—
the destruction of the sexual partner—may not have been
appropriate in the conditions obtaining at the time of the
experimental procedures. Further experiments will be made
with differing procedures and other partners in the near
future. Meanwhile Wayne Golden continues to function at
normal efficiency, provided control is not withdrawn at
any time, and apparently will do so indefinitely.

Guesting Time

BY R. A. LAFFERTY

Hordes of aliens descending upon the Earth, the armed forces helpless against them, governments crumbling under the impact of the invasion, the invaders quartered in our homes, walking all over us, grinding us under their heels . . . Can anyone find anything good to say about these things? If anyone can, it's R. A. Lafferty—and sure enough, he does, in "Guesting Time," one of the most charming and funny stories of alien contact ever written.

The usual biographic line quoted for Lafferty—that he is a retired electrical engineer who has spent almost his entire life in Oklahoma—can make him sound dull, but in actuality he is one of the least dull people alive, possessing a wickedly boisterous sense of humor, an enormous store of offbeat erudition, and one of the most outlandish imaginations in all of SF. Lafferty began writing in 1960, and in the years that followed turned out a seemingly endless string of mad and marvelous tall tales like "Narrow Valley," "Slow Tuesday Night," and "Thus We Frustrate Charlemagne"—some of the freshest and funniest short stories ever published. His first novel followed in 1968: Past Master, an intricate and lyrical novel that pits Sir Thomas More against the supposedly Utopian snares of a far-future world. Past Master was a Nebula and Hugo finalist that year, but another fine Lafferty novel, also published in 1968, was almost totally ignored, although it is one of Lafferty's best handlings of the alien theme: The Reefs of Earth, a good-humoredly grotesque story of exiled and orphaned alien children who must adapt to life on Earth—or perhaps force Earth to adapt to them. By turns boisterous, wistfully sad, wildly funny, gently insightful, and outrageously bloodthirsty, an odd blending of SF, children's fantasy, folklore, backwoods melodrama, and Grand

41

Guignol, The Reefs of Earth *baffled the critics of the day (particularly the English intellectual critics, who labeled it the work of an illiterate madman), but has held up well, and will reward any reader interested in a unique slant on human-alien interactions. That same unique slant is to be found in many of Lafferty's short stories about aliens (too numerous to describe here—see the reading list at the back of the anthology), and in many of his novels as well, particularly that marvelously paranoid fantasy* The Devil Is Dead.

Lafferty's other books include Fourth Mansions, Arrive at Easterwine, Okla Hannali, The Fall of Rome, The Flame Is Green, *and three short story collections,* Nine Hundred Grandmothers, Strange Doings, *and* Does Anyone Else Have Something Further to Add? *Lafferty won the Hugo Award in 1973 for his short story "Eurema's Dam."*

*Things were a bit crowded where they came from—
and were getting that way here!*

Winston, the Civil Servant in Immigration and Arrivals, was puzzled when he came that morning. There were several hundred new people behind the cyclone fences, and no arrivals had been scheduled.

"What ships landed?" he called out. "Why were they unscheduled?"

"No ships landed, sir," said Potholder, the senior guard.

"Then how did these people get here? Walk down from the sky?" Winston asked snappishly.

"Yes, sir, I guess so. We don't know who they are or how they keep coming here. They say they are from Skandia."

"We have few Scandinavian arrivals, and none of such appearance as this," said Winston. "How many are there?"

"Well, sir, when we first noticed them there were seven, and they hadn't been there a moment before."

"Seven? You're crazy. There are hundreds."

"Yes, sir. I'm crazy. A minute after there were seven, there were seventeen. But no more had come from anywhere. Then there were sixty. We separated them into groups of ten and watched them very closely. None crossed from one group to another, none came from anywhere else. But soon there were fifteen, then twenty-five, then thirty in each group. And there's a lot more of them there now than when you started to talk to me a moment ago, Mr. Winston."

"Corcoran is my superior and will be here in a minute," Winston said. "He'll know what to do."

"Mr. Corcoran left just before you arrived, sir," said

43

Potholder. "He watched it awhile, and then went away babbling."

"I always admired his quick grasp of a situation," said Winston. He also went away babbling.

There were about a thousand of those Skandia people, and a little later there were nine times that many. They weren't dowdy people, but the area wouldn't hold any more. The fences all went down, and the Skandias spread out into the city and towns and country. This was only the beginning of it. About a million of them materialized there that morning, then the same thing happened at ten thousand other Ports of Entry of Earth.

"Mama," said Trixie, "there are some people here who want to use our bathroom." This was Beatrice (Trixie) Trux, a little girl in the small town of Winterfield.

"What an odd request!" said Mrs. Trux. "But I suppose it is in the nature of an emergency. Let them in, Trixie. How many people are there?"

"About a thousand," said Trixie.

"Trixie, there can't be that many."

"All right, you count them."

All the people came in to use the Truxes' bathroom. There were somewhat more than a thousand of them, and it took them quite a while to use the bathroom even though they put a fifteen-second limit on each one and had a time-keeper with a bell to enforce it. They did it all with a lot of laughter and carrying on, but it took that first bunch about five hours to go through, and by that time there were a lot more new ones waiting.

"This is a little unusual," Mrs. Trux said to some of the Skandia women. "I was never short on hospitality. It is our physical resources, not our willingness, that becomes strained. There are so many of you!"

"Don't give it a thought," the Skandia women said. "It is the intent that counts, and it was so kind of you people to invite us. We seldom get a chance to go anywhere. We came a little early, but the main bunch will be along very soon. Don't you just love to go visiting?"

"Oh, yes, yes," said Mrs. Trux. "I never realized till now just how much I wanted to go visiting."

But when she saw the whole outdoors black with the new people, Mrs. Trux decided that she had better stay where she was.

Truman Trux was figuring with a pencil.

"Our lot is fifty feet by a hundred and fifty feet, Jessica," he said. "That is either seven thousand five hundred or seventy-five thousand square feet depending on how many zeroes you carry it out to."

"You were always good at math," said Mrs. Trux. "How do you do it anyhow?"

"And do you know how many people are living with us here on this lot, Jessica?" Truman asked.

"Quite a few."

"I am guessing between six and seven thousand," said Truman. "I found several more blocks of them this morning that I didn't know about. They have a complete city built in our backyard. The streets are two and a half feet wide; the houses are eight feet by eight feet with six-foot ceilings, and most of them are nine stories high. Whole families live in each room and cook there besides. They have shops and bazaars set up. They even have factories built. I know there is an entire wholesale textile district in our backyard. There are thirteen taverns and five music halls in our yard to my own knowledge, and there may be more."

"Well, some of those places are pretty small, Truman. The Little Hideout is the broom closet of the Big Hideout, and I don't know if we should count it as a separate tavern. You have to go into the Sideways Club sideways; the Thinman Club is only nine inches wide from wall to wall and it's quite a trick to bending an elbow there; and the Mouse Room is small. But the better clubs are up in our attic, Truman. Did you ever count them? The Crazy Man Carabet is up there, and the After Hours Club. Most of the other attic clubs are key clubs and I'm not a member. They've set up the Skandia Art Theater in our basement now, you know. They have continuous performances."

"I know it, Jessica, I know it."

"Their comedies are so funny that I nearly die. The trouble is that it's so crowded there that you have to laugh in when the one next to you laughs out. And I cry just like they do at their tragedies. They're all about women who can't have any more children. Why don't we have a bunch more, Truman? There's more than twenty shops in our yard where they sell nothing but fertility charms. I wonder why there aren't any children with the Skandia?"

"Ah, they say that this is just a short first visit by a few of them and they didn't presume to bring their children with them. What is that new racket superimposed on the old?"

"Oh, that's the big drums and the cymbals. They're having a political campaign to elect temporary officials for the time of their visit here. Imperial City, that's the town in our yard, and our house will elect delegates to go to Congress to represent this whole block. The elections will be tonight. Then we'll really hear some noise, they say. The big drums don't really waste space, Truman. There are people inside them and they play them from the inside. Some of our neighbors are getting a little fussy about the newcomers, but I always did like a house full of people."

"We have it now, Jessica. I never got used to sleeping in a bed with nine other people, even if they are quiet sleepers. I like people, and I am fond of new experiences. But it is getting crowded."

"We have more of the Skandia than anyone else in the block except the Skirveys. They say it's because they like us more than some of the others. Mamie Skirvey is taking four kinds of the fertility pills now. She is almost sure she will be able to have triplets. I want to too."

"All the stores are stripped, Jessica, and all the lumber yards and lumber camps; and the grain elevators will be empty in two more days. The Skandia pay for everything in money, but nobody knows what it says on it. I haven't got used to walking on men and women when I go out, but there's no avoiding it since the ground is covered with them."

"They don't mind. They're used to it. They say it's crowded where they come from."

The Winterfield *Times-Tribune Telegraph* had a piece about the Skandia:

> *The plain fact is that for two days the Earth has had ten billion visitors from Skandia, wherever that is. The plain fact is that the Earth will die of them within a week. They appear by invisible transportation, but they have shown no inclination to disappear in the same manner. Food will be gone, the very air we breathe will be gone. They speak all our languages, they are polite, friendly and agreeable. And we will perish from them.*

A big smiling man broke in on Bar-John, who was once again president of Big State Amalgamated, formerly USA.

"I'm the president of the Skandia Visitation," he boomed. "We have come partly to instruct you people and we find that you do need it. Your fertility rate is pathetic. You barely double in fifty years. Your medicine, adequate in other fields, is worse than childish in this. We find that some of the nostrums peddled to your people actually *impede* fertility. Well, get in the surgeon general and a few of the boys and we'll begin to correct the situation."

"Gedoudahere," said President Bar-John.

"I know you will not want your people to miss out on the population blessing," said the Skandia Visitation president. "We can aid you. We want you to be as happy as we are."

"Jarvis! Cudgelman! Sapsucker!" President Bar-John called out. "Shoot down this man. I'll implement the paper work on it later."

"You always say that but you never do," Sapsucker complained. "It's been getting us in a lot of trouble."

"Oh, well, don't shoot him down then if you're going to make an issue of it. I long for the old days when the simple things were done simply. Dammit, you Skandia skinner, do you know that there are nine thousand of you in the White House itself?"

"We intend to improve that this very hour," the Skandia president said. "We can erect one, two, or even three decks in these high-ceilinged rooms. I am happy to say that we will have thirty thousand of our people quartered in the White House this night."

"Do you think I like to take a bath with eight other persons—not even registered voters—in the same tub?" President Bar-John complained. "Do you think I like to eat off a plate shared by three or four other people? Or to shave, by mistake, faces other than my own in the morning?"

"I don't see why not," said the Skandia Visitation president. "People are our most precious commodity. Presidents are always chosen as being those who most love the people."

"Oh, come on, fellows," said President Bar-John. "Shoot down the ever-loving son. We're entitled to a free one now and then."

Jarvis and Cudgelman and Sapsucker blazed away at the Skandia, but they harmed him not at all.

"You should have known that we are immune to that," the Skandia said. "We voted against its effect years ago. Well, since you will not cooperate, I will go direct to your people. Happy increase to you, gentlemen."

Truman Trux, having gone out from his own place for a little change, was sitting on a park bench.

He wasn't actually sitting on it, but several feet above it. In that particular place, a talkative Skandia lady sat on the bench itself. On her lap sat a sturdy Skandia man reading the *Sporting News* and smoking a pipe. On him sat a younger Skandia woman. On this younger woman sat Truman Trux, and on him sat a dark Skandia girl who was filing her fingernails and humming a tune. On her in turn sat an elderly Skandia man. As crowded as things had become, one could not expect a seat of one's own.

A fellow and his girl came along, walking on the people on the grass.

"Mind if we get on?" asked the girl.

"Quite all right," said the elderly gentleman on top. " 'Sall right," said the girl working on her nails. "Certainly," said Truman and the others, and the *Sporting News* man puffed into his pipe that it was perfectly agreeable.

There was no longer any motor traffic. People walked closely packed on streets and sidewalks. The slow stratum was the lowest, then the medium, then the fast (walking on the shoulders of the mediums and combining the three speeds). At crossings it became rather intricate, and people were sometimes piled nine high. But the Earth people, those who still went out, quickly got onto the Skandia techniques.

An Earthman, known for his extreme views, had mounted onto a monument in the park and began to harangue the people, Earth and Skandia. Truman Trux, who wanted to see and hear, managed to get a nice fifth-level seat, sitting on the shoulders of a nice Skandia girl, who sat on the shoulders of another who likewise to the bottom.

"Ye are the plague of locusts!" howled the Earthside crank. "Ye have stripped us bare!"

"The poor man!" said the Skandia girl who was Truman's understeady. "He likely has only a few children and is embittered."

"Ye have devoured our substance and stolen the very air of our life. Ye are the Apocalyptical grasshoppers, the eleventh plague."

"Here is a fertility charm for your wife," said the Skandia girl, and reached it up to Truman. "You might not need it yet, but keep it for the future. It is for those who have more than twelve. The words in Skandia say 'Why stop now?' It is very efficacious."

"Thank you," said Truman. "My wife has many charms from you good people, but not one like this. We have only one child, a young girl."

"What a shame! Here is a charm for your daughter. She cannot begin to use them too early."

"Destruction, destruction, destruction on ye all!" screamed the Earthside crank from atop the monument.

"Quite an adept," said the Skandia girl. "To what school of eloquence does he belong?"

The crowd began to break up and move off. Truman felt himself taken down one level and then another.

"Any particular direction?" asked the Skandia girl.

"This is fine," said Truman. "We're going toward my home."

"Why, here's a place almost clear," said the girl. "You'd never find anything like this at home." They were now down to the last level, the girl walking only on the horizontal bodies of those lounging on the grass. "You can get off and walk if you wish," said the girl. "Here's a gap in the walkers you can slip down into. Well, toodle."

"You mean toodle-oo?" Truman asked as he slid off her shoulders.

"That's right. I can never remember the last part of it."

The Skandia were such friendly people!

President Bar-John and a dozen other regents of the world had decided that brusqueness was called for. Due to the intermingling of Earth and Skandia populations, this would be a task for small and medium arms. The problem would be to gather the Skandia together in open spots, but on the designated day they began to gather of themselves in a million parks and plazas of the Earth.

It worked perfectly. Army units were posted everywhere and went into action.

Rifles began to whistle and machine guns to chatter. But the effect on the Skandia was not that expected.

Instead of falling wounded, they cheered everywhere.

"Pyrotechnics yet!" exclaimed a Skandia leader, mounting onto the monument in one park. "Oh, we are honored!"

But, though the Skandia did not fall from the gunshot, they had begun to diminish in their numbers. They were disappearing as mysteriously as they had appeared a week before.

"We go now," said the Skandia leader from the top of the monument. "We have enjoyed every minute of our short visit. Do not despair! We will not abandon you to your emptiness. Our token force will return home and report. In another week we will visit you in substantial numbers. We will teach you the full happiness of human proximity, the glory of fruitfulness, the blessing of adequate population. We will teach you to fill up the horrible empty places of your planet."

The Skandia were thinning out. The last of them were taking cheering farewells of disconsolate Earth friends.

"We will be back," they said as they passed their last fertility charms into avid hands. "We'll be back and teach you everything so you can be as happy as we are. Good increase to you!"

"Good increase to you!" cried the Earth people to the disappearing Skandia. Oh, it would be a lonesome world without all those nice people! With them you had the feeling that they were really close to you.

"We'll be back!" said the Skandia leader, and disappeared from the monument. "We'll be back next week and a lot more of us," and then they were gone.

"—And next time we'll bring the kids!" came the last fading Skandia voice from the sky.

And I Awoke and Found Me Here on the Cold Hill's Side

BY JAMES TIPTREE, JR.

This story deals in part with another spacer bar, but Tiptree's Little Junction Bar is more reminiscent of the hangouts in Looking for Mr. Goodbar *than Niven's quiet and exclusive Draco Tavern. No one at the Little Junction Bar, human or alien, is particularly interested in* talking.

By now, probably everyone knows that that mysterious figure James Tiptree, Jr.—for many years the B. Traven of science fiction—is really a pseudonym of Dr. Alice Sheldon, a semiretired experimental psychologist who also writes under the name Raccoona Sheldon. As Tiptree, Dr. Sheldon won two Nebula and two Hugo awards, established a reputation as one of the very best short-story writers of the seventies, and published four books: the well-received collections Ten Thousand Light Years from Home, Warm Worlds and Otherwise, *and* Stars Songs of an Old Primate, *and a novel,* Up the Walls of the World. *As Raccoona Sheldon, she recently won another Nebula for "The Screwfly Solution," a chilling story in which aliens use a clever biological weapon to wipe humanity from an otherwise undamaged—and now available—Earth.*

But both Raccoona Sheldon and James Tiptree, Jr., share—unsurprisingly enough—a common interest in aliens. As Tiptree in particular, she probably wrote more about aliens and their interrelations with humans than any other new writer of the seventies: the relentlessly mindless juggernauts of "On the Last Afternoon"; the playful sensualists and intergalactic gourmets of "Painwise"; the slithering, sluglike creatures of "The Milk of Paradise"; the galumphing, childlike Moggadeet of "Love Is the Plan the Plan Is Death"; the giddy, pregnant (with 30,000 very

51

hungry babies) daytripper of "All the Kinds of Yes"; the immense, immortal, godlike beings of "I'm Too Big But I Love to Play" and Up The Walls of the World; *the compassionate balloon-things who also inhabit that novel—all unforgettable alien portraiture.*

The thread connecting most, if not all, of Tiptree/Sheldon's alien stories is cultural contamination: the meddling of one culture with another, less advanced, one, often with disastrous results. "And I Awoke and Found Me Here on the Cold Hill's Side" is perhaps her most subtle and effective handling of that theme, and the fever-dream vividness and bright bitter colors of a night at Little Junction Bar are an experience you may have a hard time forgetting.

He was standing absolutely still by a service port, staring out at the belly of the Orion docking above us. He had on a gray uniform and his rusty hair was cut short. I took him for a station engineer.

That was bad for me. Newsmen strictly don't belong in the bowels of Big Junction. But in my first twenty hours I hadn't found anyplace to get a shot of an alien ship.

I turned my holocam to show its big World Media insigne and started my bit about What It Meant to the People Back Home who were paying for it all.

"—it may be routine work to you, sir, but we owe it to them to share—"

His face came around slow and tight, and his gaze passed over me from a peculiar distance.

"The wonders, the drama," he repeated dispassionately. His eyes focused on me. "You consummated fool."

"Could you tell me what races are coming in, sir? If I could even get a view—"

He waved me to the port. Greedily I angled my lenses up at the long blue hull blocking out the starfield. Beyond her I could see the bulge of a black and gold ship.

"That's a Foramen," he said. "There's a freighter from

53

Belye on the other side, you'd call it Arcturus. Not much traffic right now."

"You're the first person who's said two sentences to me since I've been here, sir. What are those colorful little craft?"

"Procya," he shrugged. "They're always around. Like us."

I squashed my face on the vitrite, peering. The walls clanked. Somewhere overhead aliens were off-loading into their private sector of Big Junction. The man glanced at his wrist.

"Are you waiting to go out, sir?"

His grunt could have meant anything.

"Where are you from on Earth?" he asked me in his hard tone.

I started to tell him and suddenly saw that he had forgotten my existence. His eyes were on nowhere, and his head was slowly bowing forward onto the port frame.

"Go home," he said thickly. I caught a strong smell of tallow.

"Hey, sir!" I grabbed his arm; he was in rigid tremor. "Steady, man."

"I'm waiting . . . waiting for my wife. My loving wife." He gave a short ugly laugh. "Where are you from?"

I told him again.

"Go home," he mumbled. "Go home and make babies. While you still can."

One of the early GR casualties, I thought.

"Is that all you know?" His voice rose stridently. "Fools. Dressing in their styles. Gnivo suits, Aoleelee music. Oh, I see your newscasts," he sneered. "Nixi parties. A year's salary for a floater. Gamma radiation? Go home, read history. *Ballpoint pens and bicycles*—"

He started a slow slide downward in the half gee. My only informant. We struggled confusedly; he wouldn't take one of my sobertabs but I finally got him along the service corridor to a bench in an empty loading bay. He fumbled out a little vacuum cartridge. As I was helping him unscrew it, a figure in starched whites put his head in the bay.

"I can be of assistance, yes?" His eyes popped, his face was covered with brindled fur. An alien, a Procya! I started to thank him but the red-haired man cut me off.

"Get lost. Out."

The creature withdrew, its big eyes moist. The man stuck his pinky in the cartridge and then put it up his nose, gasping deep in his diaphragm. He looked toward his wrist.

"What time is it?"

I told him.

"News," he said. "A message for the eager, hopeful human race. A word about those lovely, lovable aliens we all love so much." He looked at me. "Shocked, aren't you, newsboy?"

I had him figured now. A xenophobe. Aliens plot to take over Earth.

"Ah, Christ, they couldn't care less." He took another deep gasp, shuddered and straightened. "The hell with generalities. What time d'you say it was? All right, I'll tell you how I learned it. The hard way. While we wait for my loving wife. You can bring that little recorder out of your sleeve, too. Play it over to yourself sometime . . . when it's too late." He chuckled. His tone had become chatty—an educated voice. "You ever hear of supernormal stimuli?"

"No," I said. "Wait a minute. White sugar?"

"Near enough. Y'know Little Junction Bar in D.C.? No, you're an Aussie, you said. Well, I'm from Burned Barn, Nebraska."

He took a breath, consulting some vast disarray of the soul.

"I accidentally drifted into Little Junction Bar when I was eighteen. No. Correct that. You don't go into Little Junction by accident, any more than you first shoot skag by accident.

"You go into Little Junction because you've been craving it, dreaming about it, feeding on every hint and clue about it, back there in Burned Barn, since before you had hair in your pants. Whether you know it or not. Once you're out of Burned Barn, you can no more help going into Little Junction than a sea worm can help rising to the moon.

"I had a brand-new liquor ID in my pocket. It was early; there was an empty spot beside some humans at the bar. Little Junction isn't an embassy bar, y'know. I found out later where the high-caste aliens go—when they go out. The New Rive, the Curtain by the Georgetown Marina.

"And they go by themselves. Oh, once in a while they do the cultural-exchange bit with a few frosty couples of other aliens and some stuffed humans. Galactic Amity with a ten-foot pole.

"Little Junction was the place where the lower orders went, the clerks and drivers out for kicks. Including, my friend, the perverts. The ones who can take humans. Into their beds, that is."

He chuckled and sniffed his finger again, not looking at me.

"Ah, yes. Little Junction is Galactic Amity night, every night. I ordered . . . what? A margharita. I didn't have the nerve to ask the snotty spade bartender for one of the alien liquors behind the bar. It was dim. I was trying to stare everywhere at once without showing it. I remember those white boneheads—Lyrans, that is. And a mess of green veiling I decided was a multiple being from someplace. I caught a couple of human glances in the bar mirror. Hostile flicks. I didn't get the message, then.

"Suddenly an alien pushed right in beside me. Before I could get over my paralysis, I heard this blurry voice:

" 'You air a futeball enthushiash?'

"An alien had spoken to me. An *alien,* a being from the stars. Had spoken. To me.

"Oh, god, I had no time for football, but I would have claimed a passion for paper folding, for dumb crambo—anything to keep him talking. I asked him about his home-planet sports, I insisted on buying his drinks. I listened rapidly while he spluttered out a play-by-play account of a game I wouldn't have turned a dial for. The 'Grain Bay Pashkers.' Yeah. And I was dimly aware of trouble among the humans on my other side.

"Suddenly this woman—I'd call her a girl now—this girl said something in a high nasty voice and swung her stool into the arm I was holding my drink with. We both turned around together.

"Christ, I can see her now. The first thing that hit me was *discrepancy.* She was a nothing—but terrific. Transfigured. Oozing it, radiating it.

"The next thing was I had a horrifying hard-on just looking at her.

"I scrooched over so my tunic hid it, and my spilled

drink trickled down, making everything worse. She pawed vaguely at the spill, muttering.

"I just stared at her trying to figure out what had hit me. An ordinary figure, a soft avidness in the face. Eyes heavy, satiated-looking. She was totally sexualized. I remember her throat pulsed. She had one hand up touching her scarf, which had slipped off her shoulder. I saw angry bruises there. That really tore it, I understood at once those bruises had some sexual meaning.

"She was looking past my head with her face like a radar dish. Then she made an *ahhhh* sound that had nothing to do with me and grabbed my forearm as if it were a railing. One of the men behind her laughed. The woman said, 'Excuse me,' in a ridiculous voice and slipped out behind me. I wheeled around after her, nearly upsetting my futeball friend, and saw that some Sirians had come in.

"That was my first look at Sirians in the flesh, if that's the word. God knows I'd memorized every news shot, but I wasn't prepared. That tallness, that cruel thinness. That appalling alien arrogance. Ivory-blue, these were. Two males in immaculate metallic gear. Then I saw there was a female with them. An ivory-indigo exquisite with a permanent faint smile on those bone-hard lips.

"The girl who'd left me was ushering them to a table. She reminded me of a goddamn dog that wants you to follow it. Just as the crowd hid them, I saw a man join them too. A big man, expensively dressed, with something wrecked about his face.

"Then the music started and I had to apologize to my furry friend. And the Sellice dancer came out and my personal introduction to hell began."

The red-haired man fell silent for a minute enduring self-pity. Something wrecked about the face, I thought; it fit.

He pulled his face together.

"First I'll give you the only coherent observation of my entire evening. You can see it here at Big Junction, always the same. Outside of the Procya, it's humans with aliens, right? Very seldom aliens with other aliens. Never aliens with humans. It's the humans who want in."

I nodded, but he wasn't talking to me. His voice had a druggy fluency.

"Ah, yes, my Sellice. My first Sellice.

"They aren't really well built, y'know, under those cloaks. No waist to speak of and short-legged. But they flow when they walk.

"This one flowed out into the spotlight, cloaked to the ground in violet silk. You could only see a fall of black hair and tassels over a narrow face like a vole. She was a mole-gray. They come in all colors, their fur is like a flexible velvet all over; only the color changes startlingly around their eyes and lips and other places. Erogenous zones? Ah, man, with them it's not zones.

"She began to do what we'd call a dance, but it's no dance, it's their natural movement. Like smiling, say, with us. The music built up, and her arms undulated toward me, letting the cloak fall apart little by little. She was naked under it. The spotlight started to pick up her body markings moving in the slit of the cloak. Her arms floated apart and I saw more and more.

"She was fantastically marked and the markings were writhing. Not like body paint—alive. Smiling, that's a good word for it. As if her whole body was smiling sexually, beckoning, winking, urging, pouting, speaking to me. You've seen a classic Egyptian belly dance? Forget it—a sorry stiff thing compared to what any Sellice can do. This one was ripe, near term.

"Her arms went up and those blazing lemon-colored curves pulsed, waved, everted, contracted, throbbed, evolved unbelievably welcoming, inciting permutations. *Come do it to me, do it, do it here and here and here and now.* You couldn't see the rest of her, only a wicked flash of mouth. Every human male in the room was aching to ram himself into that incredible body. I mean it was *pain.* Even the other aliens were quiet, except one of the Sirians who was chewing out a waiter.

"I was a basket case before she was halfway through. . . . I won't bore you with what happened next; before it was over there were several fights and I got out. My money ran out on the third night. She was gone next day.

"I didn't have time to find out about the Sellice cycle then, mercifully. That came after I went back to campus and discovered you had to have a degree in solid-state electronics to apply for off-planet work. I was a premed but I got that degree. It only took me as far as First Junction then.

"Oh, god, First Junction. I thought I was in heaven—the alien ships coming in and our freighters going out. I saw them all, all but the real exotics, the tankies. You only see a few of those a cycle, even here. And the Yyeire. You've never seen that.

"Go home, boy. Go home to your version of Burned Barn. . . .

"The first Yyeir I saw I dropped everything and started walking after it like a starving hound, just breathing. You've seen the pix of course. Like lost dreams. *Man is in love and loves what vanishes.* . . . It's the scent, you can't guess that. I followed until I ran into a slammed port. I spent half a cycle's credits sending the creature the wine they call stars' tears. . . . Later I found out it was a male. That made no difference at all.

"You can't have sex with them, y'know. No way. They breed by light or something, no one knows exactly. There's a story about a man who got hold of a Yyeir woman and tried. They had him skinned. Stories—"

He was starting to wander.

"What about that girl in the bar, did you see her again?"

He came back from somewhere.

"Oh, yes. I saw her. She'd been making it with the two Sirians, y'know. The males do it in pairs. Said to be the total sexual thing for a woman, if she can stand the damage from those beaks. I wouldn't know. She talked to me a couple of times after they finished with her. No use for men whatever. She drove off the P Street bridge. . . . The man, poor bastard, he was trying to keep that Sirian bitch happy single-handed. Money helps, for a while. I don't know where he ended."

He glanced at his wrist again. I saw the pale bare place where a watch had been and told him the time.

"Is that the message you want to give Earth? Never love an alien?"

"Never love an alien—" He shrugged. "Yeah. No. Ah, Jesus, don't you see? Everything going out, nothing coming back. Like the poor damned Polynesians. We're gutting Earth, to begin with. Swapping raw resources for junk. Alien status symbols. Tape decks, Coca-Cola and Mickey Mouse watches."

"Well, there is concern over the balance of trade. Is that your message?"

"The balance of trade." He rolled it sardonically. "Did

the Polynesians have a word for it, I wonder? You don't
see, do you? All right, why are you here? I mean *you,* personally. How many guys did you climb over——"

He went rigid, hearing footsteps outside. The Procya's
hopeful face appeared around the corner. The red-haired
man snarled at him and he backed out. I started to protest.

"Ah, the silly reamer loves it. It's the only pleasure we
have left. . . . Can't you see, man? That's *us.* That's the
way we look to them, to the real ones."

"But——"

"And now we're getting the cheap C-drive, we'll be all
over just like the Procya. For the pleasure of serving as
freight monkeys and junction crews. Oh, they appreciate
our ingenious little service stations, the beautiful star folk.
They don't *need* them, y'know. Just an amusing conve-
nience. D'you know what I do here with my two degrees?
What I did at First Junction. Tube cleaning. A swab.
Sometimes I get to replace a fitting."

I muttered something; the self-pity was getting heavy.

"Bitter? Man, it's a *good* job. Sometimes I get to talk to
one of them." His face twisted. "My wife works as a——oh,
hell, you wouldn't know. I'd trade——correction, I have
traded——everything Earth offered me for just that chance.
To see them. To speak to them. Once in a while to touch
one. Once in a great while to find one low enough, per-
verted enough to want to touch me——"

His voice trailed off and suddenly came back strong.

"And so will you!" He glared at me. "Go home! Go
home and tell them to quit it. Close the ports. Burn every
god-lost alien thing before it's too late! That's what the
Polynesians didn't do."

"But surely——"

"But surely be damned! Balance of trade——balance of
life, man. I don't know if our birth rate is going, that's not
the point. Our soul is leaking out. We're bleeding to
death!"

He took a breath and lowered his tone.

"What I'm trying to tell you, this is a trap. We've hit the
supernormal stimulus. Man is exogamous——all our history
is one long drive to find and impregnate the stranger. Or
get impregnated by him, it works for women too. Anything different-colored, different nose, ass, anything, man
has to fuck it or die trying. That's a drive, y'know, it's built

in. Because it works fine as long as the stranger is human. For millions of years that kept the genes circulating. But now we've met aliens we can't screw, and we're about to die trying. . . . Do you think I can touch my wife?"

"But—"

"Look. Y'know, if you give a bird a fake egg like its own but bigger and brighter-marked, it'll roll its own egg out of the nest and sit on the fake? That's what we're doing."

"You've only been talking about sex." I was trying to conceal my impatience. "Which is great, but the kind of story I'd hoped—"

"Sex? No, it's deeper." He rubbed his head, trying to clear the drug. "Sex is only part of it, there's more. I've seen Earth missionaries, teachers, sexless people. Teachers—they end cycling waste or pushing floaters, but they're hooked. They stay. I saw one fine-looking old woman, she was servant to a Cu'ushbar kid. A defective—his own people would have let him die. That wretch was swabbing up its vomit as if it was holy water. Man, it's deep . . . some cargo-cult of the soul. We're built to dream outwards. They laugh at us. They don't have it."

There were sounds of movement in the next corridor. The dinner crowd was starting. I had to get rid of him and get there; maybe I could find the Procya. A side door opened and a figure started toward us. At first I thought it was an alien and then I saw it was a woman wearing an awkward body-shell. She seemed to be limping slightly. Behind her I could glimpse the dinner-bound throng passing the open door.

The man got up as she turned into the bay. They didn't greet each other.

"The station employs only happily wedded couples," he told me with that ugly laugh. "We give each other . . . comfort."

He took one of her hands. She flinched as he drew it over his arm and let him turn her passively, not looking at me. "Forgive me if I don't introduce you. My wife appears fatigued."

I saw that one of her shoulders was grotesquely scarred.

"Tell them," he said, turning to go. "Go home and tell them." Then his head snapped back toward me and he added quietly, "And stay away from the Syrtis desk or I'll kill you."

They went away up the corridor.

I changed tapes hurriedly with one eye on the figures passing that open door. Suddenly among the humans I caught a glimpse of two sleek scarlet shapes. My first real aliens! I snapped the recorder shut and ran to squeeze in behind them.

Angel's Egg

BY EDGAR PANGBORN

*The late Edgar Pangborn was never a tremendously pro-
lific writer (five SF novels, one or two mainstream novels,
and a baker's dozen or so of short pieces), but nevertheless
he is one of that select crew of underappreciated authors
(one thinks of Cordwainer Smith, Jack Vance, Philip K.
Dick, Avram Davidson, Fritz Leiber, Richard McKenna)
who have had an enormous underground effect on the field
simply by impressing the hell out of other writers, and
numerous authors-in-the-egg. Pangborn wrote about "little
people" for the most part, only rarely focusing on the
famous and powerful. He was one of only three or four
working SF authors capable of writing about small-town
people and rural people with insight and sympathy (most
SF is urban in orientation), and he was also one of the very
few who could get inside the minds of both the very young
and the very old with equal ease and compassion. He had
a depth and breadth of humanity that have rarely been
matched inside the field or out, and he will be missed.*

*Pangborn's masterpiece, Davy—the best postholocaust
novel ever written, only Miller's A Canticle for Leibowitz
giving it any competition—would by itself be enough to
guarantee him a distinguished place in the history of the
genre, but there were also novels like A Mirror for Observers—his International Fantasy Award winner, in which
alien observers from two opposing philosophical camps vie
for the soul of a brilliant human boy—West of the Sun,
The Judgement of Eve, The Company of Glory, and short
works like "A Master of Babylon," "Longtooth," and the
story that follows, "Angel's Egg," one of the classic stories
of alien contact.*

*The stories in this anthology contain many ethical aliens,
from Budrys's well-intentioned castaways to Knight's So-*

cratic law-giver, but the aliens in "Angel's Egg" go beyond mere ethical responsibility—they are good creatures, benign and benevolent in a fashion that is literally unworldly.

This is an example of a characteristic theme that runs throughout Pangborn's work: that a race of morally superior, more highly evolved creatures will help humanity to help itself out of the jungle—not (as in the UFO-believer Space Brothers mythos) by magically solving our problems for us, or by imposing an alien Pax Romana, but by teaching us, ironically, to become more human. It can be traced from "Angel's Egg" through A Mirror for Observers to "Mount Charity," and turns up, in somewhat different keys, in "The Wrens in Grandpa's Whiskers," "A Better Mousehole," and West of the Sun as well. Pangborn was sometimes accused of naïveté and cock-eyed optimism on these very grounds, but I don't think the charge is true, or rather, it is not all of the truth. Pangborn knew perfectly well the kind of deviltry that we are all capable of—he just refused to conclude that that's all we are capable of. And by so doing, he helped us all to learn how to be a little more human, in the best sense of the word.

Pangborn's most recent book is Still I Persist in Wondering, a collection of short stories set in the Davy universe, published posthumously in 1978.

LETTER OF RECORD, BLAINE TO MC CARRAN,
DATED AUGUST 10, 1951

Mr. Cleveland McCarran
Federal Bureau of Investigation
Washington, D.C.

Dear Sir:

In compliance with your request I enclose herewith a
transcript of the pertinent sections of the journal of Dr.
David Bannerman deceased. The original document is being held at this office until proper disposition can be determined.

Our investigation has shown no connection between Dr.
Bannerman and any organization, subversive or otherwise.
So far as we can learn, he was exactly what he seemed, an
inoffensive summer resident, retired, with a small independent income—a recluse to some extent, but well spoken
of by local tradesmen and other neighbors. A connection
between Dr. Bannerman and the type of activity that concerns your Department would seem most unlikely.

The following information is summarized from the earlier parts of Dr. Bannerman's journal, and tallies with the
results of our own limited inquiry. He was born in

65

1898 at Springfield, Massachusetts, attended public school there, and was graduated from Harvard College in 1922, his studies having been interrupted by two years' military service. He was wounded in action in Argonne, receiving a spinal injury. He earned a doctorate in biology in 1926. Delayed aftereffects of his war injury necessitated hospitalization, 1927–8. From 1929 to 1948 he taught elementary sciences in a private school in Boston. He published two textbooks in introductory biology, 1929 and 1937. In 1948 he retired from teaching: a pension and a modest income from textbook royalties evidently made this possible. Aside from the spinal deformity, which caused him to walk with a stoop, his health is said to have been fair. Autopsy findings suggested that the spinal condition must have given him considerable pain; he is not known to have mentioned this to anyone, not even to his physician, Dr. Lester Morse. There is no evidence whatever of drug addiction or alcoholism.

At one point early in his journal Dr. Bannerman describes himself as "a naturalist of the puttering type—I would rather sit on a log than write monographs: it pays off better." Dr. Morse, and others who knew Dr. Bannerman personally, tell me that this conveys a hint of his personality.

I am not qualified to comment on the material of this journal, except to say I have no evidence to support (or to contradict) Dr. Bannerman's statements. The journal has been studied only by my immediate superiors, by Dr. Morse, and by myself. I take it for granted you will hold the matter in strictest confidence.

With the journal I am enclosing a statement by Dr. Morse, written at my request for our records and for your information. You will note that he says, with some qualifications, that "death was not inconsistent with an embolism." He has signed a death certificate on that basis. You will recall from my letter of August 5 that it was Dr. Morse who discovered Dr. Bannerman's body. Because he was a close personal friend of the deceased, Dr. Morse did not feel able to perform the autopsy himself. It was done by a Dr. Stephen Clyde of this city, and was virtually negative as regards cause of death, neither confirming nor contradicting Dr. Morse's original tentative diagnosis. If you wish to read the autopsy report in full I shall be glad to forward a copy.

Dr. Morse tells me that so far as he knows, Dr. Bannerman had no near relatives. He never married. For the last twelve summers he occupied a small cottage on a back road about twenty-five miles from this city, and had few visitors. The neighbor, Steele, mentioned in the journal is a farmer, aged sixty-eight, of good character, who tells me he "never got really acquainted with Dr. Bannerman."

At this office we feel that unless new information comes to light, further active investigation is hardly justified.

Respectfully yours,
GARRISON BLAINE
Capt., State Police
Augusta, Me.

Encl.: Extract from Journal of David Bannerman, dec'd.
Statement by Lester Morse, M.D.

LIBRARIAN'S NOTE: The following document, originally attached as an unofficial "rider" to the foregoing letter, was donated to this institution in 1994 through the courtesy of Mrs. Helen McCarran, widow of the martyred first president of the World Federation. Other personal and state papers of President McCarran, many of them dating from the early period when he was employed by the FBI, are accessible to public view at the Institute of World History, Copenhagen.

PERSONAL NOTE,
BLAINE TO MC CARRAN,
DATED AUGUST 10, 1951

Dear Cleve:

Guess I didn't make it clear in my other letter that that bastard Clyde was responsible for my having to drag you into this. He is something to handle with tongs. Happened thusly— When he came in to heave the autopsy report at me, he was already having pups just because it was so completely negative (he does have certain types of honesty), and he caught sight of a page or two of the journal on my desk. Doc Morse was with me at the time. I fear we both got upstage with him (Clyde has that effect, and we were both in a State of Mind anyway), so right away the old drip thinks he smells something subversive. Belongs to the atomize-'em-NOW-WOW-WOW school of thought—nuf sed? He went into a grand whuff-whuff about referring to Higher Authority, and I knew that meant your hive, so I wanted to get ahead of the letter I knew he'd write. I suppose his literary effort couldn't be just sort of quietly transferred to File 13, otherwise known as the Appropriate Receptacle?

He can say what he likes about my character, if any, but even I never supposed he'd take a sideswipe at his professional colleague. Doc Morse is the best of the best and would not dream of suppressing any evidence important to us, as you say Clyde's letter hints. What Doc did do was to tell Clyde, pleasantly, in the privacy of my office, to go take a flying this-and-that at the moon. I only wish I'd thought of the expression myself. So Clyde rushes off to tell teacher. See what I mean about the tongs? However (knock on wood) I don't think Clyde saw enough of the journal to get any notion of what it's all about.

As for that journal, damn it, Cleve, I don't know. If you have any ideas I want them, of course. I'm afraid I believe in angels, myself. But when I think of the effect on local opinion if the story ever gets out—brother! Here was this old Bannerman living alone with a female angel and they wuzn't even common-law married. Aw, gee. . . . And the flood of phone calls from other crackpots anxious to explain it all to me. Experts in the care and feeding of angels. Methods of angel-proofing. Angels right outside the window a minute ago. Make Angels a Profitable Enterprise in Your Spare Time! ! !

When do I see you? You said you might have a week clear in October. If we could get together maybe we could make sense where there is none. I hear the cider promises to be good this year. Try and make it. My best to Ginny and the other young fry, and Helen of course.

Respeckfully yourn,
GARRY.

P.S. If you do see any angels down your way, and they aren't willing to wait for a Republican administration, by all means have them investigated by the Senate—then we'll *know* we're all nuts.

G.

EXTRACT FROM JOURNAL
OF DAVID BANNERMAN,
JUNE 1–JULY 29, 1951

June 1

It must have been at least three weeks ago when we had that flying-saucer flurry. Observers the other side of Katahdin saw it come down this side; observers this side saw it come down the other. Size anywhere from six inches to sixty feet in diameter (or was it cigar-shaped?) and speed whatever you please. Seem to recall that witnesses agreed on a rosy-pink light. There was the inevitable gobbledegookery of official explanation designed to leave everyone impressed, soothed, and disappointed. I paid scant attention to the excitement and less to the explanations—naturally, I thought it was just a flying saucer. But now Camilla has hatched out an angel.

It would have to be Camilla. Perhaps I haven't mentioned my hens enough. In the last day or two it has dawned on me that this journal may be of importance to other eyes than mine, not merely a lonely man's plaything to blunt the edge of mortality: an angel in the house makes a difference. I had better show consideration for possible readers.

I have eight hens, all yearlings except Camilla: this is her third spring. I boarded her two winters at my neighbor Steele's farm when I closed this shack and shuffled my chilly bones off to Florida, because even as a pullet she had a manner which overbore me. I could never have eaten Camilla: if she had looked at the axe with that same expression of rancid disapproval (and she would), I should have felt I was beheading a favorite aunt. Her only concession to sentiment is the annual rush of maternity to the brain—normal, for a case-hardened White Plymouth Rock.

This year she stole a nest successfully in a tangle of blackberry. By the time I located it, I estimated I was about two weeks too late. I had to outwit her by watching from a window—she is far too acute to be openly trailed from feeding-ground to nest. When I had bled and pruned my way to her hideout she was sitting on nine eggs and hating my guts. They could not be fertile, since I keep no rooster, and I was about to rob her when I saw the ninth egg was nothing of hers. It was a deep blue and transparent, with flecks of inner light that made me think of the

first stars in a clear evening. It was the same size as
Camilla's own. There was an embryo, but I could make
nothing of it. I returned the egg to Camilla's bare and fe-
vered breastbone and went back to the house for a long,
cool drink.

That was ten days ago. I know I ought to have kept
a record: I examined the blue egg every day, watching how
some nameless life grew within it. The angel has been out
of the shell three days now. This is the first time I have
felt equal to facing pen and ink.

I have been experiencing a sort of mental lassitude unfamiliar to me. Wrong word: not so much lassitude as a
preoccupation, with no sure clue to what it is that preoc-
cupies me. By reputation I am a scientist of sorts. Right
now I have no impulse to look for data; I want to sit quiet
and let truth come to a relaxed mind if it will. Could be
merely a part of growing older, but I doubt that. The
broken pieces of the wonderful blue shell are on my desk. I
have been peering at them—into them—for the last ten
minutes or more. Can't call it study: my thought wanders
into their blue, learning nothing I can retain in words. It
does not convey much to say I have gone into a vision of
open sky—and of peace, if such a thing there be.

The angel chipped the shell deftly in two parts. This was
evidently done with the aid of small horny outgrowths on
her elbows; these growths were sloughed off on the second
day. I wish I had seen her break the shell, but when I
visited the blackberry tangle three days ago she was already out. She poked her exquisite head through Camilla's
neck feathers, smiled sleepily, and snuggled back into darkness to finish drying off. So what could I do, more than
save the broken shell and wriggle my clumsy self out of
there? I had removed Camilla's own eggs the day before—
Camilla was only moderately annoyed. I was nervous about
disposing of them, even though they were obviously
Camilla's, but no harm was done. I cracked each one to be
sure. Very frankly rotten eggs and nothing more.

In the evening of that day I thought of rats and weasels,
as I should have done earlier. I prepared a box in the
kitchen and brought the two in, the angel quiet in my
closed hand. They are there now. I think they are comfortable.

Three days after hatching, the angel is the length of my
forefinger, say three inches tall, with about the relative

proportions of a six-year-old girl. Except for head, hands, and probably the soles of her feet, she is clothed in down the color of ivory; what can be seen of her skin is a glowing pink—I do mean glowing, like the inside of certain seashells. Just above the small of her back are two stubs which I take to be infantile wings. They do not suggest an extra pair of specialized fore limbs. I think they are wholly differentiated organs; perhaps they will be like the wings of an insect. Somehow, I never thought of angels buzzing. Maybe she won't. I know very little about angels. At present the stubs are covered with some dull tissue, no doubt a protective sheath to be discarded when the membranes (if they are membranes) are ready to grow. Between the stubs is a not very prominent ridge—special musculature, I suppose. Otherwise her shape is quite human, even to a pair of minuscule mammalian buttons just visible under the down; how that can-make sense in an egg-laying organism is beyond my comprehension. (Just for the record, so is a Corot landscape; so is Schubert's *Unfinished;* so is the flight of a hummingbird, or the otherworld of frost on a window pane.) The down on her head has grown visibly in three days and is of different quality from the body down—later it may resemble human hair, as a diamond resembles a chunk of granite. . . .

A curious thing has happened. I went to Camilla's box after writing that. Judy* was already lying in front of it, unexcited. The angel's head was out from under the feathers, and I thought—with more verbal distinctness than such thoughts commonly take, "So here I am, a naturalist of middle years and cold sober, observing a three-inch oviparous mammal with down and wings." The thing is— she giggled. Now, it might have been only amusement at my appearance, which to her must be enormously gross and comic. But another thought formed unspoken: "I am no longer lonely." And her face (hardly bigger than a dime) immediately changed from laughter to a brooding and friendly thoughtfulness.

Judy and Camilla are old friends. Judy seems untroubled by the angel. I have no worries about leaving them alone together. I must sleep.

---

* Dr. Bannerman's dog, mentioned often earlier in the journal. A nine-year-old English setter. According to an entry of May 15, 1951, she was then beginning to go blind.—BLAINE.

I made no entry last night. The angel was talking to me, and when that was finished I drowsed off immediately on a cot that I have moved into the kitchen so as to be near them.

I had never been strongly impressed by the evidence for extrasensory perception. It is fortunate my mind was able to accept the novelty, since to the angel it is clearly a matter of course. Her tiny mouth is most expressive but moves only for that reason and for eating—not for speech. Probably she could speak to her own kind if she wished, but I dare say the sound would be outside the range of my hearing as well as of my understanding.

Last night after I brought the cot in and was about to finish my puttering bachelor supper, she climbed to the edge of the box and pointed, first at herself and then at the top of the kitchen table. Afraid to let my vast hand take hold of her, I held it out flat and she sat in my palm. Camilla was inclined to fuss, but the angel looked over her shoulder and Camilla subsided, watchful but no longer alarmed.

The tabletop is porcelain, and the angel shivered. I folded a towel and spread a silk handkerchief on top of that; the angel sat on this arrangement with apparent comfort, near my face. I was not even bewildered. Possibly she had already instructed me to blank out my mind. At any rate, I did so, without conscious effort to that end.

She reached me first with visual imagery. How can I make it plain that this had nothing in common with my sleeping dreams? There was no weight of symbolism from my littered past; no discoverable connection with any of yesterday's commonplaces; indeed, no actual involvement of my personality at all. I saw. I was moving vision, though without eyes or other flesh. And while my mind saw, it also knew where my flesh was, slumped at the kitchen table. If anyone had entered the kitchen, if there had been a noise of alarm out in the hen house, I should have known it.

There was a valley such as I have not seen (and never will) on Earth. I have seen many beautiful places on this planet—some of them were even tranquil. Once I took a slow steamer to New Zealand and had the Pacific as a plaything for many days. I can hardly say how I knew this was not Earth. The grass of the valley was an earthly green;

a river below me was a blue-and-silver thread under fa-
miliar-seeming sunlight; there were trees much like pine
and maple, and maybe that is what they were. But it was
not Earth. I was aware of mountains heaped to strange
heights on either side of the valley—snow, rose, amber,
gold. Perhaps the amber tint was unlike any mountain
color I have noticed in this world at midday.

Or I may have known it was not Earth simply because
her mind—dwelling within some unimaginable brain
smaller than the tip of my little finger—told me so.

I watched two inhabitants of that world come flying to
rest in the field of sunny grass where my bodiless vision
had brought me. Adult forms, such as my angel would
surely be when she had her growth, except that both of
these were male and one of them was dark-skinned. The
latter was also old, with a thousand-wrinkled face, knowing and full of tranquility; the other was flushed and lively
with youth; both were beautiful. The down of the brown-
skinned old one was reddish-tawny; the other's was ivory
with hints of orange. Their wings were true membranes,
with more variety of subtle iridescence than I have seen
even in the wings of a dragonfly; I could not say that any
color was dominant, for each motion brought a ripple of
change. These two sat at their ease on the grass. I realized
that they were talking to each other, though their lips did
not move in speech more than once or twice. They would
nod, smile, now and then illustrate something with twin-
kling hands.

A huge rabbit lolloped past them. I knew (thanks to my
own angel's efforts, I supposed) that this animal was of the
same size as our common wild ones. Later, a blue-green
snake three times the size of the angels came flowing
through the grass; the old one reached out to stroke its
head carelessly, and I think he did it without interrupting
whatever he was saying.

Another creature came, in leisured leaps. He was monstrous, yet I felt no alarm in the angels or in myself. Imagine a being built somewhat like a kangaroo up to the head,
about eight feet tall, and katydid-green. Really, the thick
balancing tail and enormous legs were the only kangaroolike features about him; the body above the massive thighs
was not dwarfed but thick and square; the arms and hands
were quite humanoid: the head was round, manlike except
for its face—there was only a single nostril and his mouth

was set in the vertical; the eyes were large and mild. I received an impression of high intelligence and natural gentleness. In one of his manlike hands two tools so familiar and ordinary that I knew my body by the kitchen table had laughed in startled recognition. But, after all, a garden spade and rake are basic. Once invented—I expect we did it ourselves in the Neolithic Age—there is little reason why they should change much down the millennia.

This farmer halted by the angels, and the three conversed awhile. The big head nodded agreeably. I believe the young angel made a joke; certainly the convulsions in the huge green face made me think of laughter. Then this amiable monster turned up the grass in a patch a few yards square, broke the sod and raked the surface smooth, just as any competent gardener might do—except that he moved with the relaxed smoothness of a being whose strength far exceeds the requirements of his task. . . .

I was back in my kitchen with everyday eyes. My angel was exploring the table. I had a loaf of bread there and a dish of strawberries and cream. She was trying a breadcrumb; seemed to like it fairly well. I offered the strawberries; she broke off one of the seeds and nibbled it but didn't care so much for the pulp. I held up the great spoon with sugary cream; she steadied it with both hands to try some. I think she liked it. It had been most stupid of me not to realize that she would be hungry. I brought wine from the cupboard; she watched inquiringly, so I put a couple of drops on the handle of a spoon. This really pleased her: she chuckled and patted her tiny stomach, though I'm afraid it wasn't awfully good sherry. I brought some crumbs of cake, but she indicated that she was full, came close to my face, and motioned me to lower my head.

She reached me until she could press both hands against my forehead—I felt it only enough to know her hands were there—and she stood so a long time, trying to tell me something.

It was difficult. Pictures come through with relative ease, but now she was transmitting an abstraction of a complex kind: my clumsy brain really suffered in the effort to receive. Something did come across. I have only the crudest way of passing it on. Imagine an equilateral triangle; place the following words one at each corner—"recruiting," "collecting," "saving." The meaning she wanted to convey ought to be near the center of the triangle.

I had also the sense that her message provided a partial explanation of her errand in this lovable and damnable world.

She looked weary when she stood away from me. I put out my palm and she climbed into it, to be carried back to the nest.

She did not talk to me tonight, nor eat, but she gave a reason, coming out from Camilla's feathers long enough to turn her back and show me the wing stubs. The protective sheaths have dropped off; the wings are rapidly growing. They are probably damp and weak. She was quite tired and went back into the warm darkness almost at once.

Camilla must be exhausted, too. I don't think she has been off the nest more than twice since I brought them into the house.

June 4

Today she can fly.

I learned it in the afternoon, when I was fiddling about in the garden and Judy was loafing in the sunshine she loves. Something apart from sight and sound called me to hurry back to the house. I saw my angel through the screen door before I opened it. One of her feet had caught in a hideous loop of loose wire at a break in the mesh. Her first tug of alarm must have tightened the loop so that her hands were not strong enough to force it open.

Fortunately I was able to cut the wire with a pair of shears before I lost my head; then she could free her foot without injury. Camilla had been frantic, rushing around fluffed up, but—here's an odd thing—perfectly silent. None of the recognized chicken noises of dismay: if an ordinary chick had been in trouble she would have raised the roof.

The angel flew to me and hovered, pressing her hands on my forehead. The message was clear at once: "No harm done." She flew down to tell Camilla the same thing.

Yes, in the same way. I saw Camilla standing near my feet with her neck out and head low, and the angel put a hand on either side of her scraggy comb. Camilla relaxed, clucked in the normal way, and spread her wings for a shelter. The angel went under it, but only to oblige Camilla, I think—at least, she stuck her head through the wing feathers and winked.

She must have seen something else, then, for she came out and flew back to me and touched a finger to my cheek, looked at the finger, saw it was wet, put it in her mouth, made a face, and laughed at me.

We went outdoors into the sun (Camilla too), and the angel gave me an exhibition of what flying ought to be. Not even Schubert can speak of joy as her first free flying did. At one moment she would be hanging in front of my eyes, radiant and delighted; the next instant she would be a dot of color against a cloud. Try to imagine something that would make a hummingbird seem a bit dull and sluggish.

They do hum. Softer than a hummingbird, louder than a dragonfly.

Something like the sound of hawk moths—*Heinmaris thisbe*, for instance: the one I used to call Hummingbird Moth when I was a child.

I was frightened, naturally. Frightened first at what might happen to her, but that was unnecessary; I don't think she would be in danger from any savage animal except possibly Man. I saw a Cooper's hawk slant down the invisible toward the swirl of color where she was dancing by herself; presently she was drawing iridescent rings around him; then, while he soared in smaller circles, I could not see her, but (maybe she felt my fright) she was again in front of me, pressing my forehead in the now familiar way. I knew she was amused and caught the idea that the hawk was a "lazy character." Not quite the way I'd describe *Accipiter Cooperi*, but it's all in the point of view. I believe she had been riding his back, no doubt with her speaking hands on his terrible head.

And later I was frightened by the thought that she might not want to return to me. Can I compete with sunlight and open sky? The passage of that terror through me brought her back swiftly, and her hands said with great clarity: "Don't ever be afraid of anything—it isn't necessary for you."

Once this afternoon I was saddened by the realization that old Judy can take little part in what goes on now. I can well remember Judy running like the wind. The angel must have heard this thought in me, for she stood a long time beside Judy's drowsy head, while Judy's tail thumped cheerfully on the warm grass. . . .

In the evening the angel made a heavy meal on two or three cake crumbs and another drop of sherry, and we had what was almost a sustained conversation. I will write it in that form this time, rather than grope for anything more exact. I asked her, "How far away is your home?"

"My home is here."

"Thank God—but I meant, the place your people came from."

"Ten light-years."

"The images you showed me—that quiet valley—that is ten light-years away?"

"Yes. But that was my father talking to you, through me. He was grown when the journey began. He is two hundred and forty years old—our years, thirty-two days longer than yours."

Mainly I was conscious of a flood of relief: I had feared, on the basis of terrestrial biology, that the explosively rapid growth after hatching must foretell a brief life. But it's all right—she can outlive me, and by a few hundred years, at that. "Your father is here now, on this planet—shall I see him?"

She took her hands away—listening, I believe. The answer was: "No. He is sorry. He is ill and cannot live long. I am to see him in a few days, when I fly a little better. He taught me for twenty years after I was born."

"I don't understand. I thought—"

"Later, friend. My father is grateful for your kindness to me."

I don't know what I thought about that. I felt no faintest trace of condescension in the message. "And he was showing me things he had seen with his own eyes, ten light-years away?"

"Yes." Then she wanted me to rest awhile; I am sure she knows what a huge effort it is for my primitive brain to function in this way. But before she ended the conversation by humming down to her nest she gave me this, and I received it with such clarity that I cannot be mistaken: "He says that only fifty million years ago it was a jungle there, just as Terra is now."

June 8

When I woke four days ago the angel was having breakfast, and little Camilla was dead. The angel watched me run sleep out of my eyes, watched me discover Camilla, and then flew to me. I received this: "Does it make you unhappy?"

"I don't know exactly." You can get fond of a hen, especially a cantankerous and homely old one whose personality has a lot in common with your own.

"She was old. She wanted a flock of chicks, and I couldn't stay with her. So I—" Something obscure here: probably my mind was trying too hard to grasp it—". . . so I saved her life." I could make nothing else out of it. She said "saved."

Camilla's death looked natural, except that I should have expected the death contractions to muss the straw, and that hadn't happened. Maybe the angel had arranged the old lady's body for decorum, though I don't see how her muscular strength would have been equal to it—Camilla weighed at least seven pounds.

As I was burying her at the edge of the garden and the angel was humming over my head, I recalled a thing which, when it happened, I had dismissed as a dream. Merely a moonlight image of the angel standing in the nest box with her hands on Camilla's head, then pressing her mouth gently on Camilla's throat, just before the hen's head sank down out of my line of vision. Probably I actually waked and saw it happen. I am somehow unconcerned—even, as I think more about it, pleased. . . .

After the burial the angel's hands said, "Sit on the grass and we'll talk. . . . Question me. I'll tell you what I can. My father asks you to write it down."

So that is what we have been doing for the last four days. I have been going to school, a slow but willing pupil. Rather than enter anything in this journal (for in the evenings I was exhausted), I made notes as best I could. The angel has gone now to see her father and will not return until morning. I shall try to make a readable version of my notes.

Since she had invited questions, I began with something which had been bothering me, as a would-be naturalist, exceedingly. I couldn't see how creatures no larger than the adults I had observed could lay eggs as large as Camilla's. Nor could I understand why, if they were hatched in an almost adult condition and able to eat a varied diet, she had any use for that ridiculous, lovely, and apparently functional pair of breasts. When the angel grasped my difficulty she exploded with laughter—her kind, which buzzed her all over the garden and caused her to fluff my hair on the wing and pinch my earlobe. She lit on a rhubarb leaf and gave a delectably naughty representation of herself

as a hen laying an egg, including the cackle. She got me
to bumbling helplessly—my kind of laughter—and it was
some time before we could quiet down. Then she did her
best to explain.

They are true mammals, and the young—not more than
two or at most three in a lifetime averaging two hundred
and fifty years—are delivered in very much the human way.
The baby is nursed—human fashion—until his brain begins
to respond a little to their unspoken language; that takes
three to four weeks. Then he is placed in an altogether different medium. She could not describe that clearly, because
there was very little in my educational storehouse to help me
grasp it. It is some gaseous medium that arrests bodily
growth for an almost indefinite period, while mental
growth continues. It took them, she says, about seven thousand years to perfect this technique after they first hit on
the idea; they are never in a hurry. The infant remains
under this delicate and precise control for anywhere from
fifteen to thirty years, the period depending not only on his
mental vigor but also on the type of lifework he tentatively
elects as soon as his brain is knowing enough to make a
choice. During this period his mind is guided with unwavering patience by teachers who—

It seems those teachers know their business. This was
peculiarly difficult for me to assimilate, although the fact
came through clearly enough. In their world, the profession
of teacher is more highly honored than any other—can
such a thing be possible?—and so difficult to enter that
only the strongest minds dare attempt it. (I had to rest
awhile after absorbing that.) An aspirant must spend fifty
years (not including the period of infantile education) in
merely getting ready to begin, and the acquisition of fac-
tual knowledge, while not understressed, takes only a small
proportion of those fifty years. Then—if he's good enough
—he can take a small part in the elementary instruction of
a few babies, and if he does well on that basis for another
thirty or forty years, he is considered a fair beginner. . . .
Once upon a time I lurched around stuffy classrooms trying to insert a few predigested facts (I wonder how many
of them *were* facts?) into the minds of bored and preoccupied adolescents, some of whom may have liked me moderately well. I was even able to shake hands and be nice
while their terribly well-meaning parents explained to me
how they ought to be educated. So much of our human

effort goes down the drain of futility, I sometimes wonder how we ever got as far as the Bronze Age. Somehow we did, though, and a short way beyond.

After that preliminary stage of an angel's education is finished, the baby is transferred to more ordinary surroundings, and his bodily growth completes itself in a very short time. Wings grow abruptly (as I have seen), and he reaches a maximum height of six inches (our measure). Only then does he enter on that lifetime of two hundred and fifty years, for not until then does his body begin to age. My angel has been a living personality for many years but will not celebrate her first birthday for almost a year. I like to think of that.

At about the same time that they learned the principles of interplanetary travel (approximately twelve million years ago) these people also learned how, by use of a slightly different method, growth could be arrested at any point short of full maturity. At first the knowledge served no purpose except in the control of illnesses which still occasionally struck them at that time. But when the long periods of time required for space travel were considered, the advantages became obvious.

So it happens that my angel was born ten light-years away. She was trained by her father and many others in the wisdom of seventy million years (that, she tells me, is the approximate sum of their *recorded* history), and then she was safely seated and cherished in what my super-amœbic brain regarded as a blue egg. Education did not proceed at that time; her mind went to sleep with the rest of her. When Camilla's temperature made her wake and grow again, she remembered what to do with the little horny bumps provided for her elbows. And came out—into this planet, God help her.

I wondered why her father should have chosen any combination so unreliable as an old hen and a human being. Surely he must have had plenty of excellent ways to bring the shell to the right temperature. Her answer should have satisfied me immensely, but I am still compelled to wonder about it. "Camilla was a nice hen, and my father studied your mind while you were asleep. It was a bad landing, and much was broken—no such landing was ever made before after so long a journey: forty years. Only four other grown-ups could come with my father.

Three of them died *en route* and he is very ill. And there were nine other children to care for."

Yes, I knew she'd said that an angel thought I was good enough to be trusted with his daughter. If it upsets me, all I need do is look at her and then in the mirror. As for the explanation, I can only conclude there must be more that I am not ready to understand. I was worried about those nine others, but she assured me they were all well, and I ought not to ask more about them at present. . . .

Their planet, she says, is closely similar to this. A trifle larger, moving in a somewhat longer orbit around a sun like ours. Two gleaming moons, smaller than ours—their orbits are such that two-moon nights come rarely. They are magic, and she will ask her father to show me one, if he can. Their year is thirty-two days longer than ours; because of a slower rotation, their day has twenty-six of our hours. Their atmosphere is mainly nitrogen and oxygen in the proportions familiar to us; slightly richer in some of the rare gases. The climate is now what we should call tropical and subtropical, but they have known glacial rigors like those in our world's past. There are only two great continental land masses, and many thousands of large islands.

Their total population is only five billion. . . .

Most of the forms of life we know have parallels there—some quite exact parallels: rabbits, deer, mice, cats. The cats have been bred to an even higher intelligence than they possess on our Earth; it is possible, she says, to have a good deal of intellectual intercourse with their cats, who learned several million years ago that when they kill, it must be done with lightning precision and without torture. The cats had some difficulty grasping the possibility of pain in other organisms, but once that educational hurdle was passed, development was easy. Nowadays many of the cats are popular storytellers; about forty million years ago they were still occasionally needed as a special police force, and served the angels with real heroism.

It seems my angel wants to become a student of animal life here on Earth. I, a teacher!—but bless her heart for the notion, anyhow. We sat and traded animals for a couple of hours last night. I found it restful, after the mental struggle to grasp more difficult matters. Judy was something new to her. They have several luscious monsters on that planet but, in her view, so have we. She told me of a

blue sea snake fifty feet long (relatively harmless) that
bellows cowlike and comes into the tidal marshes to lay
black eggs; so I gave her a whale. She offered a bat-winged,
day-flying ball of mammalian fluff as big as my head and
weighing under an ounce; I matched her with a marmoset.
She tried me with a small-sized pink brontosaur (very
rare), but I was ready with the duck-billed platypus, and
that caused us to exchange some pretty smart remarks
about mammalian eggs; she bounced. All trivial in a way;
also, the happiest evening in my fifty-three tangled years
of life.

She was a trifle hesitant to explain these kangaroolike
people, until she was sure I really wanted to know. It
seems they are about the nearest parallel to human life on
that planet; not a near parallel, of course, as she was careful to explain. Agreeable and always friendly souls (though
they weren't always so, I'm sure) and of a somewhat more
alert intelligence than we possess. Manual workers, mainly, because they prefer it nowadays, but some of them are
excellent mathematicians. The first practical spaceship was
invented by a group of them, with some assistance. . . .

Names offer difficulties. Because of the nature of the
angelic language, they have scant use for them except for
the purpose of written record, and writing naturally plays
little part in their daily lives—no occasion to write a letter
when a thousand miles is no obstacle to the speech of
your mind. An angel's formal name is about as important
to him as, say, my Social Security number is to me. She
has not told me hers, because the phonetics on which their
written language is based have no parallel in my mind. As
we would speak a friend's name, an angel will project the
friend's image to his friend's receiving mind. More pleasant
and more intimate, I think—although it was a shock to me
at first to glimpse my own ugly mug in my mind's eye.
Stories are occasionally written, if there is something in
them that should be preserved precisely as it was in the
first telling; but in their world the true storyteller has a
more important place than the printer—he offers one of
the best of their quieter pleasures; a good one can hold his
audience for a week and never tire them.

"What is this 'angel' in your mind when you think of
me?"

"A being men have imagined for centuries, when they

thought of themselves as they might like to be and not as they are."

I did not try too painfully hard to learn much about the principles of space travel. The most my brain could take in of her explanation was something like: "Rocket—then phototropism." Now, that makes scant sense. So far as I know, phototropism—movement toward light—is an organic phenomenon. One thinks of it as a response of protoplasm, in some plants and animal organisms (most of them simple), to the stimulus of light; certainly not as a force capable of moving inorganic matter. I think that whatever may be the principle she was describing, this word "phototropism" was merely the nearest thing to it in my reservoir of language. Not even the angels can create understanding out of blank ignorance. At least I have learned not to set neat limits to the possible.

(There was a time when I did, though. I can see myself, not so many years back, like a homunculus squatting at the foot of Mt. McKinley, throwing together two handfuls of mud and shouting, "Look at the big mountain *I* made!")

And if I did know the physical principles which brought them here, and could write them in terms accessible to technicians resembling myself, I would not do it.

Here is a thing I am afraid no reader of this journal will believe: These people, as I have written, learned their method of space travel some twelve million years ago. But this is the first time they have ever used it to convey them to another planet. The heavens are rich in worlds, she tells me; on many of them there is life, often on very primitive levels. No external force prevented her people from going forth, colonizing, conquering, as far as they pleased. They could have populated a galaxy. They did not, and for this reason: they believed they were not ready. More precisely: *Not good enough.*

Only some fifty million years ago, by her account, did they learn (as we may learn eventually) that intelligence without goodness is worse than high explosive in the hands of a baboon. For beings advanced beyond the level of Pithecanthropus, intelligence is a cheap commodity—not too hard to develop, hellishly easy to use for unconsidered ends. Whereas goodness is not to be achieved without unending effort of the hardest kind, within the self, whether the self be man or angel.

It is clear even to me that the conquest of evil is only

one step, not the most important. For goodness, so she tried to tell me, is an altogether positive quality; the part of living nature that swarms with such monstrosities as cruelty, meanness, bitterness, greed, is not to be filled by a vacuum when these horrors are eliminated. When you clear away a poisonous gas, you try to fill the room with clean air. Kindness, for only one example: one who can define kindness only as the absence of cruelty has surely not begun to understand the nature of either.

They do not aim at perfection, these angels: only at the attainable. . . . That time fifty million years ago was evidently one of great suffering and confusion. War and all its attendant plagues. They passed through many centuries while advances in technology merely worsened their condition and increased the peril of self-annihilation. They came through that, in time. War was at length so far outgrown that its recurrence was impossible, and the development of wholly rational beings could begin. Then they were ready to start growing up, through millennia of self-searching, self-discipline, seeking to derive the simple from the complex, discovering how to use knowledge and not be used by it. Even then, of course, they slipped back often enough. There were what she refers to as "eras of fatigue." In their dimmer past, they had had many dark ages, lost civilizations, hopeful beginnings ending in dust. Earlier still, they had come out of the slime, as we did.

But their period of deepest uncertainty and sternest self-appraisal did not come until twelve million years ago, when they knew a universe could be theirs for the taking and knew they were not yet good enough.

They are in no more hurry than the stars. She tried to convey something, tentatively, at this point, which was really beyond both of us. It had to do with time (not as I understand time) being perhaps the most essential attribute of God (not as I was ever able to understand that word). Seeing my mental exhaustion, she gave up the effort and later told me that the conception was extremely difficult for her, too—not only, I gathered, because of her youth and relative ignorance. There was also a hint that her father might not have wished her to bring my brain up to a hurdle like that one. . . .

Of course, they explored. Their little spaceships were roaming the ether before there was anything like Man on this earth—roaming and listening, observing, recording;

never entering nor taking part in the life of any home but their own. For five million years they even forbade themselves to go beyond their own solar system, though it would have been easy to do so. And in the following seven million years, although they traveled to incredible distances, the same stern restraint was in force. It was altogether unrelated to what we should call fear—that, I think, is as extinct in them as hate. There was so much to do at home!—I wish I could imagine it. They mapped the heavens and played in their own sunlight.

Naturally, I cannot tell you what goodness is. I know only, moderately well, what it seems to mean to us human beings. It appears that the best of us can, with enormous difficulty, achieve a manner of life in which goodness is reasonably dominant, by a not too precarious balance, for the greater part of the time. Often, wise men have indicated they hope for nothing better than that in our present condition. We are, in other words, a fraction alive; the rest is in the dark. Dante was a bitter masochist, Beethoven a frantic and miserable snob, Shakespeare wrote potboilers. And Christ said, "My Father, if it be possible, let this cup pass from me."

But give us fifty million years—I am no pessimist. After all, I've watched one-celled organisms on the slide and listened to Brahms's Fourth. Night before last I said to the angel, "In spite of everything, you and I are kindred."

She granted me agreement.

She was lying on my pillow this morning so that I could see her when I waked.

Her father has died, and she was with him when it happened. There was again that thought-expression that I could interpret only to mean that his life had been "saved." I was still sleep-bound when my mind asked: "What will you do?"

"Stay with you, if you wish it, for the rest of your life." Now, the last part of the message was clouded, but I am familiar with that—it seems to mean there is some further element that eludes me. I could not be mistaken about the part I did receive. It gives me amazing speculations. After all, I am only fifty-three; I might live for another thirty or forty years. . . .

She was preoccupied this morning, but whatever she felt about her father's death that might be paralleled by sadness in a human being was hidden from me. She did say her father was sorry he had not been able to show me a two-moon night.

One adult, then, remains in this world. Except to say that he is two hundred years old and full of knowledge, and that he endured the long journey without serious ill effects, she has told me little about him. And there are ten children, including herself.

Something was sparkling at her throat. When she was aware of my interest in it she took it off, and I fetched a magnifying glass. A necklace; under the glass, much like our finest human workmanship, if your imagination can reduce it to the proper scale. The stones appeared similar to the jewels we know: diamonds, sapphires, rubies, emeralds, the diamonds snapping out every color under heaven; but there were two or three very dark-purple stones unlike anything I know—not amethysts, I am sure. The necklace was strung on something more slender than cobweb, and the design of the joining clasp was too delicate for my glass to help me. The necklace had been her mother's, she told me; as she put it back around her throat I thought I saw the same shy pride that any human girl might feel in displaying a new pretty.

She wanted to show me other things she had brought, and flew to the table where she had left a sort of satchel an inch and a half long—quite a load for her to fly with, but the translucent substance is so light that when she rested the satchel on my finger I scarcely felt it. She arranged a few articles happily for my inspection, and I put the glass to work again. One was a jeweled comb; she ran it through the down on her chest and legs to show me its use. There was a set of tools too small for the glass to interpret; I learned later they were a sewing kit. A book, and some writing instrument much like a metal pencil: imagine a book and pencil that could be used comfortably by hands hardly bigger than the paws of a mouse—that is the best I can do. The book, I understand, is a blank record for her use as needed.

And finally, when I was fully awake and dressed and we had finished breakfast, she reached in the bottom of the satchel for a parcel (heavy for her) and made me understand it was a gift for me. "My father made it for you, but I put in the stone myself, last night." She unwrapped it. A ring, precisely the size for my little finger.

I broke down, rather. She understood that, and sat on

my shoulder petting my earlobe till I had command of my-self.

I have no idea what the jewel is. It shifts with the light from purple to jade-green to amber. The metal resembles platinum in appearance except for a tinge of rose at certain angles of light. . . . When I stare into the stone, I think I see—never mind that now. I am not ready to write it down, and perhaps never will be; anyway, I must be sure.

We improved our housekeeping later in the morning. I showed her over the house. It isn't much—Cape Codder, two rooms up and two down. Every corner interested her, and when she found a shoe box in the bedroom closet, she asked for it. At her direction, I have arranged it on a chest near my bed and near the window, which will be always open; she says the mosquitoes will not bother me, and I don't doubt her. I unearthed a white silk scarf for the bottom of the box; after asking my permission (as if I could want to refuse her anything!) she got her sewing kit and snipped off a piece of the scarf several inches square, folded it on itself several times, and sewed it into a narrow pillow an inch long. So now she had a proper bed and a room of her own. I wish I had something less coarse than silk, but she insists it's nice.

We have not talked very much today. In the afternoon she flew out for an hour's play in the cloud country; when she returned she let me know that she needed a long sleep. She is still sleeping, I think; I am writing this downstairs, fearing the light might disturb her.

Is it possible I can have thirty or forty years in her company? I wonder how teachable my mind still is. I seem to be able to assimilate new facts as well as I ever could; this ungainly carcass should be durable, with reason-able care. Of course, facts without a synthetic imagination are no better than scattered bricks; but perhaps my imag-ination—

I don't know.

Judy wants to be let out. I shall turn in when she comes back. I wonder if poor Judy's life could be—the word is certainly "saved." I must ask.

June 10

Last night when I stopped writing I did go to bed but I was restless, refusing sleep. At some time in the small hours—there was light from a single room—she flew over to me. The tensions dissolved like an illness, and my mind was able to respond with a certain calm.

I made plain (what I am sure she already knew) that I would never willingly part company with her, and then she gave me to understand that there are two alternatives for the remainder of my life. The choice, she says, is altogether mine, and I must take time to be sure of my decision.

I can live out my natural span, whatever it proves to be, and she will not leave me for long at any time. She will be there to counsel, teach, help me in anything good I care to undertake. She says she would enjoy this; for some reason she is, as we'd say in our language, fond of me. We'd have fun.

Lord, the books I could write! I fumble for words now, in the usual human way: whatever I put on paper is a miserable fraction of the potential: the words themselves are rarely the right ones. But under her guidance—

I could take a fair part in shaking the world. With words alone. I could preach to my own people. Before long, I would be heard.

I could study and explore. What small nibblings we have made at the sum of available knowledge! Suppose I brought in one leaf from outdoors, or one common little bug—in a few hours of studying it with her I'd know more of my own specialty than a flood of the best textbooks could tell me.

She has also let me know that when she and those who came with her have learned a little more about the human picture, it should be possible to improve my health greatly, and probably my life expectancy. I don't imagine my back could ever straighten, but she thinks the pain might be cleared away, possibly without drugs. I could have a clearer mind, in a body that would neither fail nor torment me.

Then there is the other alternative.

It seems they have developed a technique by means of which any unresisting living subject whose brain is capable of memory at all can experience a total recall. It is a by-product, I understand, of their silent speech, and a very recent one. They have practiced it for only a few thousand years, and since their own understanding of the phenomenon is very incomplete, they classify it among their experimental techniques. In a general way, it may somewhat resemble that reliving of the past that psychoanalysis can sometimes bring about in a limited way for therapeutic purposes; but you must imagine that sort of thing tremendously magnified and clarified, capable of including every detail that has ever registered on the subject's brain; and the end result is very different. The purpose is not therapeutic, as we would understand it: quite the opposite. The end result is death. Whatever is recalled by this process is transmitted to the receiving mind, which can retain it and record any or all of it if such a record is desired; but to the subject who recalls it, it is a flowing away, without return. Thus it is not a true "remembering" but a giving. The mind is swept clear, naked of all its past, and, along with memory, life withdraws also. Very quietly. At the end, I suppose it must be like standing without resistance in the engulfment of a flood tide, until finally the waters close over.

That, it seems, is how Camilla's life was "saved." Now, when I finally grasped that, I laughed, and the angel of course caught my joke. I was thinking about my neighbor Steele, who boarded the old lady for me in his hen house for a couple of winters. Somewhere safe in the angelic records there must be a hen's-eye image of the patch in the seat of Steele's pants. Well—good. And, naturally, Camilla's view of me, too: not too unkind, I hope—she couldn't help the expression on her rigid little face, and I don't believe it ever meant anything.

At the other end of the scale is the saved life of my angel's father. Recall can be a long process, she says, depending on the intricacy and richness of the mind recalling; and in all but the last stages it can be halted at will. Her father's recall was begun when they were still far out in space and he knew that he could not long survive the journey. When that journey ended, the recall had progressed so far that very little actual memory remained to him of his life on that other planet. He had what must be called a "deductive memory"; from the material of the years not yet given away, he could reconstruct what must have been; and I assume the other adult who survived the passage must have been able to shelter him from errors that loss of memory might involve. This, I infer, is why he could not show me a two-moon night. I forgot to ask her whether the images he did send me were from actual or deductive memory. Deductive, I think, for there was a certain dimness about them not present when my angel gives me a picture of something seen with her own eyes.

Jade-green eyes, by the way—were you wondering?

In the same fashion, my own life could be saved. Every aspect of existence that I ever touched, that ever touched me, could be transmitted to some perfect record. The nature of the written record is beyond me, but I have no doubt of its relative perfection. Nothing important, good or bad, would be lost. And they need a knowledge of humanity, if they are to carry out whatever it is they have in mind.

It would be difficult, she tells me, and sometimes painful. Most of the effort would be hers, but some of it would have to be mine. In her period of infantile education, she elected what we should call zoology as her lifework; for that reason she was given intensive theoretical training in this technique. Right now, I guess she knows more than anyone else on this planet not only about what makes a hen tick but about how it feels to be a hen. Though a beginner, she is in all essentials already an expert. She can help me, she thinks (if I choose this alternative)—at any rate, ease me over the toughest spots, soothe away resistance, keep my courage from too much flagging.

For it seems that this process of recall is painful to an advanced intellect (she, without condescension, calls us very advanced) because, while all pretense and self-delusion are stripped away, there remains conscience, still functioning by whatever standards of good and bad the individual has developed in his lifetime. Our present knowledge of our own motives is such a pathetically small beginning!—hardly stronger than an infant's first effort to focus his eyes. I am merely wondering how much of my life (if I choose this way) will seem to me altogether hideous. Certainly plenty of the "good deeds" that I still cherish in memory like so many well-behaved cherubs will turn up with the leering aspect of greed or petty vanity or worse.

Not that I am a bad man, in any reasonable sense of the term; not a bit of it. I respect myself; no occasion to grovel and beat my chest; I'm not ashamed to stand comparison with any other fair sample of the species. But there you are: I *am* human, and under the aspect of eternity so far, plus this afternoon's newspaper, that is a rather serious thing.

Without real knowledge, I think of this total recall as something like a passage down a corridor of myriad images—now dark, now brilliant; now pleasant, now horrible—guided by no certainty except an awareness of the open blind door at the end of it. It could have its pleasing moments and its consolations. I don't see how it could ever approximate the delight and satisfaction of living a few more years in this world with the angel lighting on my shoulder when she wishes, and talking to me.

I had to ask her of how great value such a record would be to them. Very great. Obvious enough—they can be of little use to us, by their standards, until they understand us; and they came here to be of use to us as well as to themselves. And understanding us, to them, means knowing us inside out with a completeness such as our most dedicated and laborious scholars could never imagine. I remember those twelve million years; they will not touch us until they are certain no harm will come of it. On our tortured planet, however, there is a time factor. They know that well enough, of course. . . . Recall cannot begin unless the subject is willing or unresisting; to them, that has to mean willing, for any being with intellect enough to make a considered choice. Now, I wonder how many they could find who would be honestly willing to make that uneasy journey into death, for no reward except an assurance that they were serving their own kind and the angels?

More to the point, I wonder if I would be able to achieve such willingness myself, even with her help?

When this had been explained to me, she urged me again to make no hasty decision. And she pointed out to me what my thoughts were already groping at—why not both alternatives, within a reasonable limit of time? Why couldn't I have ten or fifteen years or more with her and then undertake the total recall—perhaps not until my physical powers had started toward senility? I thought that over.

This morning I had almost decided to choose that most welcome and comforting solution. Then the mailman brought my daily paper. Not that I needed any such reminder.

In the afternoon I asked her if she knew whether, in the present state of human technology, it would be possible for our folly to actually destroy this planet. She did not know, for certain. Three of the other children have gone away to different parts of the world, to learn what they can about that. But she had to tell me that such a thing has happened before, elsewhere in the heavens. I guess I

won't write a letter to the papers advancing an explanation
for the occasional appearance of a nova among the stars.
Doubtless others have hit on the same hypothesis without
the aid of angels.

And that is not all I must consider. I could die by
accident or sudden disease before I had begun to give my
life.

Only now, at this very late moment, rubbing my sweaty
forehead and gazing into the lights of that wonderful ring,
have I been able to put together some obvious facts in the
required synthesis.

I don't know, of course, what forms their assistance to
us will take. I suspect human beings won't see or hear
much of the angels for a long time to come. Now and
then disastrous decisions may be altered, and those who
believe themselves wholly responsible won't quite know
why their minds worked that way. Here and there, maybe
an influential mind will be rather strangely nudged into a
better course. Something like that. There may be sudden
new discoveries and inventions of kinds that will tend to
neutralize the menace of our nastiest playthings. But whatever the angels decide to do, the record and analysis of my
not too atypical life will be an aid: it could even be the
small weight deciding the balance between triumph and
failure. That is fact one.

Two: my angel and her brothers and sisters, for all their
amazing level of advancement, are of perishable protoplasm, even as I am. Therefore, if this ball of earth becomes a ball of flame, they also will be destroyed. Even if
they have the means to use their spaceship again or to build
another, it might easily happen that they would not learn
their danger in time to escape. And for all I know, this
could be tomorrow. Or tonight.

So there can no longer be any doubt as to my choice,
and I will tell her when she wakes.

July 9

Tonight* there is no recall—I am to rest awhile. I see it
is almost a month since I last wrote in this journal. My

---

* At this point Dr. Bannerman's handwriting alters curiously.
From here on he used a soft pencil instead of a pen, and the script
shows signs of haste. In spite of this, however, it is actually much
clearer, steadier, and easier to read than the earlier entries in his
normal hand.—BLAINE.

total recall began three weeks ago, and I have already been able to give away the first twenty-eight years of my life.

Since I no longer require normal sleep, the recall begins at night, as soon as the lights begin to go out over there in the village and there is little danger of interruption. Daytimes, I putter about in my usual fashion. I have sold Steele my hens, and Judy's life was saved a week ago; that practically winds up my affairs, except that I want to write a codicil to my will. I might as well do that now, right here in this journal, instead of bothering my lawyer. It should be legal.

TO WHOM IT MAY CONCERN: I hereby bequeath to my friend Lester Morse, M.D., of Augusta, Maine, the ring which will be found at my death on the fifth finger of my left hand; and I would urge Dr. Morse to retain this ring in his private possession at all times, and to make provision for its disposal, in the event of his own death, to some person in whose character he places the utmost faith.

(Signed) DAVID BANNERMAN*

Tonight she has gone away for a while, and I am to rest and do as I please until she returns. I shall spend the time filling in some blanks in this record, but I am afraid it will be a spotty job, unsatisfactory to any readers who are subject to the blessed old itch for facts. Mainly because there is so much I no longer care about. It is troublesome to try to decide what things would be considered important by interested strangers.

Except for the lack of any desire for sleep, and a bodily weariness that is not at all unpleasant, I notice no physical effects thus far. I have no faintest recollection of anything that happened earlier than my twenty-eighth birthday. My deductive memory seems rather efficient, and I am sure I could reconstruct most of the story if it were worth the bother: this afternoon I grubbed around among some old letters of that period, but they weren't very interesting. My knowledge of English is unaffected; I can still read scientific German and some French, because I had occasion to use those languages fairly often after I was twenty-

---

* In spite of superficial changes in the handwriting, this signature has been certified genuine by an expert graphologist.—BLAINE.

eight. The scraps of Latin dating from high school are quite gone. So are algebra and all but the simplest propositions of high-school geometry: I never needed 'em. I can remember thinking of my mother after twenty-eight, but do not know whether the image this provides really resembles her; my father died when I was thirty-one, so I remember him as a sick old man. I believe I had a younger brother, but he must have died in childhood.*

Judy's passing was tranquil—pleasant for her, I think. It took the better part of a day. We went out to an abandoned field I know, and she lay in the sunshine with the angel sitting by her, while I dug a grave and then rambled off after wild raspberries. Toward evening the angel came and told me it was finished. And most interesting, she said. I don't see how there can have been anything distressing about it for Judy; after all, what hurts us worst is to have our favorite self-deceptions stripped away.

As the angel has explained it to me, her people, their cats, those kangaroo-folk, Man, and just possibly the cats on our planet (she hasn't met them yet) are the only animals she knows who are introspective enough to develop self-delusion and related pretenses. I suggested she might find something of the sort, at least in rudimentary form, among some of the other primates. She was immensely interested and wanted to learn everything I could tell her about monkeys and apes. It seems that long ago on the other planet there used to be clumsy, winged creatures resembling the angels to about the degree that the large anthropoids resemble us. They became extinct some forty million years ago, in spite of enlightened efforts to keep their kind alive. Their birth rate became insufficient for replacement, as if some necessary spark had simply flickered out; almost as if nature, or whatever name you prefer for the unknown, had with gentle finality written them off. . . .

I have not found the recall painful, at least not in retrospect. There must have been sharp moments, mercifully forgotten, along with their causes, as if the process had gone on under anesthesia. Certainly there were plenty of incidents in my first twenty-eight years that I should not care to offer to the understanding of any but the angels. Quite often I must have been mean, selfish, base in any

---

* Dr. Bannerman's mother died in 1918 of influenza. His brother (three years older, not younger) died of pneumonia, 1906.—BLAINE.

number of ways, if only to judge by the record since twenty-eight. Those old letters touch on a few of these things. To me, they now matter only as material for a record which is safely out of my hands.

However, to any persons I may have harmed, I wish to say this: you were hurt by aspects of my humanity which may not, in a few million years, be quite so common among us all. Against these darker elements I struggled, in my human fashion, as you do yourselves. The effort is not wasted.

It was a week after I told the angel my decision before she was prepared to start the recall. During that week she searched my present mind more closely than I should have imagined was possible: she had to be sure. During that week of hard questions I dare say she learned more about my kind than has ever gone on record even in a physician's office; I hope she did. To any psychiatrist who might question that, I offer a naturalist's suggestion: it is easy to imagine, after some laborious time, that we have noticed everything a given patch of ground can show us; but alter the viewpoint only a little—dig down a foot with a spade, say, or climb a tree branch and look downward—it's a whole new world.

When the angel was not exploring me in this fashion, she took pains to make me glimpse the satisfactions and million rewarding experiences I might have if I chose the other way. I see how necessary that was; at the time it seemed almost cruel. She had to do it, for my own sake, and I am glad that I was somehow able to stand fast to my original choice. So was she, in the end; she has even said she loves me for it. What that troubling word means to her is not within my mind: I am satisfied to take it in the human sense.

Some evening during the week—I think it was June 12—Lester dropped around for sherry and chess. Hadn't seen him in quite a while, and haven't since. There is a moderate polio scare this summer, and it keeps him on the jump. The angel retired behind some books on an upper shelf—I'm afraid it was dusty—and had fun with our chess. She had a fair view of your bald spot, Lester; later she remarked that she liked your looks, and can't you do something about that weight? She suggested an odd expedient, which I believe has occurred to your medical self from time to time—eating less.

Maybe she shouldn't have done what she did with those chess games. Nothing more than my usual blundering happened until after my first ten moves; by that time I suppose she had absorbed the principles and she took over, slightly. I was not fully aware of it until I saw Lester looking like a boiled duck: I had imagined my astonishing moves were the result of my own damn cleverness.

Seriously, Lester, think back to that evening. You've played in stiff amateur tournaments; you know your own abilities and you know mine. Ask yourself whether I could have done anything like that without help. I tell you again, I didn't study the game in the interval when you weren't here. I've never had a chess book in the library, and if I had, no amount of study would take me into your class. Haven't that sort of mentality—just your humble sparring partner, and I've enjoyed it on that basis, as you might enjoy watching a prima donna surgeon pull off some miracle you wouldn't dream of attempting yourself. Even if your game had been way below par that evening (I don't think it was), I could never have pinned your ears back three times running, without help. That evening you were a long way out of *your* class, that's all.

I couldn't tell you anything about it at the time—she was clear on that point—so I could only bumble and preen myself and leave you mystified. But she wants me to write anything I choose in this journal, and somehow, Lester, I think you may find the next few decades pretty interesting. You're still young—some ten years younger than I. I think you'll see many things that I do wish I myself might see come to pass—or I would so wish if I were not convinced that my choice was the right one.

Most of those new events will not be spectacular, I'd guess. Many of the turns to a better way will hardly be recognized at the time for what they are, by you or anyone else. Obviously, our nature being what it is, we shall not jump into heaven overnight. To hope for that would be as absurd as it is to imagine that any formula, ideology, theory of social pattern, can bring us into utopia. As I see it, Lester—and I think your consulting-room would have told you the same even if your own intuition were not enough—there is only one battle of importance: Armageddon. And Armageddon field is within each self, world without end.

At the moment I believe I am the happiest man who ever lived.

July 20

All but the last ten years now given away. The physical fatigue (still pleasant) is quite overwhelming. I am not troubled by the weeds in my garden patch—merely a different sort of flowers where I had planned something else. An hour ago she brought me the seed of a blown dandelion, to show me how lovely it was—I don't suppose I had ever noticed. I hope whoever takes over this place will bring it back to farming: they say the ten acres below the house used to be good potato land—nice early ground.

It is delightful to sit in the sun, as if I were old.

After thumbing over earlier entries in this journal, I see I have often felt quite bitter toward my own kind. I deduce that I must have been a lonely man—much of the loneliness self-imposed. A great part of my bitterness must have been no more than one ugly by-product of a life spent too much apart. Some of it doubtless came from objective causes, yet I don't believe I ever had more cause than any moderately intelligent man who would like to see his world a pleasanter place than it ever has been. My angel tells me that the pain in my back is due to an injury received in some early stage of the world war that still goes on. That could have soured me, perhaps. It's all right—it's all in the record.

She is racing with a hummingbird—holding back, I think, to give the ball of green fluff a break.

Another note for you, Lester. I have already indicated that my ring is to be yours. I don't want to tell you what I have discovered of its properties, for fear it might not give you the same pleasure and interest that it has given me. Of course, like any spot of shifting light and color, it is an aid to self-hypnosis. It is much, much more than that, but— find out for yourself, at some time when you are a little protected from everyday distractions. I know it can't harm you, because I know its source.

By the way, I wish you would convey to my publishers my request that they either discontinue manufacture of my *Introductory Biology* or else bring out a new edition revised in accordance with some notes you will find in the top left drawer of my library desk. I glanced through that book after my angel assured me that I wrote it, and I was amazed. However, I'm afraid my notes are messy (I call them mine by a poetic license), and they may be too advanced for the present day—though the revision is main-

ly a matter of leaving out certain generalities that ain't so.
Use your best judgment: it's a very minor textbook, and the
thing isn't too important. A last wriggle of my personal
vanity.

July 27

I have seen a two-moon night.

It was given to me by that other grown-up, at the end
of a wonderful visit, when he and six of those nine other
children came to see me. It was last night, I think—yes,
must have been. First there was a murmur of wings above
the house; my angel flew in, laughing; then they were here,
all about me. Full of gaiety and colored fire, showing off
in every way they knew would please me. Each one had
something graceful and friendly to say to me. One brought
me a moving image of the St. Lawrence seen at morning
from half a mile up—clouds—eagles; now, how could he
know that would delight me so much? And each one
thanked me for what I had done.

But it's been so easy!

And at the end the old one—his skin is quite black, and
his down is white and grey—gave the remembered image
of a two-moon night. He saw it some sixty years ago.

I have not even considered making an effort to describe
it—my fingers will not hold this pencil much longer tonight.
Oh—soaring buildings of white and amber, untroubled
countryside, silver on curling rivers, a glimpse of open sea;
a moon rising in clarity, another setting in a wreath of
cloud, between them a wide wandering of unfamiliar stars;
and here and there the angels, worthy after fifty million
years to live in such a night. No, I cannot describe anything
like that. But, you human kindred of mine, I can do something better. I can tell you that this two-moon night, glori-
ous as it was, was no more beautiful than a night under a
single moon on this ancient and familiar Earth might be—
if you will imagine that the rubbish of human evil has been
cleared away and that our own people have started at last
on the greatest of all explorations.

July 29

Nothing now remains to give away but the memory of
the time that has passed since the angel came. I am to rest
as long as I wish, write whatever I want to. Then I shall

get myself over to the bed and lie down as if for sleep. She tells me that I can keep my eyes open: she will close them for me when I no longer see her.

I remain convinced that our human case is hopeful. I feel sure that in only a few thousand years we may be able to perform some of the simpler preparatory tasks, such as casting out evil and loving our neighbors. And if that should prove to be so, who can doubt that in another fifty million years we might well be only a little lower than the angels?

LIBRARIAN'S NOTE: As is generally known, the original of the Bannerman Journal is said to have been in the possession of Dr. Lester Morse at the time of the latter's disappearance in 1964, and that disappearance has remained an unsolved mystery to the present day. McCarran is known to have visited Captain Garrison Blaine in October 1951, but no record remains of that visit. Captain Blaine appears to have been a bachelor who lived alone. He was killed in line of duty, December 1951. McCarran is believed not to have written about nor discussed the Bannerman affair with anyone else. It is almost certain that he himself removed the extract and related papers from the files (unofficially, it would seem!) when he severed his connections with the FBI in 1957; at any rate, they were found among his effects after his assassination and were released to the public, considerably later, by Mrs. McCarran.

The following memorandum was originally attached to the extract from the Bannerman Journal; it carries the McCarran initialing.

Aug. 11, 1951

The original letter of complaint written by Stephen Clyde, M.D., and mentioned in the accompanying letter of Captain Blaine, has unfortunately been lost, owing perhaps to an error in filing.

Personnel presumed responsible have been instructed not to allow such error to be repeated except if, as, and/or when necessary.

C. McC.

On the margin of this memorandum there was a penciled

notation, later erased. The imprint is sufficient to show the unmistakable McCarran script. The notation read in part as follows: *Far be it from a McC. to lose his job except if, as, and/or*—the rest is undecipherable, except for a terminal word which is regrettably unparliamentary.

STATEMENT
BY LESTER MORSE, M.D.,
DATED AUGUST 9, 1951

On the afternoon of July 30, 1951, acting on what I am obliged to describe as an unexpected impulse, I drove out to the country for the purpose of calling on my friend Dr. David Bannerman. I had not seen him nor had word from him since the evening of June 12 of this year.

I entered, as was my custom, without knocking. After calling to him and hearing no response, I went upstairs to his bedroom and found him dead. From superficial indications I judged that death must have taken place during the previous night. He was lying on his bed on his left side, comfortably disposed as if for sleep but fully dressed, with a fresh shirt and clean summer slacks. His eyes and mouth were closed, and there was no trace of the disorder to be expected at even the easiest natural death. Because of these signs I assumed, as soon as I had determined the absence of breath and heartbeat and noted the chill of the body, that some neighbor must have found him already, performed these simple rites out of respect for him, and probably notified a local physician or other responsible person. I therefore waited (Dr. Bannerman had no telephone), expecting that someone would soon call.

Dr. Bannerman's journal was on a table near his bed, open to that page on which he has written a codicil to his will. I read that part. Later, while I was waiting for others to come, I read the remainder of the journal, as I believe he wished me to do. The ring he mentions was on the fifth finger of his left hand, and it is now in my possession. When writing that codicil Dr. Bannerman must have overlooked, or forgotten, the fact that in his formal will, written some months earlier, he had appointed me executor. If there are legal technicalities involved, I shall be pleased to cooperate fully with the proper authorities.

The ring, however, will remain in my keeping, since

that was Dr. Bannerman's expressed wish, and I am not prepared to offer it for examination or discussion under any circumstances.

The notes for a revision of one of his textbooks were in his desk, as noted in the journal. They are by no means "messy"; nor are they particularly revolutionary except in so far as he wished to rephrase, as theory or hypothesis, certain statements that I would have supposed could be regarded as axiomatic. This is not my field, and I am not competent to judge. I shall take up the matter with his publishers at the earliest opportunity.*

So far as I can determine, and bearing in mind the results of the autopsy performed by Stephen Clyde, M.D., the death of Dr. David Bannerman was not inconsistent with the presence of an embolism of some type not distinguishable on postmortem. I have so stated on the certificate of death. It would seem to be not in the public interest to leave such questions in doubt. I am compelled to add one other item of medical opinion for what it may be worth:

I am not a psychiatrist, but, owing to the demands of general practice, I have found it advisable to keep as up to date as possible with current findings and opinion in this branch of medicine. Dr. Bannerman possessed, in my opinion, emotional and intellectual stability to a better degree than anyone else of comparable intelligence in the entire field of my acquaintance, personal and professional. If it is suggested that he was suffering from a hallucinatory psychosis, I can only say that it must have been of a type quite outside my experience and not described, so far as I know, anywhere in the literature of psychopathology.

Dr. Bannerman's house, on the afternoon of July 30, was in good order. Near the open, unscreened window of his bedroom there was a coverless shoe box with a folded silk scarf in the bottom. I found no pillow such as Dr. Bannerman describes in the journal, but observed that a small section had been cut from the scarf. In this box, and near it, there was a peculiar fragrance, faint, aromatic, and very sweet, such as I have never encountered before and therefore cannot describe.

* LIBRARIAN'S NOTE: But it seems he never did. No new edition of *Introductory Biology* was ever brought out, and the textbook has been out of print since 1952.

It may or may not have any bearing on the case that, while I remained in his house that afternoon, I felt no sense of grief or personal loss, although Dr. Bannerman had been a loved and honored friend for a number of years. I merely had, and have, a conviction that after the completion of some very great undertaking, he had found peace.

Oh, To Be a Blobel!

BY PHILIP K. DICK

A dedicated investigator of the elusive nature of reality, an intrepid explorer of alternate states of consciousness, a wickedly effective and acidulous satirist, Philip K. Dick has written some of the most brilliant novels and short stories in the history of the genre. Dick is famous for his obsessed, paranoid characters, elaborately intricate plots, wildly original concepts, and macabre social backgrounds, and for vivid flashes of irony and sardonic black humor. He is perhaps best known for The Man in the High Castle, *his Hugo-winning novel of an alternate America under the Nazi thumb, but other Dick novels such as* Ubik, *with its endless dovetailing layers of reality and illusion,* Martian Time-Slip, *with its frightening perspectives into a schizoid world, and* The Three Stigmata of Palmer Eldrich, *in which humanity's entire "reality" is swallowed—lock, stock, and cosmos—by a protean alien drug pusher from Proxima, all have their followings as well, and some have been elevated almost to "cult" status on college campuses. Dick's other books include* Do Androids Dream of Electric Sheep?, Time Out of Joint, Our Friends from Frolix 8, Solar Lottery, The Zap Gun, Now Wait for Last Year, Dr. Bloodmoney, *and two collections,* The Preserving Machine *and* The Best of Philip K. Dick. *His latest books are* A Scanner Darkly *and* Confessions of a Crap Artist. *Enormously popular in Europe and among the counterculture, Dick is probably the only SF writer ever to have a major article devoted to him in* Rolling Stone, *and certainly the only SF author ever to write a scene in which a character has to argue with his toaster before it will let him eat breakfast.*

Many stories have been written about war with aliens, but what happens afterward, when the peace treaties have been signed and the warships have gone home? Here Dick gives us a glimpse of the Veterans of Unnatural Wars of the future, and suggests that while war is hell, détente isn't necessarily so hot either.

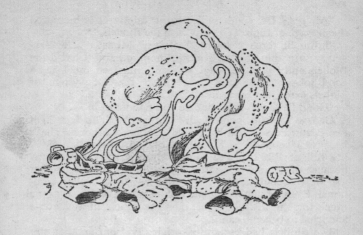

He put a twenty-dollar platinum coin into the slot and the analyst, after a pause, lit up. Its eyes shone with sociability and it swiveled about in its chair, picked up a pen and pad of long yellow paper from its desk and said,

"Good morning, sir. You may begin."

"Hello, Doctor Jones. I guess you're not the same Doctor Jones who did the definitive biography of Freud; that was a century ago." He laughed nervously; being a rather poverty-stricken man he was not accustomed to dealing with the new fully homeostatic psychoanalysts. "Um," he said, "should I free-associate or give you background material or just what?"

Dr. Jones said, "Perhaps you could begin by telling me who you are und warum mich—why you have selected me."

"I'm George Munster of catwalk 4, building WEF-395, San Francisco condominium established 1996."

"How do you do, Mr. Munster?" Dr. Jones held out its hand, and George Munster shook it. He found the hand to be of a pleasant body temperature and decidedly soft. The grip, however, was manly.

"You see," Munster said, "I'm an ex-GI, a war veteran. That's how I got my condominium apartment at WEF-395; veterans' preference."

"Ah yes," Dr. Jones said, ticking faintly as it measured the passage of time. "The war with the Blobels."

"I fought three years in that war," Munster said, nervously smoothing his long black thinning hair. "I hated the Blobels and I volunteered; I was only nineteen and I had a good job—but the crusade to clear the Sol System of Blobels came first in my mind."

"Um," Dr. Jones said, ticking and nodding.

George Munster continued, "I fought well. In fact I got two decorations and a battlefield citation. Corporal. That's because I single-handedly wiped out an observation satellite full of Blobels; we'll never know exactly how many because of course, being Blobels, they tend to fuse together and unfuse confusingly." He broke off, then, feeling emotional. Even remembering and talking about the war was too much for him . . . he lay back on the couch, lit a cigarette and tried to become calm.

The Blobels had emigrated originally from another star system, probably Proxima. Several thousand years ago they had settled on Mars and on Titan, doing very well at agrarian pursuits. They were developments of the original unicellular amoeba, quite large and with a highly organized nervous system, but still amoeba, with pseudopodia, reproducing by binary fission, and in the main offensive to Terran settlers.

The war itself had broken out over ecological considerations. It had been the desire of the Foreign Aid Department of the UN to change the atmosphere on Mars, making it more usable for Terran settlers. This change, however, had made it unpalatable for the Blobel colonies already there; hence the squabble.

And, Munster reflected, it was not possible to change *half* the atmosphere of a planet, the Brownian movement being what it was. Within a period of ten years the altered atmosphere had diffused throughout the planet, bringing suffering—at least so they alleged—to the Blobels. In retaliation, a Blobel armada had approached Terra and had put into orbit a series of technically sophisticated satellites designed eventually to alter the atmosphere of Terra. This alteration had never come about because of course the War Office of the UN had gone into action; the satellites had been detonated by self-instructing missiles . . . and the war was on.

Dr. Jones said, "Are you married, Mr. Munster?"

"No, sir," Munster said. "And—" He shuddered. "You'll see why when I've finished telling you. See, Doctor—" He stubbed out his cigarette. "I'll be frank. I was a Terran spy. That was my task; they gave the job to me because of my bravery in the field . . . I didn't ask for it."

"I see," Dr. Jones said.

"Do you?" Munster's voice broke. "Do you know what was necessary in those days in order to make a Terran into a successful spy among the Blobels?"

Nodding, Dr. Jones said, "Yes, Mr. Munster. You had to relinquish your human form and assume the repellent form of a Blobel."

Munster said nothing; he clenched and unclenched his fist, bitterly. Across from him Dr. Jones ticked.

That evening, back in his small apartment at WEF-395, Munster opened a fifth of Teacher's scotch, sat by himself sipping from a cup, lacking even the energy to get a glass down from the cupboard over the sink.

What had he gotten out of the session with Dr. Jones today? Nothing, as nearly as he could tell. And it had eaten deep into his meager financial resources . . . meager because—

Because for almost twelve hours out of the day he reverted, despite all the efforts of himself and the Veterans' Hospitalization Agency of the UN, to his old wartime Blobel shape. To a formless unicellularlike blob, right in the middle of his own apartment at WEF-395.

His financial resources consisted of a small pension from the War Office; finding a job was impossible, because as soon as he was hired the strain caused him to revert there on the spot, in plain sight of his new employer and fellow workers.

It did not assist in forming successful work relationships.

Sure enough, now, at eight in the evening, he felt himself once more beginning to revert; it was an old and familiar experience to him, and he loathed it. Hurriedly, he sipped the last of the cup of scotch, put the cup down on a table . . . and felt himself slide together into a homogenous puddle.

The telephone rang.

"I can't answer," he called to it. The phone's relay picked up his anguished message and conveyed it to the calling party. Now Munster had become a single transparent gelatinous mass in the middle of the rug; he undulated toward the phone—it was still ringing, despite his statement to it, and he felt furious resentment; didn't he have enough troubles already, without having to deal with a ringing phone?

Reaching it, he extended a pseudopodium and snatched the receiver from the hook. With great effort he formed his plastic substance into the semblance of a vocal apparatus, resonating dully. "I'm busy," he resonated in a low booming fashion into the mouthpiece of the phone. "Call later." *Call,* he thought as he hung up, *tomorrow morning. When I've been able to regain my human form.*

The apartment was quiet, now.

Sighing, Munster flowed back across the carpet, to the window, where he rose into a high pillar in order to see the view beyond; there was a light-sensitive spot on his outer surface, and although he did not possess a true lens he was able to appreciate—nostalgically—the sight of San Francisco Bay, the Golden Gate Bridge, the playground for small children which was Alcatraz Island.

Dammit, he thought bitterly. *I can't marry; I can't live a genuine human existence, reverting this way to the form the War Office bigshots forced me into back in the war times....*

He had not known then, when he accepted the mission, that it would leave this permanent effect. They had assured him it was "only temporary, for the duration," or some such glib phrase. *Duration my ass,* Munster thought with furious, impotent resentment. *It's been* eleven years, *now.*

The psychological problems created for him, the pressure on his psyche, were immense. Hence his visit to Dr. Jones.

Once more the phone rang.

"Okay," Munster said aloud, and flowed laboriously back across the room to it. "You want to talk to me?" he said as he came closer and closer; the trip, for someone in Blobel form, was a long one. "I'll talk to you. You can even turn on the vidscreen and *look* at me." At the phone he snapped the switch which would permit visual communication as well as auditory. "Have a good look," he said, and displayed his amorphous form before the scanning tube of the video.

Dr. Jones's voice came: "I'm sorry to bother you at your

home, Mr. Munster, especially when you're in this, um, awkward condition . . ." The homeostatic analyst paused. "But I've been devoting time to problem-solving vis-à-vis your condition. I may have at least a partial solution."

"What?" Munster said, taken by surprise. "You mean to imply that medical science can now—"

"No, no," Dr. Jones said hurriedly. "The physical aspects lie out of my domain; you must keep that in mind, Munster. When you consulted me about your problems it was the psychological adjustment that—"

"I'll come right down to your office and talk to you," Munster said. And then he realized that he could not; in his Blobel form it would take him days to undulate all the way across town to Dr. Jones's office. "Jones," he said desperately, "you see the problems I face. I'm stuck here in this apartment every night beginning about eight o'clock and lasting through until almost seven in the morning . . . I can't even visit you and consult you and get help—"

"Be quiet, Mr. Munster," Dr. Jones interrupted. "I'm trying to tell you something. *You're not the only one in this condition.* Did you know that?"

Heavily, Munster said, "Sure. In all, eighty-three Terrans were made over into Blobels at one time or another during the war. Of the eighty-three—" He knew the facts by heart. "Sixty-one survived and now there's an organization called Veterans of Unnatural Wars of which fifty are members. I'm a member. We meet twice a month, revert in unison . . ." He started to hang up the phone. So this was what he had gotten for his money, this stale news. "Goodbye, Doctor," he murmured.

Dr. Jones whirred in agitation. "Mr. Munster, I don't mean other Terrans. I've researched this in your behalf, and I discover that according to captured records at the Library of Congress fifteen *Blobels* were formed into pseudo-Terrans to act as spies for *their* side. Do you understand?"

After a moment Munster said, "Not exactly."

"You have a mental block against being helped," Dr. Jones said. "But here's what I want, Munster; you be at my office at eleven in the morning tomorrow. We'll take up the solution to your problem then. Good night."

Wearily, Munster said, "When I'm in my Blobel form my wits aren't too keen, Doctor. You'll have to forgive me." He hung up, still puzzled. So there were fifteen Blobels walking around on Titan this moment, doomed to occupy human forms—so what? How did that help him?

Maybe he would find out at eleven tomorrow.

When he strode into Dr. Jones's waiting room he saw, seated in a deep chair in a corner by a lamp, reading a copy of *Fortune*, an exceedingly attractive young woman.

Automatically, Munster found a place to sit from which he could eye her. Stylish dyed-white hair braided down the back of her neck . . . he took in the sight of her with delight, pretending to read his own copy of *Fortune*. Slender legs, small and delicate elbows. And her sharp, clearly featured face. The intelligent eyes, the thin, tapered nostrils—a truly lovely girl, he thought. He drank in the sight of her . . . until all at once she raised her head and stared coolly back at him.

"Dull, having to wait," Munster mumbled.

The girl said, "Do you come to Dr. Jones often?"

"No," he admitted. "This is just the second time."

"I've never been here before," the girl said. "I was going to another electronic fully homeostatic psychoanalyst in Los Angeles and then late yesterday Dr. Bing, my analyst, called me and told me to fly up here and see Dr. Jones this morning. Is this one good?"

"Um," Munster said. "I guess so." *We'll see*, he thought. *That's precisely what we don't know, at this point.*

The inner office door opened and there stood Dr. Jones. "Miss Arrasmith," it said, nodding to the girl. "Mr. Munster." It nodded to George. "Won't you both come in?"

Rising to her feet, Miss Arrasmith said, "Who pays the twenty dollars then?"

But the analyst had become silent; it had turned off.

"I'll pay," Miss Arrasmith said, reaching into her purse.

"No, no," Munster said. "Let me." He got out a twenty-dollar piece and dropped it into the analyst's slot.

At once, Dr. Jones said, "You're a gentleman, Mr. Munster." Smiling, it ushered the two of them into its office. "Be seated, please. Miss Arrasmith, without preamble please allow me to explain your—condition to Mr. Munster." To Munster it said, "Miss Arrasmith is a Blobel."

Munster could only stare at the girl.

"Obviously," Dr. Jones continued, "presently in human form. This, for her, is the state of involuntary reversion. During the war she operated behind Terran lines, acting for the Blobel War League. She was captured and held, but then the war ended and she was neither tried nor sentenced."

"They released me," Miss Arrasmith said in a low, carefully controlled voice. "Still in human form. I stayed here out of shame. I just couldn't go back to Titan and—" Her voice wavered.

"There is great shame attached to this condition," Dr. Jones said, "for any high-caste Blobel."

Nodding, Miss Arrasmith sat clutching a tiny Irish linen handkerchief and trying to look poised. "Correct, Doctor. I did visit Titan to discuss my condition with medical authorities there. After expensive and prolonged therapy with me they were able to induce a return to my natural form for a period of—" She hesitated. "About one-fourth of the time. But the other three-fourths . . . I am as you perceive me now." She ducked her head and touched the handkerchief to her right eye.

"Jeez," Munster protested, "you're lucky; a human form is infinitely superior to a Blobel form—I ought to know. As a Blobel you have to creep along . . . you're like a big jellyfish, no skeleton to keep you erect. And binary fission —it's lousy, I say really lousy, compared to the Terran form of—you know. Reproduction." He colored.

Dr. Jones ticked and stated, "For a period of about six hours your human forms overlap. And then for about one hour your Blobel forms overlap. So all in all, the two of you possess seven hours out of twenty-four in which you both possess identical forms. In my opinion—" It toyed with its pen and paper. "Seven hours is not too bad. If you follow my meaning."

After a moment Miss Arrasmith said, "But Mr. Munster and I are natural enemies."

"That was years ago," Munster said.

"Correct," Dr. Jones agreed. "True, Miss Arrasmith is basically a Blobel and you, Munster, are a Terran, but—" It gestured. "Both of you are outcasts in either civilization; both of you are stateless and hence gradually suffering a loss of ego-identity. I predict for both of you a gradual deterioration ending finally in severe mental illness. Unless you two can develop a rapprochement." The analyst was silent, then.

Miss Arrasmith said softly, "I think we're very lucky, Mr. Munster. As Dr. Jones said, we do overlap for seven hours a day . . . we can enjoy that time together, no longer in wretched isolation." She smiled up hopefully at him, re-arranging her coat. Certainly, she had a nice figure; the somewhat low-cut dress gave an ideal clue to that.

Studying her, Munster pondered.

"Give him time," Dr. Jones told Miss Arrasmith. "My analysis of him is that he will see this correctly and do the right thing."

Still rearranging her coat and dabbing at her large, dark eyes, Miss Arrasmith waited.

The phone in Dr. Jones's office rang, a number of years later. He answered it in his customary way. "Please, sir or madam, deposit twenty dollars if you wish to speak to me."

A tough male voice on the other end of the line said, "Listen, this is the UN Legal Office and we don't deposit twenty dollars to talk to anybody. So trip that mechanism inside you, Jones."

"Yes sir," Dr. Jones said, and with his right hand tripped the lever behind his ear that caused him to come on free.

"Back in 2037," the UN legal expert said, "did you ad-vise a couple to marry? A George Munster and a Vivian Arrasmith, now Mrs. Munster?"

"Why, yes," Dr. Jones said, after consulting his built-in memory banks.

"Had you investigated the legal ramifications of their issue?"

"Um well," Dr. Jones said, "that's not my worry."

"You can be arraigned for advising any action contrary to UN law."

"There's no law prohibiting a Blobel and a Terran from marrying."

The UN legal expert said, "All right, Doctor, I'll settle for a look at their case histories."

"Absolutely not," Dr. Jones said. "That would be a breach of ethics."

"We'll get a writ and sequester them, then."

"Go ahead." Dr. Jones reached behind his ear to shut himself off.

"Wait. It may interest you to know that the Munsters now have four children. And, following the Mendelian Law, the offspring comprise a strict one, two, one ratio. One Blobel girl, one hybrid boy, one hybrid girl, one Ter-ran girl. The legal problem arises in that the Blobel Su-

preme Council claims the pure-blooded Blobel girl as a
citizen of Titan and also suggests that one of the two
hybrids be donated to the council's jurisdiction." The UN
legal expert explained, "You see, the Munsters' marriage
is breaking up; they're getting divorced and it's sticky
finding which laws obtain regarding them and their issue."

"Yes," Dr. Jones admitted, "I would think so. What has
caused their marriage to break up?"

"I don't know and don't care. Possibly the fact that both
adults and two of the four children rotate daily between
being Blobels and Terrans; maybe the strain got to be too
much. If you want to give them psychological advice, consult them. Good-bye." The UN legal expert rang off.

Did I make a mistake, advising them to marry? Dr.
Jones asked itself. *I wonder if I shouldn't look them up;
I owe at least that to them.*

Opening the Los Angeles phonebook, it began thumbing
through the *M*'s.

These had been six difficult years for the Munsters.

First, George had moved from San Francisco to Los
Angeles; he and Vivian had set up their household in a
condominium apartment with three instead of two rooms.
Vivian, being in Terran form three-fourths of the time,
had been able to obtain a job; right out in public she gave
jet flight information at the Fifth Los Angeles Airport.
George, however—

His pension comprised an amount only one-fourth that
of his wife's salary and he felt it keenly. To augment it,
he had searched for a way of earning money at home.
Finally in a magazine he had found this valuable ad:

MAKE SWIFT PROFITS IN YOUR OWN CONDO! RAISE GIANT
BULLFROGS FROM JUPITER, CAPABLE OF EIGHTY-FOOT
LEAPS. CAN BE USED IN FROG-RACING (where legal)
AND

So in 2038 he had bought his first pair of frogs imported
from Jupiter and had begun raising them for swift profits,
right in his own condominium apartment building, in a
corner of the basement that Leopold the partially homeostatic janitor let him use gratis.

But in the relatively feeble Terran gravity the frogs were
capable of enormous leaps, and the basement proved too

small for them; they ricocheted from wall to wall like green ping-pong balls and soon died. Obviously it took more than a portion of the basement at QEK-604 Apartments to house a crop of the damned things, George realized.

And then, too, their first child had been born. It had turned out to be pure-blooded Blobel; for twenty-four hours a day it consisted of a gelatinous mass and George found himself waiting in vain for it to switch over to a human form, even for a moment.

He faced Vivian defiantly in this matter, during a period when both of them were in human form.

"How can I consider it my child?" he asked her. "It's— an alien life form to me." He was discouraged and even horrified. "Dr. Jones should have foreseen this; maybe it's *your* child—it looks just like you."

Tears filled Vivian's eyes. "You mean that insultingly."

"Damn right I do. We fought you creatures—we used to consider you no better than Portuguese sting rays." Gloomily, he put on his coat. "I'm going down to Veterans of Unnatural Wars Headquarters," he informed his wife. "Have a beer with the boys." Shortly, he was on his way to join with his old wartime buddies, glad to get out of the apartment house.

VUW Headquarters was a decrepit cement building in downtown Los Angeles left over from the twentieth century and sadly in need of paint. The VUW had little funds because most of its members were, like George Munster, living on UN pensions. However, there was a pool table and an old 3-D television set and a few dozen tapes of popular music and also a chess set. George generally drank his beer and played chess with his fellow members, either in human form or in Blobel form; this was one place in which both were accepted.

This particular evening he sat with Pete Ruggles, a fellow veteran who also had married a Blobel female, reverting, as Vivian did, to human form.

"Pete, I can't go on. I've got a gelatinous blob for a child. My whole life I've wanted a kid, and now what have I got? Something that looks like it washed up on the beach."

Sipping his beer—he too was in human form at the moment—Pete answered, "Criminy, George, I admit it's a mess. But you must have known what you were getting into when you married her. And my god, according to Mendel's Law, the next kid—"

"I mean," George broke in, "I don't respect my own wife; that's the basis of it. I think of her as a *thing*. And myself, too. We're both things." He drank down his beer in one gulp.

Pete said meditatively, "But from the Blobel standpoint—"

"Listen, whose side are you on?" George demanded.

"Don't yell at me," Pete said, "or I'll deck you."

A moment later they were swinging wildly at each other. Fortunately Pete reverted to Blobel form in the nick of time; no harm was done. Now George sat alone, in human shape, while Pete oozed off somewhere else, probably to join a group of the boys who had also assumed Blobel form.

Maybe we can found a new society somewhere on a remote moon, George said to himself moodily. *Neither Terran nor Blobel.*

I've got to go back to Vivian, George resolved. *What else is there for me? I'm lucky to find her; I'd be nothing but a war veteran guzzling beer here at VUW Headquarters every damn day and night, with no future, no hope, no real life . . .*

He had a new money-making scheme going, now. It was a home mail-order business; he had placed an ad in the *Saturday Evening Post* for MAGIC LODE-STONES REPUTED TO BRING YOU LUCK. FROM ANOTHER STAR-SYSTEM ENTIRELY! The stones had come from Proxima and were obtainable on Titan; it was Vivian who had made the commercial contact for him with her people. But so far, few people had sent in the dollar-fifty.

I'm a failure, George said to himself.

Fortunately the next child, born in the winter of 2039, showed itself to be a hybrid; it took human form 50 percent of the time, and so at last George had a child who was—occasionally, anyhow—a member of his own species.

He was still in the process of celebrating the birth of Maurice when a delegation of their neighbors at QEK-604 Apartments came and rapped on their door.

"We've got a petition here," the chairman of the delegation said, shuffling his feet in embarrassment, "asking that you and Mrs. Munster leave QEK-604."

"But why?" George asked, bewildered. "You haven't objected to us up until now."

"The reason is that now you've got a hybrid youngster who will want to play with ours, and we feel it's unhealthy for our kids to—"

George slammed the door in their faces.

But still, he felt the pressure, the hostility from the people on all sides of them. *And to think,* he thought bitterly, *that I fought in the war to save these people. It sure wasn't worth it.*

An hour later he was down at VUW Headquarters once more, drinking beer and talking with his buddy Sherman Downs, also married to a Blobel.

"Sherman, it's no good. We're not wanted; we've got to emigrate. Maybe we'll try it on Titan, in Viv's world."

"Chrissakes," Sherman protested, "I hate to see you fold up, George. Isn't your electromagnetic reducing belt beginning to sell, finally?"

For the last few months, George had been making and selling a complex electronic reducing gadget which Vivian had helped him design; it was based in principle on a Blobel device popular on Titan but unknown on Terra. And this had gone over well; George had more orders than he could fill. But—

"I had a terrible experience, Sherm," George confided. "I was in a drugstore the other day, and they gave me a big order for my reducing belt, and I got so excited—" He broke off. "You can guess what happened. I reverted. Right in plain sight of a hundred customers. And when the buyer saw that he canceled the order for the belts. It was what we all fear . . . you should have seen how their attitude toward me changed."

Sherm said, "Hire someone to do your selling for you. A full-blooded Terran."

Thickly, George said, *"I'm* a full-blooded Terran, and don't you forget it. Ever."

"I just mean—"

"I know what you meant," George said. And took a swing at Sherman. Fortunately he missed and in the excitement both of them reverted to Blobel form. They oozed angrily into each other for a time, but at last fellow veterans managed to separate them.

"I'm as much a Terran as anyone," George thought-radiated in the Blobel manner to Sherman. "And I'll flatten anyone who says otherwise."

In Blobel form he was unable to get home; he had to phone Vivian to come and get him. It was humiliating.

Suicide, he decided. *That's the answer.*

How best to do it? In Blobel form he was unable to feel pain; best to do it then. Several substances would dissolve him . . . he could for instance drop himself into a heavily chlorinated swimming pool, such as QEK-604 maintained in its recreation room.

Vivian, in human form, found him as he reposed hesitantly at the edge of the swimming pool, late one night.

"George, I beg you—go back to Dr. Jones."

"Naw," he boomed dully, forming a quasi-vocal apparatus with a portion of his body. "It's no use, Viv. I don't *want* to go on." Even the belts; they had been Viv's idea, rather than his. He was second even there . . . behind her, falling constantly further behind each passing day.

Viv said, "You have so much to offer the children."

That was true. "Maybe I'll drop over to the UN War Office," he decided. "Talk to them, see if there's anything new that medical science has come up with that might stabilize me."

"But if you stabilize as a Terran," Vivian said, "what would become of me?"

"We'd have *eighteen entire hours* together a day. All the hours you take human form!"

"But you wouldn't want to stay married to me. Because, George, then you could meet a Terran woman."

It wasn't fair to her, he realized. So he abandoned the idea.

In the spring of 2041 their third child was born, also a girl, and like Maurice a hybrid. It was Blobel at night and Terran by day.

Meanwhile, George found a solution to some of his problems.

He got himself a mistress.

At the Hotel Elysium, a rundown wooden building in the heart of Los Angeles, he and Nina arranged to meet one another.

"Nina," George said, sipping Teacher's scotch and seated beside her on the shabby sofa which the hotel provided, "you've made my life worth living again." He fooled with the buttons of her blouse.

"I respect you," Nina Glaubman said, assisting him with

the buttons. "In spite of the fact—well, you are a former enemy of our people."

"God," George protested, "we must not think about the old days—we have to close our minds to our pasts." *Nothing but our future,* he thought.

His reducing-belt enterprise had developed so well that now he employed fifteen full-time Terran employees and owned a small modern factory on the outskirts of San Fernando. If UN taxes had been reasonable he would by now be a wealthy man . . . brooding on that, George wondered what the tax rate was in Blobel-run lands, on Io, for instance. Maybe he ought to look into it.

One night at VUW Headquarters he discussed the subject with Reinholt, Nina's husband, who of course was ignorant of the modus vivendi between George and Nina.

"Reinholt," George said with difficulty, as he drank his beer, "I've got big plans. This cradle-to-grave socialism the UN operates . . . it's not for me. It's cramping me. The Munster Magic Magnetic Belt is—" He gestured. "More than Terran civilization can support. You get me?"

Coldly, Reinholt said, "But George, you are a Terran; if you immigrate to Blobel-run territory with your factory you'll be betraying your—"

"Listen," George told him, "I've got one authentic Blobel child, two half-Blobel children, and a fourth on the way. I've got strong *emotional* ties with those people out there on Titan and Io."

"You're a traitor," Reinholt said, and punched him in the mouth. "And not only that," he continued, punching George in the stomach, "you're running around with my wife. I'm going to kill you."

To escape, George reverted to Blobel form; Reinholt's blows passed harmlessly deep into his moist, jellylike substance. Reinholt then reverted too, and flowed into him murderously, trying to consume and absorb George's nucleus.

Fortunately fellow veterans pried their two bodies apart before any permanent harm was done.

Later that night, still trembling, George sat with Vivian in the living room of their eight-room suite at the great new condominium apartment building ZGF-900. It had been a close call, and now of course Reinholt would tell Viv; it was only a question of time. The marriage, as far as George could see, was over. This perhaps was their last moment together.

"Viv," he said urgently, "you have to believe me; I love you. You and the children—plus the belt business, naturally—are my complete life." A desperate idea came to him. "Let's immigrate now, tonight. Pack up the kids and go to Titan, right this minute."

"I can't go," Vivian said. "I know how my people would treat me, and treat you and the children, too. George, *you* go. Move the factory to Io. I'll stay here." Tears filled her dark eyes.

"Hell," George said, "what kind of life is that? With you on Terra and me on Io—that's no marriage. And who'll get the kids?" Probably Viv would get them . . . but his firm employed top legal talent—perhaps he could use it to solve his domestic problems.

The next morning Vivian found out about Nina. And hired an attorney of her own.

"Listen," George said on the phone, talking to his top legal talent, Henry Ramarau. "Get me custody of the fourth child; it'll be a Terran. And we'll compromise on the two hybrids; I'll take Maurice and she can have Kathy. And naturally she gets that blob, that first so-called child. As far as I'm concerned it's hers anyhow." He slammed the receiver down and then turned to the board of directors of his company. "Now where were we?" he demanded. "In our analysis of Io tax laws."

During the next weeks the idea of a move to Io appeared more and more feasible from a profit and loss standpoint.

"Go ahead and buy land on Io," George instructed his business agent in the field, Tom Hendricks. "And get it cheap; we want to start right." To his secretary, Miss Nolan, he said, "Now keep everyone out of my office until further notice. I feel an attack coming on. From anxiety over this major move off Terra to Io." He added, "And personal worries."

"Yes, Mr. Munster," Miss Nolan said, ushering Tom Hendricks out of George's private office. "No one will disturb you." She could be counted on to keep everyone out while George reverted to his wartime Blobel shape, as he often did, these days; the pressure on him was immense.

When, later in the day, he resumed human form, George learned from Miss Nolan that a Dr. Jones had called.

"I'll be damned," George said, thinking back to six years ago. "I thought it'd be in the junk pile by now." To Miss Nolan he said, "Call Doctor Jones, notify me when you have it; I'll take a minute off to talk to it." It was like old times, back in San Francisco.

Shortly, Miss Nolan had Dr. Jones on the line.

"Doctor," George said, leaning back in his chair and swiveling from side to side and poking at an orchid on his desk. "Good to hear from you."

The voice of the homeostatic analyst came in his ear, "Mr. Munster, I note that you now have a secretary."

"Yes," George said, "I'm a tycoon. I'm in the reducing-belt game; it's somewhat like the flea collar that cats wear. Well, what can I do for you?"

"I understand you have four children now—"

"Actually three, plus a fourth on the way. Listen, that fourth, doctor, is vital to me; according to Mendel's Law it's a full-blooded Terran and by god I'm doing everything in my power to get custody of it." He added, "Vivian—you remember her—is now back on Titan. Among her own people, where she belongs. And I'm putting some of the finest doctors I can get on my payroll to stabilize me; I'm tired of this constant reverting, night and day; I've got too much to do for such nonsense."

Dr. Jones said, "From your tone I can see you're an important, busy man, Mr. Munster. You've certainly risen in the world, since I saw you last."

"Get to the point, doctor," George said impatiently. "Why'd you call?"

"I, um, thought perhaps I could bring you and Vivian together again."

"Bah," George said contemptuously. "That woman? Never. Listen, doctor, I have to ring off; we're in the process of finalizing on some basic business strategy, here at Munster, Incorporated."

"Mr. Munster," Dr. Jones asked, "is there another woman?"

"There's another Blobel," George said, "if that's what you mean." And he hung up the phone. *Two Blobels are better than none,* he said to himself. *And now back to business . . .* He pressed a button on his desk and at once Miss Nolan put her head into the office. "Miss Nolan," George said, "get me Hank Ramarau; I want to find out—"

"Mr. Ramarau is waiting on the other line," Miss Nolan said. "He says it's urgent."

Switching to the other line, George said, "Hi, Hank. What's up?"

"I've just discovered," his top legal adviser said, "that to operate your factory on Io you must be a citizen of Titan."

"We ought to be able to fix that up," George said.

"But to be a citizen of Titan—" Ramarau hesitated. "I'll break it to you easy as I can, George. You have to be a Blobel."

"Dammit, I am a Blobel," George said. "At least part of the time. Won't that do?"

"No," Ramarau said, "I checked into that, knowing of your affliction, and it's got to be one hundred percent of the time. Night *and* day."

"Hmmm," George said. "This is bad. But we'll overcome it, somehow. Listen, Hank, I've got an appointment with Eddy Fullbright, my medical coordinator; I'll talk to you after, okay?" He rang off and then sat scowling and rubbing his jaw. *Well*, he decided, *if it has to be it has to be. Facts are facts, and we can't let them stand in our way.*

Picking up the phone he dialed his doctor Eddy Fullbright.

The twenty-dollar platinum coin rolled down the chute and tripped the circuit. Dr. Jones came on, glanced up and saw a stunning, sharp-breasted young woman whom it recognized—by means of a quick scan of its memory banks—as Mrs. George Munster, the former Vivian Arrasmith.

"Good day, Vivian," Dr. Jones said cordially. "But I understood you were on Titan." It rose to its feet, offering her a chair.

Dabbing at her large, dark eyes, Vivian sniffled, "Doctor, everything is collapsing around me. My husband is having an affair with another woman . . . all I know is that her name is Nina and all the boys down at VUW Headquarters are talking about it. Presumably she's a Terran. We're both filing for divorce. And we're having a dreadful legal battle over the children." She arranged her coat modestly. "I'm expecting. Our fourth."

"This I know," Dr. Jones said. "A full-blooded Terran this time, if Mendel's Law holds . . . although it only applied to litters."

Mrs. Munster said miserably, "I've been on Titan talking to legal and medical experts, gynecologists, and especially marital guidance counselors; I've had all sorts of advice during the past month. Now I'm back on Terra but I can't find George—he's *gone*."

"I wish I could help you, Vivian," Dr. Jones said. "I talked to your husband briefly, the other day, but he spoke only in generalities . . . evidently he's such a big tycoon now that it's hard to approach him."

"And to think," Vivian sniffled, "that he achieved it all because of an idea *I* gave him. A Blobel idea."

"The ironies of fate," Dr. Jones said. "Now, if you want to keep your husband, Vivian—"

"I'm determined to keep him, Dr. Jones. Frankly I've undergone therapy on Titan, the latest and most expensive . . . it's because I love George so much, even more than I love my own people or my planet."

"Eh?" Dr. Jones said.

"Through the most modern developments in medical science in the Sol System," Vivian said, "I've been stabilized, Doctor Jones. Now I am in human form twenty-four hours a day instead of eighteen. I've renounced my natural form in order to keep my marriage with George."

"The supreme sacrifice," Dr. Jones said, touched.

"Now, if I can only *find* him, doctor—"

At the ground-breaking ceremonies on Io, George Munster flowed gradually to the shovel, extended a pseudopodium, seized the shovel, and with it managed to dig a symbolic amount of soil. "This is a great day," he boomed hollowly, by means of the semblance of a vocal apparatus into which he had fashioned the slimy, plastic substance which made up his unicellular body.

"Right, George," Hank Ramarau agreed, standing nearby with the legal documents.

The Ionan official, like George a great transparent blob, oozed across to Ramarau, took the documents and boomed, "These will be transmitted to my government. I'm sure they're in order, Mr. Ramarau."

"I guarantee you," Ramarau said to the official, "Mr. Munster does not revert to human form at any time; he's made use of some of the most advanced techniques in medical science to achieve this stability at the unicellular phase of his former rotation. Munster would never cheat."

"This historic moment," the great blob that was George Munster thought-radiated to the throng of local Blobels attending the ceremonies, "means a higher standard of living for Ionans who will be employed; it will bring prosperity to this area, plus a proud sense of national achievement in the manufacture of what we recognize to be a native invention, the Munster Magic Magnetic Belt."

The throng of Blobels thought-radiated cheers.

"This is a proud day in my life," George Munster informed them, and began to ooze by degrees back to his car, where his chauffeur waited to drive him to his permanent hotel room at Io City.

Someday he would own the hotel. He was putting the profits from his business in local real estate; it was the patriotic—and the profitable—thing to do, other Ionans, other Blobels, had told him.

"I'm finally a successful man," George Munster thought-radiated to all close enough to pick up his emanations.

Amid frenzied cheers he oozed up the ramp and into his Titan-made car.

Be Merry

BY ALGIS BUDRYS

*Here the aliens are benign and civilized, ethical creatures
with the best of intentions, who in fact visit us only by
accident—and still, in spite of themselves, they bring death
and destruction and ruin down upon the Earth, as efficiently and as devastatingly as any jackbooted conquering horde.
But, as Budrys suggests in the novelette that follows, one
of the finest alien-contact stories ever written, cultural contamination cuts both ways, and creatures adrift in the same
leaky boat soon find that it doesn't matter much who
helps you pull the oar—except for those aboard who refuse to pull at all.*

*Algis Budrys published his first SF story in 1952, and
by the end of that decade had firmly established himself
as one of the very finest writers of his generation. His most
famous novel is probably* Rogue Moon, *published in 1960,
in which explorers discover a huge, enigmatic alien artifact
on the Moon, one that quickly and horribly kills anyone
who dares to tamper with it—a forerunner, along with
Sturgeon's "There Is No Defense," of stories-to-come like
Clarke's* Rendezvous with Rama, *Pohl's* Gateway, *Silverberg's* Man in the Maze, *Saberhagen's* Berserker, *and Mar-
tin's "The Stone City." At shorter lengths, two of Budrys's
best-known stories of alien contact are "All for Love,"
which pits humanity against a two-hundred-and-fifty-mile-
high spaceship that has landed in the Colorado desert, and
"Silent Brother," in which we enter into a strange but
ultimately beneficial kind of symbiosis with an alien race.
Budrys's other books include* Who?—*which was made into
a movie starring Elliott Gould—*The Falling Torch, *and*

Some Will Not Die. *His most recent books are* Michaelmas
—*one of the three or four best SF novels of 1977—and*
Blood and Burning, *a collection of his short fiction. Budrys
is also one of SF's most astute critics—his reviews appeared
for years in* Galaxy, *and now appear regularly in* The
Magazine of Fantasy and Science Fiction.

Our Old Man is a good Old Man. His name is Colston McCall, and I don't know what he used to do before. Now he's chief of policing for the Western District of Greater New York, and he knows what's important and what isn't.

I was sitting under a big pine tree, feeling weak and dizzy. I had taken a load of aspirin, and my stomach wasn't feeling right. But it was a nice sunny day. I could feel the soft, lumpy bark giving in to the weight of my back. The branches made a sweet, shady canopy.

The ground was soft under the spongy pine needles, too, and it felt good sitting there, looking out over the meadows. There were wild flowers growing.

We might have had that ground plowed up, and people planting things. But there weren't enough people to plow up everything, and we had as many fields going as we had machinery for. We were doing our best. It still took a lot of people who had to go into the warehouses for packaged food that hadn't spoiled. There just wasn't any way we could have been organized better. We all had something useful to do, all of us who weren't in beds. I shouldn't have been sitting under any tree.

But it was a beautiful day, and I had been hurting bad all night and morning. The doctors in the hospital had given me a piece of paper saying I only had to work when I wanted to. I guess that means I only had to work when I could stand it, but if they had written it out that way it would have made a sadist out of anybody who asked me if I would do something for him. We've gotten very careful. Very considerate, in nice practical ways. Our manners are lousy, because there's no time to be polite, but it's true what people used to say—the fewer people are, the more important people become. I remember what it was like back before the Klarri had their accident, but I can't believe how mean people used to be to each other. I remember specific things they did to each other, and it gets me boiling mad because that's how I'd feel if somebody tried to do that kind of thing to me these days. It's how we'd all feel.

I think some of the things that used to make us sick, before, came from living like that. I think that if I was fifteen years younger and just coming to make my own way in the world we have now, I wouldn't have my trouble, and I wouldn't have to sit here thinking. I mean, a man like me who had come so well through the Klarri sicknesses should have had a lot to do in this world, and instead I was shutting off because of something the old world had done to me.

I wished I wasn't sitting under the tree. I wished I wasn't trying to soak it all in. I know that if I could, I would soak in all the sun and pine trees and wild flowers in the world, just for me.

I had thrown away the note the doctor had given me on the back of a page torn off a calendar pad. Well, you don't keep a note like that. Not when it's been written with a pencil stub by the light of a gasoline lantern in a big tent. Not when the doctor's so tired, and the people in the tent are so bad off from sicknesses nobody knows. I mean you don't walk around with something like that in your pocket. I would rather just sit here for a while and feel guilty.

But, you know, you can't keep that up very long. You know all you're doing is playing with yourself, because any time you feel guilty for having something simple and clear-cut like cancer, you're really just pretending you can afford luxuries. I didn't have to feel guilty about anything, not one blessed thing. But it's human to feel guilty, and the thing about any kind of pain isn't the pain. It's that it turns you back to that wet, helpless thing you were when you were born. You know the sky and the earth have gone soft and could smother you or swallow you any time. You know it's not that way for anybody else. Other people are still doing things in a world that will still be there and be dependable tomorrow. But you're not. You've poled your raft to a one-man island of jelly. So you enjoy the chance to put splinters into yourself. And that's playing.

I was just starting to get up when Artel, my partner, came walking to me from the Old Man's house. "Ed," he said. "Mr. McCall wants to talk to us."

"Right," I said, and the two of us walked back. Facing this way, I could see all the tents, and the houses that had been turned into offices, and the tracks of trucks and people cutting back and forth across what used to be the front and back lawns of the development. The whole thing was turning into a plain of mud, but at least there was a decent amount of space between the houses and a decent amount of open ground to put up tents and prefabs on, instead of everything jammed together the way it was in the cities and towns.

It was rotten in the cities and towns. Not just the fires, or the other kinds of trouble you get when a bunch of close-packed people get awfully sick and lose their heads. We were over that, but still when you went into someplace where the buildings were like walls along the street and everything should have been alive and working, selling shoes and groceries, the feeling of death would come over you and you couldn't do anything useful. They used to talk about how people were all moving out of the cities, before. Maybe because they already had something like that kind of feeling. Anyway, this place where the Old Man had set up was a development out along Route 46, and back in there up in the hills, there were lakes and wild animals, and you had a better feeling. You had better contact with the permanent things of the world.

"Is he sending us out on something?" I asked Artel.

"Yes."

Artel didn't ever talk much. The Old Man had teamed us up about a year ago, and it worked well. Klarri are a lot like us. Their arms and legs are longer in proportion to their bodies, and their shoulders are wider. They have long, narrow skulls, with all the cerebral cortex formed over what would be the back of the brain in a human, so if you're a highbrow among the Klarri, you're a bigdome. When they haven't washed for a few hours, there's a light, rusty deposit that forms on their skins and turns them that color. And nobody likes the way their teeth look. If a human being had teeth like that, he had some bad vitamin deficiency when he was a kid. But they're decent people. When they look at a hospital, I think they feel exactly the way we would if spaceships of ours had brought pestilence to a whole world of theirs.

There's one other thing about Klarri. Their kids all walk bent forward, and so do some of their adults, because that's the way their spines are. But they have a lot of trouble with that. It's like appendicitis with humans, and there isn't a Klarr who isn't aware that he could have severe back trouble almost any time. So there's a lot of them have had a fusing operation on the lower spinal column, either because they became crippled, or they started to feel little twinges and they got worried and had it done right away. It's just like people. Only instead of appendicitis scars, the ones who've had the fusing operation have this funny way of walking and standing as if they were about to fall over backwards. Artel was like that, but he also had to wear a back brace because he'd been hurt in the lifeboat crash that killed his wife and children. Back braces are faster than re-fusing operations.

You see, there can't be any doubt about it any longer. You do the best you can. We don't much believe in theory anymore. You can be as civilized as the Klarri, and know you shouldn't go around contaminating other people's worlds, but when your faster-than-light ship breaks down and you've got to ditch, you pile into the lifeboats and you ditch. If you're really lucky you've had your FTL breakdown within reaching distance of a solar system, and the solar system's got a planet you can live on; you come down any way you can, and you don't put decontamination high on your priority list. Life is hard; it's hard for Klarri, it's hard for humans. You spend each day living with whatever happened the day before, and that's it—that's how it is in all Creation, for everything with brains enough.

II

Colston McCall was a big man—there must have been a time when he weighed close to two hundred fifty pounds. He was way over six feet tall, and now he was all muscle and bones except for a little bit of a belly. He was about fifty or fifty-five, I guess, and he would lean back in his chair and look at a problem and solve it in a voice that must have been hell on his help in the days when he was running some kind of company. Whenever he raised his voice and called out a man's name, that man would get there quickly.

We went through into his office, and he looked up and waved us toward a couple of folding metal chairs. "Sit down, men." We did, with Artel straddling his chair backwards the way cowboys did in movie saloons.

"How are you feeling, Ed?"

"All right."

The Old Man looked straight at me for just a second. "Can you go twenty miles to someplace where there might not be any doctors?"

Well, the only other answer to that is, "No, sir, I'm ready to lie down and die," so I didn't say that.

"All right. There's a town down the coast where nobody's sick."

Artel sat up straight. "I beg your pardon?"

The Old Man laid his hand down flat on a small stack of papers. "These people have never asked for any medicines. Now, I don't know what that means. We first contacted them about two and a half years ago. One of our scouts found a party from their town foraging through the highway discount houses down along Route 35, there."

I nodded. That was the usual pattern in those days. The towns were all gutted on the inside, and any survivors had to start spreading out and looking for supplies outside. But that was a mug's game. You burned up what fuel you had, running emptier and emptier trucks farther and farther, coming back with less and less. What happened after that was they'd pool their remaining fuel, load everybody into the trucks and come busting up north, because everybody had the idea the big city had to be different.

The Old Man went on: "Well, it turned out that, for

once in a great while, these were the kind of people who'd stay put if we'd promise to send food down. So that's how it's been ever since."

And pretty grateful we were, too, I thought.

"Well, that was all right," the Old Man said, "but it's getting to be too much of a good thing, maybe. They're not complaining at all. You've got to figure any medical supplies they might have had left would be pretty much down to basics by now. Your antibiotics and your other fancy drugs either don't exist anymore or have turned to mush. Well, hell, you know that."

We knew. It was the biggest problem we had; things were tightening up pretty badly. And it wasn't any use being able to grow penicillin or any of those fermentation drugs you don't need much of a plant for. All that stuff was just so much extra peanut butter on the sandwich for the strains of bug we had now.

"But these people don't seem to have noticed that. They don't even complain about their food; they take whatever the trucks bring, they never ask for more, they never ask for anything different from what they get. I don't like it when people don't gripe about what we can deliver. And these people just take it and go away with it and never say a word."

"How many people?" I asked.

"A hundred and eighty-odd. I cut down their ration by three percent just to see what would happen. They haven't reacted at all. About the medicine, I had one of the drivers ask them if they needed a doctor, and they said no. They didn't say they had a doctor, and they didn't say they were all healthy. They just said 'No' and walked away."

"They're either very lucky or very generous," Artel said.

The Old Man gave him a quick look. "I'm always ready to believe in those things up to a point. But now I'd like to know if maybe there's something they haven't told anybody about."

Artel nodded.

I wanted to know about the food part. "What kind of a town is it?" I asked. "What kind of people are they? Could they be fishing or farming?"

"Not in that country," the Old Man said. "They're just property owners—squatters, some of them, but it's a community. All friends and relatives, all townies. Real estate agents, storekeepers, tree surgeons—all they know is how to sell cars and salt water taffy to each other." He sounded angry. The same thing angered us all: it had turned out farming was more than scratching the ground and dropping seeds into it. And it's slow, besides being hard to learn. He'd tell you just the opposite, but your hungry townsman would rather die than farm.

It sounds good, to just wave a hand and say, "Let there be light again." But *that's* the kind of thing that drives you wild. The Four Horsemen of the Apocalypse are ducks, and they nibble you to death.

"No, I don't believe it," the Old Man said, slapping the inventory control forms again. "Go down there and find out about it. Come back and tell me about it. Quietly."

"Of course," Artel said. "It wouldn't do to raise false hopes."

"Or even real ones." That was what made him a leader and me and Artel troopers. Our Old Man likes to go softly. He might not have been a top man before, when you had to move bing, bing, bing because the competition was clicking along right behind you. But he was good for us now.

You want to keep it soft. You want to take it slow and easy, and you have to know what to let slide. Cancer, they say, used to hit twenty-five percent of the population in one of its forms or another. They had been pretty close to cures, before. They weren't any closer now, because you can afford to ignore something like that when you've had diseases that each kill sixty, seventy percent in one summer.

You don't even care whether it was all the Klarri's fault or not. They were in awful trouble, too, cast away on an uncharted shoal, with our diseases beating the hell out of their survivors, and them with fewer biochemists than we had. I mean—what are you going to do? You could have some kind of lurching war and string them all up to lampposts, but there were better things to do with the energy, especially now that the first impact had passed and most of us that were going to die of each other were pretty much dead. If somebody was to put me in a time machine and send me back, the people then ought to shoot me down like a mad dog in the streets; I was carrying more kinds of death in me than anybody ever dreamed of, before. And if it wasn't for this home-grown thing of my own, I'd count as a healthy man by today's way of judging. So you don't worry about yesterday. You take what you have, and you work with it today.

"All right," the Old Man said. "Go down there, the two of you. Maybe we've got a miracle." That was as close as any one of the three of us got to laughing and clapping each other on the back and crying hallelujah.

I went down to the hospital while Artel waited for me. I walked through to the back, to where the dispensary was. The idea was, if you were well enough to walk in and ask for medicine, you had better be sick enough to walk by all those beds and still want medicine. I saw them all; the ones with the sores, and the ones with the twisted limbs, the ones with the blind eyes, and the ones with the hemorrhages. I heard them and I smelled them, human and Klarri.

These were survivors. The losers were dead. These were the ones you could expect still had a chance to live, if they could be kept strong enough to avoid things like pneumonia and the other killers of the weakened. I still had some kind of low-grade lymph node trouble. My arms would go to sleep, and I couldn't squeeze anything very hard without having my fingers go numb for hours afterward. While they were trying to do something about whatever bug it was that made my lymphatic system react, they found this other thing that had been living in me for quite some time already.

It didn't matter. I was around yet to walk down between the beds. Now, my Mary had drowned in her own blood. And I'd had this kid, about six, with his own little two-wheeler. A sidewalk bike, with solid rubber wheels, that was supposed to be for just diddling around in front of the house. Kind of a first step after graduating from a trike. There was an ice cream store that was open on Sundays fourteen blocks away from where we lived, and about ten days before the Klarri lifeboats came showering in from the sky, this kid and I had gone to that ice cream store, with me on my Sears, Roebuck three-speed and him on that boneshaker of his. Six years old, and pumping away like mad with just a little four-inch crank sprocket that gave him no speed at all, and me reminding him to slow down and pace himself, and him grinning over at me as he went bouncing over the potholes in the alleys. Good little kid.

The dispenser nodded when he saw me coming. He was a young Klarr, usually with his head bent over a medical dictionary; the wall had human and Klarr anatomical charts, and there was a human clerk putting together the mimeographed pages of a new medical text. We were beginning to shape up. For a long time, now, the Old Man hadn't been letting them put Klarr and human patients at separate ends of the tents. The idea was, if you were a doctor in the ward, by now you ought to be able to work most of the problems you saw no matter who had them. You'd have maybe one or two Klarr patients in the hospital at any time. It meant something that you'd always have more Klarr than that on the staff, or studying to join it.

Anyway, I showed the dispenser my Special Branch requisition permit, and he punched another notch on the edge of it and gave me a plastic bottle with twenty-five aspirins, and I said thank you and went back out through the tent. There was a supply truck running down to Trenton that would come within twenty or twenty-five miles of this place we were going to. Artel had drawn a couple of bikes from the transport pool for us on his permit and was just lashing them on to the side of the truck. We got in and we rode in the back, on top of a bunch of cases and bags. Artel made a kind of a hump-back pad out of bean sacks for himself and lay down on his stomach. I wedged myself into a nice tight fit where I wouldn't be bounced around too much, and after a while we took off.

III

The name of the town was Ocean Heights. After the truck dropped us, we moved toward it through some very pretty country, using the Garden State Parkway for a while. We had good gear; Artel's bike was a Peugeot and mine was a Raleigh, both of them fifteen-speed lightweights with high pressure tires and strapped pedals; they weren't specially comfortable, but they were very fast on any kind of decent surface, and with all that gearing to choose from, hill-and-dale touring was a snap.

We each had a .22 hunting rifle—the Old Man would have had our hearts if we'd carried anything to kill more people with—and some food, some tools and a water bottle apiece. We looked very technological, and you feel pretty good when you've got good gear. So we were both pretty well off in our own minds as we went zipping along, through the pine woods and along that smooth asphalt track. When we cut off and got onto Route 35, of course, we started running into signs of taffy salesman life—lots of roadside stands and one saloon painted Day-Glo orange, and a lot of garden tool and outboard motor shops, along with great big discount centers. All of it looked shabby, beat up, and just a shell. There was nothing left in the discount houses but phonograph records, and little plastic pots to raise rubber plants in, and games made by the Wham-O Manufacturing Company. The wind was in off the ocean, and that was all right too.

It started to get dark while we were still five miles away from Ocean Heights. That was the way we wanted it.

We took ourselves a couple of miles farther, and then we cut out up a side road, into the woods. We found a good place to leave the bikes and made a little bit of a camp. It was good getting off the bike. Artel was walking very slowly, and he was leaning farther over backwards than ever. I didn't remark on it; I guess I've already said that in our own eyes from ten or fifteen years before, we'd all seemed like very rude people. Artel sighed when we were finally able to sit down and lean against something. So did I, I guess.

We sat down close together. Artel had one of those squeeze type flashlights that generates its own power. We put my windbreaker over our heads to muffle the light and we studied the map, laying out a heading for Ocean Heights from where we were. We'd be able to walk it in not much more than a couple of hours. We got our compass headings straight in our heads, and then we were able to come out from under the windbreaker, which was all right with me. One of the reasons Artel and I could work as a team was because I didn't mind his smell. (That was what I said; actually, I liked it). But not in big doses like this. It was like eating a pound of milk chocolate.

We'd done this kind of thing before; we knew what we were doing. A couple of hours from now, when it was still dark and we could expect most people to be thinking of sleep, we'd get moving, so that by the time we hit the place it would be tight-fast in dreamland. We'd ghost around and find out what we could. Get the lay of the land, figure an escape route and boltholes if we needed them. It sounds like playing Indians, but it's the kind of technique you work out when you're dealing with unknown people these days. You can't even tell in advance sometimes whether they're humans or Klarri; that was originally why a Special Branch team had to have at least one of each.

We sat in the woods and waited until it was time to move. We didn't talk much as a rule. For one thing, what had happened to Artel's respiratory system gave him a lot of trouble with breath control. For another thing, life's too simple to need a lot of conversation. But it was lonely out there, and nightfall bothers me. "Listen," I asked Artel, "do you think your people will ever find you?"

"Pretty unlikely," he said after a while. "The volume they'd have to search is mighty big." After a while he added: "It'd be better if they didn't. We'd be as deadly now to our home as we were to you." I could see him smile a little. "We Klarri here have traded too much back and forth with Earth. We've become much more like you than like our people."

He folded his arms with his hands over his shoulders, the way they do. "I don't see much difference between us, in anything, really. Our machinery may be a little better. But most of us don't understand it any better than you understand yours. We lose ships, once in a while. We don't find them any more often than you'd expect. We have to pretend this isn't so, because otherwise we couldn't sell tickets to each other."

"Travel agents about the same anyplace, I guess," I said.

He shrugged. "Civilization's about the same anyplace. You take a ship from one star to another, and you say to yourself, 'Here's something my father couldn't do.' It's true. My father couldn't do either. Nor lose an interstellar passenger ship. And end with only a few thousand survivors from it. And have a whole future to solve."

He pushed himself down and lay on his back for a minute, with his hands behind his head, looking up. "I'm glad I don't have to imagine how they're going to do it." He didn't sound particularly worried; well, it wasn't our problem. I'd heard humans and Klarri talk about things like what'll happen when we build spaceships again. It's a cinch they won't be rockets; they'll be a lot like the Klarr ships, I guess. But where will they go? Looking for planets where Klarri and humans from Earth could start the same business of living together, or contacting the Klarr worlds, or what? What would happen if we met Klarri from some political faction that didn't like our Klarri? Well, there are damn fools everywhere, I guess. When the real problems really came, they'd more than likely have some shape of their own, and they'd either be solved or flubbed in some way that was possible to their own time.

"You heard about this new idea?" Artel said cautiously. "There's some biochemist with a hypothesis. He says that with two or three generations of gene manipulation, it might be possible to have Klarr- and human-descended compromise people who could breed true with each other. Think there's anything to that?"

"I've heard that. What do I know?' 'It shouldn't have, but the idea made my stomach turn. I guess Artel felt the same way.

"It's an idea," Artel said, and I could see he didn't like it any better than I did. But that was one of those things the two of us didn't have to worry about. And I appreciated what he was trying to do. You try to make as much contact as you can. Probably the Old Man had put us together originally because we were both lonely in the same way. Everybody wants to see a team as good as possible. Just for its own sake; not just because so many of the Klarr ships had happened to hit the Western Hemisphere. Other places, there'd been so few Klarr, I think they killed them all during the pestilence feelings. There were people who talked about national pride being involved; they said a lot of things like that, maybe getting ready to hand the next generation something they could go to war about.

Talk's all right in its place. Now we'd done some, Artel and I just waited in the woods.

IV

At about ten o'clock we started to slide into the outskirts of Ocean Heights. These Jersey coast towns are all a lot alike. There's always a highway paralleling the ocean, leaving a strip maybe three miles wide with feeder roads running down to the Atlantic. Follow the feeder road and you find you're on the main street of some town that was in its heyday in 1880. Right up near the water there'll be a strip of big Steamboat Gothic summer homes; frame and shingle construction, three, four storeys high, with lots of cupolas, and gingerbread, and maybe even an imitation widow's walk. Big verandas, hollow wooden columns and lots of etched glass in the ground-floor windows. Some people think that's a sign of gracious living. I think it just proves how much we wanted mass production.

Closer in toward town there'll be a lot of stores. Some of them will have bright new cast stone or aluminum fronts, but the buildings are all fifty years old behind them. There'll be a couple of yellow fire-brick structures, with almost anything in on their ground floors now, that used to be the A & P and the Woolworth's. Those moved out to the shopping center back in the 1950s. There'll be a couple of movie theaters, and one of them was closed long before the trouble hit the town itself. There's a Masonic Temple, churches of various Christian denominations, a hotel for little old ladies and salesmen. Used car lots full of stuff carrying ten dollars' worth of paint over the salt rust. A railroad track. A couple of television repair stores, and a weekly four-page newspaper dedicated to getting people to shop at home.

On the ocean there are some seafood restaurants, a miniature golf course and a building that looks like a horse barn but in the summertime houses a wheel of fortune and a couple of dart-toss games, with most of the stalls standing empty even in the height of the season. The parking lot for the oceanfront amusements is where the dog track used to be. The boardwalk is falling down everywhere. There are piles and sheets of rusty iron sticking up out of the beaches farther along, where the boardwalk used to reach. The people say it's the Republican legislators from the inland counties, with their blue laws, that killed these towns. If you approach from the beach, the first thing you notice is the plastic-coated paper from the frozen custard stands. It doesn't mash up and wash into the ground at all; it just turns gray.

We slid on in through the outskirts. Artel said: "It was bad here."

Looked like it. There were a lot of burnt pits full of bricks and pieces of charred timber, with dead trees standing around them, where there had been fires. There was all sorts of trash in the gutters, swept in from the fires and the general scraps that blow around and pile up when nobody collects them. The gutters were clogged with odd pieces of wood, tarpaper, sand and gravel. The sewer grates were all choked, and the streets were broken down. Rainwater and frost had broken up the asphalt and undermined the cement. Some of the streets had been laid in brick, and they now looked as if long walls had collapsed onto the ground. It wasn't unless you looked hard, toward the ocean, that you could see the occasional lantern burning and could believe that anyone lived on beyond this mess.

We found only one street that was really open. It had truck ruts in it, with trash smashed down into them, and unmarked sand washed into pools in other places. The last supply run had been a couple of weeks ago, and it looked as if our trucks were the only things that came and went. Once we had found the main drag this way, we moved off away from it and worked our way along the back streets. We came across dead cars, and the weathered tumble-down of barricades. Once I tripped over a shotgun with a broken stock; the wood grainy from rainwater and sunlight, the barrels just tubes of rust. "You'd think they'd have cleaned up the useful things," Artel said.

"It's broken."

"But it could have been fixed."

"No, not here," I said. The soil was sand, just one great big bar that the Atlantic had raised over thousands of years of pounding itself up against the rock coast of what were now the northern counties, and you couldn't raise anything on it but scrub pine. West of the line running from New York down to Camden you were off the interstate highways and main railroads. The only thing you could do with this part of the world was sleep in it and play in it, and sell taffy to each other. We'd passed a horse-racing track coming in. Big looming plant, standing dirty in the darkness. Its parking lots had been full of cars, and there was a smell, originally trapped in all that wet upholstery, that hung in the air. That was as far as they'd gotten—the people trying to get out of the city. They were turned back by the local cops, cursing and sweating, and thanking God there was someplace to point to where all those people could go to die.

Farther in toward the town we passed the Women's Club

building—a big place with a phony Grecian front, that the local people had probably tried to make into a supplementary hospital at this end of town. We padded on up the steps, and there were three-year-old bodies right up against the doors, inside. We backed off.

"We won't find anyone living right around here," Artel said. Twenty years from now, the Women's Club building and the cinderblock walls of the bowling alley down the street would be all that stuck up out of the second growth. There'd be trees growing out of the sewers.

We crossed the railroad tracks, and we stood there as if we'd just sat straight up in bed in the middle of the night. The first thing I noticed was the smell of fresh paint. But there was plenty of other stuff to hit you, all at once.

It must have been one of the best parts of the town to begin with. The houses were brick, two and three storeys high. They were all set in the middle of very nice lots, and most of them had those Georgian fronts that spell class. In daylight, we might have seen soot and patches in some of the brickwork, but we didn't see it now. All the outlines were crisp and sharp; there wasn't a warped board or a sagging roof anywhere here. There were neat, well-located privies in the backyards, we found as we started to move around. The fronts of them were made out of brick and had shrubs planted around them.

It was all like that. The hedges were trimmed. The lawns were like velvet. There wasn't a chipped place in any sidewalk, nor litter on the grass, or anything.

There were lanterns burning upstairs in two or three of the houses. "What the hell?" I said. There were eight or ten solid blocks of this stuff. All it needed was a wall around it.

"This is 'way off the supply route," Artel said. "To see this part, you'd have to do what we did. You notice the trees—how thick they are? I think they even had airplanes in mind when they picked this spot."

"Listen," I said. From one of the houses, through a window open to the soft night air, you could hear it: *"Bella figlia del amore . . ."*

"What is that?" Artel asked.

"Opera. Somebody's got a windup phonograph."

"Or a generator."

"But no bulldozer to bury his dead with."

Artel looked back over his shoulder toward the other side of the railroad tracks. "That is different."

We kept moving, with faint music. There was no other living sound. No night birds, no cats in love, no dogs. There wasn't any sound of people sneaking through yards. This town didn't have teenagers who liked to visit each other. All these people were locked up tight in their little clean town-within-a-town, most of them sleeping the sleep of the innocent. The innocent and the healthy.

We worked our way closer toward the ocean. We were only a block away from it. The waves were rolling in to the shore regularly and gently, making the only steady sound we could hear, now that we were out of range of the phonograph. I looked back over my shoulder, and I could see nothing but those few upstairs lights, some of which had been put out since we had gone by. Solid citizens turning in. I thought they were lantern lights. They might have been lightbulbs on low voltage. We were getting more questions than answers out of this town.

We got down to the beach, and we found another dirty fringe—a motel with its windows broken out, a playground with scrub bushes growing up among the teeter-totters and the monkey bars, a flight of wooden steps tumbled down the stone jumble of the sea wall. If you had been going by in a boat you would have never known about that neat little clean patch with its edged flower beds and its un-littered streets.

There was a big, dark building just inland of the play-ground. Flat-sided and square, it was two storeys high, and the ground-floor windows were well over the height of a man's head, long and very narrow. If this was a war, and the building was at a crossroads, I would have reported it for a bunker. The sign over the doorway said "Ocean Heights Professional Bldg." The double doors were at the head of a flight of stairs set back and flanked by solid masonry. I could have defended it from the inside with one machine gun. There was a padlock hanging on the doors, closing a chain looped through the handles.

"There was a gambling casino in Ocean Heights during World War II," Artel said. He was the one who'd gone through the Old Man's background file on the town. "It was closed by state investigators in 1947."

"We've found it." Going by the delicately scalloped, once white-painted directory board bolted to the wall beside the stairs, an architect and a real estate agent had set up offices in it after the space became available. There was no sound in it now, and no lights. But I noticed something, and it made me wonder. I pulled in a deep breath through my nose.

"It's not empty," I said.

"I agree," Artel said. "I have that feeling. And yet I can't say why." In the starlight, I could see him shake his head quickly. "It bothers me. It was built to be a hiding place. They might be doing almost anything in there."

"Let's look around some more," I said.

"If you say so," Artel said hesitantly.

The other thing we found was down at the beach. It was something looming, most of it under the water, the waves phosphorescing weakly against the one side that we could see. It stretched away into the darkness, and its curved sides went up like the biggest dead whale in the world. I could see a long strut extending out over the water at a shallow angle, and the round circle of a landing pad hanging at a crazy angle from the end of it. It was a crashed Klarri lifeboat.

"What happened to the people in it, I wonder," Artel said.

"They're in that building back there. Locked up and kept out of sight," I said. I had smelled them, the scent seeping out weakly through the double doors and God knew how many other barriers inside. "What do you want to do about it?"

It was up to him. They were his people. If he wanted us to go in there and break them out now, I didn't see any way for me not to help him. Maybe we could get away with it; I wasn't crazy about the idea of trying to do all that without making any noise, but it was up to him. "Anything you say."

"Come off it, Ed. We don't know anywhere near enough about the situation in this place. We haven't found what we were sent for." Artel sounded a little mad. He had a right to be. I'd as good as said he wasn't a team man. I felt bad about having been rude. "Come on—let's go back to camp," he said. "We had a plan and let's follow it." Artel slipped off into the darkness.

I followed him. We didn't say anything more to each other that night. We got back to our camp and sacked out.

A team is a little bit like a marriage. I don't care what anybody says, sometimes it's better not to talk it out. It makes you feel like hell for a while, but you've got an even chance the next morning one or the other of you will say something in a friendly way and then the other one will feel relieved and it will be all over.

V

In the morning we went in straight. There's no point to horsing around. If we'd had things like phone taps, snooper microphones and truth serum to work with, we might have decided on something different. But life's too simple these days for any of that kind of stuff to be worth a damn. We'd just ask them questions, and then see what their lies added up to.

Coming down the main drag on our bikes, we went through the dead shopping district of the town and then cut right on a concrete street a couple of blocks in from the ocean. I figured we'd be coming up to signs of life soon.

What we heard first was the sound of a ball bat from some field two or three blocks away and off to our right, somewhere near where the clean patch of houses was. We couldn't see anything, but we could hear kids yell; it was the kind of noise you get from a schoolyard at recess time.

We made another half a block, still going by houses that were all abandoned, and then we heard some little kid yelling "Daddy! Daddy! Daddy!" The sound of fast little feet on the floor of a veranda went clattering in echoes along the street, and then a screen door slammed shut. We'd finally been spotted. We stopped and began walking our bikes up the middle of the street.

About a hundred fifty yards ahead there was a traffic light hanging from guy wires over an intersection. There were a couple of gas stations there, and the drive-in apron of an ice cream stand. It made a kind of open place where you might expect people to gather when you unloaded your supply truck. Between there and us there were a couple of houses that might be lived in. They didn't have any broken glass in their windows, and there were light-colored streaks of unpainted putty in places along the sash. They didn't look neat, but they looked livable. They looked about the way you might expect houses to look in a town, if it wasn't a town on its feet enough to have that nice little residential section tucked away back there.

A screen door slammed again, and this time we caught the direction of the sound. It was coming from a couple of houses down and to our right. It was a big green three-storey house, and we could see faces at the windows, but the glass was dirty, and we couldn't tell much about them. What we could see was the man coming out from the veranda and walking down the front steps. He stood there for a minute as we came closer.

He was a tall, thin, oldish-looking man with a checked shirt and suit pants, wearing glasses and carrying a pipe in his hand. He looked seedy and comfortable, with the pants hanging down flat and butt-sprung behind, and the knees baggy in front. He waved a hand at us in a nice neighborly way, and then he walked around the side of the house. There was a sudden hammering of metal on metal—a wild, carrying sound—and all the other noises we'd been hearing stopped. The only things to listen to were the steady wash of the ocean off to our left and the grit of our tires on the street. The man came back from around the house just as we reached his front walk. He had bushy salt-and-pepper hair growing out of the sides and back of his head, and a streak of it growing back from his forehead; his hairline was shaped like a thick-tined pitchfork, and he reminded me of all the retired men who might come around to your place in the summertime and help you build a rose arbor for a few dollars.

"Howdy!" he said. "Didn't hear you coming." He was looking closely at Artel. I had the feeling he was having trouble making up his mind whether Artel could possibly be a Klarr.

"Howdy," I said. "My name's Ed Dorsey. This is my partner, Loovan Artel. Artel's his first name. What was all that racket?"

The man came forward and stuck out his hand. "My name's Walter Sherman. Got one of those iron fire-alarm rings set up next to the house. I kinda let people know when we've got company. Pleased to meet you." He shook my hand, and then he gave Artel another look, very fast.

He thought it over and shook Artel's hand. "Pleased to meet *you*."

"My pleasure," Artel said, grinning a little.

Sherman blinked once. He was trying to act right. He was doing pretty well, I thought, considering he hadn't ever before seen a Klarr wearing human clothes and riding a bicycle. Sherman looked all right, too. He was getting old, but there was a nice glint in his eyes and good color in his face. His hair wasn't dead and dull, and the whites of his eyes were clear. He didn't move or talk like a man who was anywhere near sitting down and waiting to get older. He looked like an upstanding gent, and you don't get to see very many of those any more.

I took a quick look around.

There were people beginning to show up. One or two of them were coming out of nearby houses, but most of them were beginning to gather down at the intersection under the traffic light, coming up side streets and back from where the clean houses were. Just looking down that way, if you were a supply truck driver, say, you'd guess that they had all come out of the houses down there. "We're from Philadelphia," I said to Sherman. "Survey team." Artel and I got cards out of our shirt pockets and showed them to him. They were signed "F. X. Daley, United States Commissioner, Philadelphia District."

"We're just starting to check this part of the country," I said as Sherman took the cards in his hand and studied them, peering and blinking with the pipe in his mouth. The pipe was cold and empty—had been for years, probably. "We'd just like to find out a little bit about this community —how many people, what kind of social organization . . . that kind of thing."

"That's right, sir," Artel said. "We'd appreciate your cooperation. Or if you'd rather direct us right away to your mayor or whoever's in charge, why, we'll get out of your front yard and let you go back to what you were doing."

"Oh, no—that's all right," Sherman said, handing us back the cards. "I imagine there'll be some people from our town council here in a minute. Glad to help."

There wasn't any doubt we were bothering him. He was talking off the top of his head and thinking very hard about something else. I wondered for a minute if these people had some way of knowing there wasn't anything in

Philadelphia—not a blessed thing—but it didn't seem likely. One of the hardest things to be sure of in this world is nothing.

"Well, come in and—" He waved with his pipe toward the steps of his veranda. "Ah, why don't you sit down?" He was looking at the touring saddles on our bikes. "I imagine it might be nice to rest yourselves on something flat."

He tried to chuckle. He was trying to be pleasant, he really was. But we had caught him off base very bad by not coming into town with a truck engine roaring ahead of us, and by not both of us being human.

We sat down on his front steps. We left our bikes up on their kick stands, with the .22's strapped down on the carriers, just like any survey team would have.

"You—ah—people look bushed," Sherman said. "You come all the way from Philadelphia on those bikes?"

I nodded. "Easy stages, yeah," I told him. "There's a lot to check out." He looked a lot healthier than either one of us, that was for sure.

"We ought to explain," Artel said. "It's the people who can't do a regular day's work they can spare for things like surveys." Like me, he was watching the bunch of people coming toward us. They were walking fast. Not running; just coming on at a good pace. There were young and old, and a few kids, a good mixed human crowd coming to the railroad station to watch the streamliner go by. A good, healthy crowd. Even not running, they were moving faster than any bunch of people I'd seen in years. They looked good; clean, eager. They looked the way people ought to look when something exciting is happening. You could see the front ones slow down and frown as they made out what Artel was.

A freckled man in suntans and a rainhat, with squint wrinkles around his blue eyes, came through them as they began to gather into a clump on Sherman's front lawn. "Hi, Walt!" he said as he came up to us. "I see you got company."

"Couple of government men from Philadelphia," Sherman said.

"Philadelphia, eh?" he said, shaking hands with us as we

stood up. "My name's Luther Koning. Pleased to meet you both."

"Luther's sort of like our mayor," Sherman explained.

Whatever he was, he was the man we'd come to see. I guessed he was about fifty; all long, flat muscle under that weather-tight skin, and able to act as if it was nothing unusual to see a Klarr walking around instead of being in that big, silent building out behind the abandoned playground. He had fast reactions, Koning did, and where other people had slowed to a walk and stopped, he had come on forward.

"Glad to meet you," I said. I told him my name, and I told him: "This is Artel, my partner."

"Mm-hmm," Koning said. "Well, I can see that," he said in an agreeable enough voice, looking over at the bicycles and the two rifles. "Two equally intelligent races in the same jam, after all. They waste their strength in fighting, there's no hope at all. So they work together. It makes sense." He looked at me and then at Artel. "You look tired—both of you. Things still aren't so good in the big city, huh?"

"Things aren't so good anywhere, Mr. Koning," Artel said. "But we're trying to make them better. That's why we're here."

"Why *are* you here?" Koning grinned again. "We're standing here talking, and for all I know you two are anxious to get something done right away."

"They've got ID cards here from Philadelphia," Walter Sherman said. He had gotten a chance to settle down some, and his voice was easier. But he was really fast in getting that across to Koning, even though he said it in a careless voice. "Gave me a turn, coming in that way. On bicycles." He chuckled: "Real fancy machines, those are. Smart idea. Saves on gasoline." I think the point he was trying to make was that we were dissimilar from the people who came in trucks, and that we might not even know about any other organization.

"We're just trying to find out if you people need anything," I said harmlessly to Koning. I was watching the crowd. There were thirty or forty of them, and it seemed to me that any time you can collect twenty percent of the total population at the drop of a hat, you're dealing with an excitable population. But they didn't look jumpy the way a crowd of sick-nervous people might. You don't see the kind of shuffling and fevery face-jerking you get sometimes. These people weren't looking for excitement. Sick people need excitement because it interrupts their misery. When they get it, they lose their dignity; it's a dose of the stuff they crave, and when you pour it out in front of them they can't hide how much they need it. These people weren't like that. They didn't need to be a mob. But they were very, very interested. Like members of the same club, and a famous guest-lecturer. There wasn't a Klarr among them. That would have struck me even if I hadn't known about the special building.

I couldn't make this crowd out. I kept looking at them; men of all ages, housewife-types in cotton print dresses, some of them with water-spotted aprons around their middles where they'd been washing up the breakfast dishes. There were young men in T-shirts, who looked as if they'd been working around the yard, and older men who were like Sherman and Koning in looking like they'd lived useful, cheerful lives, and had a lot of useful time in them. It was the kind of crowd that gives you the feeling life is comfortable and pleasant all the time. There wasn't another one like it in the whole world.

It bothered the hell out of me. Some of the kids had brought their gloves and started a game of catch out beyond the fringes of the crowd. Other kids were circulating back and forth; you couldn't get their attention with a conversation on a veranda, but they were either going to be where the attraction was, whatever it was, or they were going to spread the news. Some of them had been up to Sherman's house and back down to the intersection several times already. Now one of them on the edges of the crowd yelled: "Here comes Tully!" Koning turned around as if he'd been shot, but he recovered nicely.

"Hey! Let's keep it down; we're trying to talk here," he said. But he kept looking sideways over at a man ambling along the sidewalk, so Artel and I did too.

VI

Tully was like one of those men you'll see sitting on a beachfront bench staring out over the water. Nobody can do anything for or to them. They're past the big tussle. He had given up trying to look as if God never made pot bellies, and was wearing loose-weaved light pants with a big, comfortable waistline and baggy legs. He had rubber-soled cloth shoes on and bright socks that you could see showing under the flipping cuffs of his pants. He had broad-strap suspenders holding up his pants, and he was wearing a short-sleeved, bright shirt. His bare arms were thin and knobby, tanned an even darker and shinier brown than Koning's face was under his freckles. He was wearing a headband with a transparent green eyeshade. There was a fringe of white hair around his stuck-out ears, and the top of his skull was tanned and glistening. He had a big, amiable grin. He walked along as if he had all the time in the world, knowing that he was a center of interest, too, and the rest of the show would wait for him.

Neither Koning nor Sherman said a word. People will do that. People think that if they stop, time stops.

Tully ambled into the crowd, still grinning, and the crowd drifted out of his way. There wasn't anything obtrusive about it; it wasn't like the Red Sea parting for Moses into two straight-edged and shiny walls. It was just that they drifted out of his way, easily and naturally as if everybody in town knew from a baby that you didn't stand close to Tully. Tully walked forward, still grinning.

He cocked his undersized, round-chinned, round face up at the veranda. He looked at Artel, and then he looked past Koning and me at Sherman. When he spoke, his voice was high, like the cackle of a chicken with the biggest egg in the yard. "Ah-heh, Doc. Heard you had one of them Hammerheads visiting on your porch." He looked Artel up and down. "Looks like a prime example, considerin' how puny critters are these days."

He looked at me now. His eyes under the shade were small and black, and smart. "His partner don't look so good either, does he?" He stood there with his little squirrel-paw hands hooked into the front of his trousers, and when he began to laugh, first his cheeks quivered, and then the loose skin in his neck, and then his belly under the shirt, and then he was bouncing on the balls of his feet. But he didn't make any noise. He flapped with laughter as he ran his eyes around from Sherman and quickly across Artel and me to Koning, and then he began to turn very slowly and his glance didn't miss one of the people around him. And then he walked away. He went back down the sidewalk the way he'd come, his hands still hooked in the waistband of his pants, his back shaking a little bit, the suspenders tight across his wizened shoulders, and a reflection of sunlight bouncing off the curved sheen of his eyeshade.

"Well," Artel said in an amused and careless voice, "I see every town has its character."

Koning rubbed his hand across the back of his neck, where the skin was seamed and granulated from years of exposure to sunlight. His jaw was out; I could see his lower teeth. They were wet and brown, and snaggled by oncoming age. The breath was pushing out steadily through his nostrils, making a very thin whistle. He took off his khaki rainhat and ran his hand over his scalp. He put the hat back on, all without taking his eyes off Tully. The crowd was looking up at us expectantly, and I believe half of them were holding their breath.

"I didn't know you were a doctor," I said to Sherman, as if this were interesting but not vital. Of all the things that had been happening to us since Sherman had given the alarm, this was the one that I couldn't make out to have not noticed. "Want to make a note of that, Artel?" I went on. "It's good news. It means we won't have to send one of our own in." Artel nodded and took a pad of mimeographed form sheets out of his pocket. He got out a pencil, licked the tip and made an X-mark in a box.

"Doctor present. Right," he mumbled boredly.

"By the way, doctor, congratulations," I said to Sherman. "You must be doing a fine job here. These people look fine."

Sherman said quickly: "Now, wait—you're getting the wrong idea. I'm no doctor. We don't have any doctor. That's just something that crazy old coot calls everybody." His glance flickered over to Koning.

"I ought to lock—no, God damn it, I . . . can't . . ." Koning wasn't talking to me. He was talking directly to Sherman.

Whatever it was, it had them completely shaken up. I can imagine how they must have planned for snoopers in advance, sitting around a kitchen table and nerving each other. *Well, listen, Luther—what'll we do if somebody comes around asking questions?* "We'll handle it, Walt. *After all, it's our town, we live here. The important things are all kept out of sight, and how would they know what*

*questions to ask? Don't you worry about it, Walt. You just
always let me do most of the talking, and I'll make sure
they don't find out anything but what we want them to
know.*" That was exactly how it had gone between them;
it's the kind of conversation smart, decent men with a
secret have held between themselves since time knows
when. And it had worked, back when things were looser.

They were looking at each other like two men tied to
opposite ends of a rope, and the middle of the rope hooked
over a spur of rock on the side of a twenty-thousand-foot
mountain.

"Oh. Sorry, Mr. Sherman," I said. "Artel, looks like
you're going to have to start a new form."

"Yeah. Before I do that—Mr. Sherman, do you have
very many seniles in your population? Will you require any
special supplies—tranquilizers or that sort of thing?" Artel
asked.

"Well, I wouldn't know," Sherman said doggedly. "And
Tully don't seem to do any harm, as long as you don't pay
him any mind."

"We've been very lucky here," Koning said. He was
beginning to get back to himself. He was talking a little
fast, and the wrinkles at the corners of his eyes weren't
completely relaxed. But he was doing a good job of recov-
ering. "We're all healthy people here. Oh, once in a while
somebody mashes his thumb with a hammer or something.
But that's not anything that can't be taken care of. We live
nice and quiet. It's good. When I look back on how it was
in the old days, I've got to say we live better. That's a
terrible thing, when you think of how this town used to
have twenty-five thousand people in it and mighty few of
them ready to be dead. But now we've got through the bad
time, things are pretty good. For the live ones. Meaning no
insult, maybe a lot better than they are for you outside."

He was looking steadily at Sherman. And he had come
to something in his mind. He wasn't back on his heels anymore. He was nervous, and he didn't like to trust his own
improvisations any better than anybody else would. But he
was going to go with it, whatever it was. He wasn't looking to Artel and me for his cues any longer. You could see
that happening in him; you could hear it in his voice.
"Look, gentlemen," he said, stepping back and smiling. "I
got taken up here in a hurry, and there's a couple of little

things that I'd like to finish up, if that's all right with the two of you. I mean, this isn't any kind of an emergency. It's a surprise, but it isn't an emergency. So if you could excuse me for about a half hour, I could come back then and I'd have the rest of the day clear to talk to you. I'm sure Mr. Sherman can keep you entertained, and maybe fill you in on some of the background. Just the general stuff; I'll be back in time to give you the specifics. How would that be?" He grinned at Sherman with everything but his eyes. "Why don't you take them inside, Walt? Millie could maybe give them a little refreshment."

"Well, I don't know——" Sherman looked at Koning as if he had gone just as wild as Tully. "I mean, the house is a mess . . ."

It was sad, watching a man turn into a nervous house-wife right in front of my eyes.

"No, you go ahead and take them inside," Koning said. "Don't worry about the house." He grinned again. "Relax, Walt! You're just not used to company," he chuckled.

Sherman nodded slowly. "All right," he said, "take your word on that."

His face went through a spasm; I think he started to grin back, and then realized immediately he couldn't make it stick. I didn't dare look over at Artel myself, for fear we'd lay ourselves open in the same way.

The crowd was livening up again; Koning's starting some kind of action was taking the dismay of Tully out of them. The kids, of course, hadn't stayed quiet for more than a minute. Some of them were back to playing catch, and some of the others had drifted on down the street after Tully—I didn't know whether on purpose after Tully or just happening to be headed in the same direction. I noticed nobody had tried giving Tully any catcalls or josh-ing, not even the kids.

It was a nice town; they were polite to their sick ones.

"It sounds like a practical idea," I said. "And I sure could use a cool drink, Mr. Sherman. How about you, Artel?"

Artel nodded. "Yes."

"Oh, well, sure," Sherman said. "No problem about that. Got a good well down by where the Nike site used to be. Deep, government-dug well. Lucky that way, too, we were. Lots of good water."

"Well, that would be fine!" I said.

I could hear Koning sigh just a little bit. "Okay! So it's all settled—Doc here'll take care of you two fellows till I get back, and everything'll work out just fine." Koning turned and trotted down the steps. "Be seeing you!"

I waved a hand cheerfully after him. So did Artel. "Well," Sherman said. "Let's—let's go inside." So we did.

VII

A blonde young woman of maybe twenty-five was waiting in the hall, carrying a baby over her shoulder, one arm around it and the spread fingers of her other hand supporting it over the fresh, clean diaper. There were a couple of other kids clustered around her; a girl maybe a year older than the baby, and a boy in a T-shirt and corduroy rompers who was just under school age. He had little shoes on, scuffed up around the toes since the time this morning his mother had coated them with some of that polish that comes in a bottle with a dabber. The little girl had her arms around her mother's knees and her face buried in the side of her skirt. Sherman said: "This is my wife, Millie. And my kids. That's LaVonne, and Walt, and the baby's name is Lucille. Millie, this is Mr.—" He looked over at me.

"Dorsey. I'm very pleased to meet you. This is my partner—"

"Loovan Artel. Loovan's his family name," Sherman said.

Millie Sherman nodded, looking at Artel. Her eyes were very big, and the corners of her mouth kept twitching. Finally she said, "Oh."

"It's all *right*, Millie," Sherman soothed.

"We just need a place to sit, Mrs. Sherman," Artel said gently. "Until Mr. Koning gets back."

"That's right, honey," Sherman said, throwing Artel a grateful glance. "Luther just asked me to give these men some refreshment until he gets back. He asked me to bring 'em in."

Putting the seal of authority on it seemed to buck her up, some. "Oh." She wet her lips. "Well, won't you come in?" She pulled the boy Walter out of the way and stood back against the wall. We were in one of those narrow foyer things that runs through toward the back of the house and has doors opening off it into the main rooms, and a flight of stairs going up.

"Let's go straight on through to the kitchen. I'm sure you fellows don't mind," Sherman said.

"Not at all," Artel said, and we followed him toward the back of the house. I threw a glance into the living room as we went by. There were couches and a lot of chairs up against the walls, with a coffee table in front of each couch. There were books on the tables, bound in bright-colored cheap cloth. Novels.

The kitchen was big, with a chrome-legged table, wooden cabinets and a lot of chrome-legged chairs with padded plastic seats and backs. Next to the capped stub of a gas-pipe coming up through the floor was a cast iron wood range, and in the sink was a big, galvanized iron pan with the washing water in it. The drinking water was in a regular office-type water cooler with a big glass bottle held upside down in it. And in one corner, standing spindly legged, was a kerosene refrigerator. "Well, now, that's something," I said, nodding toward it. "You people are really starting to get straightened around here." Sherman's eyes followed mine. He looked at the refrigerator as if all hope were lost.

"I have to have it," he said.

"Oh? Are you a diabetic?" I said.

What happened to his face now was like nothing I could recognize, but if he had been made out of strings, I could have heard them snap. The look he gave me was damn near unbearable; I might have been a cobra.

Without taking his eyes off me, he said to his wife: "Millie, I'm sure you and the kids have things to do elsewhere. I can take care of these gentlemen by myself. You go on, Millie. You go on, now."

Millie nodded and backed out of the room, taking the kids with her. The kitchen had a swinging door on it, and it swung shut.

"What do you mean, am I a diabetic? All the diabetics are dead."

"It's just that refrigerators and insulin go together in this house, doctor," I said. "And before you tell me again you're not a doctor, any fool can see Koning doesn't care any more whether we find out or not. Artel, you figure his office is across the hall from that waiting room?"

"Uh-huh. I could smell the antiseptics."

"Look, Dr. Sherman, why don't you relax?" I said. "Koning told you that, and I'm telling you that. So you're getting it from both sides, and you might as well believe it. Let's sit down and just wait. We can talk if you like. Koning's obviously gone to do something."

"Town council meeting, I guess," Sherman said desperately.

"I figured something like that. Take it easy. Doc—it's us that may have our heads in a noose. Artel, drift out there and see what his office looks like, will you?" Artel nodded and went out. I could hear Millie Sherman gasping out in the hall and Artel murmuring something reassuring that ended in " 'scuse me, ma'am, kids . . ."

Sherman sank down in one of the kitchen chairs. He held his head in his hands with his elbows on his knees. "You had to bring one of them in with you," he mumbled.

I pulled another chair away from the kitchen table and sat down. "Well sure, doctor. He's a United States citizen. At least where we come from he is, and he's got just as much right to walk these streets as I have."

"You don't realize what you're doing to us."

"No, I don't, except I know guilt when I see it. But it's a pretty good question who's doing what to whom."

Sherman's head came up fast. "What do you mean? What do you know?"

"Whatever we know, we'll know a lot more, and if we never go back to tell our Old Man about it, why that'll tell him something, too."

I started to talk very fast. I had him on the ropes, and win, lose or even, I was going to press that as long as Koning would let me. "What do you people think you're doing here, Sherman? Living in some little world of your own? You may think so, all fenced off behind a bunch of skeletons and burnt-out houses, but there's a whole goddamned world out there, and in the middle of the night sometimes you know it. This is just one town. *One* town, in a whole country. On a continent. On a world. We're not just dying out there—we're living and breathing, too. You think it's *fun* for me and Artel to come down here and play patsy with you people? There's no time for that."

He was white and sweating. He was shaking his head back and forth. "No. No, this is a good town. You're not the only people we've seen. We've seen other people from outside. You're all sick—all of you. You're weak, and you're in pain. I've been watching the way you move, Dorsey. You treat your bones like glass. I can imagine what it's like out there. You lived through it—you were the lucky ones, and look at you! Your livers and your kidneys must be like old pieces of sponge. Your lungs are in rags. And maybe, maybe if you get halfway decent food, and enough rest, and enough time, you'll slowly get back toward what you were. But most of you will never make it. Your kids might—for those of you who've got the energy for parenthood, and those of you who can successfully transmit immunities to your offspring. What's your infant mortality rate, Dorsey? What's your live birth rate? Who takes care of your kids? Who educates them? Who keeps up the public sanitation? How many psychotics have you got?"

Artel came back into the kitchen. "All he's got in his layout is surgical stuff. He's a bonesetter. Just about the only medicines he has are aspirin, iodine and Vaseline. Funniest doctor's office I've ever seen. Well, Koning told us. But it's no surprise they thought they ought to hide it." Artel got a chair for himself and sat down watching Dr. Sherman with a sleepy, unwavering expression. "I'm sorry your wife and children are so upset by me," he said. Sherman nodded blindly, not looking up from the floor.

"Boy's by my first wife," he said. "I married late. Always figured it would be too big a change in my life. Got older, changed my mind."

"You've been very fortunate," Artel said.

"I know it. There isn't another family in town with two survivors. You think I didn't know the odds, when I finally realized what we had on our hands? What do you think I wouldn't have done to save Mary and the boy both? It was hopeless in the hospital by then. I voted to dynamite the place, it was so bad. Didn't matter—if they'd all voted with me, there wasn't time nor sense or strength to do it. Man, you can know how to swim, but when the wave hits you the next thing you know you're smashed up against the shells on the shore. I came home and I barricaded this place. Had big pans full of carbolic acid, soaked rags in it and stuffed them in the windows. Had spray guns full of disinfectant. You could barely breathe in here. What good was it? I wasn't even thinking. We were all out of our heads. We were sick, and we were using it all up. When it started, we were using up the antibiotics as if we could always order another truckload in the morning. Had lab technicians—*technicians*—working up slides, and had all the doctors out on the floor. We did everything backwards. We couldn't believe—" Sherman held his head and laughed. "We couldn't believe what was going to happen. We couldn't act like we believed what was going to happen. I mean, if we'd let ourselves think about what was going to happen—"

He stood up quickly. "I never got you your water." He went to a cabinet over the sink and got out some glasses.

"We kept listening to the radios, telling ourselves somebody somewhere would announce treatments. I had a radio with me everywhere I went, in my shirt pocket. I listened to that radio night and day, had my pockets full of batteries. When I couldn't get stations anymore, I kept it on anyhow—kept it on wanting to know if WRKO would get back on the air." He pushed the glasses clunking under the spigot of the water fountain.

"I wasn't listening for any announcement. I was just listening to the cities die. Every time a station went off the air, I'd say to myself 'There, you smart people at Massachusetts General. There, you fancy labs down at Johns Hopkins. There, Columbia Presbyterian Medical Center—you couldn't find it either.' That's how we were—you remember how you were?" He came over to us and pushed the glasses into our hands. "Here. Here." Water slopped on my wrist.

VIII

Sherman went back to his chair. He sat there looking at us. His hands turned the pipe over and over, and the ferocity had taken hold of him. "Luther wanted me to give you the background. All right, I'll give you the background. What do you think happens to the organization of a place like this? The water mains lead from a reservoir that belongs to a town fifteen miles away. What happens when they close the valves up there because they're scared they'll need it all to themselves? What happens to your food storage when your refrigeration goes? How much do you think we had stored around here, when we could always bring everything down from Newark in a couple of hours? What happens when you realize that's all there is, hah, and you're not going to bring any more from anyplace else, 'cause nobody's producing any more, nobody's packing it, nobody's putting it on trains? By God, they fought for it in the dark! They broke into houses where fat people lived, sometimes before and sometimes after they set fire to a block on account of pestilence.

"It's dead, it's dead out there," he said, pointing. "You came in through it. You saw it. You lived through it where you were, but you were in a goddamned metropolis with the rivers to scoop water out of and the warehouses jammed up. Do you know what we had to do to clear the site for that well you're drinking from now? They were dead! They were all dead, and we'd come crawling through the gutters, we'd come through three-hour journeys that took a block. We didn't clear them out. We—we as good as burrowed through them. We were twisted around them like snakes." He looked up. "Of course, it's all clean and neat now," he smiled. "Everything's clean and neat. This is a model community." He wiped out his eye sockets with the backs of his hands. There was sweat drenching his shirt under the arms.

"Drink your water," he said.

"Thank you," I said. I took a hearty swallow. "I gather you didn't save your Mary."

"No," he said bitterly, outraged at my manners. "I didn't save my Mary."

Well, I hadn't even intended for him to get some of my point. But it would have been nice if he'd been able to realize you couldn't buy anything with that story these days. They were always like that, when you contacted them. The loners—the ones we pick up in open countryside because they used to be farmers—would run around our town for days, telling their particular story over and over again.

It always took them a while to understand that nobody was listening. The communities we'd contact couldn't believe that the rest of the world was just like them. They all had this vision that theirs was the only town blighted, even though nothing that used power or fuel or the cooperation of large groups of people could be seen in the world any longer. We had all run screaming. We had all spent everything we had, trying to run, trying to learn an answer, trying to hide, trying to wipe out. You could only be glad the world's military was still shocked from what the air defense missiles had done to the incoming Klarr lifeboats,

because if they'd been full of their usual spirit we would
have found some excuse for unloading that stockpile on
ourselves, too. The only special grief Ocean Heights might
have would be from having that lifeboat land on their door-
step and provide them with five hundred-odd immediate
centers of cross-infection instead of their having to wait
their turn from the winds and the refugees. But I figured
that silent building farther down canceled that excuse, too.
And besides, Mary is a common name.

"Look, doctor," I said, "we've got cards from the United
States government. You remember the United States. We
obviously represent the return of some kind of social organization to the world. You see us—you see what kind of shape
we're in. You say you've seen other people. What's more,
you can't tell me somebody in town doesn't know how to
build a crystal set. There isn't much to pick up, but there's
something. You're trying to tell me you're cut off, but
you're not—you know what kind of shape the world's in,
even if what you know is only little bits and pieces. We're
sitting right here in your kitchen working on the little bits
and pieces we know, and it adds up bad. It adds up real
bad, doctor, just from what you've given us. What's going
on in this town?"

Sherman shook his head miserably. "I can't tell you," he
whispered.

"You've been trying to," Artel said. "You're doing everything but putting it into words." Sherman's glance jerked
over toward him and met pity. I don't know whether he
could tell that's what it was on a Klarr face or not. "Doctor,
you have a great secret in this town. But you are its only
sentry. It's possible to get as far as your house without
being detected. And then you call attention to yourself by
hammering on a gong. When you and Koning talk to each
other in front of us, you make sure we notice every lie.
You think Tully told us about you? We didn't need Tully
for that. But it was you and Koning who told us Tully is
important—you and Koning, and all your other neighbors
and friends. When you tell us how things were in this town,
you're apologizing in advance for what we'll know when
we put all the pieces together." Sherman was going whiter
and whiter. The wood of the pipe was creaking in his
hands as he squeezed them and the skin slipped damply

over it. "You couldn't fool anybody who's the least bit interested," Artel finished up, still gently. "You know that. You've always known that."

I put down my water glass and walked over to the refrigerator. "He marched us by the waiting room because it was smart not to let us sit there and figure out he was a doctor, so we wouldn't ask him any medical questions. He walked us right in here into the kitchen. Where the refrigerator is." I opened it.

Sherman cried out: "We couldn't get two! We could only find one, and it made sense to keep it in the kitchen!"

I nodded. "And there was a fuel problem, too," I said. I could afford to be understanding. I didn't have the foggiest notion yet what the hell he meant. "It's a hard world; we've got to economize."

I was looking through the refrigerator, and it was dark enough in there so that I was having trouble. There were a couple of heads of lettuce, wrapped in cellophane with the New York seal on them, and some leftovers in plastic covered dishes, half a sausage . . . and, up close to the weak cooling coils, a half-pint cream bottle with a homemade rubber diaphragm stretched over its mouth.

I took it out and held it up to the light. It was three-quarters full of a just faintly yellow liquid with white clouds stirring around the bottom.

Sherman stared at it and me and Artel. Then he jumped up and made a lunge for it. He had his hand open, and he was trying to slap it away and smash it. His eyes were bulging. His face looked like it was a foot wide and made of chalk. "No, let me!" he panted as I ducked it out of his reach. "Please!"

First, I stepped back from him, so that he fell clumsily against the standing cabinet, and then as he put his hands down to catch his balance, I said: "All right," quietly, and held the bottle out. He straightened up, and I carefully put it into his hands. He stood looking down at it, and just as suddenly as he'd jumped up, tears began to fall on his shirtsleeves. Woebegone, he carefully put it back in the refrigerator and closed the door. He turned around and leaned his back against it. He took a long, gasping breath, and then he sniffed sharply. Well, anyone will when they're crying.

I looked over at Artel.

"That's the kind of setup they use when they want to measure out doses for injections."

Artel nodded. "He'd do his sterilization in here, on the stove." He began opening cabinet doors, and on the second try he found the leatherette-covered tin case with the syringes and the needles carefully nested. I turned to Sherman. "We've been in this town what—forty-five minutes? That's how long it took you folks to lead us straight to the wonder drug. Sure this is a good town." Sherman kept his eyes on the floor. He had shrunk inside his clothes. He was shuddering, and he was still weeping. I looked over at Artel. Artel shook his head—he couldn't tell what that stuff was either.

IX

"That's it, huh, doctor?" I asked. "The stuff in that bottle replaces all other kinds of medicines. You come into Dr. Sherman's office with, say, liver flukes, a bad heart and a broken arm. He sets your arm, and he goes back into the kitchen and comes back with a syringe full of this stuff and squirts it into you, and you walk out smiling, all cured. You come in with spots in front of your eyes, a roaring in your ears and a swelling in your armpit. Doctor gives you the needle, and six hours later you're dancing with your best girl. Doc, is that the way it is?"

"Don't make fun of it," Sherman whispered.

He was down to that. It was all he had left. We had broken him—well, no; the three of us together, and this town, and this world had broken him. That'll happen, if you let it, every time. Sherman was saying: "It's specific against Klarr-transmitted infectious diseases and allergic reactions. And it has broad-spectrum applications in treating the older forms of infectious disease. It won't repair a damaged heart, no. But it reduces that heart's burden."

He looked at Artel and winced the way he would have if he were hit with a gust of windy rain. "It may be a panacea," he explained. "In a matter of hours after a three cubic centimeter injection, the subject is completely free of everything that can possibly be destroyed by an antibody. I'm—I'm trying to make myself clear to you. The human body reacts to the stuff by manufacturing counteragents which not only destroy it, but every other invading organism. At least, I've never seen the infectious disease that one dose isn't effective for. I—" He waved his hand in the air. "The population's too small for me to have seen examples of all the sicknesses that humans could get. But it's never failed me yet. And the reaction's nearly permanent. The only people we routinely need it for is the new babies. There's no disease in this town, Mr. Loovan." The tears were starting in his eyes again; not the big, steady running wetness on his face he'd shown before, but he had to keep blinking. "You see, the human body has its defense mechanisms. And this stuff stimulates them. Fantastically." He shook his head violently and turned to me, because Artel had kept looking at him deadpan.

"You can see it, Dorsey! You must know that the normal human being's body is constantly engaged in staving off all sorts of potential illnesses. At any time, a great deal of the human mechanism's functioning is directed toward the destruction of invading microorganisms and the filtering and disposal of the resultant wastes. And I'm sure I don't have to tell you how vulnerable the organism is if it has been exhausted. And I don't have to tell you how debilitating even simple illnesses are; at some time in your life you must have had a common cold, or a reaction to an infected tooth, or a cut. Can you imagine how much energy was constantly being drained from your system by things as commonplace as that? Energy that could have gone to doing work or maintaining the growth and repair functions of your body?" He was shifting back and forth between the two of us now. We kept looking at him blankly because there wasn't any need to encourage him and we weren't planning to interrupt him. And he kept trying to get through to us—trying to get us to smile, or pat his hand and say, "It's all *right*."

"Can you imagine what the population of this town is like? It's free to devote full energy to life. There's none of that gray, dragging stuff they used to come in to me with in the old days, that I couldn't diagnose, and made them miserable, and I'd write tonics for. Do you realize how much tension has been wiped out of their lives? They're not nagged by a hundred little illnesses. They're not terrified by sudden stomach twinges and mysterious rashes or coughing spells. They don't find themselves spitting or passing blood. They don't worry themselves into stomach ulcers, and they don't come down with nervous diseases. When you add that to the fact that they no longer have many of the old social tensions . . . Don't you see? It's like a miracle for them! It's like perpetual springtime—they're alive— they're vital. They don't tire as fast, they don't mope—"

"And they laugh all the time," I said. "Artel and I could see that; running and dancing and singing and clapping their hands when they saw us. Like a bunch of happy South Sea islanders in a book. Nature's Children."

Sherman ducked his head again. "They were pretty well off until you showed up," he muttered.

"No arthritis, doctor?" Artel said. "No athlete's foot, no kidney stones?"

"I didn't say that," the doctor said. "If you had something like that before the Klarri came, there's nothing that can be done for you except to make you generally healthier. That helps." His head came up a little farther. "There is something interesting about that, though. I don't see any new cases starting. You can't tell with a sample this size, but it just may be we won't have any of that after this generation.

"There's a lot I don't know about it. What I've got does the job it has to. But I'm not going to pretend to you that my extraction methods are exact. I haven't got the time or equipment to isolate the precise effective fraction, whatever it is. I've got a bundle of stuff there, and some part of it does the job. The rest doesn't do any harm." He was starting to gather the little pieces of himself back together again. Talking shop was doing him good. Well, that had to be one of his reasons for talking shop.

"What does it do for cancer, Doc?" I asked.

"I think it prevents it. I know it doesn't cure it."

"That's fine, doctor." I looked at him from a long way away. I had an idea I was about to smash him again.

I looked over at Artel. He had caught it in the doctor's choices of words. It was sad to see his face. "Doctor— where do you get this stuff?"

He had nearly made himself forget it. He had been talking, and talking, and all the time his mind had been putting the screens back up. He stared at me as if I'd belched in church, and then he took a little half step away from Artel; a little, sidling, sheepish step I'm sure he didn't know he was performing. "I extract it from human-infected Klarr blood," he said, his mouth blowing each word in its own bubble. Artel sighed and bowed his head.

I'd had my next question ready, too, and I was pretty sure of the answer to that one, but I had to stop and study him for a minute. Then I said, "And everybody in town knows where it comes from?"

Sherman nodded, two or three times, slowly. "All the adults. I *wish* you hadn't brought in Mr. Loovan."

"I think we'd better move, Artel."

He wasn't keeping all his mind on the spot we were in, but he nodded. "Yo." We pushed open the swinging door.

"Wait!" Sherman cried behind us. "If you try to run for it, they're *bound* to kill you."

Artel was moving quickly up the foyer. "We know that," I said over my shoulder. That kind of talk annoys me. I didn't need him to teach me my business. Sherman's wife and his kids were hanging over the banister three-quarters of the way up the stairs, staring down at us. Artel hit the front door as hard as he could, slamming it back against the wall, and then kneed the screen door open so that it spanged against the outside wall. The people standing around out there jumped. Well, that was the effect that he wanted.

"Good-bye, Mister Boogeyman!" the little girl piped as Artel hit the veranda with his boots clattering. I went just as fast behind him, slamming both doors shut. Artel didn't slow; you never want to do that. I jumped the steps and picked up speed, so that we reached the crowd side by side. We went right by our bikes, picked the biggest man in the group, and stood with our toes practically on his. "Where do we find Luther Koning?" I barked in his face. The rest of the people were falling back. Artel and I were both glowering and obviously beside ourselves with rage. The man took a step back, and we took a step forward. Artel reached down and grabbed his belt. "Come on, you! You're fooling with the government!" The man waved vaguely down the street toward the intersection.

"Right!" I said. "Let's go, buddy." Artel pushed the man back firmly, letting go of his belt, and the two of us swung down the sidewalk, marching side by side, our feet coming down regular as heartbeats, our faces grim, our arms swinging. Kids and housewives scattered out of our way. "You can't—!" somebody protested.

"Well, then, you run tell him," I said, and we kept going.

"Dorsey! Loovan!" Sherman shouted, coming down his veranda steps, his feet thudding across the lawn as he cut over to us. We kept marching. He came panting up to us. He was trying to keep up, but he lost speed as he turned to try to talk to us. I kept my eyes on the people down at the intersection; there were a fair number of them down there, and I saw one of them notice us coming and freeze.

"Dorsey!" Sherman panted. "You don't understand. It's not just—" He tripped over the cover of a water meter, stumbled, and lost pace. He came trotting up even with us again. "Loovan—" Then he realized he'd picked the wrong one to tell the rest of it to. "Dorsey! We were dying. We were too weak to move. We hadn't eaten in days. We hadn't eaten enough in weeks, and all that time we'd been burning with fever. My wife was lying dead upstairs. For three days. And I couldn't get up there. I had the boy in my office, on the examining table. I was lying on the floor. I couldn't reach him. I had him strapped down. He was crying. I couldn't reach him. We were all like that."

"So were we," I said. I had run out of patience with him entirely.

But Sherman wanted to make his point. I had been waiting for him to tell me where their captive Klarrs were, and it seemed to me at the time that would be the only other interesting thing he could have left to tell us. Instead, he kept babbling on: "You weren't lost and cut off from the rest of the world! Do you know how bad the human animal wants to live? Do you know what it will do to keep alive? Do you know what it will keep trying to do, right up to the last minute? As long as it has its teeth and claws?"

I was listening for any footsteps coming up fast and determined behind us. I was paying most of my attention to that. There weren't any. We'd left them standing there. Now we were almost up to the intersection. The fourth corner was a big saloon-hotel thing, and I guess it was a town hall now, because I could see Koning and a bunch of other men come out quickly through the doors and stop dead, watching us. There was a grinning, jumping figure with them, pointing at us coming on and slapping his broomstick thigh, making the flapping cloth of his pants billow as if he had no bones at all.

"It was Tully!" Sherman puffed out. "There was a lot of Klarr-killing going on for a while. Then we got too weak, and we gave it up. But Tully wounded one someplace where they'd both crawled to die, I guess. Starving to death, both of them. Tully must have been just as far out of his head—just as far back to being a dying animal as you can get. You know what I mean?" he pleaded. "You know how Tully was? It was just him and this dying Klarr. It was Tully. It was Tully that was the animal. But it was Tully then that had sense enough to come and save me—and save little Walt—after he was back to being a man again." He barely got it out. "It was Tully who found out. I just refined his discovery. Made it nice and medical and sanitary. But you see how it is—they *can't* let the two of you go!"

Artel had stopped dead. He had turned to salt in the blink of an eye. "Move. Move," I said to him, "you've got to move," still looking straight ahead, stopping dead with him. Whatever we did, we had to do it together. "If you don't move, none of this gets back." We moved.

Now there were about fifteen or twenty people at the intersection. They were all men. They were wound up tight, moving their feet and hands back and forth. They stood on the corner in front of the hotel as we marched off the end of the sidewalk and across the street toward them.

Tully was bouncing and grinning at the crowd's left. He had a lot of energy; a lot of drive. You had to figure him for spunk. For him to be the historical personage he was, he had to have had the persistence to have haggled hot raw meat with loose teeth in a mouth full of open sores.

You won't often find that kind of grit, even in your really desperate person. Even so, the nearest man to him was drawn a little away from him. Like the others in the crowd, he was watching Artel and me, but he kept darting side glances at Tully, too.

We walked up to Koning, who was trying to keep his face blank and was keeping it tense instead. I looked only at him; straight into his eyes. It was important to hit him before he could say or do anything. I said casually: "Well, it worked out the way you were hoping. Sherman cracked wide open and told us all about it. So you didn't do it. It's all out of your hands and off your mind."

Koning started to frown. "What do you mean by that?"

Artel said, "Look, Mr. Koning," with his voice patient, "if you really didn't want it taken off you, you would have made sure to ask the supply trucks for some drugs now and then. Whether Doc wanted to deprive the poor sick outside world or not."

"Now you can just be mayor," I said. "That'll be a lot easier, won't it?"

"Well, we've got things to do, Mr. Koning," Artel said. "Let's go, Ed. That building's four blocks down and over to our right."

Sherman had been trying to catch his breath over to my right for the last few moments. He said: "I never—"

I gave him something that might pass for a smile. "We know where the lifeboat is, too, Dr. Sherman. And those over there." I waved my hand in the direction of the neat houses, off beyond the bulk of the hotel. "Well, you can see we have to open that casino building, Mr. Koning. Care to come along?"

Koning's jaw flexed a couple of times. He looked around, and once you do that, of course, you've lost it.

He took a deep breath. And then nodded hastily, looking back at the crowd. "All right. Okay."

Artel and I stepped out. We walked down the middle of the street, with Koning walking along beside us, and having to compromise between a casual walk and a trot, until he finally settled for keeping in step with us. Doc Sherman tagged along. One or two other people started to follow, and then the rest of them, and with the group that had slowly followed us down from Sherman's house, it made a respectable bunch. Tully had set out down the sidewalk. He was keeping pace with us the best he could. He kept trying to attract the attention of people who passed near him. I could hear him saying: "Where do you think you're going, you chicken punk?" He said it to young and old, irrespective of sex. "Where do you think you're going, you chicken punk?" I could hear it as a fading mutter in the background. People were looking at him and then looking away. They were dodging around him, and twitching their feet nearer the center of the street. Except for him, nobody was talking.

X

In daylight, the building was painted green. Not new—from before. Artel and I trotted up the steps. Koning pushed himself ahead and unlocked the doors into the lobby. The crowd waited out in the street.

The lobby was dark and musty. It was floored in a checkerboard pattern of red and brown vinyl tiles with a black rubber runner laid down over them. There were office doors opening on the lobby, but Koning went ahead toward a flight of stairs leading to the left. "Lantern around here somewhere," he said.

"Never mind," Artel said, taking his flashlight out of his windbreaker. We went up the stairs with it whirring. At the top of the stairs there was another set of double doors. Koning unlocked those. The smell kept getting stronger.

There was some light coming in from one window near us. They had bricked up the rest from the inside. The entire second floor was one big room from here on back, and the open window was on this side of the row of bars and cyclone fencing they had put in from one wall to the other. Artel shone his light in through the bars.

We could see six iron cots with mattresses on them. There were two Klarri lying on two of them. The mattresses were turned back and rolled over on three others. There was another Klarr sitting on the edge of the remaining bed. He was wearing what was left of his shipboard clothes, I guess.

"All right, unlock that," I told Koning, pointing to the pipe-and-cyclone-mesh gate that went from floor to ceiling. Some master craftsman had worked hard and expertly, custom-building that. Koning nodded, went over to it and trembled the key into the lock. He pushed in on the gate, and it swung back. He turned around and looked at Artel and me expectantly.

"I don't think anything much is going to happen to you, Koning," I said. "We don't mess with communities if we can possibly help it. We all had to live through a bad time, and we all found out things about ourselves."

Koning nodded.

"We didn't find out what you found out. I'll give you that," I said.

"But that was just luck," Artel said; he took a deep breath

before each phrase. "Just your luck. Instead of somebody else's, somewhere else."

Koning shook his head. "Listen—that Tully—"

"I'm sure Artel understands," I said. "After all, you couldn't do anything to Tully."

Koning said bitterly: "The son of a bitch kept reminding us and mocking us. He'd ask us if our arms were sore from Doc's needle."

"I wish you'd go away," Artel told him.

Koning nodded again and went around us to go back down the stairs. He went down quickly, and then we could hear his footsteps in the lobby, and the sound of him going out through the double doors outside. He was not a bad man. Not the sort who would eat the flesh of a Klarr, no matter how hungry. Just the sort who would take a Klarr's blood to make medicine out of it. And take. And take.

As soon as it was all quiet, Artel began to tremble. He shook like a leaf. He put one hand on my shoulder and squeezed. "Oh, Ed."

"Easy, easy, easy."

"Chicken punks," Artel muttered.

The Klarr who'd been sitting on his bed had gotten up. He came shuffling forward, peering ahead.

"Artel, I don't see any reason why it might not work the other way. Maybe I'm wrong, but I don't see why Klarr-infected human blood fractions wouldn't do it for your people."

"They didn't try that, though, did they?" Artel said with his eyes shut.

"Well, they couldn't," I said. "They needed these Klarri to stay infected."

Artel nodded. "I understand that."

The other two Klarri had noticed something was different and had turned over on their beds. I speak a pretty good version of Klarr. "Hey," I said to them. "We're policemen. You can come out."

"What are we going to do with them, Ed?" Artel said.

"Move 'em into one of the houses. I'll stay with them until you send a truck down to pick them up. If you take a bike out to the Camden route, you'll probably be up at the Old Man's maybe late tonight, tomorrow morning for sure."

Artel nodded. "All right." He put his hand back on my shoulder as the white-haired Klarr came closer, got to the gate, and stood in it with one hand on each upright, leaning forward and looking out at us.

"I am Eredin Mek, Sub-Assistant Navigating Officer. My companions here are very weak and may be frightened. Could one of you go in and speak to them, please?" He came closer.

"Go ahead, Artel," I said, and he ducked through the gate and walked quickly toward the back of the cell.

"Is it possible to go outside?" Eredin asked me.

"Certainly," I said.

"I'd like that."

We walked together to the stairs, and then, with him putting one hand on the banister and the other over my shoulders, we got down the stairs and out into the lobby. I could see the crowd milling around outside, and for a minute I thought we were in trouble again, but their backs were to the glass doors. Then we got out through those, and stood at the head of the steps. Tully was across the street. He was standing on the sidewalk, and he was saying something to the people. They were ducking their heads away from him.

Tully saw Eredin and me. He pointed over at us. "Hey, critter!" That made them raise their heads. They all turned, and when they saw Eredin leaning against me, they sighed like an extra wave. Sherman and Koning were in the middle of them, pale. They could all see what it meant, the Klarr up there on the steps with me, stinking and sick, but out. Only Tully didn't see what it meant to him. He thought he still had something going for him.

He laughed. "Hey, critter! I b'lieve you're even scrawnier than me! What's the matter—ain't we been feedin' you right?" He looked around for his effect.

"Who is that man?" Eredin muttered, peering, groping like any sensible person will when he's weak and is in a world he doesn't understand; like somebody senile. "What's he saying?"

Klarr is a language that made my answer come out: "He is the savior of their tribe."

"Yah!" Tully was crying out. "Yah, ya bunch of needle-pushing arm-wipers—"

"Ah, God!" Sherman groaned and turned and rammed back through the crowd toward Tully. Then they were all as if they were being yanked on strings. They clustered suddenly around the squirrel-cheeked man in the green sun-shade. I could see Koning's face. The veins were standing out; his mouth was wide open, and what was coming out of him and all of them was what you might hear if all the lovers in the world were inside one big megaphone. The people at the back of the crowd tried to push in. The whole mass of them fell against a tall hedge.

Eredin looked up at me, squinting, his eyes watering; there had to be a lot of things he couldn't know the reasons for. "They—they kept taking our blood," he complained.

"I know," I said. I patted him on the shoulder.

Pattern

BY FREDRIC BROWN

Although the late Fredric Brown did write novels (his two most acclaimed novels are the very funny Martians, Go Home—*in which humanity is visited with a plague of interplanetary voyeurs—and* What Mad Universe), *he was primarily known for his expertise in writing short-short stories, an exceedingly difficult and demanding skill in which he has seldom been equaled and rarely—if ever—surpassed. In the space of very few words, sometimes fewer words than are used in this story introduction, Brown could create a whole world or milieu, people it with well-defined characters, and follow them through a satisfyingly complex plot to an often stunning climax—squeezing down into a thousand or two thousand words what most authors would have milked for ten thousand words, and what some authors would have turned into a 300-page novel.*

In the typically terse story that follows, Brown's aliens deliver the unkindest cut of all, human ego being what it is: they ignore us.

Miss Macy sniffed. "Why is everyone worrying so? They're not *doing* anything to us, are they?"

In the cities, elsewhere, there was blind panic. But not in Miss Macy's garden. She looked up calmly at the monstrous mile-high figures of the invaders.

A week ago, they'd landed, in a spaceship a hundred miles long that had settled down gently in the Arizona desert. Almost a thousand of them had come out of that spaceship and were now walking around.

But, as Miss Macy pointed out, they hadn't hurt anything or anybody. They weren't quite *substantial* enough to affect people. When one stepped on you or stepped on a house you were in, there was sudden darkness and until he moved his foot and walked on you couldn't see; that was all.

They had paid no attention to human beings and all attempts to communicate with them had failed, as had all attacks on them by the army and the air force. Shells fired at them exploded right inside them and didn't hurt them. Not even the H-bomb dropped on one of them while he was crossing a desert area had bothered him in the slightest.

They had paid no attention to us at all.

"And that," said Miss Macy to her sister who was also Miss Macy since neither of them was married, "is proof that they don't mean us any harm, isn't it?"

"I hope so, Amanda," said Miss Macy's sister. "But look what they're doing now."

It was a clear day, or it had been one. The sky had been bright blue and the almost humanoid heads and shoulders of the giants, a mile up there, had been quite clearly visible. But now it was getting misty, Miss Macy saw as she fol-

175

lowed her sister's gaze upward. Each of the two big figures in sight had a tanklike object in his hands and from these objects clouds of vaporous matter were emerging, settling slowly toward Earth.

Miss Macy sniffed again. "Making clouds. Maybe that's how they have fun. *Clouds* can't hurt us. Why do people worry so?"

She went back to her work.

"Is that a liquid fertilizer you're spraying, Amanda?" her sister asked.

"No," said Miss Macy. "It's insecticide."

An Honorable Death

BY GORDON R. DICKSON

*Even within SF, the way writers think about aliens—the
unstated consensus opinion as to what contact with aliens
would be like—has undergone a slow evolution over the
years. In the twenties and early thirties, aliens were most
frequently depicted as monsters, horrific bug-eyed creatures
with snapping lobster claws who would crash in through
doors to abduct young Earthwomen, for reasons either
dietary or romantic—and it has taken Hollywood forty
years to even begin to rise above this level. Within SF, however, writers like Stanley G. Weinbaum (his story "A Martian Odyssey" in particular had terrific impact on readers
and fellow authors), Raymond Z. Gallun, and Eric Frank
Russell, among others, helped to "humanize" the alien: no
longer was our reaction to the alien—or the alien's reaction to us, for that matter—one of automatic hostility or
revulsion. Other possibilities, other relationships, became
possible.*

*Sometime during the forties, a new consensus opinion
began to solidify, shaped in the main by John W. Campbell,
the editor of* Astounding *(later* Analog*), who encouraged
his writers to adopt it. This consensus opinion survived as
the predominant way to characterize aliens throughout the
fifties, and is still with us today, though less common—in
Damon Knight's words, "John Campbell . . . would not
publish any story in which another race turned out to be
more advanced, smarter, or in any other way better than
us." Now when Earthmen traveled to other planets, they
did so most frequently in the guise of Kiplingesque colonial
administrators. Far worlds became analogues of British
India, colonies of an expanding Terran Empire whose people were superior in technology, pluck, and moral values
to the alien races they ruled. And if Earthmen were the*

177

colonial overlords, commercial factors, plantation owners, British East India Company agents, then it was left to the aliens to become the swarming native hordes, "niggers," obsequious, sly, and unchristian, not to be trusted. (It is interesting to note that when alien stories started coming back into vogue in the middle and late seventies—after a decade in which few had been written, particularly by younger authors; after years of political and psychological chaos and economic collapse; after people had begun to talk of "the Decline of the West"; after Vietnam—it was most often the aliens who came to us, came to us in huge, enigmatic machines far beyond the powers of our technology [cf. Clarke's Rendezvous with Rama, Benford and Eklund's If the Stars Are Gods, Benford's In the Ocean of Night, Varley's Titan, Tiptree's Up the Walls of the World, Pohl's Gateway, Dozois's Strangers, Dann's Starhiker, etc.], reducing us to the role of provincial natives.)

There were many exceptions to this consensus opinion, of course. Over at Planet Stories (where the paper solar systems often seemed as crowded and chummy as an Elks' picnic, chockablock with dozens of alien races), or at Galaxy and F&SF, humans and aliens seemed to be on somewhat more even terms, and although there was inter-species hostility and warfare aplenty in the pages of these magazines too, the aliens sometimes even won. Even within the pages of Astounding itself, there were many exceptions, for Campbell was not always consistent with his policy—and sometimes even in works that hewed to the letter of the law, the spirit was heretical or half-hearted (in Clement's work, for instance, while the Earthmen are usually technologically superior to the aliens, they are much too civilized to be convincing as imperialistic aggressors). For the most part, however, the rule held. It sometimes seemed that many SF writers were ignorant of, or oblivious to, Santayana's famous dictum that "those who cannot remember the past are condemned to repeat it"—especially as, in the real world, colonial empires were breaking up all around them.

Not all SF writers were unaware of the lessons of history, however—"An Honorable Death," written in 1961, is a forerunner of stories to come: a beautifully subtle examination of the seeds planted by intolerance, insensitivity, and pride, and their inevitable grim harvest.

Gordon R. Dickson is probably best known for his Dorsai *series about mercenary soldiers of the future, but he is also the author of several beautiful and insightful stories about human-alien interaction, among them "Black Charlie," "Dolphin's Way," and the brilliant novella "Jean Dupres." He won a Hugo Award in 1965 for his short novel "Soldier, Ask Not," and a Nebula Award in 1966 for his novelette "Call Him Lord." His* books include Dorsai, Soldier, Ask Not, The Tactics of Mistake, The Book of Gordon R. Dickson, The Dragon and the George, SF Greats, *and* Ancient, My Enemy. *His most recent books are* Time Storm, The Far Call, *and* Pro, *an illustrated novel.*

From the arboretum at the far end of the patio to the landing stage of the transporter itself, the whole household was at sixes and sevens over the business of preparing the party for the celebration. As usual, Carter was having to oversee everything himself, otherwise it would not have gone right; and this was all the harder in that, of late, his enthusiasms seemed to have run down somewhat. He was conscious of a vague distaste for life as he found it, and all its parts. He would be forty-seven this fall. Could it be the imminent approach of middle age, seeking him out even in the quiet backwater of this small, suburban planet? Whatever it was, things were moving even more slowly than usual this year. He had not even had time to get into his costume of a full dress suit (19th–20th cent.) with tails, which he had chosen as not too dramatic, and yet kinder than most dress-ups to his tall, rather awkward figure—when the chime sounded, announcing the first arrival.

Dropping the suit on his bed, he went out, cutting across the patio toward the gathering room, where the landing stage of the transporter was—and almost ran headlong into one of the original native inhabitants of the planet, standing like a lean and bluish post with absolute rigidity in the center of the pretty little flagstone path.

"What are *you* doing here?" cried Carter.

The narrow, indigo, horselike face leaned confidentially down toward Carter's own. And then Carter recognized the great mass of apple blossoms, like a swarming of creamy-winged moths, held to the inky chest.

"Oh—" began Carter, on a note of fury. Then he threw up his hands and took the mass of branches. Peering around the immovable alien and wincing, he got a glimpse of his imported apple tree. But it was not as badly violated as he had feared. "Thank you. Thank you," he said, and waved the native out of the way.

But the native remained. Carter stared—then saw that in addition to the apple blossoms the thin and hairless creature, though no more dressed than his kind ever were, had in this instance contrived belts, garlands, and bracelets of native flowers for himself. The colors and patterns would be arranged to convey some special meaning—they always did. But right at the moment Carter was too annoyed and entirely too rushed to figure them out, though he did think it a little unusual the native should be holding a slim shaft of dark wood with a fire-hardened point. Hunting was most expressly forbidden to the natives.

"Now what?" said Carter. The native (a local chief, Carter suddenly recognized) lifted the spear and unexpectedly made several slow, stately hops, with his long legs flicking up and down above the scrubbed white of the flagstones—like an Earthly crane at its mating. "Oh, now, don't tell me you want to dance!"

The native chief ceased his movements and went back to being a post again, staring out over Carter's head as if at some horizon, lost and invisible beyond the iridescences of Carter's dwelling walls. Carter groaned, pondered, and glanced anxiously ahead toward the gathering room, from which he could now hear the voice of Ona, already greeting the first guest with female twitters.

"All right," he told the chief. "All right—this once. But only because it's Escape Day Anniversary. And you'll have to wait until after dinner."

The native stepped aside and became rigid again. Carter hurried past into the gathering room, clutching the apple blossoms. His wife was talking to a short, brown-bearded man with an ivory-tinted guitar hanging by a broad, tan band over one red-and-white, checked-shirted shoulder.

"Ramy!" called Carter, hurrying up to them. The landing stage of the transporter, standing in the middle of the room, chimed again. "Oh, take these will you, dear?" He thrust the apple blossoms into Ona's plump, bare arms. "The chief. In honor of the day. You know how they are—and I had to promise he could dance after dinner." She stared, her soft, pale face upturned to him. "I couldn't help it."

He turned and hurried to the landing stage, from the small round platform of which were now stepping down a short, academic, elderly man with wispy gray hair and a rather fat, button-nosed woman of the same age, both wearing the ancient Ionian chiton as their costume. Carter had warned Ona against wearing a chiton, for the very reason that these two might show up in the same dress. He allowed himself a small twinge of satisfaction at the thought of her ballroom gown as he went hastily now to greet them.

"Doctor!" he said. "Lidi! Here you are!" He shook hands with the doctor. "Happy Escape Day to both of you."

"I was sure we'd be late," said Lidi, holding firmly to the folds of her chiton with both hands. "The public terminal on Arcturus Five was so crowded. And the doctor won't hurry no matter what I say—" She looked over at her husband, but he, busy greeting Ona, ignored her.

The chime sounded again and two women, quite obviously sisters in spite of the fact that they were wearing dissimilar costumes, appeared on the platform. One was dressed in a perfectly ordinary everyday kilt and tunic—no costume at all. The other wore a close, unidentifiable sort of suit of some gray material and made straight for Carter.

"Cart!" she cried, taking one of his hands in both of her own and pumping it heartily. "Happy Escape Day." She beamed at him from a somewhat plain, strong-featured face, sharply made up. "Ani and I—" She looked around for her sister and saw the kilt and tunic already drifting in rather dreamlike and unconscious fashion toward the perambulating bar at the far end of the room. "I," she corrected herself hastily, "couldn't wait to get here. Who else is coming?"

"Just what you see, Totsa," said Carter, indicating those present with a wide-flung hand. "We thought a small party this year—a little, quiet gathering—"

"So nice! And what do you think of my costume?" She revolved slowly for his appraisal.

"Why—good, very good."

"Now!" Totsa came back to face him. "You can't guess what it is at all."

"Of course I can," said Carter heartily.

"Well, then, what is it?"

"Oh, well, perhaps I won't tell you, then," said Carter.

A small head with wispy gray hair intruded into the circle of their conversation. "An artistic rendering of the space suitings worn by those two intrepid pioneers who this day, four hundred and twenty years ago, burst free in their tiny ship from the iron grip of Earth's prisoning gravitation?"

Totsa shouted in triumph. "I knew you'd know, doctor! Trust a philosophical researcher to catch on. Carter hadn't the slightest notion. Not an inkling!"

"A host is a host is a host," said Carter. "Excuse me, I've got to get into my own costume."

He went out again and back across the patio. The outer air felt pleasantly cool on his warm face. He hoped that the implications of his last remark—that he had merely been being polite in pretending to be baffled by the significance of her costume—had got across to Totsa, but probably it had not. She would interpret it as an attempt to cover up his failure to recognize her costume by being cryptic. The rapier was wasted on the thick hide of such a woman. And to think he once . . . you had to use a club. And the worst of it was, he *had* grasped the meaning of her costume immediately. He had merely been being playful in refusing to admit it . . .

The native chief was still standing unmoved where Carter had left him, still waiting for his moment.

"Get out of the way, can't you?" said Carter irritably, as he shouldered by.

The chief retreated one long ostrichlike step until he stood half obscured in the shadow of a trellis of roses. Carter went on into the bedroom.

His suit was laid out for him and he climbed into the clumsy garments, his mind busy on the schedule of the evening ahead. The local star that served as this planet's sun (one of the Pleiades, Asterope) would be down in an hour and a half, but the luminosity of the interstellar space in this galactic region made the sky bright for hours after a setting, and the fireworks could not possibly go on until that died down.

Carter had designed the set piece of the finale himself—a vintage space rocket curving up from a representation of the Earth, into a firmament of stars, and changing into a star itself as it dwindled. It would be unthinkable to waste this against a broad band of glowing rarefied matter just above the western horizon.

Accordingly, there was really no choice about the schedule. At least five hours before the thought of fireworks could be entertained. Carter, hooking his tie into place around his neck before a section of his bedroom wall set on reflection, computed in his head. The cocktail session now starting would be good for two and a half, possibly three hours. He dared not stretch it out any longer than that or Ani would be sure to get drunk. As it was, it would be bad enough with a full cocktail session and wine with the dinner. But perhaps Totsa could keep her under control. At any rate—three, and an hour and a half for dinner. No matter how it was figured, there would be half an hour or more to fill in there.

Well—Carter worked his way into his dress coat—he could make his usual small speech in honor of the occasion. And—oh, yes, of course—there was the chief. The native dances were actually meaningless, boring things, though Carter had been quite interested in them at first, but then his was the inquiring type of mind. Still, the others might find it funny enough, or interesting for a single performance.

Buttoning up his coat, he went back out across the patio, feeling more kindly toward the native than he had since the moment of his first appearance. Passing him this time, Carter thought to stop and ask, "Would you like something to eat?"

Remote, shiny, mottled by the shadow of the rose leaves, the native neither moved nor answered, and Carter hurried on with a distinct feeling of relief. He had always made it a point to keep some native food on hand for just such an emergency as this—after all, they got hungry, too. But it was a definite godsend not to have to stop now, when he was so busy, and see the stuff properly prepared and provided for this uninvited and unexpected guest.

The humans had all moved out of the gathering room by the time he reached it and into the main lounge with its more complete bar and mobile chairs. On entering, he saw that they had already split up into three different and, in a way, inevitable groups. His wife and the doctor's were at gossip in a corner; Ramy was playing his guitar and singing in a low, not unpleasant, though hoarse voice to

Ani, who sat drink in hand, gazing past him with a half
smile into the changing colors of the wall behind him.
Totsa and the doctor were in a discussion at the bar. Carter joined them.

"—and I'm quite prepared to believe it," the doctor was
saying in his gentle, precise tones as Carter came up.
"Well, very good, Cart." He nodded at Carter's costume.

"You think so?" said Carter, feeling his face warm
pleasantly. "Awkward getup, but—I don't know, it just
struck me this year." He punched for a lime brandy and
watched with pleasure as the bar disgorged the brimming
glass by his waiting hand.

"You look armored in it, Cart," Totsa said.

"Thrice-armed is he—" Carter acknowledged the compli-
ment and sipped on his glass. He glanced at the doctor to
see if the quotation had registered, but the doctor was already leaning over to receive a refill in his own glass.

"Have you any idea what this man's been telling me?"
demanded Totsa, swiveling toward Carter. "He insists
we're doomed. Literally doomed!"

"I've no doubt we are—" began Carter. But before he
could expand on this agreement with the explanation that
he meant it in the larger sense, she was foaming over him
in a tidal wave of conversation.

"Well, I don't pretend to be unobjective about it. After
all, who are we to survive? But really—how ridiculous!
And you back him up just like that, *blindly,* without the
slightest notion of what he's been talking about!"

"A theory only, Totsa," said the doctor, quite unruffled.

"I wouldn't honor it by even calling it a theory!"

"Perhaps," said Carter, sipping on his lime brandy, "if I
knew a little more about what you two were—"

"The point," said the doctor, turning a little, politely,
toward Carter, "has to do with the question of why, on all
these worlds we've taken over, we've found no other race
comparable to our own. We may," he smiled, "of course
be unique in the universe. But this theory supposes that
any contact between races of differing intelligences must
inevitably result in the death of the inferior race. Conse-
quently, if we met our superiors—" He gave a graceful
wave of his hand.

"I imagine it could," said Carter.

"Ridiculous!" said Totsa. "As if we couldn't just avoid
contact altogether if we wanted to!"

"That's a point," said Carter. "I imagine negotiations—"

"We," said Totsa, "who burst the bonds of our Earthly home, who have spread out among the stars in a scant four hundred years, are hardly the type to turn up our toes and just die!"

"It's all based on an assumption, Cart"—the doctor put his glass down on the bar and clasped his small hands before him—"that the racial will to live is dependent upon what might be called a certain amount of emotional self-respect. A race of lesser intelligence or scientific ability could hardly be a threat to us. But a greater race, the theory goes, must inevitably generate a sort of death-wish in all of us. We're too used to being top dog. We must conquer or—"

"Absolutely nonsense!" said Totsa.

"Well, now, you can't just condemn the idea offhand like that," Carter said. "Naturally, I can't imagine a human like myself ever giving up, either. We're too hard, too wolfish, too much the last-ditch fighters. But I imagine a theory like this might well hold true for other, lesser races." He cleared his throat. "For example, I've had quite a bit of contact since we came here with the natives which were the dominant life form on this world in its natural state—"

"Oh, natives!" snapped Totsa scornfully.

"You might be surprised, Totsa!" said Carter, heating up a little. An inspiration took hold of him. "And, in fact, I've arranged for you to do just that. I've invited the local native chief to dance for us after dinner. You might just find it very illuminating."

"Illuminating? How?" pounced Totsa.

"That," said Carter, putting his glass down on the bar with a very slight flourish, "I'll leave you to find out for yourself. And now, if you don't mind, I'm going to have to make my hostly rounds of the other guests."

He walked away, glowing with a different kind of inner warmth. He was smiling as he came up to Ramy, who was still singing ballads and playing his guitar for Totsa's sister.

"Excellent," Carter said, clapping his hands briefly and sitting down with them as the song ended. "What was that?"

"Richard the Lion-Hearted wrote it," said Ramy hoarsely. He turned to the woman. "Another drink, Ani?"

Carter tried to signal the balladeer with his eyes, but Ramy had already pressed the buttons on the table beside their chairs, and a little moto unit from the bar was already on its way to them with the drinks emerging from its interior. Carter sighed inaudibly and leaned back in his chair. He could warn Totsa to keep an eye on Ani a little later.

He accepted another drink himself. The sound of voices in the room was rising as more alcohol was consumed. The only quiet one was Ani. She sat, engaged in the single-minded business of imbibing, and listened to the conversation between Ramy and himself, as if she was—thought Carter suddenly—perhaps one step removed, beyond some glasslike wall, where the real sound and movement of life came muted, if at all. The poetry of this flash of insight—for Carter could think of no other way to describe it—operated so strongly upon his emotions that he completely lost the thread of what Ramy was saying and was reduced to noncommittal noises by way of comment.

I should take up my writing again, he thought to himself.

As soon as a convenient opportunity presented itself, he excused himself and got up. He went over to the corner where the women were talking.

"—Earth," Lidi was saying, "the doctor and I will never forget it. Oh, Cart—" She twisted around to him as he sat down in a chair opposite. "You must take this girl to Earth sometime. Really."

"Do you think she's the back-to-nature type?" said Carter, with a smile.

"No, stop it!" Lidi turned back to Ona. "Make him take you!"

"I've mentioned it to him. Several times," said Ona, putting down the glass in her hand with a helpless gesture on the end table beside her.

"Well, you know what they say," smiled Carter. "Everyone talks about Earth but nobody ever goes there anymore."

"The doctor and I went. And it was memorable. It's not what you see, of course, but the insight you bring to it. I'm only five generations removed from people living right there on the North American continent. And the doctor had cousins in Turkey when he was a boy. Say what you like, the true stock thins out as generation succeeds generation away from the home world."

"And it's not the expense anymore," put in Ona. "Everyone's rich nowadays."

"Rich! What an uncomfortable word!" said Lidi. "You should say *capable,* dear. Remember, our riches are merely the product of our science, which is the fruit of our own capabilities."

"Oh, you know what I mean!" said Ona. "The point is, Cart won't go. He just won't."

"I'm a simple man," Carter said. "I have my writing, my music, my horticulture, right here. I feel no urge to roam"—he stood up—"except to the kitchen right now, to check on the caterers. If you'll excuse me—"

"But you haven't given your wife an answer about taking her to Earth one of these days!" cried Lidi.

"Oh, we'll go, we'll go," said Carter, walking off with a good-humored wave of his hand.

As he walked through the west sunroom to the dining area and the kitchen (homey word!) beyond, his cheerfulness dwindled somewhat. It was always a ticklish job handling the caterers, now that they were all artists doing the work for the love of it and not to be controlled by the price they were paid. Carter would have liked to wash his hands of that end of the party altogether and just leave them to operate on their own. But what if he failed to check and then something went wrong? It was his own artistic conscience operating, he thought, that would not give him any rest.

The dining room was already set up in classic style with long table and individual chairs. He passed the gleam of its tableware and went on through the light screen into the kitchen area. The master caterer was just in the process of directing his two apprentices to set up the heating tray on which the whole roast boar, papered and gilded, would be kept warm in the centerpiece position on the table during the meal. He did not see Carter enter; and Carter himself stopped to admire, with a sigh of relief, the boar itself. It was a masterwork of the carver's art and had been built up so skillfully from its component chunks of meat that no one could have suspected it was not the actual animal itself.

Looking up at this moment, the caterer caught sight of him and came over to see what he wanted. Carter advanced a few small, tentative suggestions, but the response was so artificially polite that after a short while Carter was glad to leave him to his work.

Carter wandered back through the house without returning directly to the lounge. With the change of the mood that the encounter with the caterer had engendered, his earlier feelings of distaste with life—a sort of melancholy—had come over him. He thought of the people he had invited almost with disgust. Twenty years ago, he would not have thought himself capable of belonging to such a crowd. Where were the great friends, the true friends, that as a youngster he had intended to acquire? Not that it was the fault of those in the lounge. They could not help being what they were. It was the fault of the times, which made life too easy for everybody; and—yes, he would be honest—his own fault, too.

His wanderings had brought him back to the patio. He remembered the chief and peered through the light dusk at the trellis under the light arch of which the native stood.

Beyond, the house was between the semienclosed patio and the fading band of brilliance in the west. Deep shadow lay upon the trellis itself and the native under it. He was almost obscured by it, but a darkly pale, vertical line of reflection from his upright spear showed that he had made no move. A gush of emotion burst within Carter. He took a single step toward the chief, with the abrupt, spontaneous urge to thank him for coming and offering to dance. But at that moment, through the open doorway of his bedroom, sounded the small metallic chimes of his bedside clock, announcing the twenty-first hour, and he turned hastily and crossed through the gathering room, into the lounge.

"Hors d'oeuvres! Hors d'oeuvres!" he called cheerfully, flinging the lounge door wide. "Hors d'oeuvres, everybody! Time to come and get it!"

Dinner could not go off otherwise than well. Everyone was half tight and hungry. Everyone was talkative. Even Ani had thrown off her habitual introversion and was smiling and nodding, quite soberly, anyone would swear. She was listening to Ona and Lidi talking about Lidi's grown-up son when he had been a baby. The doctor was in high spirits, and Ramy, having gotten his guitar playing out of his system earlier with Ani, was ready to be companionable. By the time they had finished the rum-and-butter pie, everyone was in a good mood, and even the caterer, peering through a momentary transparency of the kitchen wall, exchanged a beam with Carter.

Carter glanced at his watch. Only twenty minutes more! The time had happily flown, and, far from having to fill it in, he would have to cut his own speech a little short. If it were not for the fact that he had already announced it, he would have eliminated the chief's dance—no, that would not have done, either. He had always made a point of getting along with the natives of this world. "It's their home, too, after all," he had always said.

He tinkled on a wineglass with a spoon and rose to his feet.

Faces turned toward him and conversation came to a reluctant halt around the table. He smiled at his assembled guests.

"As you know," said Carter, "it has always been my custom at these little gatherings—and old customs are the best—to say a few"—he held up a disarming hand—"a very few words. Tonight I will be even briefer than usual." He stopped and took a sip of water from the glass before him.

"On this present occasion, the quadricentennial of our great race's Escape into the limitless bounds of the universe, I am reminded of the far road we have come; and the far road—undoubtedly—we have yet to go. I am thinking at the moment"—he smiled, to indicate that what he was about to say was merely said in good fellowship—"of a new theory expressed by our good doctor here tonight. This theory postulates that when a lesser race meets a greater, the lesser must inevitably go to the wall. And that, since it is pretty generally accepted that the laws of chance ensure our race eventually meeting *its* superior, *we* must inevitably and eventually go to the wall."

He paused and warmed them again with the tolerance of his smile.

"May I say *nonsense!*

"Now, let no one retort that I am merely taking refuge in the blind attitude that reacts with the cry, 'It can't happen to us.' Let me say I believe it *could* happen to us, but it won't. And why not? I will answer that with one word. Civilization.

"These overmen—if indeed they ever show up—must, even as we, be civilized. *Civilized.* Think of what that word means! Look at the seven of us here. Are we not educated, kindly, sympathetic people? And how do we treat the races inferior to us that we have run across?

"I'm going to let you answer these questions for yourselves, because I now invite you to the patio for cognac and coffee—and to see one of the natives of this planet, who has expressed a desire to dance for you. Look at him as he dances, observe him, consider what human gentleness and consideration are involved in the gesture that included him in this great festival of ours." Carter paused. "And consider one other great statement that has echoed down the corridors of time—*As ye have done to others, so shall ye be done by!*"

Carter sat down, flushed and glowing, to applause, then rose immediately to precede his guests, who were getting up to stream toward the patio. Walking rapidly, he outdistanced them as they passed the gathering room.

For a second, as he burst out through the patio doorway, his eyes were befuddled by the sudden darkness. Then his vision cleared as the others came through the doorway behind him and he was able to make out the inky shadow of the chief, still barely visible under the trellis.

Leaving Ona to superintend the seating arrangements in the central courtyard of the patio, he hurried toward the trellis. The native was there waiting for him.

"Now," said Carter, a little breathlessly, "it must be a short dance, a very short dance."

The chief lowered his long, narrow head, looking down at Carter with what seemed to be an aloofness, a sad dignity, and suddenly Carter felt uncomfortable.

"Um—well," he muttered, "you don't have to cut it *too* short."

Carter turned and went back to the guests. Under Ona's direction, they had seated themselves in a small semicircle of chairs, with snifter glasses and coffee cups. A chair had been left for Carter in the middle. He took it and accepted a glass of cognac from his wife.

"Now?" asked Totsa, leaning toward him.

"Yes—yes, here he comes," said Carter, and directed their attention toward the trellis.

The lights had been turned up around the edge of the courtyard, and as the chief advanced unto them from the darkness, he seemed to step all at once out of a wall of night.

"My," said Lidi, a little behind and to the left of Carter, "isn't he big!"

"*Tall*, rather," said the doctor, and coughed dryly at her side.

The chief came on into the center of the lighted courtyard. He carried his spear upright in one hand before him, the arm half bent at the elbow and half extended, advancing with exaggeratedly long steps and on tiptoe—in a manner unfortunately almost exactly reminiscent of the classical husband sneaking home late at night. There was a sudden titter from Totsa, behind Carter. Carter flushed.

Arrived in the center of the patio before them, the chief halted, probed at the empty air with his spear in several directions, and began to shuffle about with his head bent toward the ground.

Behind Carter, Ramy said something in a low voice. There was a strangled chuckle and the strings of the guitar plinked quietly on several idle notes.

"Please," said Carter, without turning his head.

There was a pause, some more indistinguishable murmuring from Ramy, followed again by his low, hoarse, and smothered chuckle.

"Perhaps—" said Carter, raising his voice slightly, "perhaps I ought to translate the dance as he does it. All these dances are stories acted out. This one is apparently called 'An Honorable Death.' "

He paused to clear his throat. No one said anything. Out in the center of the patio, the chief was standing crouched, peering to right and left, his neck craned like a chicken's.

"You see him now on the trail," Carter went on. "The silver-colored flowers on his right arm denote the fact that it *is* a story of death that he is dancing. The fact that they are below the elbow indicates it is an honorable, rather than dishonorable, death. But the fact that he wears nothing at all on the other arm below the elbow tells us this is the full and only story of the dance."

Carter found himself forced to clear his throat again. He took a sip from his snifter glass.

"As I say," he continued, "we see him now on the trail, alone." The chief had now begun to take several cautious steps forward, and then alternate ones in retreat, with some evidence of tension and excitement. "He is happy at the moment because he is on the track of a large herd of local game. Watch the slope of his spear as he holds it in his hand. The more it approaches the vertical, the happier he is feeling—"

Ramy murmured again and his coarse chuckle rasped on Carter's ears. It was echoed by a giggle from Totsa and even a small, dry bark of a laugh from the doctor.

"—the happier he is feeling," repeated Carter loudly. "Except that, paradoxically, the line of the absolute vertical represents the deepest tragedy and sorrow. In a little paper I did on the symbolism behind these dance movements, I advanced the theory that when a native strikes up with his spear from the absolute vertical position, it is because some carnivore too large for him to handle has already downed him. He's a dead man."

The chief had gone into a flurry of movement.

"Ah," said Carter, on a note of satisfaction. The others were quiet now. He let his voice roll out a little. "He has made his kill. He hastens home with it. He is very happy. Why shouldn't he be? He is successful, young, strong. His mate, his progeny, his home await him. Even now it comes into sight."

The chief froze. His spear point dropped.

"But what is this?" cried Carter, straightening up dramatically in his chair. "What has happened? He sees a stranger in the doorway. It is the Man of Seven Spears who—this is a superstition, of course"—Carter interrupted himself—"who has, in addition to his own spear, six other magic spears which will fly from him on command and kill anything that stands in his way. What is this unconquerable being doing inside the entrance of the chief's home without being invited?"

The wooden spear point dropped abruptly, almost to the ground.

"The Man of Seven Spears tells him," said Carter. "He, the Man of Seven Spears, has chosen to desire the flowers about our chief's house. Therefore he has taken the house, killing all within it—the mate and the little ones—that their touch may be cleansed from flowers that are his. Everything is now his."

The soft, tumbling sound of liquid being poured filled in the second of Carter's pause.

"Not too much—" whispered someone.

"What can our chief do?" said Carter sharply. The chief was standing rigid with his head bent forward and his forehead pressed against the perfectly vertical shaft of his spear, now held upright before him. "He is sick—we would say he is weeping, in human terms. All that meant anything to him is now gone. He cannot even revenge himself on the Man of Seven Spears, whose magic weapons make him invincible." Carter, moved by the pathos in his own voice, felt his throat tighten on the last words.

"Ona, dear, do you have an antacid tablet?" the doctor's wife whispered behind him.

"He stands where he has stopped!" cried Carter fiercely. "He has no place else to go. The Man of Seven Spears ignores him, playing with the flowers. For eventually, without moving, without food or drink, he will collapse and die, as all of the Man of Seven Spears' enemies have died. For one, two, three days he stands there in his sorrow; and late on the third day the plan for revenge he has longed for comes to him. He cannot conquer his enemy— but he can eternally shame him, so that the Man of Seven Spears, in his turn, will be forced to die.

"He goes into the house." The chief was moving again. "The Man of Seven Spears sees him enter, but pays no attention to him, for he is beneath notice. And it's a good thing for our chief this is so—or else the Man of Seven Spears would call upon all his magic weapons and kill him on the spot. But he is playing with his new flowers and pays no attention.

"Carrying his single spear," went on Carter, "the chief goes in to the heart of his house. Each house has a heart, which is the most important place in it. For if the heart is destroyed, the house dies, and all within it. Having come to the heart of the house, which is before its hearth fire, the chief places his spear butt down on the ground and holds it upright in the position of greatest grief. He stands there pridefully. We can imagine the Man of Seven Spears, suddenly realizing the shame to be put upon him, rushing wildly to interfere. But he and all of his seven spears are too slow. The chief leaps into the air—"

Carter checked himself. The chief was still standing with his forehead pressed against the spear shaft.

"He leaps into the air," repeated Carter, a little louder.

And at that moment the native *did* bound upward, his long legs flailing, to an astonishing height. For a second he seemed to float above the tip of his spear, still grasping it —and then he descended like some great, dark, stricken bird, heavily upon the patio. The thin shaft trembled and shook, upright, above his fallen figure.

Multiple screams exploded and the whole company was on their feet. But the chief, slowly rising, gravely removed the spear from between the arm and side in which he had cleverly caught it while falling; and, taking it in his other hand, he stalked off into the shadows toward the house.

A babble of talk burst out behind Carter. Over all the other voices, Lidi's rose like a half-choked fountain.

"—absolutely! Heart failure! I never was so upset in my life—"

"Cart!" said Ona bitterly.

"Well, Cart," spoke Totsa triumphantly in his ear. "What's the application of all this to what you told me earlier?"

Carter, who had been sitting stunned, exploded roughly out of his chair.

"Oh, don't be such a *fool!*" He jerked himself away from them into the tree-bound shadows beyond the patio.

Behind him—after some few minutes—the voices lowered to a less excited level, and then he heard a woman's footsteps approaching him in the dark.

"Cart?" said his wife's voice hesitantly.

"What?" asked Carter, not moving.

"Aren't you coming back?"

"In a while."

There was a pause.

"Cart?"

"What?"

"Don't you think—"

"No, I don't think!" snarled Carter. "She can go to bloody hell!"

"But you can't just call her a fool—"

"She *is* a fool! They're all fools—every one of them!

I'm a fool, too, but I'm not a stupid damn bloody fool like all of them!"

"Just because of some silly native dance!" said Ona, almost crying.

"Silly?" said Carter. "At least it's something. He's got a dance to do. That's more than the rest of them in there have. And it just so happens that dance is pretty important to him. You'd think they might like to learn something about that, instead of sitting back making their stupid jokes!"

His little explosion went off into the darkness and fell unanswered.

"Please come back, Cart," Ona said, after a long moment.

"At least he has something," said Carter. "At least there's that for him."

"I just can't face them if you don't come back."

"All right, goddammit," said Carter. "I'll go back."

They returned in grim fashion to the patio. The chair tables had been cleared and rearranged in a small circle. Ramy was singing a song and they were all listening politely.

"Well, Cart, sit down here!" invited the doctor heartily as Carter and Ona came up, indicating the chair between himself and Totsa. Carter dropped into it.

"This is one of those old sea ballads, Cart," said Totsa.

"Oh?" asked Carter, clearing his throat, "Is it?"

He sat back, punched for a drink and listened to the song. It echoed out heartily over the patio with its refrain of *"Haul away, Joe!"* but he could not bring himself to like it.

Ramy ended and began another song. Lidi, her old self again, excused herself a moment and trotted back into the house.

"Are you really thinking of taking a trip Earthside—" the doctor began, leaning confidentially toward Carter— and was cut short by an ear-splitting scream from within the house.

Ramy broke off his singing. The screams continued and all of them scrambled to their feet and went crowding toward the house.

They saw Lidi—just outside the dark entrance to the gathering room—small, fat and stiffly standing, and screaming again and again, with her head thrown back. Almost at her feet lay the chief, with the slim shaft of the spear sticking up from his body. Only, this time, it was actually through him.

The rest flooded around Lidi and she was led away, still screaming, by the doctor. Everyone else gathered in horrified fascination about the native corpse. The head was twisted on one side and Carter could just see one dead eye staring up, it seemed, at him alone, with a gleam of sly and savage triumph.

"Horrible!" breathed Totsa, her lips parted. "Horrible!"

But Carter was still staring at that dead eye. Possibly, the thought came to him, the horrendous happenings of the day had sandpapered his perceptions to an unusually suspicious awareness. But just possibly . . .

Quietly, and without attracting undue attention from the others, he slipped past the group and into the dimness of the gathering room, where the lights had been turned off. Easing quietly along the wall until he came to the windows overlooking the patio, he peered out through them.

A considerable number of the inky natives were emerging from the greenery of the garden and the orchard beyond and approaching the house. A long, slim, fire-hardened spear gleamed in the hand of each. It occurred to Carter like a blow that they had probably moved into position surrounding the house while the humans' attention was all focused on the dancing of their chief.

His mind clicking at a rate that surprised even him, Carter withdrew noiselessly from the window and turned about. Behind him was the transporter, bulky in the dimness. As silently as the natives outside, he stole across the floor and mounted onto its platform. The transporter could move him to anywhere in the civilized area of the galaxy at a second's notice. And one of the possible destinations was the emergency room of police headquarters on Earth itself. Return, with armed men, could be equally instantaneous. Much better this way, thought Carter with a clarity he had never in his life experienced before; much better than giving the alarm to the people within, who would undoubtedly panic and cause a confusion that could get them all killed.

Quietly, operating by feel in the darkness, Carter set the

controls for police headquarters. He pressed the Send button.

Nothing happened.

He stared at the machine in the impalpable darkness. A darker spot upon the thin lacquered panel that covered its front and matched it to the room's decor caught his eye. He bent down to investigate.

It was a hole. Something like a ritual thrust of a fire-hardened wooden spear appeared to have gone through the panel and into the vitals of the transporter. The machine's delicate mechanism was shattered and broken and pierced.

The Reality Trip

BY ROBERT SILVERBERG

Once we got beyond seeing aliens as either menaces or saviors, it was almost inevitable that we would begin having romantic liaisons with them instead. But unlike Phil Dick's story, where the alien-human match is an arranged, cold-blooded thing, entered into reluctantly by both parties, or Tiptree's story, where the aliens are only interested in a quick wham-bam-thank-you-human pickup, the alien in the Silverberg story that follows—a rather decent sort, trying hard to do the Right Thing—gets involved in a relationship instead, with all the classical implications, and we are treated to a passionate tale of star-crossed love and interspecies seduction—even if the passion (and the seducing) is somewhat one-sided.

An elegant man with a dapper beard and a coolly sardonic sense of humor, Robert Silverberg can lay claim to more than 450 fiction and nonfiction books, and 3,000 magazine pieces. Within SF, Silverberg rose to his greatest prominence during the New Wave and post–New Wave periods—roughly 1965 to 1975—winning four Nebula Awards and a Hugo Award, publishing dozens of major novels and anthologies, and editing New Dimensions, *one of the most influential anthology series of the seventies. Unlike many of the other major writers of that chaotic decade—for instance: Disch, Ellison, Brunner, Malzberg, Russ, Spinrad, Ballard, Wilhelm, Moorcock, Sladek, Effinger, and many others—who were too preoccupied with sociological concerns and near-future utopian/dystopian scenarios to write very much about aliens, Silverberg managed to produce a body of important work on the theme of human/alien relations as well as some of the sharpest (and most elegantly bleak) sociological/dystopian speculation of the seventies. His best alien novel is probably*

Downward to the Earth, *a skilled and loving homage to Joseph Conrad that also features Silverberg's most attractive aliens: the serene, nonviolent, elephantlike nildoror, who are locked into an intricate cycle of rebirth and metamorphosis with the sullen, carnivorous sulidor. Also excellent are* Nightwings, *his novel of a bizarre far-future society coming to terms with alien invasion,* The Man in the Maze *and* "Flies," *with their godlike, enigmatic aliens, and* "Sundance," *that tour de force of compressed plotting that may or may not document human aggression and genocide against the docile alien Eaters.*

Silverberg's other books include Dying Inside—*considered by many critics to be one of the best novels of the seventies*—The Book of Skulls, The World Inside, Unfamiliar Territory, Born with the Dead, Up the Line, Tower of Glass, The Best of Robert Silverberg *and* Shadrach in the Furnace, *as well as a large number of first-rate anthologies. After four years of self-imposed "retirement," Silverberg is writing again*—*his latest novel,* Lord Valentine's Castle, *sold to hardcover for a six-figure sum, one of the highest advances in genre history.*

I am a reclamation project for her. She lives on my floor of the hotel, a dozen rooms down the hall: a lady poet, private income. No, that makes her sound too old, a middle-aged eccentric. Actually she is no more than thirty. Taller than I am, with long kinky brown hair and a sharp, bony nose that has a bump on the bridge. Eyes are very glossy. A studied raggedness about her dress; carefully chosen shabby clothes. I am in no position really to judge the sexual attractiveness of Earthfolk but I gather from remarks made by men living here that she is not considered good-looking. I pass her often on my way to my room. She smiles fiercely at me. Saying to herself, no doubt, You poor lonely man. Let me help you bear the burden of your unhappy life. Let me show you the meaning of love, for I too know what it is like to be alone.

Or words to that effect. She's never actually said any such thing. But her intentions are transparent. When she sees me, a kind of hunger comes into her eyes, part maternal, part (I guess) sexual, and her face takes on a wild crazy intensity. Burning with emotion. Her name is Elizabeth Cooke. "Are you fond of poetry, Mr. Knecht?" she asked me this morning, as we creaked upward together in the ancient elevator. And an hour later she knocked at my door. "Something for you to read," she said. "I wrote them." A sheaf of large yellow sheets, stapled at the top; poems printed in smeary blue mimeography. *The Reality Trip*, the collection was headed. *Limited Edition: 125 Copies.* "You can keep it if you like," she explained. "I've got lots more." She was wearing bright corduroy slacks and a flimsy pink shawl through which her breasts plainly showed. Small tapering breasts, not very functional-looking. When she saw me studying them her nostrils flared momentarily and she blinked her eyes three times swiftly. Tokens of lust?

I read the poems. Is it fair for me to offer judgment on them? Even though I've lived on this planet eleven of its years, even though my command of colloquial English is quite good, do I really comprehend the inner life of poetry? I thought they were all quite bad. Earnest, plodding poems, capturing what they call slices of life. The world around her, the cruel, brutal, unloving city. Lamenting the failure of people to open to one another. The title poem began this way:

> *He was on the reality trip. Big black man,*
> *bloodshot eyes, bad teeth. Eisenhower jacket,*
> *frayed. Smell of cheap wine. I guess a knife*
> *in his pocket. Looked at me mean. Criminal*
> *record. Rape, child-beating, possession of drugs.*
> *In his head saying, slavemistress bitch, and me in*
> *my head saying, black brother, let's freak in to-*
> *gether, let's trip on love—*

And so forth. Warm, direct emotion; but is the urge to love all wounded things a sufficient center for poetry? I don't know. I did put her poems through the scanner and transmit them to Homeworld, although I doubt they'll learn much from them about Earth. It would flatter Elizabeth to know that while she has few readers here, she has acquired some ninety light-years away. But of course I can't tell her that.

She came back a short while ago. "Did you like them?" she asked.

"Very much. You have such sympathy for those who suffer."

I think she expected me to invite her in. I was careful not to look at her breasts this time.

The hotel is on West Twenty-third Street. It must be over a hundred years old; the façade is practically baroque and the interior shows a kind of genteel decay. The place has a bohemian tradition. Most of its guests are permanent residents and many of them are artists, novelists, playwrights, and such. I have lived here nine years. I know a number of the residents by name, and they me, but I have discouraged any real intimacy, naturally, and everyone has respected that choice. I do not invite others into my room. Sometimes I let myself be invited to visit theirs, since one of my responsibilities on this world is to get to know something of the way Earthfolk live and think. Elizabeth is the first to attempt to cross the invisible barrier of privacy I surround myself with. I'm not sure how I'll handle that. She moved in about three years ago; her attentions became noticeable perhaps ten months back, and for the last five or six weeks she's been a great nuisance. Some kind of confrontation is inevitable: either I must tell her to leave me alone, or I will find myself drawn into a situation impossible to tolerate. Perhaps she'll find someone else to feel even sorrier for, before it comes to that.

My daily routine rarely varies. I rise at seven. First Feeding. Then I clean my skin (my outer one, the Earthskin, I mean) and dress. From eight to ten I transmit data to Homeworld. Then I go out for the morning field trip: talking to people, buying newspapers, often some library research. At one I return to my room. Second Feeding. I transmit data from two to five. Out again, perhaps to the theater, to a motion picture, to a political meeting. I must soak up the flavor of this planet. Often to saloons; I am equipped for ingesting alcohol, though of course I must get rid of it before it has been in my body very long, and I drink and listen and sometimes argue. At midnight back to my room. Third Feeding. Transmit data from one to four in the morning. Then three hours of sleep, and at seven the cycle begins anew. It is a comforting schedule. I don't know how many agents Homeworld has on Earth, but I like to think that I'm one of the most diligent and useful. I miss very little. I've done good service, and, as they say here, hard work is its own reward. I won't deny that I hate the physical discomfort of it and frequently give way to real despair over my isolation from my own kind. Sometimes I even think of asking for a transfer to Home-world. But what would become of me there? What services could I perform? I have shaped my life to one end: that of dwelling among the Earthfolk and reporting on their ways. If I give that up, I am nothing.

Of course there is the physical pain. Which is consider-able.

The gravitational pull of Earth is almost twice that of Homeworld. It makes for a leaden life for me. My inner organs always sagging against the lower rim of my cara-pace. My muscles cracking with strain. Every movement a willed effort. My heart in constant protest. In my eleven years I have as one might expect adapted somewhat to the conditions; I have toughened, I have thickened. I suspect that if I were transported instantly to Homeworld now I would be quite giddy, baffled by the lightness of everything. I would leap and soar and stumble, and might even miss this crushing pull of Earth. Yet I doubt that. I suffer here; at all times the weight oppresses me. Not to sound too self-pitying about it. I knew the conditions in advance. I was placed in simulated Earth gravity when I volunteered, and was given a chance to withdraw, and I decided to go any-way. Not realizing that a week under double gravity is not the same thing as a lifetime. I could always have stepped out of the simulation chamber. Not here. The eternal drag on every molecule of me. The pressure. My flesh is always in mourning.

And the outer body I must wear. This cunning disguise. Forever to be swaddled in thick masses of synthetic flesh, smothering me, engulfing me. The soft slippery slap of it against the self within. The elaborate framework that holds it erect, by which I make it move: a forest of struts and braces and servoactuators and cables, in the midst of which I must unendingly huddle, atop my little platform in the gut. Adopting one or another of various uncomfortable positions, constantly shifting and squirming, now jabbing myself on some awkwardly placed projection, now trying to make my inflexible body flexibly to bend. Seeing the world by periscope through mechanical eyes. Enwombed in this mountain of meat. It is a clever thing; it must look convincingly human, since no one has ever doubted me, and it ages ever so slightly from year to year, graying a bit at the temples, thickening a bit at the paunch. It walks. It talks. It takes in food and drink, when it has to. (And deposits them in a removable pouch near my leftmost arm.) And I within it. The hidden chess player; the invisible rider. If I dared, I would periodically strip myself of this cloak of flesh and crawl around my room in my own guise. But it is forbidden. Eleven years now and I have not been outside my protoplasmic housing. I feel sometimes that it has come to adhere to me, that it is no longer merely around me but by now a part of me.

In order to eat I must unseal it at the middle, a process that takes many minutes. Three times a day I unbutton myself so that I can stuff the food concentrates into my true gullet. Faulty design, I call that. They could just as easily have arranged it so I could pop the food into my Earthmouth and have it land in my own digestive tract. I suppose the newer models have that. Excretion is just as troublesome for me; I unseal, reach in, remove the cubes of waste, seal my skin again. Down the toilet with them. A nuisance.

And the loneliness! To look at the stars and know Homeworld is out there somewhere! To think of all the others, mating, chanting, dividing, abstracting, while I live out my days in this crumbling hotel on an alien planet, tugged down by gravity and locked within a cramped counterfeit body—always alone, always pretending that I am not what I am and that I am what I am not, spying, questioning, recording, reporting, coping with the misery of solitude, hunting for the comforts of philosophy—

In all of this there is only one real consolation, aside, that is, from the pleasure of knowing that I am of service to Homeworld. The atmosphere of New York City grows grimier every year. The streets are full of crude vehicles belching undigested hydrocarbons. To the Earthfolk, this stuff is pollution, and they mutter worriedly about it. To me it is joy. It is the only touch of Homeworld here: that sweet soup of organic compounds adrift in the air. It intoxicates me. I walk down the street breathing deeply, sucking the good molecules through my false nostrils to my authentic lungs. The natives must think I'm insane. Tripping on auto exhaust! Can I get arrested for overenthusiastic public breathing? Will they pull me in for a mental checkup?

Elizabeth Cooke continues to waft wistful attentions at me. Smiles in the hallway. Hopeful gleam of the eyes. "Perhaps we can have dinner together some night soon, Mr. Knecht. I know we'd have so much to talk about. And maybe you'd like to see the new poems I've been doing." She is trembling. Eyelids flickering tensely; head held rigid on long neck. I know she sometimes has men in her room, so it can't be out of loneliness or frustration that she's cultivating me. And I doubt that she's sexually attracted to my outer self. I believe I'm being accurate when I say that women don't consider me sexually magnetic. No, she loves me because she pities me. The sad shy bachelor at the end of the hall, dear unhappy Mr. Knecht; can I bring some brightness into his dreary life? And so forth. I think that's how it is. Will I be able to go on avoiding her? Perhaps I should move to another part of the city. But I've lived here so long; I've grown accustomed to this hotel. Its easy ways do much to compensate for the hardships of my post. And my familiar room. The huge many-paned window; the cracked green floor tiles in the bathroom; the lumpy patterns of replastering on the wall above my bed. The high ceiling; the funny chandelier. Things that I love. But of course I can't let her try to start an affair with me. We are supposed to observe Earthfolk, not to get involved with them. Our disguise is not that difficult to penetrate at close range. I must keep her away somehow. Or flee.

Incredible! There is another of us in this very hotel!

As I learned through accident. At one this afternoon, returning from my morning travels: Elizabeth in the lobby, as though lying in wait for me, chatting with the manager. Rides up with me in the elevator. Her eyes looking into mine. "Sometimes I think you're afraid of me," she begins. "You mustn't be. That's the great tragedy of human life, that people shut themselves up behind walls of fear and never let anyone through, anyone who might care about them and be warm to them. You've got no reason to be afraid of me." I do, but how to explain that to her? To sidestep prolonged conversation and possible entanglement I get off the elevator one floor below the right one.

Let her think I'm visiting a friend. Or a mistress. I walk slowly down the hall to the stairs, using up time, waiting so she will be in her room before I go up. A maid bustles by me. She thrusts her key into a door on the left: a rare *faux pas* for the usually competent help here, she forgets to knock before going in to make up the room. The door opens and the occupant, inside, stands revealed. A stocky, muscular man, naked to the waist. "Oh, excuse me," the maid gasps, and backs out, shutting the door. But I have seen. My eyes are quick. The hairy chest is split, a dark gash three inches wide and some eleven inches long, beginning between the nipples and going past the navel. Visible within is the black shiny surface of a Homeworld carapace. My countryman, opening up for Second Feeding. Dazed, numbed, I stagger to the stairs and pull myself step by leaden step to my floor. No sign of Elizabeth. I stumble into my room and throw the bolt. Another of us here? Well, why not? I'm not the only one. There may be hundreds in New York alone. But in the same hotel? I remember, now, I've seen him occasionally: a silent, dour man, tense, hunted-looking, unsociable. No doubt I appear the same way to others. Keep the world at a distance. I don't know his name or what he is supposed to do for a living.

We are forbidden to make contact with fellow Homeworlders except in case of extreme emergency. Isolation is a necessary condition of our employment. I may not introduce myself to him; I may not seek his friendship. It is worse now for me, knowing that he is here, than when I was entirely alone. The things we could reminisce about! The friends we might have in common! We could reinforce one another's endurance of the gravity, the discomfort of our disguises, the vile climate. But no. I must pretend I know nothing. The rules. The harsh, unbending rules. I to go about my business, he his; if we meet, no hint of my knowledge must pass.

So be it. I will honor my vows. But it may be difficult.

He goes by the name of Swanson. Been living in the hotel eighteen months; a musician of some sort, according to the manager. "A very peculiar man. Keeps to himself; no small talk, never smiles. Defends his privacy. The other day a maid barged into his room without knocking and I thought he'd sue. Well, we get all sorts here." The manager thinks he may actually be a member of one of the old European royal families, living in exile, or something similarly romantic. The manager would be surprised.

I defend my privacy too. From Elizabeth, another assault on it.

In the hall outside my room. "My new poems," she said. "In case you're interested." And then: "Can I come in? I'd read them to you. I love reading out loud." And: "Please don't always seem so terribly afraid of me. I don't bite, David. Really I don't. I'm quite gentle."

"I'm sorry."

"So am I." Anger, now, lurking in her shiny eyes, her thin taut lips. "If you want me to leave you alone, say so, I will. But I want you to know how cruel you're being. I don't *demand* anything from you. I'm just offering some friendship. And you're refusing. Do I have a bad smell? Am I so ugly? Is it my poems you hate and you're afraid to tell me?"

"Elizabeth—"

"We're only on this world such a short time. Why can't we be kinder to each other while we are? To love, to share, to open up. The reality trip. Communication, soul to soul." Her tone changed. An artful shading. "For all I know, women turn you off. I wouldn't put anybody down for that. We've all got our ways. But it doesn't have to be a sexual thing, you and me. Just talk. Like, opening the channels. Please? Say no and I'll never bother you again, but don't say no, please. That's like shutting a door on life, David. And when you do that, you start to die a little."

Persistent. I should tell her to go to hell. But there is the loneliness. There is her obvious sincerity. Her warmth, her eagerness to pull me from my lunar isolation. Can there be harm in it? Knowing that Swanson is nearby, so close yet sealed from me by iron commandments, has intensified my sense of being alone. I can risk letting Elizabeth get closer to me. It will make her happy; it may make me happy; it could even yield information valuable to Homeworld. Of course I must still maintain certain barriers.

"I don't mean to be unfriendly. I think you've misunderstood, Elizabeth. I haven't really been rejecting you. Come in. Do come in." Stunned, she enters my room. The first guest ever. My few books; my modest furnishings; the ultrawave transmitter, impenetrably disguised as a piece of sculpture. She sits. Skirt far above the knees. Good legs, if I understand the criteria of quality correctly. I am determined to allow no sexual overtures. If she tries anything, I'll resort to—I don't know—hysteria. "Read me your new poems," I say. She opens her portfolio. Reads.

> *In the midst of the hipster night of doubt and*
> *Emptiness, when the bad-trip god came to me with*
> *Cold hands, I looked up and shouted yes at the*
> *Stars. And yes and yes again. I groove on yes;*
> *The devil grooves on no. And I waited for you to*
> *Say yes, and at last you did. And the world said*
> *The stars said the trees said the grass said the*
> *Sky said the streets said yes and yes and yes—*

She is ecstatic. Her face is flushed; her eyes are joyous. She has broken through to me. After two hours, when it becomes obvious that I am not going to ask her to go to bed with me, she leaves. Not to wear out her welcome. "I'm so glad I was wrong about you, David," she whispers. "I couldn't believe you were really a life-denier. And you're not." Ecstatic.

I am getting into very deep water.

We spend an hour or two together every night. Sometimes in my room, sometimes in hers. Usually she comes to me, but now and then, to be polite, I seek her out after Third Feeding. By now I've read all her poetry; we talk instead of the arts in general, politics, racial problems. She has a lively, well-stocked, disorderly mind. Though she probes constantly for information about me, she realizes how sensitive I am, and quickly withdraws when I parry her. Asking about my work; I reply vaguely that I'm doing research for a book, and when I don't amplify she drops it, though she tries again, gently, a few nights later. She drinks a lot of wine, and offers it to me. I nurse one glass through a whole visit. Often she suggests we go out together for dinner; I explain that I have digestive problems and prefer to eat alone, and she takes this in good grace but immediately resolves to help me overcome those problems, for soon she is asking me to eat with her again. There is an excellent Spanish restaurant right in the hotel, she says. She drops troublesome questions. Where was I born? Did I go to college? Do I have family somewhere?

Have I ever been married? Have I published any of my writings? I improvise evasions. Nothing difficult about that, except that never before have I allowed anyone on Earth such sustained contact with me, so prolonged an opportunity to find inconsistencies in my pretended identity. What if she sees through?

And sex. Her invitations grow less subtle. She seems to think that we ought to be having a sexual relationship, simply because we've become such good friends. Not a matter of passion so much as one of communication: we talk, sometimes we take walks together, we should do *that* together too. But of course it's impossible. I have the external organs but not the capacity to use them. Wouldn't want her touching my false skin in any case. How to deflect her? If I declare myself impotent she'll demand a chance to try to cure me. If I pretend homosexuality she'll start some kind of straightening therapy. If I simply say she doesn't turn me on physically she'll be hurt. The sexual thing is a challenge to her, the way merely getting me to talk with her once was. She often wears the transparent pink shawl that reveals her breasts. Her skirts are hip high. She doses herself with aphrodisiac perfumes. She grazes my body with hers whenever opportunity arises. The tension mounts; she is determined to have me.

I have said nothing about her in my reports to Homeworld. Though I do transmit some of the psychological data I have gathered by observing her.

"Could you ever admit you were in love with me?" she asked tonight.

And she asked, "Doesn't it hurt you to repress your feelings all the time? To sit there locked up inside yourself like a prisoner?"

And, "There's a physical side of life too, David. I don't mind so much the damage you're doing to me by ignoring it. But I worry about the damage you're doing to you."

Crossing her legs. Hiking her skirt even higher.

We are heading toward a crisis. I should never have let this begin. A torrid summer has descended on the city, and in hot weather my nervous system is always at the edge of eruption. She may push me too far. I might ruin everything. I should apply for transfer to Homeworld before I cause trouble. Maybe I should confer with Swanson. I think what is happening now qualifies as an emergency.

Elizabeth stayed past midnight tonight. I had to ask her finally to leave: work to do. An hour later she pushed an envelope under my door. Newest poems. Love poems. In a shaky hand: *"David you mean so much to me. You mean the stars and nebulas. Cant you let me show my love? Cant you accept happiness? Think about it. I adore you."*

What have I started?

103°F. today. The fourth successive day of intolerable heat. Met Swanson in the elevator at lunch time; nearly blurted the truth about myself to him. I must be more careful. But my control is slipping. Last night, in the worst of the heat, I was tempted to strip off my disguise. I could no longer stand being locked in here, pivoting and ducking to avoid all the machinery festooned about me. Resisted the temptation; just barely. Somehow I am more sensitive to the gravity too. I have the illusion that my carapace is developing cracks. Almost collapsed in the street this afternoon. All I need: heat exhaustion, whisked off to the hospital, routine fluoroscope exam. "You have a very odd skeletal structure, Mr. Knecht." Indeed. Dissecting me, next, with three thousand medical students looking on. And then the United Nations called in. Menace from outer space. Yes. I must be more careful. I must be more careful. I must be more—

Now I've done it. Eleven years of faithful service destroyed in a single wild moment. Violation of the Fundamental Rule. I hardly believe it. How was it possible that I—that I—with my respect for my responsibilities—that I could have—even considered, let alone actually done—

But the weather was terribly hot. The third week of the heat wave. I was stifling inside my false body. And the gravity: was New York having a gravity wave too? That terrible pull, worse than ever. Bending my internal organs out of shape. Elizabeth a tremendous annoyance: passionate, emotional, teary, poetic, giving me no rest, pleading for me to burn with a brighter flame. Declaring her love in sonnets, in rambling hip epics, in haiku. Spending two hours in my room, crouched at my feet, murmuring about the hidden beauty of my soul. "Open yourself and let love come in," she whispered. "It's like giving yourself to God. Making a commitment; breaking down all walls. Why not? For love's sake, David, why not?" I couldn't tell her why not, and she went away, but about midnight she was back knocking at my door. I let her in. She wore an ankle-length silk housecoat, gleaming, threadbare. "I'm stoned," she said hoarsely, voice an octave too deep. "I had to bust three joints to get up the nerve. But here I am. David, I'm sick of making the turnoff trip. We've been so wonderfully close, and then you won't go the last stretch of the way." A cascade of giggles. "Tonight you will. Don't fail me. Darling." Drops the housecoat. Naked underneath it: narrow waist, bony hips, long legs, thin thighs, blue veins crossing her breasts. Her hair wild and kinky. A sorceress. A seeress. Berserk. Approaching me, eyes slit-wide, mouth open, tongue flickering snakily. How fleshless she is! Beads of sweat glistening on her flat chest. Seizes my wrists; tugs me roughly toward the bed. We tussle a little. Within my false body I throw switches, nudge levers. I am stronger than she is. I pull free, breaking her hold with an effort. She stands flat-footed in front of me, glaring, eyes fiery. So vulnerable, so sad in her nudity. And yet so fierce. "David! David! David!" Sobbing. Breathless. Pleading with her eyes and the tips of her breasts. Gathering her strength; now she makes the next lunge, but I see it coming and let her topple past me. She lands on the bed, burying her face in the pillow, clawing at the sheet. "Why? Why why why WHY?" she screams.

In a minute we will have the manager in here. With the police.

"Am I so hideous? I love you, David, do you know what that word means? Love. Love." Sits up. Turns to me. Imploring. "Don't reject me," she whispers. "I couldn't take that. You know, I just wanted to make you happy, I figured I could be the one, only I didn't realize how unhappy you'd make me. And you just stand there. And you don't say anything. What are you, some kind of machine?"

"I'll tell you what I am," I said.

That was when I went sliding into the abyss. All control lost; all prudence gone. My mind so slathered with raw emotion that survival itself means nothing. I must make things clear to her, is all. I must show her. At whatever expense. I strip off my shirt. She glows, no doubt thinking I will let myself be seduced. My hands slide up and down my bare chest, seeking the catches and snaps. I go through the intricate, cumbersome process of opening my body. Deep within myself something is shouting NO NO NO NO NO, but I pay no attention. The heart has its reasons.

Hoarsely: "Look, Elizabeth. Look at me. This is what I am. Look at me and freak out. The reality trip."

My chest opens wide.

I push myself forward, stepping between the levers and struts, emerging halfway from the human shell I wear. I have not been this far out of it since the day they sealed me in, on Homeworld. I let her see my gleaming carapace. I wave my eyestalks around. I allow some of my claws to show. "See? See? Big black crab from outer space. That's what you love, Elizabeth. That's what I am. David Knecht's just a costume, and this is what's inside it." I have gone insane. "You want reality? Here's reality, Elizabeth. What good is the Knecht body to you? It's a fraud. It's a machine. Come on, come closer. Do you want to kiss me? Should I get on you and make love?"

During this episode her face has displayed an amazing range of reactions. Open-mouthed disbelief at first, of course. And frozen horror: gagging sounds in throat, jaws agape, eyes wide and rigid. Hands fanned across breasts. Sudden modesty in front of the alien monster? But then, as the familiar Knecht-voice, now bitter and impassioned, continues to flow from the black thing within the sundered chest, a softening of her response. Curiosity. The poetic sensibility taking over. Nothing human is alien to me: Terence, quoted by Cicero. Nothing alien is alien to me. Eh? She will accept the evidence of her eyes. "What are you? Where did you come from?" And I say, "I've violated the Fundamental Rule. I deserve to be plucked and thinned. We're not supposed to reveal ourselves. If we get into some kind of accident that might lead to exposure, we're supposed to blow ourselves up. The switch is right here." She comes close and peers around me, into the cavern of David Knecht's chest. "From some other planet? Living here in disguise?" She understands the picture. Her shock is fading. She even laughs. "I've seen worse than you on acid," she says. "You don't frighten me now, David. David? Shall I go on calling you David?"

This is unreal and dreamlike to me. I have revealed myself, thinking to drive her away in terror; she is no longer aghast, and smiles at my strangeness. She kneels to get a better look. I move back a short way. Eyestalks fluttering: I am uneasy, I have somehow lost the upper hand in this encounter.

She says, "I knew you were unusual, but not like this. But it's all right. I can cope. I mean, the essential personality, that's what I fell in love with. Who cares that you're a crab-man from the Green Galaxy? Who cares that we can't be real lovers? I can make that sacrifice. It's your soul I dig, David. Go on. Close yourself up again. You don't look comfortable this way." The triumph of love. She will not abandon me, even now. Disaster. I crawl back into Knecht and lift his arms to his chest to seal it. Shock is glazing my consciousness: the enormity, the audacity. What have I done? Elizabeth watches, awed, even delighted. At last I am together again. She nods. "Listen," she tells me, "you can trust me. I mean, if you're some kind of spy, checking out the Earth, I don't care. *I don't care.* I won't tell anybody. Pour it all out, David. Tell me about yourself. Don't you see, this is the biggest thing that ever happened to me. A chance to show that love isn't just physical, isn't just chemistry, that it's a soul trip, that it crosses not just racial lines but the lines of the whole damned species, the planet itself—"

It took several hours to get rid of her. A soaring, intense conversation, Elizabeth doing most of the talking. She putting forth theories of why I had come to Earth, me nodding, denying, amplifying, mostly lost in horror at my own perfidy and barely listening to her monologue. And the humidity turning me into rotting rags. Finally: "I'm down from the pot, David. And all wound up. I'm going out for a walk. Then back to my room to write for a while. To put this night into a poem before I lose the power of it. But I'll come to you again by dawn, all right? That's maybe five hours from now. You'll be here? You won't do anything foolish? Oh, I love you so much, David! Do you believe me? Do you?"

When she was gone I stood a long while by the window, trying to reassemble myself. Shattered. Drained. Remembering her kisses, her lips running along the ridge marking the place where my chest opens. The fascination of the abomination. She will love me even if I am crustaceous beneath.

I had to have help.

I went to Swanson's room. He was slow to respond to my knock; busy transmitting, no doubt. I could hear him within, but he didn't answer. "Swanson?" I called. "Swanson?" Then I added the distresss signal in the Homeworld tongue. He rushed to the door. Blinking, suspicious. "It's all right," I said. "Look, let me in. I'm in big trouble." Speaking English, but I gave him the distress signal again.

"How did you know about me?" he asked.

"The day the maid blundered into your room while you were eating, I was going by. I saw."

"But you aren't supposed to——"

"Except in emergencies. This is an emergency." He shut off his ultrawave and listened intently to my story. Scowling. He didn't approve. But he wouldn't spurn me. I had been criminally foolish, but I was of his kind, prey to the same pains, the same lonelinesses, and he would help me.

"What do you plan to do now?" he asked. "You can't harm her. It isn't allowed."

"I don't want to harm her. Just to get free of her. To make her fall out of love with me."

"How? If showing yourself to her didn't——"

"Infidelity," I said. "Making her see that I love someone else. No room in my life for her. That'll drive her away. Afterwards it won't matter that she knows: who'd believe her story? The FBI would laugh and tell her to lay off the LSD. But if I don't break her attachment to me I'm finished."

"Love someone else? Who?"

"When she comes back to my room at dawn," I said, "she'll find the two of us together, dividing and abstracting. I think that'll do it, don't you?"

So I deceived Elizabeth with Swanson.

The fact that we both wore male human identities was irrelevant, of course. We went to the room and stepped out of our disguises—a bold, dizzying sensation!—and suddenly we were just two Homeworlders again, receptive to one another's needs. I left the door unlocked. Swanson and I crawled up on my bed and began the chanting. How strange it was, after these years of solitude, to feel those vibrations again! And how beautiful. Swanson's vibrissae touching mine. The interplay of harmonies. An underlying sternness to his technique—he was contemptuous of me for my idiocy, and rightly so—but once we passed from the chanting to the dividing all was forgiven, and as we moved into the abstracting it was truly sublime. We climbed through an infinity of climactic emptyings. Dawn crept upon us and found us unwilling to halt even for rest.

A knock at the door. Elizabeth.

"Come in," I said.

A dreamy, ecstatic look on her face. Fading instantly when she saw the two of us entangled on the bed. A questioning frown. "We've been mating," I explained. "Did you think I was a complete hermit?" She looked from Swanson to me, from me to Swanson. Hand over her mouth. Eyes anguished. I turned the screw a little tighter. "I couldn't stop you from falling in love with me, Elizabeth. But I really do prefer my own kind. As should have been obvious."

"To have her here now, though—when you knew I was coming back—"

"Not *her*, exactly. Not *him* exactly either, though."

"—so cruel, David! To ruin such a beautiful experience." Holding forth sheets of paper with shaking hands. "A whole sonnet cycle," she said. "About tonight. How beautiful it was, and all. And now—and now—" Crumpling the pages. Hurling them across the room. Turning. Running out, sobbing furiously. Hell hath no fury like. *"David!"* A smothered cry. And slamming the door.

She was back in ten minutes. Swanson and I hadn't quite finished donning our bodies yet; we were both still unsealed. As we worked, we discussed further steps to take: he felt honor demanded that I request a transfer back to Homeworld, having terminated my usefulness here through tonight's indiscreet revelation. I agreed with him to some degree but was reluctant to leave. Despite the bodily torment of life on Earth I had come to feel I belonged here. Then Elizabeth entered, radiant.

"I mustn't be so possessive," she announced. "So bourgeois. So conventional. I'm willing to share my love." Embracing Swanson. Embracing me. "A *ménage à trois*," she said. "I won't mind that you two are having a physical relationship. As long as you don't shut me out of your lives completely. I mean, David, we could never have been physical anyway, right, but we can have the other aspects of love, and we'll open ourselves to your friend also. Yes? Yes? Yes?"

Swanson and I both put in applications for transfer, he to Africa, me to Homeworld. It would be some time before we received a reply. Until then we were at her mercy. He was blazingly angry with me for involving him in this, but what choice had I had? Nor could either of us avoid Elizabeth. We were at her mercy. She bathed both of us in shimmering waves of tender emotion; wherever we turned, there she was, incandescent with love. Lighting up the darkness of our lives. You poor lonely creatures. Do you suffer much in our gravity? What about the heat? And the winters. Is there a custom of marriage on your planet? Do you have poetry?

A happy threesome. We went to the theater together. To concerts. Even to parties in Greenwich Village. "My friends," Elizabeth said, leaving no doubt in anyone's mind that she was living with both of us. Faintly scandalous doings; she loved to seem daring. Swanson was sullenly obliging, putting up with her antics but privately haranguing me for subjecting him to all this. Elizabeth got out another mimeographed booklet of poems, dedicated to both of us. *Triple Tripping,* she called it. Flagrantly erotic. I quoted a few of the poems in one of my reports to Homeworld, then lost heart and hid the booklet in the closet. "Have you heard about your transfer yet?" I asked Swanson at least twice a week. He hadn't. Neither had I.

Autumn came. Elizabeth, burning her candle at both ends, looked gaunt and feverish. "I have never known such happiness," she announced frequently, one hand clasping Swanson, the other me. "I never think about the strangeness of you anymore. I think of you only as people. Sweet, wonderful, lonely people. Here in the darkness of this horrid city." And she once said, "What if everybody here is like you, and I'm the only one who's really human? But that's silly. You must be the only ones of your kind here. The advance scouts. Will your planet invade ours? I do hope so! Set everything to rights. The reign of love and reason at last!"

"How long will this go on?" Swanson muttered.

At the end of October his transfer came through. He left without saying good-bye to either of us and without leaving a forwarding address. Nairobi? Addis Ababa? Kinshasa?

I had grown accustomed to having him around to share the burden of Elizabeth. Now the full brunt of her affection fell on me. My work was suffering; I had no time to file my reports properly. And I lived in fear of her gossiping. What was she telling her Village friends? ("You know David? He's not really a man, you know. Actually inside him there's a kind of crab-thing from another solar system. But what does that matter? Love's a universal phenomenon. The truly loving person doesn't draw limits around the planet.") I longed for my release. To go home; to accept my punishment; to shed my false skin. To empty my mind of Elizabeth.

My reply came through the ultrawave on November 13. Application denied. I was to remain on Earth and continue my work as before. Transfers to Homeworld were granted only for reasons of health.

I debated sending a full account of my treason to Homeworld and thus bringing about my certain recall. But I hesitated, overwhelmed with despair. Dark brooding seized me. "Why so sad?" Elizabeth asked. What could I say? That my attempt at escaping from her had failed? "I love you," she said. "I've never felt so *real* before." Nuzzling against my cheek. Fingers knotted in my hair. A seductive whisper. "David, open yourself up again. Your chest, I mean. I want to see the inner you. To make sure I'm not frightened of it. Please? You've only let me see you once." And then, when I had: "May I kiss you, David?" I was appalled. But I let her. She was unafraid. Transfigured by happiness. She is a cosmic nuisance, but I fear I'm getting to like her.

Can I leave her? I wish Swanson had not vanished. I need advice.

Either I break with Elizabeth or I break with Homeworld. This is absurd. I find new chasms of despondency every day. I am unable to do my work. I have requested a transfer once again, without giving details. The first snow of the winter today.

Application denied.

"When I found you with Swanson," she said, "it was a terrible shock. An even bigger blow than when you first came out of your chest. I mean, it was startling to find out you weren't human, but it didn't hit me in any emotional way, it didn't threaten me. But then, to come back a few hours later and find you with one of your own kind, to know that you wanted to shut me out, that I had no place in your life— Only we worked it out, didn't we?" Kissing me. Tears of joy in her eyes. How did this happen? Where did it all begin? Existence was once so simple. I have tried to trace the chain of events that brought me from there to here, and I cannot. I was outside of my false body for eight hours today. The longest spell so far. Elizabeth is talking of going to the islands with me for the winter. A secluded cottage that her friends will make available. Of course, I must not leave my post without permission. And it takes months simply to get a reply.

Let me admit the truth: I love her.

January 1. The new year begins. I have sent my resignation to Homeworld and have destroyed my ultrawave equipment. The links are broken. Tomorrow, when the city offices are open, Elizabeth and I will go to get the marriage license.

Rule Golden

BY DAMON KNIGHT

With his long rippling white beard, down to his chest in the most recent photograph we've seen, Damon Knight looks the part of patriarch of SF—a role he also has the credentials to play, as founder of the Science Fiction Writers of America, cofounder of the prestigious Milford Writers Conference, author of the first important book of SF criticism (In Search of Wonder), *editor of* Orbit (*the longest-running original anthology series in the history of the field), and a multitalented professional whose career as writer, editor, critic, and anthologist spans almost forty years.*

Knight, however, rarely acts like a patriarch—rather than maintaining a solemn and sober demeanor at all times, he has been known to engage in peanut fights during dull cocktail parties, is lightning fast on the draw with a squirt-gun, and more than once has lightened the hypertense atmosphere of writer's workshops by spraying the ulcerated participants with silly-string or bombarding them with superballs. Nor is his mind at all safely fossilized and dead, as a proper patriarch's should be. Knight's mind is still alive and supple and growing, his curiosity is restless and insatiable, his range of interests enormous; he has a particular knack for turning problems on their heads, for seeing things from unexpected and valuable angles, for penetrating to the heart of mazes with one needle-sharp thrust.

One of the subjects he has been examining for years with that special clarity of vision, and from his own unique perspectives, is that of human-alien interaction.

Damon Knight has probably written more about alien contact than any other writer of his generation, with the possible exception of Theodore Sturgeon. Certainly it would have been possible to fill this entire anthology with noth-

223

ing but Knight's alien stories, all presenting alien contact from different angles: in "To Serve Man" the aliens eat us; in "Idiot Stick" they use us as hired hand labor in a project that could result in our own destruction; in "Four in One" the alien literally swallows the human characters, merging with them in bizarre symbiosis; in "Babel II" aliens inadvertently destroy our ability to communicate with one another; in "The Enemy" a young girl and an alien "monster" engage in a deadly conflict on an airless world; in "The Earth Quarter" expatriate Earthmen are restricted to ghettos on other worlds by the alien races who distrust them; in "Double Meaning" the alien's fondness for puns is the cause of an imperialistic Earth's undoing; in "Man in the Jar" an alien bellhop struggles to deal with a very dangerous customer; and in "Stranger Station," perhaps Knight's most famous contact story, an Earthman and an alien, isolated together for months, strive to alter one another through hate and love.

In "Rule Golden," a story at the top of even Knight's high standard, we are forced to live up to one of our own most ancient laws—with odd and disquieting results.

Knight's books include A for Anything, Hell's Pavement, The Best of Damon Knight, The Other Foot, Turning On, Off Center, In Deep, the Orbit series, and a large number of other first-rate anthologies. He won the Hugo Award in 1956 for In Search of Wonder, his pioneering book of critical essays. His latest books are Turning Points, an anthology of critical pieces; The Futurians, a history of the early days of SF; and Rule Golden and Other Stories, a collection. A novel, The World and Thorrin, is forthcoming.

I

A man in Des Moines kicked his wife when her back was turned. She was taken to the hospital, suffering from a broken coccyx.

So was he.

In Kansas City, Kansas, a youth armed with a .22 killed a schoolmate with one shot through the chest, and instantly dropped dead of heart failure.

In Decatur two middleweights named Packy Morris and Leo Oshinsky simultaneously knocked each other out.

In St. Louis, a policeman shot down a fleeing bank robber and collapsed. The bank robber died; the policeman's condition was described as critical.

I read those items in the afternoon editions of the Washington papers, and although I noted the pattern, I wasn't much impressed. Every newspaperman knows that runs of coincidence are a dime a dozen; *everything* happens that way—plane crashes, hotel fires, suicide pacts, people giving away all their money; name it and I can show you an epidemic of it in the files.

What I was actually looking for were stories originating in two places: my home town and Chillicothe, Missouri. Stories with those datelines had been carefully cut out of the papers before I got them, so, for lack of anything better, I read everything datelined near either place. And that was how I happened to catch the Des Moines, Kansas City, Decatur and St. Louis items—all of those places will fit into a two-hundred-mile circle drawn with Chillicothe as its center.

I had asked for, but hadn't got, a copy of my own paper. That made it a little tough, because I had to sit there, in a Washington hotel room at night—and if you know a lonelier place and time, tell me—and wonder if they had really shut us down.

I knew it was unlikely. I knew things hadn't got that bad in America yet, by a long way. I knew they *wanted* me to sit there and worry about it, but I couldn't help it.

Ever since *La Prensa,* every newspaper publisher on this continent has felt a cold wind blowing down his back.

That's foolishness, I told myself. Not to wave the flag too much or anything, but the free speech tradition in this country is too strong; we haven't forgotten Peter Zenger.

And then it occurred to me that a lot of editors must have felt the same way, just before their papers were suppressed on the orders of an American president named Abraham Lincoln.

So I took one more turn around the room and got back into bed, and although I had already read all the papers from bannerlines to box scores, I started leafing through them again, just to make a little noise. Nothing to do.

I had asked for a book, and hadn't got it. That made sense, too; there was nothing to do in that room, nothing to distract me, nothing to read except newspapers—and how could I look at a newspaper without thinking of the *Herald-Star?*

My father founded the *Herald-Star*—the *Herald* part, that is, the *Star* came later—ten years before I was born. I inherited it from him, but I want to add that I'm not one of those publishers by right of primogeniture whose only function consists in supplying sophomoric by-lined copy for the front page; I started on the paper as a copy boy and I can still handle any job in a city room.

It was a good newspaper. It wasn't the biggest paper in the Middle West, or the fastest growing, or the loudest; but we'd had two Pulitzer Prizes in the last fifteen years, we kept our political bias on the editorial page, and up to now we had never knuckled under to anybody.

But this was the first time we had picked a fight with the U.S. Department of Defense.

Ten miles outside Chillicothe, Missouri, the department had a little thousand-acre installation with three laboratory buildings, a small airfield, living quarters for a staff of two hundred and a one-storey barracks. It was closed down in 1968 when the Phoenix-bomb program was officially abandoned.

Two years and ten months later, it was opened up again. A new and much bigger barracks went up in place of the old one; a two-company garrison moved in. Who else or what else went into the area, nobody knew for certain; but rumors came out.

We checked the rumors. We found confirmation. We published it, and we followed it up. Within a week we had a full-sized crusade started; we were asking for a congressional investigation, and it looked as if we might get it.

Then the President invited me and the publishers of twenty-odd other antiadministration dailies to Washington. Each of us got a personal interview with The Man; the secretary of defense was also present, to evade questions.

They asked me, as a personal favor and in the interests of national security, to kill the Chillicothe series.

After asking a few questions, to which I got the answers I expected, I politely declined.

And here I was.

The door opened. The guard outside looked in, saw me on the bed, and stepped back out of sight. Another man walked in: stocky build, straight black hair turning gray; about fifty. Confident eyes behind rimless bifocals.

"Mr. Dahl. My name is Carlton Frisbee."

"I've seen your picture," I told him. Frisbee was the undersecretary of defense, a career man, very able; he was said to be the brains of the department.

He sat down facing me. He didn't ask permission, and he didn't offer to shake hands, which was intelligent of him.

"How do you feel about it now?" he asked.

"Just the same."

He nodded. After a moment he said, "I'm going to try to explain our position to you, Mr. Dahl."

I grinned at him. "The word you're groping for is 'awkward.' "

"No. It's true that we can't let you go in your present state of mind, but we can keep you. If necessary, you will be killed, Mr. Dahl. That's how important Chillicothe is."

"Nothing," I said, "is that important."

He cocked his head at me. "If you and your family lived in a community surrounded by hostile savages, who were kept at bay only because you had rifles—and if someone proposed to give them rifles—well?"

"Look," I said, "let's get down to cases. You claim that a new weapon is being developed at Chillicothe, is that right? It's something revolutionary, and if the Russians got it first we would be sunk, and so on. In other words, the Manhattan Project all over again."

"Right."

"Okay. Then why has Chillicothe got twice the military guard it had when it was an atomic research center, and a third of the civilian staff?"

He started to speak.

"Wait a minute, let me finish. Why, of the fifty-one scientists we have been able to trace to Chillicothe, are there seventeen linguists and philologists, three organic chemists, five physiologists, *twenty-six psychologists, and not one single physicist?*"

"In the first place—were you about to say something?"

"All right, go ahead."

"You know I can't answer those questions factually, Mr. Dahl, but speaking conjecturally, can't you conceive of a psychological weapon?"

"You can't answer them at all. My third question is, why have you got a wall around that place—not just a stockade, a wall, with guard towers on it? Never mind speaking conjecturally. Now I'll answer your question. Yes, I can conceive of psychological experimentation that you might call weapons research, I can think of several possibilities, and there isn't a damn one of them that wouldn't have to be used on American citizens before you could get anywhere near the Russians with it."

His eyes were steady behind the bright lenses. He didn't say, "We seem to have reached a deadlock," or "Evidently it would be useless to discuss this any further"; he simply changed the subject.

"There are two things we can do with you, Mr. Dahl; the choice will be up to you. First, we can indict you for treason and transfer you to a federal prison to await trial. Under the revised Alien and Sedition Act, we can hold you incommunicado for at least twelve months, and, of course, no bail will be set. I feel bound to point out to you that in this case, it would be impossible to let you come to trial until after the danger of breaching security at Chillicothe is past. If necessary, as I told you, you would die in prison.

"Second, we can admit you to Chillicothe itself as a press representative. We would, in this case, allow you full access to all nontechnical information about the Chillicothe project as it develops with permission to publish as soon as security is lifted. You would be confined to the project until that time, and I can't offer you any estimate of how long it might be. In return, you would be asked to write letters plausibly explaining your absence to your staff and to close friends and relatives, and—providing that you find Chillicothe to be what we say it is and not what you suspect—to work out a series of stories for your newspaper which will divert attention from the project."

He seemed to be finished. I said, "Frisbee, I hate to tell you this, but you're overlooking a point. Let's just suppose for a minute that Chillicothe is what I think it is. How do I know that once I got inside I might not somehow or other find myself writing that kind of copy whether I felt like it or not?"

He nodded. "What guarantees would you consider sufficient?"

I thought about that. It was a nice point. I was angry enough, and scared enough, to feel like pasting Frisbee a good one and then seeing how far I could get; but one thing I couldn't figure out, and that was why, if Frisbee wasn't at least partly on the level, he should be here at all.

If they wanted me in Chillicothe, they could drag me there.

After a while I said, "Let me call my managing editor and tell him where I'm going. Let me tell him that I'll call him again—*on a video circuit*—within three days after I get there, when I've had time to inspect the whole area. And that if I don't call, or if I look funny or sound funny, he can start worrying."

He nodded again. "Fair enough." He stood up. "I won't ask you to shake hands with me now, Mr. Dahl; later on I hope you will." He turned and walked to the door, unhurried, calm, imperturbable, the way he had come in.

Six hours later I was on a westbound plane.

That was the first day.

The second day, an inexplicable epidemic broke out in the slaughterhouses of Chicago and surrounding areas. The symptoms were a sudden collapse followed by nausea, incontinence, anemia, shock, and, in some cases, severe pain in the occipital and cervical regions. Or: as one victim, an AF of L knacker with twenty-five years' experience in the nation's abattoirs, succinctly put it: "It felt just like I was hit in the head."

Local and federal health authorities immediately closed down the affected slaughterhouses, impounded or banned the sale of all supplies of fresh meat in the area, and launched a sweeping investigation. Retail food stores sold out their stocks of canned, frozen and processed meats early in the day; seafood markets reported their largest volume of sales in two decades. Eggs and cheese were in short supply.

Fifty-seven guards, assistant wardens and other minor officials of the federal penitentiary at Leavenworth, Kansas, submitted a group resignation to Warden Hermann R. Longo. Their explanation of the move was that all had experienced a religious conversion, and that assisting in the forcible confinement of other human beings was inconsonant with their beliefs.

Near Louisville, Kentucky, neighbors attracted by cries for help found a forty-year-old woman and her twelve-year-old daughter both severely burned. The woman, whose clothing was not even scorched although her upper body was covered with first and second degree burns, admitted pushing the child into a bonfire, but in her hysterical condition was unable to give a rational account of her own injuries.

There was also a follow-up on the Des Moines story about the man who kicked his wife. Remember that I didn't say he had a broken coccyx; I said he was suffering from one. A few hours after he was admitted to the hospital he stopped doing so, and he was released into police custody when X-rays showed no fracture.

Straws in the wind.

At five thirty that morning, I was waking up my manag-

ing editor, Eli Freeman, with a monitored long-distance
call—one of Frisbee's bright young men waiting to cut me
off if I said anything I shouldn't. The temptation was
strong, just the same, but I didn't.

From six to eight thirty I was on a plane with three
taciturn guards. I spent most of the time going over the
last thirty years of my life, and wondering how many people would remember me two days after they wrapped my
obituary around their garbage.

We landed at the airfield about a mile from the project
proper, and after one of my hitherto silent friends had finished a twenty-minute phone call, a limousine took us over
to a long, temporary-looking frame building just outside
the wall. It took me only until noon to get out again; I had
been fingerprinted, photographed, stripped, examined, X-
rayed, urinalyzed, blood-tested, showered, disinfected, and
given a set of pinks to wear until my own clothes had
been cleaned and fumigated. I also got a numbered badge
which I was instructed to wear on the left chest at all
times, and an identity card to keep in my wallet when I
got my wallet back.

Then they let me through the gate, and I saw Chillicothe.

I was in a short cul-de-sac formed by the gate and two
walls of masonry, blank except for firing slits. Facing
away from the gate I could see one of the three laboratory
buildings a good half mile away. Between me and it was a
geometrical forest of poles with down-pointing reflectors
on their crossbars. Floodlights.

I didn't like that. What I saw a few minutes later I liked
even less. I was bouncing across the flat in a jeep driven
by a stocky, moon-faced corporal; we passed the first building, and I saw the second.

There was a ring of low pillboxes around it. And their
guns pointed *inward*, toward the building.

Major General Parst was a big, bald man in his fifties,
whose figure would have been more military if the Prus-
sian corset had not gone out of fashion. I took him for a
Pentagon soldier; he had the Pentagon smoothness of manner, but there seemed to be a good deal more under it
than the usual well-oiled vacancy. He was also, I judged, a
very worried man.

"There's just one thing I'd like to make clear to you at
the beginning, Mr. Dahl. I'm not a grudge-holding man,

and I hope you're not either, because there's a good chance that you and I will be seeing a lot of each other during the next three or four years. But I thought it might make it a little easier for you to know that you're not the only one with a grievance. You see this isn't an easy job, it never has been. I'm just stating the fact: it's been considerably harder since your newspaper took an interest in us." He spread his hands and smiled wryly.

"Just what is your job, General?"

"You mean, what is Chillicothe." He snorted. "I'm not going to waste my breath telling you."

My expression must have changed.

"Don't misunderstand me—I mean that if I told you, you wouldn't believe me. I didn't myself. I'm going to have to show you." He stood up, looking at his wristwatch. "I have a little more than an hour. That's more than enough for the demonstration, but you're going to have a lot of questions afterward. We'd better start."

He thumbed his intercom. "I'll be in Section One for the next fifteen minutes."

When we were in the corridor outside he said, "Tell me something, Mr. Dahl: I suppose it occurred to you that if you were right in your suspicions of Chillicothe, you might be running a certain personal risk in coming here, in spite of any precautions you might take?"

"I considered the possibility. I haven't seen anything to rule it out yet."

"And still, I gather that you chose this alternative almost without hesitation. Why was that, if you don't mind telling me?"

It was a fair question. There's nothing very attractive about a federal prison, but at least they don't saw your skull open there, or turn your mind inside out with drugs. I said, "Call it curiosity."

He nodded. "Yes. A very potent force, Mr. Dahl. More mountains have been moved by it than by faith."

We passed a guard with a T44, then a second, and a third. Finally Parst stopped at the first of three metal doors. There was a small pane of thick glass set into it at eye-level, and what looked like a microphone grill under that. Parst spoke into the grill: "Open up Three, sergeant."

"Yes, sir."

I followed Parst to the second door. It slid open as we reached it and we walked into a large, empty room. The door closed behind us with a thud and a solid *click*. Both sounds rattled back startlingly; the room was solid metal, I realized—floor, walls and ceiling.

In the opposite wall was another heavy door. To my left was a huge metal hemisphere, painted the same gray as the walls, with a machine gun's snout projecting through a horizontal slit in a deadly and impressive manner.

Echoes blurred the general's voice: "This is Section One. We're rather proud of it. The only entrance to the central room is here, but each of the three others that adjoin it is covered from a gun turret like that one. The gun rooms are accessible only from the corridors outside."

He motioned me over to the other door. "This door is double," he said. "It's going to be an airlock eventually, we hope. All right, sergeant."

The door slid back, exposing another one a yard farther in; like the others, it had a thick inset panel of glass.

Parst stepped in and waited for me. "Get ready for a shock," he said.

I loosened the muscles in my back and shoulders; my wind isn't what it used to be, but I can still hit. *Get ready for one yourself,* I thought, *if this is what I think it is.*

I walked into the tiny room, and heard the door thump behind me. Parst motioned to the glass pane.

I saw a room the size of the one behind me. There was a washbasin in it, and a toilet, and what looked like a hammock slung across one corner, and a wooden table with papers and a couple of pencils or crayons on it.

And against the far wall, propped upright on an ordinary lunch-counter stool, was something I couldn't recognize at all; I saw it and I didn't see it. If I had looked away then, I couldn't possibly have told anyone what it looked like.

Then it stirred slightly, and I realized that it was alive.

I saw that it had eyes.

I saw that it had arms.

I saw that it had legs.

Very gradually the rest of it came into focus. The top was about four feet off the floor, a small truncated cone about the size and shape of one of those cones of string that some merchants keep to tie packages. Under that came the eyes, three of them. They were round and oyster-gray, with round black pupils, and they faced in different directions. They were set into a flattened bulb of flesh that just fitted under the base of the cone; there was no nose, no ears, no mouth, and no room for any.

The cone was black; the rest of the thing was a very dark, shiny blue-gray.

The head, if that is the word, was supported by a thin neck from which a sparse growth of fuzzy spines curved down and outward, like a botched attempt at feathers. The neck thickened gradually until it became the torso. The torso was shaped something like a bottle gourd, except that the upper lobe was almost as large as the lower. The upper lobe expanded and contracted evenly, all around, as the thing breathed.

Between each arm and the next, the torso curved inward to form a deep vertical gash.

There were three arms and three legs, spaced evenly around the body so that you couldn't tell front from back. The arms sprouted just below the top of the torso, the legs from its base. The legs were bent only slightly to reach the floor; each hand, with five slender, shapeless fingers, rested on the opposite-number thigh. The feet were a little like a chicken's . . .

I turned away and saw Parst; I had forgotten he was there, and where I was, and who I was. I don't recall planning to say anything, but I heard my own voice, faint and hoarse:

"Did you *make* that?"

II

"Stop it!" he said sharply.

I was trembling. I had fallen into a crouch without realizing it, weight on my toes, fists clenched.

I straightened up slowly and put my hands into my pockets. "Sorry."

The speaker rasped.

"Is everything all right, sir?"

"Yes, sergeant," said Parst. "We're coming out." He turned as the door opened, and I followed him, feeling all churned up inside.

Halfway down the corridor I stopped. Parst turned and looked at me.

"Ithaca," I said.

Three months back there had been a Monster-from-Mars scare in and around Ithaca, New York; several hundred people had seen, or claimed to have seen, a white wingless aircraft hovering over various out-of-the-way places; and over thirty, including one very respectable Cornell professor, had caught sight of something that wasn't a man in the woods around Cayuga Lake. None of these people had got close enough for a good look, but nearly all of them agreed on one point—the thing walked erect, but had too many arms and legs. . . .

"Yes," said Parst. "That's right. But let's talk about it in my office, Mr. Dahl."

I followed him back there. As soon as the door was shut I said, "Where did it come from? Are there any more of them? What about the ship?"

He offered me a cigarette. I took it and sat down, hitting the chair by luck.

"Those are just three of the questions we can't answer," he said. "He claims that his home world revolves around a sun in our constellation of Aquarius; he says that it isn't visible from Earth. He also—"

I said, "He talks—? You've taught him to speak English?" For some reason that was hard to accept; then I remembered the linguists.

"Yes. Quite well, considering that he doesn't have vocal cords like ours. He uses a tympanum under each of those vertical openings in his body—those are his mouths. His name is Aza-Kra, by the way. I was going to say that he also claims to have come here alone. As for the ship, he says it's hidden, but he won't tell us where. We've been searching that area, particularly the hills near Cayuga and the lake itself, but we haven't turned it up yet. It's been suggested that he may have launched it under remote control and put it into an orbit somewhere outside the atmosphere. The Lunar Observatory is watching for it, and so are the orbital stations, but I'm inclined to think that's a dead end. In any case, that's not my responsibility. He had some gadgets in his possession when he was captured, but even those are being studied elsewhere. Chillicothe is what you saw a few minutes ago, and that's all it is. God knows it's enough."

His intercom buzzed. "Yes."

"Dr. Meshevski would like to talk to you about the technical vocabularies, sir."

"Ask him to hold it until the conference if he possibly can."

"Yes, sir."

"Two more questions we can't answer," Parst said, "are what his civilization is like and what he came here to do. I'll tell you what he says. The planet he comes from belongs to a galactic union of highly advanced, peace-loving races. He came here to help us prepare ourselves for membership in that union."

I was trying hard to keep up, but it wasn't easy. After a moment I said, "Suppose it's true?"

He gave me the cold eye.

"All right, suppose it's true." For the first time, his voice was impatient. "Then suppose the opposite. Think about it for a minute."

I saw where he was leading me, but I tried to circle around to it from another direction; I wanted to reason it out for myself. I couldn't make the grade; I had to fall back on analogies, which are a kind of thinking I distrust.

You were a cannibal islander, and a missionary came along. He meant well, but you thought he wanted to steal your yamfields and your wives, so you chopped him up and ate him for dinner.

Or:

You were a West Indian, and Columbus came along. You treated him as a guest, but he made a slave of you, worked you till you dropped, and finally wiped out your whole nation, to the last woman and child.

I said, "A while ago you mentioned three or four years as the possible term of the project. Did you—?"

"That wasn't meant to be taken literally," he said. "It may take a lifetime." He was staring at his desktop.

"In other words, if nothing stops you, you're going to go right on just this way, sitting on this thing. Until What's-his-name dies, or his friends show up with an army, or something else blows it wide open."

"That's right."

"Well, damn it, don't you see that's the one thing you can't do? Either way you guess it, that won't work. If he's friendly—"

Parst lifted a pencil in his hand and slapped it palm down against the desktop. His mouth was tight. "It's *necessary*," he said.

After a silent moment he straightened in his chair and spread the fingers of his right hand at me. "One," he said, touching the thumb: "weapons. Leaving everything else aside, if we can get one strategically superior weapon out of him, or the theory that will enable us to build one, then we've *got* to do it and we've *got* to do it in secret."

The index finger. "Two: the spaceship." Middle finger. "Three: the civilization he comes from. If they're planning to attack us we've got to find that out, and when, and how, and what we can do about it." Ring finger. "Four: Aza-Kra himself. If we don't hold him in secret we can't hold him at all, and how do we know what he might do if we let him go? There isn't a single possibility we can rule out. Not one."

He put the hand flat on the desk. "Five, six, seven, eight, nine, ten, infinity. Biology, psychology, sociology, ecology, chemistry, physics, right down the line. Every science. In any one of them we might find something that would mean the difference between life and death for this country or this whole planet."

He stared at me for a moment, his face set. "You don't have to remind me of the other possibilities, Dahl. I know what they are; I've been on this project for thirteen weeks. I've also heard of the Golden Rule, and the Ten Commandments, and the Constitution of the United States. But this is *the survival of the human race* we're talking about."

I opened my mouth to say "That's just the point," or something equally stale, but I shut it again; I saw it was no good. I had one argument—that if this alien ambassador was what he claimed to be, then the whole world had to know about it; any nation that tried to suppress that knowledge, or dictate the whole planet's future, was committing a crime against humanity. That, on the other hand, if he was an advance agent for an invasion fleet, the same thing was true only a great deal more so.

Beyond that I had nothing but instinctive moral conviction; and Parst had that on his side too; so did Frisbee and the president and all the rest. Being who and what they were, they had to believe as they did. Maybe they were right.

Half an hour later, the last thought I had before my head hit the pillow was, *Suppose there isn't any Aza-Kra? Suppose that thing was a fake, a mechanical dummy?*

But I knew better, and I slept soundly.

That was the second day. On the third day, the front pages of the more excitable newspapers were top heavy with forty-eight-point headlines. There were two Chicago stories. The first, in the early afternoon editions, announced that every epidemic victim had made a complete recovery, that health department experts had been unable to isolate any disease-causing agent in the stock awaiting slaughter, and that although several cases not involving stockyard employees had been reported, not one had been traced to consumption of infected meat. A Chicago epidemiologist was quoted as saying, "It could have been just a gigantic coincidence."

The later story was a lulu. Although the slaughterhouses had not been officially reopened or the ban on fresh-meat sales rescinded, health officials allowed seventy of the previous day's victims to return to work as an experiment. Within half an hour every one of them was back in the hospital, suffering from a second, identical attack.

Oddly enough—at first glance—sales of fresh meat in areas outside the ban dropped slightly in the early part of the day ("They *say* it's all right, but you won't catch me taking a chance"), rose sharply in the evening ("I'd better stock up before there's a run on the butcher shops").

Warden Longo, in an unprecedented move, added his resignation to those of the fifty-seven "conscience" employees of Leavenworth. Well known as an advocate of prison reform, Longo explained that his subordinates' example had convinced him that only so dramatic a gesture could focus the American public's attention upon the injustice and inhumanity of the present system.

He was joined by two hundred and three of the federal institution's remaining employees, bringing the total to more than eighty percent of Leavenworth's permanent staff.

The movement was spreading. In Terre Haute, Indiana eighty employees of the federal penitentiary were reported to have resigned. Similar reports came from the State prisons of Iowa, Missouri, Illinois and Indiana, and from city and county correctional institutions from Kansas City to Cincinnati.

The war in Indochina was crowded back among the stockmarket reports. Even the official announcements that the first Mars rocket was nearing completion in its sublunar orbit—front-page news at any normal time—got an inconspicuous paragraph in some papers and was dropped entirely by others.

But I found an item in a St. Louis paper about the police

man who had collapsed after shooting a criminal. He was dead.

I woke up a little before dawn that morning, having had a solid fifteen hours' sleep. I found the cafeteria and hung around until it opened. That was where Captain Ritchy-loo tracked me down.

He came in as I was finishing my second order of ham and eggs, a big, blond, swimming-star type, full of confidence and good cheer. "You must be Mr. Dahl. My name is Ritchy-loo."

I let him pump my hand and watched him sit down. "How do you spell it?" I asked him.

He grinned happily. "It is a tough one, isn't it? French. R, i, c, h, e, l, i, e, u."

Richelieu. Ritchy-loo.

I said, "What can I do for you, captain?"

"Ah, it's what I can do for *you*, Mr. Dahl. You're a VIP around here, you know. You're getting the triple-A guided tour, and I'm your guide."

I *hate* people who are cheerful in the morning.

We went out into the pale glitter of early-morning sunshine on the flat; the floodlight poles and the pillboxes trailed long, mournful shadows. There was a jeep waiting, and Ritchy-loo took the wheel himself.

We made a right turn around the corner of the building and then headed down one of the diagonal avenues between the poles. I glanced into the firing slit of one of the pillboxes as we passed it, and saw the gleam of somebody's spectacles.

"That was B building that we just came out of," said the captain. "Most of the interesting stuff is there, but you want to see everything, naturally, so we'll go over to C first and then back to A."

The huge barracks, far off to the right, looked deserted; I saw a few men in fatigues here and there, spearing stray bits of paper. Beyond the building we were heading for, almost against the wall, tiny figures were leaping rhythmically, opening and closing like so many animated scissors.

It was a well-policed area, at any rate; I watched for a while, out of curiosity, and didn't see a single cigarette paper or gum wrapper.

To the left of the barracks and behind it was a miniature town—neat one-storey cottages, all alike, all the same distance apart. The thing that struck me about it was that there were none of the signs of a permanent camp——no borders of whitewashed stones, no trees, no shrubs, no flowers. No *wives,* I thought.

"How's morale here, captain?" I asked.

"Now, it's funny you should ask me that. That happens to be my job, I'm the Company B morale officer. Well, I should say that all things considered, we aren't doing too badly. Of course, we have a few difficulties. These men are here on eighteen-month assignments, and that's a kind of a long time without passes or furloughs. We'd like to make the hitches shorter, naturally, but of course you understand that there aren't too many fresh but seasoned troops available just now."

"No."

"*But,* we do our best. Now here's C building."

Most of C building turned out to be occupied by chemical laboratories: long rows of benches covered by rank growths of glassware, only about a fifth of it working, and nobody watching more than a quarter of that.

"What are they doing here?"

"Over my head," said Ritchy-loo cheerfully. "Here's Dr. Vitale, let's ask him."

Vitale was a little sharp-featured man with a nervous blink. "This is the atmosphere section," he said. "We're trying to analyze the atmosphere which the alien breathes. Eventually we hope to manufacture it."

That was a point that hadn't occurred to me. "He can't breathe our air?"

"No, no. Altogether different."

"Well, where does he get the stuff he does breathe, then?"

The little man's lips worked. "From that cone-shaped mechanism on the top of his head. An atmosphere plant that you could put in your pocket. Completely incredible. We can't get an adequate sample without taking it off him, and we can't take it off him without killing him. We have to deduce what he breathes in from what he breathes *out.* *Very* difficult." He went away.

All the same, I couldn't see much point in it. Presumably if Aza-Kra couldn't breathe our air, we couldn't breathe his——so anybody who wanted to examine him would have to wear an oxygen tank and a breathing mask.

But it was obvious enough, and I got it in another minute. If the prisoner didn't have his own air supply, it would be that much harder for him to break out past the gun rooms and the guards in the corridors and the pillboxes and the floodlights and the wall. . . .

We went on, stopping at every door. There were store-rooms, sleeping quarters, a few offices. The rest of the rooms were empty.

Ritchy-loo wanted to go on to A building, but I was being perversely thorough, and I said we would go through the barracks and the company towns first. We did; it took us three hours, and thinned down Ritchy-loo's stream of cheerful conversation to a trickle. We looked everywhere, and of course we did not find anything that shouldn't have been there.

A building was the recreation hall. Canteen, library, gymnasium, movie theater, PX, swimming pool. It was also the project hospital and dispensary. Both sections were well filled.

So we went back to B. And it was almost noon, so we had lunch in the big air-conditioned cafeteria. I didn't look forward to it; I expected that rest and food would turn on Ritchy-loo's conversational spigot again, and if he didn't get any response to the first three or four general topics he tried, I was perfectly sure he would begin telling me jokes. Nothing of the kind happened. After a few minutes I saw why, or thought I did. Looking around the room, I saw face after face with the same blank look on it; there wasn't a smile or an animated expression in the place. And now that I was paying attention I noticed that the sounds were odd, too. There were more than a hundred people in the room, enough to set up a beehive roar, but there was so little talking going on that you could pick out individual sentences with ease, and they were all trochaic—Want some *sugar? No,* thanks. Like that.

It was infectious; I was beginning to feel it now myself —an execution-chamber kind of mood, a feeling that we were all shut up in a place that we couldn't get out of, and where something horrible was going to happen. Unless you've ever been in a group made up of people who had that feeling and were reinforcing it in each other, it's indescribable; but it was very real and very hard to take.

Ritchy-loo left half a chop on his plate; I finished mine, but it choked me.

In the corridor outside I asked him, "Is it always as bad as that?"

"You noticed it too? That place gives me the creeps, I don't know why. It's the same way in the movies, too, lately—wherever you get a lot of these people together. I just don't understand it." For a second longer he looked worried and thoughtful, and then he grinned suddenly. "I don't want to say anything against civilians, Mr. Dahl, but I think that bunch is pretty far gone."

I could have hugged him. Civilians! If Ritchy-loo was more than six months away from a summer-camp counselor's job, I was a five-star general.

We started at that end of the corridor and worked our way down. We looked into a room with an X-ray machine and a fluoroscope in it, and a darkroom, and a room full of racks and filing cabinets, and a long row of offices.

Then, Ritchy-loo opened a door that revealed two men standing on opposite sides of a desk, spouting angry German at each other. The tall one noticed us after a second, said, " 'St, 'st," to the other, and then to us, coldly, "You might, at least, knock."

"Sorry, gentlemen," said Ritchy-loo brightly. He closed the door and went on to the next on the same side. This opened into a small, bare room with nobody in it but a stocky man with corporal's stripes on his sleeve. He was sitting hunched over, elbows on knees, hands over his face. He didn't move or look up.

I have a good ear, and I had managed to catch one sentence of what the fat man next door had been saying to the tall one. It went like this: *Nein, nein, das ist bestimmt nicht die Klaustrophobie; Ich sage dir, es ist das dreifüssige Tier, das sie störrt.*

My college German came back to me when I prodded it, but it creaked a little. While I was still working at it, I asked Ritchy-loo, "What was that?"

"Psychiatric section," he said.

"You get many psycho cases here?"

"Oh, no," he said. "Just the normal percentage, Mr. Dahl. Less, in fact."

The captain was a poor liar.

"Klaustrophobie" was easy, of course. *"Dreifüssige Tier"* stopped me until I remembered that the German for "zoo" is *"Tiergarten." Dreifüssige Tier:* the three-footed beast. The triped.

The fat one had been saying to the tall one, "No, no, it

is absolutely not claustrophobia; I tell you, it's the triped that's disturbing them."

Three-quarters of an hour later we had peered into the last room in B building: a long office full of IBM machines. We had now been over every square yard of Chillicothe, and I had seen for myself that no skulduggery was going forward anywhere in it. That was the idea behind the guided tour, as Ritchy-loo was evidently aware.

He said, "Well, that just about wraps it up, Mr. Dahl. By the way, the general's office asked me to tell you that if it's all right with you, they'll set up that phone call for you for four o'clock this afternoon."

I looked down at the rough map of the building I'd been drawing as we went along. "There's one place we haven't been, captain," I said. "Section One."

"Oh, well that's right, that's right. You saw that yesterday, though, didn't you, Mr. Dahl?"

"For about two minutes. I wasn't able to take much of it in. I'd like to see it again, if it isn't too much trouble. Or even if it is."

Ritchy-loo laughed heartily. "Good enough. Just wait a second, I'll see if I can get you a clearance on it." He walked down the corridor to the nearest wall phone.

After a few moments he beckoned me over, palming the receiver. "The general says there are two research groups in there now and it would be a little crowded. He says he'd like you to postpone it if you think you can."

"Tell him that's perfectly all right, but in that case I think we'd better put off the phone call, too."

He repeated the message, and waited. Finally, "Yes. Yes, uh-huh. Yes, I've got that. All right."

He turned to me. "The general says it's all right for you to go in for half an hour and watch, but he'd appreciate it if you'll be careful not to distract the people who're working in there."

I had been hoping the general would say no. I wanted to see the alien again, all right, but what I wanted the most was time.

This was the second day I had been at Chillicothe. By tomorrow at the latest I would have to talk to Eli Freeman; and I still hadn't figured out any sure, safe way to tell him that Chillicothe was a legitimate research project, not to be sniped at by the *Herald-Star*—and make him understand that I didn't mean a word of it.

I could simply refuse to make the call, or I could tell him as much of the truth as I could before I was cut off —two words, probably—but it was a cinch that call would be monitored at the other end, too; that was part of what Ritchy-loo meant by "setting up the call." Somebody from the FBI would be sitting at Freeman's elbow . . . and I wasn't telling myself fairy tales about Peter Zenger anymore.

They would shut the paper down, which was not only the thing I wanted least in the world but a thing that would do nobody any good.

I wanted Eli to spread the story by underground channels—spread it so far, and time the release so well, that no amount of censorship could kill it.

Treason is a word every man has to define for himself.

Ritchy-loo did the honors for me at the gun-room door, and then left me, looking a little envious. I don't think he had ever been inside Section One.

There was somebody ahead of me in the tiny antechamber, I found: a short, wide-shouldered man with a sheep-dog tangle of black hair.

He turned as the door closed behind me. "Hi. Oh— you're Dahl, aren't you?" He had a young, pleasant, meaningless face behind dark-rimmed glasses. I said yes.

He put a half inch of cigarette between his lips and shook hands with me. "Somebody pointed you out. Glad to know you; my name's Donnelly. Physical psych section—very junior." He pointed through the spy-window. "What do you think of him?"

Aza-Kra was sitting directly in front of the window; his lunch-counter stool had been moved into the center of the room. Around him were four men: two on the left, sitting on folding chairs, talking to him and occasionally making notes; two on the right, standing beside a waist-high enclosed mechanism from which wires led to the upper lobe of the alien's body. The ends of the wires were taped against his skin.

"That isn't an easy question," I said.

Donnelly nodded without interest. "That's my boss there," he said, "the skinny, gray-haired guy on the right. We get on each other's nerves. If he gets that setup operating this session, I'm supposed to go in and take notes. He won't, though."

"What is it?"

"Electroencephalograph. See, his brain isn't in his head, it's in his upper thorax there. Too much insulation in the way. We can't get close enough for a good reading without surgery. I say we ought to drop it till we get permission, but Hendricks thinks he can lick it. Those two on the other side are interviewers. Like to hear what they're saying?"

He punched one of two buttons set into the door beside the speaker grill, under the spy-window. "If you're ever in here alone, remember you can't get out while this is on. You turn on the speaker here, it turns off the one in the gun room. They wouldn't be able to hear you ask to get out."

Inside, a monotonous voice was saying, ". . . have that here, but what exactly do you mean by . . ."

"I ought to be in physiology," Donnelly said, lowering his voice. "They have all the fun. You see his eyes?"

I looked. The center one was staring directly toward us; the other two were tilted, almost out of sight around the curve of that bulb of blue-gray flesh.

". . . in other words, just what is the nature of this energy, is it—uh—transmitted by waves, or . . ."

"He can look three ways at once," I said.

"Three, with binocular," Donnelly agreed. "Each eye can function independently or couple with the one on either side. So he can have a series of overlapping monocular images, all the way around, or he can have up to three binocular images. They focus independently, too. He could read a newspaper and watch for his wife to come out of the movie across the street."

"Wait a minute." I said. "He has *six* eyes, not three?"

"Sure. Has to, to keep the symmetry and still get binocular vision."

"Then he hasn't got any front or back," I said slowly.

"No, that's right. He's trilaterally symmetrical. Drive you crazy to watch him walk. His legs work the same way as his eyes—any one can pair up with either of the others. He wants to change direction, he doesn't have to turn around. I'd hate to try to catch him in an open field."

"How did they catch him?" I asked.

"Luckiest thing in the world. Found him in the woods with two broken ankles. Now look at his hands. What do you see?"

The voice inside was still droning; evidently it was a long question. "Five fingers," I said.

"Nope." Donnelly grinned. "One finger, four thumbs. See how they appose, those two on either side of the middle finger? He's got a better hand than ours. One *hell* of an efficient design. Brain in his thorax where it's safe, six eyes on a stalk—trachea up there too, no connection with the esophagus, so he doesn't need an epiglottis. Three of everything else. He can lose a leg and still walk, lose an arm and still type, lose two eyes and still see better than we do. He can lose—"

I didn't hear him. The interviewer's voice had stopped, and Aza-Kra's had begun. It was frightening, because it was a buzzing and it was a voice.

I couldn't take in a word of it; I had enough to do absorbing the fact that there were words.

Then it stopped, and the interviewer's ordinary, flat middle western voice began again.

"—And just try to sneak up behind him," said Donnelly. "I dare you."

Again Aza-Kra spoke briefly, and this time I saw the flesh at the side of his body, where the two lobes flowed together, bulge slightly and then relax.

"He's talking with one of his mouths," I said. "I mean, one of those—" I took a deep breath. "If he breathes through the top of his head, and there's no connection between his lungs and his vocal organs, then where the hell does he get the air?"

"He belches. Not as inconvenient as it sounds. You could learn to do it if you had to." Donnelly laughed. "Not very fragrant, though. Watch their faces when he talks."

I watched Aza-Kra's instead—what there was of it: one round, expressionless, oyster-colored eye staring back at me. With a human opponent, I was thinking, there were a thousand little things that you relied on to help you: facial expressions, mannerisms, signs of emotion. But Parst had been right when he said, *There isn't a single possibility we can rule out. Not one.* And so had the fat man: *It's the triped that's disturbing them.* And Ritchy-loo: *It's the same way . . . wherever you get a lot of these people together.*

And I still hadn't figured out any way to tell Freeman what he had to know.

I thought I could arouse Eli's suspicion easily enough; we knew each other well enough for a word or a gesture to mean a good deal, I could make him look for hidden meanings. But how could I hide a message so that Eli would be more likely to dig it out than a trained FBI cryptologist?

I stared at Aza-Kra's glassy eye as if the answer were there. It was going to be a video circuit, I told myself. Donnelly was still yattering in my ear, and now the alien was buzzing again, but I ignored them both. Suppose I broke the message up into one-word units, scattered them through my converastion with Eli, and marked them off somehow—by twitching a finger, or blinking my eyelids?

A dark membrane flicked across the alien's oyster-colored eye.

A moment later, it happened again.

Donnelly was saying, ". . . intercostal membranes, apparently. But there's no trace of . . ."

"Shut up a minute, will you?" I said. "I want to hear this."

The inhuman voice, the voice that sounded like the articulate buzzing of a giant insect, was saying, "Comparison not possible, excuse me. If *(blink)* you try to understand in words you know, you *(blink)* tell yourself you wish *(blink)* to understand, but knowledge escape *(blink)* you. Can only show *(blink)* you from beginning, one *(blink)* little, another little. Not possible to carry all knowledge in one hand *(blink)*."

If you wish escape, show one hand.

I looked at Donnelly. He had moved back from the spy-window; he was lighting a cigarette, frowning at the matchflame. His mouth was sullen.

I put my left hand flat against the window. I thought, *I'm dreaming.*

The interviewer said querulously, ". . . getting us nowhere. Can't you—"

"Wait," said the buzzing voice. "Let me say, please. Ignorant man hold *(blink)* burning stick, say, this is breath *(blink)* of the wood. Then you show him flashlight—"

I took a deep breath, and held it.

Around the alien, four men went down together, folding over quietly at waist and knee, sprawling on the floor. I heard a thump behind me.

Donnelly was lying stretched out along the wall, his head tilted against the corner. The cigarette had fallen from his hand.

I looked back at Aza-Kra. His head turned slightly, the dark flesh crinkling. Two eyes stared back at me through the window.

"Now you can breathe," said the monster.

III

I let out the breath that was choking me and took another. My knees were shaking.

"What did you do to them?"

"Put them to sleep only. In a few minutes I will put the others to sleep. After you are outside the doors. First we will talk."

I glanced at Donnelly again. His mouth was ajar; I could see his lips fluttering as he breathed.

"All right," I said, "talk."

"When you leave," buzzed the voice, "you must take me with you."

Now it was clear. He could put people to sleep, but he couldn't open locked doors. He had to have help.

"No deal," I said. "You might as well knock me out, too."

"Yes," he answered, "you will do it. When you understand."

"I'm listening."

"You do not have to agree now. I ask only this much. When we are finished talking, you leave. When you are past the second door, hold your breath again. Then go to the office of General Parst. You will find there papers about me. Read them. You will find also keys to open gun room. Also, handcuffs. Special handcuffs, made to fit me. Then you will think, if Aza-Kra is not what he says, would he agree to this? Then you will come back to gun room, use controls there to open middle door. You will lay handcuffs down, where you stand now, then go back to gun room, open inside door. I will put on the handcuffs. You will see that I do it. And then you will take me with you."

. . . I said, "Let me think."

The obvious thing to do was to push the little button that turned on the audio circuit to the gun room, and yell for help; the alien could then put everybody to sleep from here to the wall, maybe, but it wouldn't do any good. Sooner or later he would have to let up, or starve to death along with the rest of us. On the other hand if I did what he asked—*anything* he asked—and it turned out to be the wrong thing, I would be guilty of the worst crime since Pilate's.

But I thought about it, I went over it again and again, and I couldn't see any loophole in it for Aza-Kra. He was leaving it up to me—if I felt like letting him out after I'd seen the papers in Parst's office, I could do so. If I didn't, I could still yell for help. In fact, I could get on the phone and yell to Washington, which would be a hell of a lot more to the point.

So where was the payoff for Aza-Kra? What was in those papers?

I pushed the button. I said, "This is Dahl. Let me out, will you please?"

The outer door began to slide back. Just in time, I saw Donnelly's head bobbing against it; I grabbed him by the shirtfront and hoisted his limp body out of the way.

I walked across the echoing outer chamber. The outermost door opened for me. I stepped through it and held my breath. Down the corridor, three guards leaned over their rifles and toppled all in a row, like precision divers. Beyond them a hurrying civilian in the cross-corridor fell heavily and skidded out of sight.

The clacking of typewriters from a nearby office had stopped abruptly. I let out my breath when I couldn't hold it any longer, and listened to the silence.

The general was slumped over his desk, head on his crossed forearms, looking pretty old and tired with his polished bald skull shining under the light. There was a faint silvery scar running across the top of his head, and I wondered whether he had got it in combat as a young man, or whether he had tripped over a rug at an embassy reception.

Across the desk from him a thin man in a gray pincheck suit was jackknifed on the carpet, half supported by a chair leg, rump higher than his head.

There were two six-foot filing cabinets in the right-hand corner behind the desk. Both were locked; the drawers of the first one were labeled alphabetically, the other was unmarked.

I unhooked Parst's key chain from his belt. He had as many keys as a janitor or a high-school principal, but not many of them were small enough to fit the filing cabinets.

I got the second one unlocked and began going through the drawers. I found what I wanted in the top one—seven fat manila folders labeled "Aza-Kra—Armor," "Aza-Kra—General information," "Aza-Kra—Power sources," "Aza-Kra—Spaceflight" and so on; and one more labeled "Directives and related correspondence."

I hauled them all out, piled them on Parst's desk and pulled up a chair.

I took "Armor" first because it was on top and because the title puzzled me. The folder was full of transcripts of interviews whose subject I had to work out as I went along. It appeared that when captured, Aza-Kra had been wearing a lightweight bulletproof body armor, made of something that was longitudinally flexible and perpendicularly rigid—in other words, you could pull it on like a suit of winter underwear, but you couldn't dent it with a sledgehammer.

They had been trying to find out what the stuff was and how it was made for almost two months and as far as I could see they had not made a nickel's worth of progress.

I looked through "Power sources" and "Spaceflight" to see if they were the same, and they were. The odd part was that Aza-Kra's answers didn't sound reluctant or evasive; but he kept running into ideas for which there weren't any words in English and then they would have to start all over again, like Twenty Questions. . . . Is it animal? vegetable? mineral? It was a mess.

I put them all aside except "General information" and "Directives." The first, as I had guessed, was a catchall for nontechnical subjects—where Aza-Kra had come from, what his people were like, his reasons for coming to this planet: all the unimportant questions; or the only questions that had any importance, depending on how you looked at it.

Parst had already given me an accurate summary of it, but it was surprisingly effective in Aza-Kra's words. *You say we want your planet. There are many planets, so many you would not believe. But if we wanted your planet, and if we could kill as you do, please understand, we are very many. We would fall on your planet like snowflakes. We would not send one man alone.*

And later: *Most young peoples kill. It is a law of nature, yes, but try to understand, it is not the only law. You have been a young people, but now you are growing older. Now*

*you must learn the other law, not to kill. That is what I
have come to teach. Until you learn this, we cannot have
you among us.*

There was nothing in the folder dated later than a
month and a half ago. They had dropped that line of questioning early.

The first thing I saw in the other folder began like this:
*You are hereby directed to hold yourself in readiness to
destroy the subject under any of the following circumstances, without further specific notification:*

1, a: If the subject attempts to escape.

1, b: If the subject kills or injures a human being.

*1, c: If the landing, anywhere in the world, of other
members of the subject's race is reported and their similarity
to the subject established beyond a reasonable doubt. . . .*

Seeing it written down like that, in the cold dead-
aliveness of black words on white paper, it was easy to
forget that the alien was a stomach-turning monstrosity,
and to see only that what he had to say was lucid and no-
ble.

But I still hadn't found anything that would persuade
me to help him escape. The problem was still there, as in-
soluble as ever. There was no way of evaluating a word
the alien said about himself. He had come alone—perhaps
—instead of bringing an invading army with him; but how
did we know that one member of his race wasn't as
dangerous to us as Perry's battleship to the Japanese? He
might be; there was some evidence that he was.

My quarrel with the Defense Department was not that
they were mistreating an innocent three-legged missionary,
but simply that the problem of Aza-Kra belonged to the
world, not to a fragment of the executive branch of the
government of the United States—and certainly not to me.

. . . There was one other way out, I realized. Instead of
calling Frisbee in Washington, I could call an arm-long list
of senators and representatives. I could call the UN
secretariat in New York; I could call the editor of every
major newspaper in this hemisphere and the head of every
wire service and broadcasting chain. I could stir up a
hornet's nest, even, as the saying goes, if I swung for it.

Wrong again: I couldn't. I opened the "Directives"
folder again, looking for what I thought I had seen there in
the list of hypothetical circumstances. There it was:

1, f: If any concerted attempt on the part of any person or group to remove the subject from Defense Department custody, or to aid him in any way is made; or if the subject's existence and presence in Defense Department custody becomes public knowledge.

That sewed it up tight, and it also answered my question about Aza-Kra. Knocking out the personnel of B building would be construed as an attempt to escape or as a concerted attempt by a person or group to remove the subject from Defense Department custody, it didn't matter which. If I broke the story, it would have the same result. They would kill him.

In effect, he had put his life in my hands: and that was why he was so sure that I'd help him.

It might have been that, or what I found just before I left the office, that decided me. I don't know; I wish I did.

Coming around the desk the other way, I glanced at the thin man on the floor and noticed that there was something under him, half hidden by his body. It turned out to be two things: a gray fedora and a pint-sized gray-leather briefcase, chained to his wrist.

So I looked under Parst's folded arms, saw the edge of a thick white sheet of paper, and pulled it out.

Under Frisbee's letterhead, it said:

By courier.

Dear General Parst:

Some possibility appears to exist that A.K. is responsible for recent disturbances in your area; please give me your thought on this as soon as possible—the decision can't be long postponed.

In the meantime you will of course consider your command under emergency status, and we count on you to use your initiative to safeguard security at all costs. In a crisis, you will consider Lieut. D. as expendable.

Sincerely yours,

CARLTON FRISBEE

cf/cf/enc.

"Enc." meant "enclosure"; I pried up Parst's arms again

and found another sheet of stiff paper, folded three times, with a paperclip on it.

It was a first lieutenant's commission, made out to Robert James Dahl, dated three days before, and with a perfect forgery of my signature at the bottom of it.

If commissions can be forged, so can court-martial records.

I put the commission and the letter in my pocket. I didn't seem to feel any particular emotion, but I noticed that my hands were shaking as I sorted through the "General information" file, picked out a few sheets and stuffed them into my pocket with the other papers. I wasn't confused or in doubt about what to do next. I looked around the room, spotted a metal locker diagonally across from the filing cabinets, and opened it with one of the General's keys.

Inside were two .45 automatics, boxes of ammunition, several loaded clips, and three odd-looking sets of handcuffs, very heavy, each with its key.

I took the handcuffs, the keys, both automatics and all the clips.

In a storeroom at the end of the corridor I found a two-wheeled dolly. I wheeled it all the way around to Section One and left it outside the center door. Then it struck me that I was still wearing the pinks they had given me when I arrived, and where the hell were my own clothes? I took a chance and went up to my room on the second floor, remembering that I hadn't been back there since morning.

There they were, neatly laid out on the bed. My keys, lighter, change, wallet and so on were on the bedside table. I changed and went back down to Section One.

In the gun room were two sprawled shapes, one beside the machine gun that poked its snout through the hemispherical blister, the other under a panel set with three switches and a microphone.

The switches were clearly marked. I opened the first two, walked out and around and laid the three sets of handcuffs on the floor in the middle room. Then I went back to the gun room, closed the first two doors and opened the third.

Soft thumping sounds came from the loudspeaker over the switch panel; then the rattling of metal, more thumps, and finally a series of rattling clicks.

I opened the first door and went back inside. Through the panel in the middle door I could see Aza-Kra; he had retreated into the inner room so that all of him was plainly visible. He was squatting on the floor, his legs drawn up. His arms were at full stretch, each wrist manacled to an ankle. He strained his arms outward to show me that the cuffs were tight.

I made one more trip to open the middle door. Then I got the dolly and wheeled it in.

"Thank you," said Aza-Kra. I got a whiff of his "breath"; as Donnelly had intimated, it wasn't pleasant.

Halfway to the airport, at Aza-Kra's request, I held my breath again. Aside from that we didn't speak except when I asked him, as I was loading him from the jeep into a limousine, "How long will they stay unconscious?"

"Not more than twenty hours, I think. I could have given them more, but I did not dare, I do not know your chemistry well enough."

We could go a long way in twenty hours. We would certainly have to.

I hated to go home, it was too obvious and there was a good chance that the hunt would start before any twenty hours were up, but there wasn't any help for it. I had a passport and a visa for England, where I had been planning to go for a publishers' conference in January, but it hadn't occurred to me to take it along on a quick trip to Washington. And now I had to have the passport.

My first idea had been to head for New York and hand Aza-Kra over to the UN there, but I saw it was no good. Extraterritoriality was just a word, like a lot of other words; we wouldn't be safe until we were out of the country, and, on second thought, maybe not then.

It was a little after eight thirty when I pulled in to the curb down the street from my house. I hadn't eaten since noon, but I wasn't hungry; and it didn't occur to me until later to think about Aza-Kra.

I got the passport and some money without waking my housekeeper. A few blocks away I parked again on a side street. I called the airport, got a reservation on the next eastbound flight, and spent half an hour buying a trunk big enough for Aza-Kra and wrestling him into it.

It struck me at the last minute that perhaps I had been counting too much on that atmosphere plant of his. Hi air supply was taken care of, but what about his respiratory waste products—would he poison himself in that tiny closed space? I asked him, and he said, "No, it is all right. I will be warm, but I can bear it."

I put the lid down, then opened it again. "I forgot about food," I said. "What do you eat, anyway?"

"At Chillicothe I ate soya bean extract. With added minerals. But I am able to go without food for long periods. Please, do not worry."

All right. I put the lid down again and locked the trunk, but I didn't stop worrying.

He was being too accommodating.

I had expected him to ask me to turn him loose, or take him to wherever his spaceship was. He hadn't brought the subject up; he hadn't asked me where we were going, or what my plans were.

I thought I knew the answer to that, but it didn't make me any happier. He didn't ask because he already knew—just as he'd known the contents of Parst's office, down to the last document; just as he'd known what I was thinking when I was in the anteroom with Donnelly.

He read minds. And he gassed people through solid metal walls.

What else did he do?

There wasn't time to dispose of the limousine; I simply left it at the airport. If the alarm went out before we got to the coast, we were sunk anyhow; if not, it wouldn't matter.

Nobody stopped us. I caught the stratojet in New York at 12:20, and five hours later we were in London.

Customs was messy, but there wasn't any other way to handle it. When we were fifth in line, I thought: *Knock them out for about an hour*—and held my breath. Nothing happened. I rapped on the side of the trunk to attract his attention, and did it again. This time it worked: everybody in sight went down like a rag doll.

I stamped my own passport, filled out a declaration form and buried it in a stack of others, put a tag on the trunk, loaded it aboard a handtruck, wheeled it outside and took a cab.

I had learned something in the process, although it certainly wasn't much: either Aza-Kra couldn't, or didn't, eavesdrop on my mind all the time—or else he was simply one step ahead of me.

Later, on the way to the harbor, I saw a newsstand and realized that it was going on three days since I had seen a paper. I had tried to get the New York dailies at the airport, but they'd been sold out—nothing on the stands but a lone copy of the Staten Island *Advance*. That hadn't struck me as odd at the time—an index of my state of mind—but it did now.

I got out and bought a copy of everything on the stand except the tipsheets—four newspapers, all of them together about equaling the bulk of one *Herald-Star*. I felt frustrated enough to ask the newsvendor if he had any papers left over from yesterday or the day before. He gave me a glassy look, made me repeat it, then pulled his face into an indescribable expression, laid a finger beside his nose, and said, " 'Arf a mo'." He scuttled into a bar a few yards down the street, was gone five minutes, and came back clutching a mare's-nest of soiled and bedraggled papers.

" 'Eere you are, guvnor. Three bob for the lot."

I paid him. "Thanks," I said, "very much."

He waved his hand expansively. "Okay, bud," he said. "T'ink nuttin' of it!"

A comedian.

The only Channel boat leaving before late afternoon turned out to be an excursion steamer—round trip, two guineas. The boat wasn't crowded; it was the tag end of the season, and a rough, windy day. I found a seat without any trouble and finished sorting out my stack of papers by date and folio.

British newspapers don't customarily report any more of our news than we do of theirs, but this week our supply of catastrophes had been ample enough to make good reading across the Atlantic. I found all three of the Chicago stories—trimmed to less than two inches apiece, but there. I read the first with professional interest, the second skeptically, and the third with alarm.

I remembered the run of odd items I'd read in that Washington hotel room, a long time ago. I remembered Frisbee's letter to Parst: *"Some possibility appears to exist that A.K. is responsible for recent disturbances in your area. . . ."*

I found two of the penitentiary stories, half smothered

by stop press, and I added them to the total. I drew an imaginary map of the United States in my head and stuck imaginary pins in it. Red ones, a little cluster: Des Moines, Kansas City, Decatur, St. Louis. Blue ones, a scattering around them: Chicago, Leavenworth, Terre Haute.

Down toward the end of the cabin someone's portable radio was muttering.

A fat youth in a checkered jacket had it. He moved over reluctantly and made room for me to sit down. The crisp, controlled BBC voice was saying, ". . . in Commons today, declared that Britain's trade balance is more favorable than at any time during the past fifteen years. In London, ceremonies marking the sixth anniversary of the death . . ." I let the words slide past me until I heard:

"In the United States, the mysterious epidemic affecting stockyard workers in the central states has spread to New York and New Jersey on the eastern seaboard. The president has requested Congress to provide immediate emergency meat-rationing legislation."

A blurred little woman on the bench opposite leaned forward and said, "Serve 'em right, too! Them with their beefsteak a day."

There were murmurs of approval.

I got up and went back to my own seat. . . . It all fell into one pattern, everything: the man who kicked his wife, the prizefighters, the policeman, the wardens, the slaughterhouse "epidemic."

It was the *lex talionis*—or the Golden Rule in reverse: Be done by as you do to others.

When you injured another living thing, both of you felt the same pain. When you killed, you felt the shock of your victim's death. You might be only stunned by it, like the slaughterhouse workers, or you might die, like the policeman and the schoolboy murderer.

So-called mental anguish counted too, apparently. That explained the wave of humanitarianism in prisons, at least partially; the rest was religious hysteria and the kind of herd instinct that makes any startling new movement mushroom.

And, of course, it also explained Chillicothe: the horrible blanketing depression that settled anywhere the civilian staff congregated—the feeling of being penned up in a place where something frightful was going to happen—and the thing the two psychiatrists had been arguing about,

the pseudoclaustrophobia . . . all that was nothing but the
reflection of Aza-Kra's feelings, locked in that cell on an
alien planet.

Be done by as you do.

And I was carrying that with me. Des Moines, Kansas
City, Decatur, St. Louis, Chicago, Leavenworth, Terre
Haute—*New York*. After that, England. We'd been in London less than an hour—but England is only four hundred-
odd miles long, from John o' Groat's to Lands End.

I remembered what Aza-Kra had said: *Now you must
learn the other law, not to kill.*

Not to kill tripeds.

My body was shaking uncontrollably; my head felt like
a balloon stuffed with cotton. I stood up and looked
around at the blank faces, the inward-looking eyes, every
man, woman and child living in a little world of his own.
I had a hysterical impulse to shout at them, *Look at you,
you idiots! You've been invaded and half conquered without a shot fired, and you don't know it!*

In the next instant I realized that I was about to burst
into laughter. I put my hand over my mouth and half ran
out on deck, giggles leaking through my fingers; I got to
the rail and bent myself over it, roaring, apoplectic. I was
utterly ashamed of myself, but I couldn't stop it; it was
like a fit of vomiting.

The cold spray on my face sobered me. I leaned over
the rail, looking down at the white water boiling along the
hull. It occurred to me that there was one practical test
still to be made: a matter of confirmation.

A middle-aged man with rheumy eyes was standing in
the cabin doorway, partly blocking it. As I shouldered
past him, I deliberately put my foot down on his.

An absolutely blinding pain shot through the toes of my
right foot. When my eyes cleared I saw that the two of us
were standing in identical attitudes—weight on one foot,
the other knee bent, hand reaching instinctively for the injury.

I had taken him for a "typical Englishman," but he
cursed me in a rattling stream of gutter French. I apolo-
gized, awkwardly but sincerely—very sincerely.

When we docked at Dunkirk I still hadn't decided what
to do.

What I had had in mind up till now was simply to get

across France into Switzerland and hold a press conference there, inviting everybody from Tass to the UP. It had to be Switzerland for fairly obvious reasons; the English or the French would clamp a security lid on me before you could say NATO, but the Swiss wouldn't dare—they paid for their neutrality by having to look *both* ways before they cleared their throats.

I could still do that, and let the UN set up a committee to worry about Aza-Kra—but at a conservative estimate it would be ten months before the committee got its foot out of its mouth, and that would be pretty nearly ten months too late.

Or I could simply go to the American consulate in Dunkirk and turn myself in. Within ten hours we would be back in Chillicothe, probably, and I'd be free of the responsibility. I would also be dead.

We got through customs the same way we'd done in London. And then I had to decide.

The cab driver put his engine in gear and looked at me over his shoulder. *"Un hôtel?"*

". . . Yes," I said. "A cheap hotel. *Un hôtel à bon marché.*"

"Entendu." He jammed down the accelerator an instant before he let out the clutch; we were doing thirty before he shifted into second.

The place he took me to was a villainous third-rate commercial-travelers' hotel, smelling of urine and dirty linen. When the porters were gone I unlocked the trunk and opened it.

We stared at each other.

Moisture was beaded on his blue-gray skin, and there was a smell in the room stronger and ranker than anything that belonged there. His eyes looked duller than they had before; I could barely see the pupils.

"Well?" I said.

"You are half right," he buzzed. "I am doing it, but not for the reason you think."

"All right; you're doing it. *Stop it.* That comes first. We'll stay here, and I'll watch the papers to make sure you do."

"At the customs, those people will sleep only an hour."

"I don't give a damn. If the gendarmes come up here, you can put them to sleep. If I have to I'll move you out to the country and we'll live under a haystack. But no matter what happens we're not going a mile farther into Europe until I know you've quit. If you don't like that, you've got two choices. Either you knock me out, and see how much good it does you, or I'll take that air machine off your head."

He buzzed inarticulately for a moment. Then, "I have to say no. It is impossible. I could stop for a time, or pretend to you that I stop, but that would solve nothing. It will be—it will do the greatest harm if I stop; you don't understand. It is necessary to continue."

I said, "That's your answer?"

"Yes. If you will let me explain—"

I stepped toward him. I didn't hold my breath, but I think half consciously I expected him to gas me. He didn't. He didn't move; he just waited.

Seen at close range, the flesh of his head seemed to be continuous with the black substance of the cone; instead of any sharp dividing line, there was a thin area that was neither one nor the other.

I put one hand over the fleshy bulb, and felt his eyes retract and close against my palm. The sensation was indescribably unpleasant, but I kept my hand there, put the other one against the far side of the cone—pulled and pushed simultaneously, as hard as I could.

The top of my head came off.

I was leaning against the top of the open trunk, dizzy and nauseated. The pain was like a white-hot wire drawn tight around my skull just above the eyes. I couldn't see; I couldn't think.

And it didn't stop; it went on and on. . . . I pushed myself away from the trunk and let my legs fold under me. I sat on the floor with my head in my hands, pushing my fingers against the pain.

Gradually it ebbed. I heard Aza-Kra's voice buzzing very quietly, not in English but in a rhythm of tone and phrasing that seemed almost directly comprehensible; if there were a language designed to be spoken by bass viols, it might sound like that.

I got up and looked at him. Shining beads of blue liquid stood out all along the base of the cone, but the seam had not broken.

I hadn't realized that it would be so difficult, that it would be so painful. I felt the weight of the two automatics in my pockets, and I pulled one out, the metal cold and heavy in my palm . . . but I knew suddenly that I couldn't do that either.

I didn't know where his brain was, or his heart. I didn't know whether I could kill him with one shot.

I sat down on the bed, staring at him. "You knew that would happen, didn't you?" I said. "You must think I'm a prize sucker."

He said nothing. His eyes were half closed, and a thin whey-colored fluid was drooling out of the two mouths I could see. Aza-Kra was being sick.

I felt an answering surge of nausea. Then the flow stopped, and a second later, the nausea stopped too. I felt angry, and frustrated, and frightened.

After a moment I got up off the bed and started for the door.

"Please," said Aza-Kra. "Will you be gone long?"

"I don't know," I said. "Does it matter?"

"If you will be gone long," he said, "I would ask that you loosen the handcuffs for a short period before you go."

I stared at him, suddenly hating him with a violence that shook me.

"No," I said, and reached for the door handle.

My body knotted itself together like a fist. My legs gave way under me, and I missed the door handle going down; I hit the floor hard.

There was no sensation in my hands or feet. The muscles of my shoulders, arms, thighs, and calves were one huge, heavy pain. And I couldn't move.

I looked at Aza-Kra's wrists, shackled to his drawn-up ankles. He had been like that for something like fourteen hours. He had cramps.

"I am sorry," said Aza-Kra. "I did not want to do that to you, but there was no other way."

I thought dazedly, *No other way to do what?*

"To make you wait. To listen. To let me explain."

I said, "I don't get it." Anger flared again, then faded under something more intense and painful. The closest English word for it is "humility"; some other language may come nearer, but I doubt it; it isn't an emotion that we like to talk about. I felt bewildered, and ashamed, and very small, all at once, and there was another component, harder to name. A . . . threshold feeling.

I tried again. "I felt the other pain, before, but not this. Is that because—"

"Yes. There must be the intention to injure or cause pain. I will tell you why. I have to go back very far. When an animal becomes more developed—many cells, instead of one—always the same things happen. I am the first man of my kind who ever saw a man of your kind. But we both have eyes. We both have ears." The feathery spines on his neck stiffened and relaxed. "Also there is another sense that always comes. But always it goes only a little way and then stops.

"When you are a young animal, fighting with the others to live, it is useful to have a sense which feels the thoughts of the enemy. Just as it is useful to have a sense which sees the shape of his body. But this sense cannot come all at once, it must grow by a little and a little, as when a surface that can tell the light from the dark becomes a true eye.

"But the easiest thoughts to feel are pain thoughts, they are much stronger than any others. And when the sense is still weak—it is part of the brain, not an organ by itself—when it is weak, only the strongest stimulus can make it work. This stimulus is hatred, or anger, or the wish to kill.

"So that just when the sense is enough developed that it could begin to be useful, it always disappears. It is not gone, it is pushed under. A very long time ago, one race discovered this sense and learned how it could be brought back. It is done by a class of organic chemicals. You have not the word. For each race a different member of the class, but always it can be done. The chemical is a catalyst, it is not used up. The change it makes is in the cells of all the body—it is permanent, it passes also to the children.

"You understand, when a race is older, to kill is not useful. With the change, true civilization begins. The first race to find this knowledge gave it to others, and those to others, and now all have it. All who are able to leave their planets. We give it to you, now, because you are ready. When you are older there will be others who are ready. You will give it to them."

While I had been listening, the pain in my arms and legs had slowly been getting harder and harder to take. I reminded myself that Aza-Kra had borne it, probably, at least ten hours longer than I had; but that didn't make it much easier. I tried to keep my mind off it but that wasn't possible; the band of pain around my head was still there, too, a faint throbbing. And both were consequences of things I had done to Aza-Kra. I was suffering with him, measure for measure.

Justice. Surely that was a good thing? Automatic instant retribution, mathematically accurate: an eye for an eye.

I said, "That was what you were doing when they caught you, then—finding out which chemical we reacted to?"

"Yes. I did not finish until after they had brought me to Chillicothe. Then it was much more difficult. If not for my accident, all would have gone much more quickly."

"The walls?"

"Yes. As you have guessed, my air machine will also make other substances and expel them with great force. Also, when necessary, it will place these substances in a—state of matter, you have not the word—so that they pass through solid objects. But this takes much power. While in Chillicothe my range was very small. Later, when I can be in the open, it will be much greater."

He caught what I was thinking before I had time to speak. He said, "Yes. You will agree. When you understand."

It was the same thing he had told me at Chillicothe, almost to the word.

I said, "You keep talking about this thing as a gift but I notice you didn't ask us if we wanted it. What kind of a gift is that?"

"You are not serious. You know what happened when I was captured."

After a moment he added, "I think if it had been possible, if we could have asked each man and woman on the planet to say yes or no, explaining everything, showing that there was no trick, that most would have said yes. For people the change is good. But for governments it is not good."

I said, "I'd like to believe you. It would be very pleasant to believe you. But nothing you can say changes the fact that this thing, this gift of yours could be a weapon. To soften us up before you move in. If you were an advance agent for an invasion fleet, this is what you'd be doing."

"You are thinking with habits," he said. "Try to think with logic. Imagine that your race is very old, with much knowledge. You have ships that cross between the stars. Now you discover this young race, these Earthmen, who only begin to learn to leave their own planet. You decide to conquer them. Why? What is your reason?"

"How do I know? It could be anything. It might be something I couldn't even imagine. For all I know you want to eat us."

His throat-spines quivered. He said slowly, "You are partly serious. You really think . . . I am sorry that you did not read the studies of the physiologists. If you had, you would know. My digestion is only for vegetable food. You cannot understand, but—with us, to eat meat is like with you, to eat excretions."

I said, "All right, maybe we have something else you want. Natural resources that you've used up. Some substance, maybe some rare element."

"This is still habit thinking. Have you forgotten my air machine?"

"—Or maybe you just want the planet itself. With us cleared off it, to make room for you."

"Have you never looked at the sky at night?"

I said, "All right. But this quiz was your idea, not mine. I *admit* that I don't know enough even to make a sensible guess at your motives. And that's the reason why I can't trust you."

He was silent a moment. Then: "Remember that the substance which makes the change is a catalyst. Also it is a very fine powder. The particles are of only a few molecules each. The winds carry it. It is swallowed and breathed in and absorbed by the skin. It is breathed out and excreted. The wind takes it again. Water carries it. It is carried by insects and by birds and animals, and by men, in their bodies and in their clothing.

"This you can understand and know that it is true. If I die another could come and finish what I have begun, but even this is not necessary. The amount of the catalyst I have already released is more than enough. It will travel slowly, but nothing can stop it. If I die now, this instant, still in a year the catalyst will reach every part of the planet."

After a long time I said, "Then what did you mean by saying that a great harm would be done, if you stopped now?"

"I meant this. Until now, only your Western nations have the catalyst. In a few days their time of crisis will come, beginning with the United States. And the nations of the East will attack."

IV

I found that I could move, inchmeal, if I sweated hard enough at it. It took me what seemed like half an hour to get my hand into my pocket, paw all the stuff out onto the floor, and get the key ring hooked over one finger. Then I had to crawl about ten feet to Aza-Kra, and when I got there my fingers simply wouldn't hold the keys firmly enough.

I picked them up in my teeth and got two of the wrist-cuffs unlocked. That was the best I could do; the other one was behind him, inside the trunk, and neither of us had strength enough to pull him out where I could get at it.

It was comical. My muscles weren't cramped, but my nervous system was getting messages that said they were—so, to all intents and purposes, it was true. I had no control over it; the human body is about as skeptical as a God-smitten man at a revival meeting. If mine had thought it was burning, I would have developed simon-pure blisters.

Then the pins and needles started, as Aza-Kra began to flex his arms and legs to get the stiffness out of them. Between us, after a while, we got him out of the trunk and unlocked the third cuff. In a few minutes I had enough freedom of movement to begin massaging his cramped muscles; but it was three-quarters of an hour before either of us could stand.

We caught the midafternoon plane to Paris, with Aza-Kra in the trunk again. I checked into a hotel, left him there, and went shopping: I bought a hideous black dress with imitation-onyx trimming, a black coat with a cape, a feather muff, a tall black hat and the heaviest mourning veil I could find. At a theatrical costumer's near the Place de l'Opéra I got a reasonably lifelike old-woman mask and a heavy wig.

When he was dressed up, the effect was startling. The tall hat covered the cone, the muff covered two of his hands. There was nothing to be done about the feet, but the skirt hung almost to the ground, and I thought he would pass with luck.

We got a cab and headed for the American consulate,

but halfway there I remembered about the photographs. We stopped off at an amusement arcade and I got my picture taken in a coin-operated machine. Aza-Kra was another problem—that mask wouldn't fool anybody without the veil—but I spotted a poorly dressed old woman and with some difficulty managed to make her understand that I was a crazy American who would pay her fifty francs to pose for her picture. We struck a bargain at a hundred.

As soon as we got into the consulate waiting room, Aza-Kra gassed everybody in the building. I locked the street door and searched the offices until I found a man with a little pile of blank passport books on the desk in front of him. He had been filling one in on a machine like a typewriter except that it had a movable plane-surface platen instead of a cylinder.

I moved him out of the way and made out two passports; one for myself, as Arthur James LeRoux; one for Aza-Kra, as Mrs. Adrienne LeRoux; I pasted on the photographs and fed them into the machine that pressed the words *"Photograph attached U.S. Consulate Paris, France"* into the paper, and then into the one that impressed the consular seal.

I signed them, and filled in the blanks on the inside covers, in the taxi on the way to the Israeli consulate. The afternoon was running out, and we had a lot to do.

We went to six foreign consulates, gassed the occupants, and got a visa stamp in each one. I had the devil's own time filling them out; I had to copy the scribbles I found in legitimate passports at each place and hope for the best. The Israeli one was surprisingly simple, but the Japanese was a horror.

We had dinner in our hotel room—steak for me, water and soy-bean paste, bought at a health-food store, for Aza-Kra. Just before we left for Le Bourget, I sent a cable to Eli Freeman:

BIG STORY WILL HAVE TO WAIT SPREAD THIS NOW ALL STOCKYARD SO-CALLED EPIDEMIC AND SIMILAR PHENOMENA DUE ONE CAUSE STEP ON SOMEBODY'S TOE TO SEE WHAT I MEAN.

Shortly after seven o'clock we were aboard a flight bound for the Middle East.

And that was the fourth day, during which a number of

things happened that I didn't have time to add to my list until later.

Commercial and amateur fishermen along the Atlantic seaboard, from Delaware Bay as far north as Portland, suffered violent attacks whose symptoms resembled those of asthma. Some—who had been using rods or poles rather than nets—complained also of sharp pains in the jaws and hard palate. Three deaths were reported.

The "epidemic" now covered roughly half the continental United States. All livestock shipments from the West had been canceled, stockyards in the affected area were full to bursting. The President had declared a national emergency.

Lobster had disappeared completely from east-coast menus.

One Robert James Dahl, described as the owner and publisher of a middle-western newspaper, was being sought by the Defense Department and the FBI in connection with the disappearance of certain classified documents.

The next day, the fifth, was Saturday. At two in the morning on a Sabbath, Tel Aviv seemed as dead as Angkor. We had four hours there, between planes; we could have spent them in the airport waiting room, but I was wakeful and I wanted to talk to Aza-Kra. There was one ancient taxi at the airport; I had the driver take us into the town and leave us there, down in the harbor section, until plane time.

We sat on a bench behind the sea wall and watched the moonlight on the Mediterranean. Parallel banks of faintly silvered clouds arched over us to northward; the air was fresh and cool.

After a while I said, "You know that I'm only playing this your way for one reason. As far as the rest of it goes, the more I think about it the less I like it."

"Why?"

"A dozen reasons. The biological angle, for one. I don't like violence, I don't like war, but it doesn't matter what I like. They're biologically necessary, they eliminate the unfit."

"Do you say that only the unfit are killed in wars?"

"That isn't what I mean. In modern war the contest isn't between individuals, it's between whole populations. Nations, and groups of nations. It's a cruel, senseless, wasteful business, and when you're in the middle of it it's hard to see any good at all in it, but it works—the survivors *survive,* and that's the only test there is."

"Our biologists do not take this view." He added, "Neither do yours."

I said, "How's that?"

"Your biologists agree with ours that war is not biological. It is social. When so many are killed, no stock improves. All suffer. It is as you yourself say, the contest is between nations. But their wars kill men."

I said, "All right, I concede that one. But we're not the only kind of animal on this planet, and we didn't get to be the dominant species without fighting. What are we supposed to do if we run into a hungry lion—argue with him?"

"In a few weeks there will be no more lions."

I stared at him. "This affects lions, too? Tigers, elephants, everything?"

"Everything of sufficient brain. Roughly, everything above the level of your insects."

"But I understood you to say that the catalyst—that it took a different catalyst for each species."

"No. All those with spines and warm blood have the same ancestors. Your snakes may perhaps need a different catalyst, and I believe you have some primitive sea creatures which kill, but they are not important."

I said, "My God." I thought of lions, wolves, coyotes, house cats, lying dead beside their prey. Eagles, hawks and owls tumbling out of the sky. Ferrets, stoats, weasels . . .

The world a big garden, for protected children.

My fists clenched. "But this is a million times worse than I had any idea. It's insane. You're upsetting the whole natural balance, you're knocking it crossways. Just for a start, what the hell are we going to do about rats and mice? That's—" I choked on my tongue. There were too many images in my mind to put any of them into words. Rats like a tidal wave, filling a street from wall to wall. Deer swarming out of the forests. The sky blackening with crows, sparrows, jays.

"It will be difficult for some years," Aza-Kra said. "Perhaps even as difficult as you now think. But you say that to fight for survival is good. Is it not better to fight against other species than among yourselves?"

"Fight!" I said. "What have you left us to fight with? How many rats can a man kill before he drops dead from shock?"

"It is possible to kill without causing pain or shock. . . . You would have thought of this, although it is a new idea for you. Even your killing of animals for food can continue. We do not ask you to become as old as we are in a day. Only to put behind you your cruelty which has no purpose."

He had answered me, as always; and as always, the answer was two-edged. It was possible to kill painlessly, yes. And the only weapon Aza-Kra had brought to Earth, apparently, was an anesthetic gas. . . .

We landed at Srinagar, in the Vale of Kashmir, at high noon: a sea of white light under a molten-metal sky.

Crossing the field, I saw a group of white-turbaned figures standing at the gate. I squinted at them through the glare; heat waves made them jump and waver, but in a moment I was sure. They were bush-bearded Sikh policemen, and there were eight of them.

I pressed Aza-Kra's arm sharply and held my breath.

A moment later we picked our way through the sprawled line of passengers to the huddle of bodies at the gate. The passport examiner, a slender Hindu, lay a yard from the Sikhs. I plucked a sheet of paper out of his hand.

Sure enough, it was a list of the serial numbers of the passports we had stolen from the Paris consulate.

Bad luck. It was only six-thirty in Paris now, and on a Saturday morning at that; we should have had at least six hours more. But something could have gone wrong at any one of the seven consulates—an after-hours appointment, or a worried wife, say. After that the whole thing would have unraveled.

"How much did you give them this time?" I asked.

"As before. Twenty hours."

"All right, good. Let's go."

He had overshot his range a little: all four of the hack drivers waiting outside the airport building were snoring over their wheels. I dumped the skinniest one in the back seat with Aza-Kra and took over.

Not for the first time, it occurred to me that without me or somebody just like me Aza-Kra would be helpless. It wasn't just a matter of getting out of Chillicothe; he couldn't drive a car or fly a plane, he couldn't pass for human by himself; he couldn't speak without giving himself away. Free, with no broken bones, he could probably

escape recapture indefinitely; but if he wanted to go anywhere he would have to walk.

And not for the first time, I tried to see into a history
book that hadn't been written yet. My name was there,
that much was certain, providing there was going to be
any history to write. But was it a name like Blondel . . . or
did it sound more like Vidkun Quisling?

We had to go south; there was nothing in any other
direction but the highest mountains in the world. We didn't
have Pakistan visas, so Lahore and Amritsar, the obvious
first choices, were out. The best we could do was Chamba,
about two hundred rail miles southeast on the Srinagar-
New Delhi line. It wasn't on the principal air routes, but
we could get a plane there to Saharanpur, which was.

There was an express leaving in half an hour, and we
took it. I bought an English-language newspaper at the
station and read it backward and forward for four hours;
Aza-Kra spent the time apparently asleep, with his cone,
hidden by the black hat, tilted out the window.

The "epidemic" had spread to five western states, plus
Quebec, Ontario and Manitoba, and parts of Mexico and
Cuba . . . plus England and France, I knew, but there was
nothing about that in my Indian paper; too early.

In Chamba I bought the most powerful battery-operated
portable radio I could find; I wished I had thought of it
sooner. I checked with the airport: there was a flight
leaving Saharanpur for Port Blair at eight o'clock.

Port Blair, in the Andamans, is Indian territory; we
wouldn't need to show our passports. What we were going
to do after that was another question.

I could have raided another set of consulates, but I
knew it would be asking for trouble. Once was bad enough;
twice, and when we tried it a third time—as we would
have to, unless I found some other answer—I was willing
to bet we would find them laying for us, with gas masks
and riot guns.

Somehow, in the few hours we were to spend at Port
Blair, I had to get those serial numbers altered by an expert.

We had been walking the black, narrow dockside streets
for two hours when Aza-Kra suddenly stopped.

"Something?"

"Wait," he said. ". . . Yes. This is the man you are looking for. He is a professional forger. His name is George Wheelwright. He can do it, but I do not know whether he will. He is a very timid and suspicious man."

"All right. In here?"

"Yes."

We went up a narrow unlighted stairway, choked with a kitchen-midden of smells, curry predominating. At the second floor landing Aza-Kra pointed to a door. I knocked.

Scufflings behind the door. A low voice: "Who's that?"

"A friend. Let us in, Wheelwright."

The door cracked open and yellow light spilled out; I saw the outline of a head and the faint gleam of a bulbous eye. "What d'yer want?"

"Want you to do a job for me, Wheelwright. Don't keep us talking here in the hall."

The door opened wider and I squeezed through into a cramped, untidy box of a kitchen. A faded cloth covered the doorway to the next room.

Wheelwright glanced at Aza-Kra and then stared hard at me; he was a little chicken-breasted wisp of a man dressed in dungarees and a striped polo shirt. "Who sent yer?"

"You wouldn't know the name. A friend of mine in Calcutta." I took out the passports. "Can you fix these?"

He looked at them carefully, taking his time. "What's wrong with 'em?"

"Nothing but the serial numbers."

"What's wrong with *them?*"

"They're on a list."

He laughed, a short, meaningless bark.

I said, "Well?"

"Who'd yer say yer friend in Calcutter was?"

"I haven't any friend in Calcutta. Never mind how I knew about you. Will you do the job or won't you?"

He handed the passports back and moved toward the door. "Mister, I haven't got the time to fool with yer. Perhaps yer having me on, or perhaps yer've made an honest mistake. There's another Wheelwright over on the north side of town. You try him." He opened the door. "Good night, both."

I pushed it shut again and reached for him, but he was a yard away in one jump, like a rabbit. He stood beside the table, arms hanging, and stared at me with a vague smile.

I said, "I haven't got time to play games, either. I'll pay you five hundred American dollars to alter these passports"—I tossed them onto the table—"or else I'll beat the living tar out of you." I took a step toward him.

I never saw a man move faster: he had the drawer open and the gun out and aimed before I finished that step. But the muzzle trembled slightly. "No nearer," he said hoarsely.

I thought, *Five minutes,* and held my breath.

When he slumped, I picked up the revolver. Then I lifted him—he weighed about ninety pounds—propped him in a chair behind the table, and waited.

In a few minutes he raised his head and goggled at me dazedly. "How'd yer do that?" he whispered.

I put the money on the table beside the passports. "Start," I said.

He stared at it, then at me. His thin lips tightened. "Go ter blazes," he said.

I stepped around the table and cuffed him backhand. I felt the blow on my own face, hard and stinging, but I did it again. I kept it up. It wasn't pleasant; I was feeling not only the blows themselves, but Wheelwright's emotional responses, the shame and wretchedness and anger, and the queasy writhing fear: Wheelwright couldn't bear pain.

At that, he beat me. When I stopped, sickened and dizzy, and said as roughly as I could, "Had enough, Wheelwright?" he answered, "Not if yer was ter kill me, yer bloody barstid."

His voice trembled, and his face was streaked with tears, but he meant it. He thought I was a government agent, trying to bully him into signing his own prison sentence, and rather than let me do it he would take any amount of punishment; prison was the one thing he feared more than physical pain.

I looked at Aza-Kra. His neck-spines were erect and quivering; I could see the tips of them at the edges of the veil. Then inspiration hit me.

I pulled him forward where the little man could see him, and lifted the veil. The feathery spines stood out clearly on either side of the corpse-white mask.

"I won't touch you again," I said. "But look at this. Can you see?"

His eyes widened; he scrubbed them with the palms of his hands and looked again.

"And this," I said. I pulled at Aza-Kra's forearm and the clawed blue-gray hand came out of the muff.

Wheelwright's eyes bulged. He flattened himself against the back of the chair.

"Now," I said, "six hundred dollars—or I'll take this mask off and show you what's behind it."

He clenched his eyes shut. His face had gone yellowish-pale; his nostrils were white.

"Get it out of here," he said faintly.

He didn't move until Aza-Kra had disappeared behind the curtain into the other room. Then, without a word, he poured and drank half a tumblerful of whisky, switched on a gooseneck lamp, produced bottles, pens and brushes from the table drawer, and went to work. He bleached away the first and last digits of both serial numbers, then painted over the areas with a thin wash of color that matched the blue tint of the paper. With a jeweler's loupe in his eye, he restored the obliterated tiny letters of the background design; finally, still using the loupe, he drew the new digits in black. From first to last, it took him thirty minutes; and his hands didn't begin to tremble until he was done.

V

The sixth day was two days—because we left Otaru at 3:30 P.M. Sunday and arrived at Honolulu at 4:00 A.M. Saturday. We had lost five hours in traversing sixty-one degrees of longitude—but we'd also gained a day by crossing the International Date Line from west to east.

On the sixth day, then, which was two days, the following things happened and were duly reported:

Be Done By As Ye Do was the title of some thousands of sermons and, by count, more than seven hundred front-page newspaper editorials from Newfoundland to Oaxaca. My cable to Freeman had come a little late; the *Herald-Star*'s announcement was lost in the ruck.

Following this, a wave of millennial enthusiasm swept the continent; Christians and Jews everywhere feasted, fasted, prayed and in other ways celebrated the imminent Second (or First) Coming of Christ. Evangelistic and fundamentalist sects garnered souls by the million.

Members of the Apostolic Overcoming Holy Church of God, the Pentecostal Fire Baptized Holiness Church and numerous other groups gave away most or all of their worldly possessions. Others were more practical. The Seventh Day Adventists, who are vegetarians, pooled capital and began an enormous expansion of their meatless-food factories, dairies and other enterprises.

Delegates to a World Synod of Christian Churches began arriving at a tent city near Smith Center, Kansas, late Saturday night. Trouble developed almost immediately between the Brethren Church of God (Reformed Dunkers) and the Two-Seed-in-the-Spirit Predestinarian Baptists—later spreading to a schism which led to the establishment of two rump synods, one at Lebanon and the other at Athol.

Five hundred Doukhobors stripped themselves mother-naked, burned their homes, and marched on Vancouver.

Roman Catholics in most places celebrated the Feast of the Transfiguration as usual, awaiting advice from Rome.

Riots broke out in Chicago, Detroit, New Orleans, Philadelphia, and New York. In each case the original disturbances were brief, but were followed by protracted vandalism and looting which local police, state police, and even National Guard units were unable to check. By midnight Sunday property damage was estimated at more than twenty million dollars. The casualty list was fantastically high. So was the proportion of police and National Guard casualties—exactly 50 percent of the total. . . .

In the British Isles, Western Europe and Scandinavia, the early symptoms of the Western Hemisphere's disaster were beginning to appear: the stricken slaughterers and fishermen, the unease in prisons, the freaks of violence.

An unprecedented number of political refugees turned up on the West German side of the Burnt Corridor early Saturday morning.

Late the same day, a clash between Sikh and Moslem guards on the India-Pakistan border near Sialkot resulted in the annihilation of both parties.

And on Sunday it hit the fighting in Indochina.

Allied and Communist units, engaging at sixty points along the eight-hundred-mile front, fell back with the heaviest casualties of the war.

Red bombers launched a successful daylight attack on

Luangprabang: successful, that is, except that nineteen out of twenty planes crashed outside the city or fell into the Nam Ou.

Forty Allied bombers took off on sorties to Yen-bay, Hanoi and Nam-dinh. None returned.

Nobody knew it yet, but the war was over.

Still other things happened but were not recorded by the press:

A man in Arizona, a horse gelder by profession, gave up his business and moved out of the county, alleging ill health.

So did a dentist in Tacoma, and another in Galveston.

In Breslau an official of the People's Police resigned his position with the same excuse; and one in Buda; and one in Pest.

A conservative Tajik tribesman of Indarab, discovering that his new wife had been unfaithful, attempted to deal with her in the traditional manner, but desisted when a critical observer would have said he had hardly begun; nor did this act of compassion bring him any relief.

And outside the town of Otaru, just two hundred and fifty miles across the Sea of Japan from the eastern shore of the Russian Socialist Federated Soviet Republic, Aza-Kra used his anesthetic gas again—on me.

I had been bone-tired when we left Port Blair shortly before midnight, but I hadn't slept all the long dark droning way to Manila; or from there to Tokyo, with the sun rising half an hour after we cleared the Philippines and slowly turning the globe underneath us to a white disk of fire; or from Tokyo north again to Otaru, bleak and windy and smelling of brine.

In all that time, I hadn't been able to forget Wheelwright except for half an hour toward the end, when I picked up an English-language broadcast from Tokyo and heard the news from the States.

The first time you burn yourself playing with matches, the chances are that if the blisters aren't too bad, you get over it fast enough; you forget about it. But the second time, it's likely to sink in.

Wheelwright was my second time; Wheelwright finished me.

It's more than painful, it's more than frightening, to

cause another living creature pain and feel what he feels. It tears you apart. It makes you the victor and the victim, and neither half of that is bearable.

It makes you love what you destroy—as you love yourself—and it makes you hate yourself as your victim hates you.

That isn't all. I had felt Wheelwright's self-loathing as his body cringed and the tears spilled out of his eyes, the helpless gut-twisting shame that was as bad as the fear; and that burden was on me too.

Wheelwright was talented. That was his own achievement; he had found it in himself and developed it and trained himself to use it. Wheelwright had courage. That was his own. But who had made Wheelwright afraid? And who had taught him that the world was his enemy?

You, and I, and every other human being on the planet, and all our two-legged ancestors before us. Because we had settled for too little. Because not more than a handful of us, out of all the crawling billions, had ever had the will to break the chain of blows, from father to daughter to son, generation after generation.

So there was Wheelwright; that was what we had made out of man: the artistry and the courage compressed to a needle-thin, needle-hard core inside him, and that only because we hadn't been able to destroy it altogether; the rest of him self-hatred, and suspicion, and resentment, and fear.

But after breakfast in Tokyo, it began to seem a little more likely that some kind of a case could be made for the continued existence of the human race. And after that it was natural to think about lions, and about the rioting that was going on in America.

For all his moral nicety, Aza-Kra had no trouble in justifying the painful extinction of carnivores. From his point of view, they were better off dead. It was regrettable, of course, but . . .

But, *sub specie aeternitatis*, was a man much different from a lion?

It was a commonplace that no other animal killed on so grand a scale as man. The problem had never come up before: could we live without killing?

I was standing with Aza-Kra at the top of a little hill that overlooked the coast road and the bay. The bus tha had brought us there was dwindling, a white speck in a cloud of dust, down the highway toward Cape Kamui.

Aza-Kra sat on a stone, his third leg grotesquely bulging the skirt of his coat. His head bent forward, as if the old woman he was pretending to be had fallen asleep, chin on massive chest; the conical hat pointed out to sea.

I said, "This is the time of crisis you were talking about, for America."

"Yes. It begins now."

"When does it end? Let's talk about this a little more. This justice. Crimes of violence—all right. They punish themselves, and before long they'll prevent themselves automatically. What about crimes of property? A man steals my wallet and runs. Or he smashes a window and takes what he wants. Who's going to stop him?"

He didn't answer for a moment; when he did the words came slowly and the pronunciation was bad, as if he were too weary to attend to it. "The wallet can be chained to your clothing. The window can be made of glass that does not break."

I said impatiently, "You know that's not what I mean. I'm talking about the problem as it affects everybody. We solve it by policemen and courts and prisons. What do we do instead?"

"I am sorry that I did not understand you. Give me a moment. . . ."

I waited.

"In your Middle Ages, when a man was insane, what did you do?"

I thought of Bedlam, and of creatures with matted hair chained to rooftops.

He didn't wait for me to speak. "Yes. And now, you are more wise?"

"A little."

"Yes. And in the beginning of your Industrial Revolution, when a factory stopped and men had no work; what was done?"

"They starved."

"And now?"

"There are relief organizations. We try to keep them alive until they can get work."

"If a man steals what he does not need," Aza-Kra said, "is he not sick? If a man steals what he must have to live, can you blame him?"

Socrates, in an onyx-trimmed dress, three-legged on a stone.

Finally I said, "It's easy enough to make us look foolish, but we have made some progress in the last two thousand years. Now you want us to go the rest of the way overnight. It's impossible; we haven't got time enough."

"You will have more time now." His voice was very faint. "Killing wastes much time. . . . Forgive me, now I must sleep."

His head dropped even farther forward. I watched for a while to see if he would topple over, but of course he was too solidly based. A tripod. I sat down beside him, feeling my own fatigue drag at my body, envying him his rest; but I couldn't sleep.

There was really no point in arguing with him, I told myself; he was too good for me. I was a savage splitting logic with a missionary. He knew more than I did; probably he was more intelligent. And the central question, the only one that mattered, couldn't be answered the way I was going at it.

Aza-Kra himself was the key, not the doctrine of non-violence, not the psychology of crime.

If he was telling the truth about himself and the civilization he came from, I had nothing to worry about.

If he wasn't, then I should have left him in Chillicothe or killed him in Paris; and if I could kill him now, that was what I should do.

And I didn't know. After all this time, I still didn't know.

I saw the bus come back down the road and disappear toward Otaru. After a long time, I saw it heading out again. When it came back from the cape the second time, I woke Aza-Kra and we slogged down the steep path to the roadside. I waved as the bus came nearer; it slowed and rattled to a halt a few yards beyond us.

Passengers' heads popped out of the windows to watch us as we walked toward the door. Most of them were Japanese, but I saw one Caucasian, leaning with both arms out of the window. I saw his features clearly, narrow pale nose and lips, blue eyes behind rimless glasses; sunlight glinting on sparse yellow hair. And then I saw the flat dusty road coming up to meet me.

*   *   *

I was lying face-up on a hard sandy slope; when I opened my eyes I saw the sky and a few blades of tough, dry grass. The first thought that came into my head was, *Now I know. Now I've had it.*

I sat up. And a buzzing voice said, "Hold your breath!"

Turning, I saw a body sprawled on the slope just below me. It was the yellow-haired man. Beyond him squatted the gray form of Aza-Kra.

"All right," he said.

I let my breath out. "What—"

He showed me a brown metal ovoid, cross-hatched with fragmentation grooves. A grenade.

"He was about to arm it. There was no time to warn you. I knew you would wish to see for yourself."

I looked around dazedly. Thirty feet above, the slope ended in a clean-cut line against the sky; beyond it was a short, narrow white stripe that I recognized as the top of the bus, still parked at the side of the road.

"We have ten minutes more before the others awaken."

I went through the man's pockets. I found a handful of change, a wallet with nothing in it but a few yen notes, and a folded slip of glossy white paper. That was all.

I unfolded the paper, but I knew what it was even before I saw the small teleprinted photograph on its inner side. It was a copy of my passport picture—the one on the genuine document, not the bogus one I had made in Paris.

On the way back, my hands began shaking. It got so bad that I had to put them between my thighs and squeeze hard; and then the shaking spread to my legs and arms and jaw. My forehead was cold and there was a football-sized ache in my belly, expanding to a white pain every time we hit a bump. The whole bus seemed to be tilting ponderously over to the right, farther and farther but never falling down.

Later, when I had had a cup of coffee and two cigarettes in the terminal lunch room, I got one of the most powerful irrational impulses I've ever known: I wanted to take the next bus back to that spot on the coast road, walk down the slope to where the yellow-haired man was, and kick his skull to flinders.

If we were lucky, the yellow-haired man might have been the only one in Otaru who knew we were here. The only way to find out was to go on to the airport and take a chance; either way, we had to get out of Japan. But it didn't end there. Even if they didn't know where we were now, they knew all the stops on our itinerary; they knew which visas we had. Maybe Aza-Kra would be able to gas the next one before he killed us, and then again maybe not.

I thought about Frisbee and Parst and the president—damning them all impartially—and my anger grew. By now, I realized suddenly, they must have understood that we were responsible for what was happening. They would have been energetically apportioning the blame for the last few days; probably Parst had already been court-martialed.

Once that was settled, there would be two things they could do next. They could publish the truth, admit their own responsibility, and warn the world. Or they could destroy all the evidence and keep silent. If the world went to hell in a bucket, at least they wouldn't be blamed for it. . . . Providing I was dead. Not much choice.

After another minute I got up and Aza-Kra followed me out to a taxi. We stopped at the nearest telegraph office and I sent a cable to Frisbee in Washington:

HAVE SENT FULL ACCOUNT CHILLICOTHE TO TRUST-WORTHY PERSON WITH INSTRUCTIONS PUBLISH EVENT MY DEATH OR DISAPPEARANCE. CALL OFF YOUR DOGS.

It was childish, but apparently it worked. Not only did we have no trouble at Otaru airport—the yellow-haired man, as I'd hoped, must have been working alone—but nobody bothered us at Honolulu or Asunción.

Just the same, the mood of depression and nervousness that settled on me that day didn't lift; it grew steadily worse. Fourteen hours' sleep in Asunción didn't mend it Monday's reports of panics and bank failures in North America intensified it, but that was incidental.

And when I slept, I had nightmares: dreams of stifling dark jungles, full of things with teeth.

We spent twenty-four hours in Asunción, with Aza-Kra pumping out enough catalyst to blanket South America seven million square miles—a territory almost as big the sprawling monster of Soviet Eurasia.

After that we flew to Capetown—and that was it. W were finished.

We had spiraled around the globe, from the Unit States to England, to France, to Israel, to India, to Japa to Paraguay, to the Union of South Africa, trailing an expanding invisible cloud behind us. Now the winds were carrying it westward from the Atlantic, south from the Mediterranean, north from the Indian Ocean, west from the Pacific.

Frigate birds and locusts, men in tramp steamers and men in jet planes would carry it farther. In a week it would have reached all the places we had missed: Australia, Micronesia, the islands of the South Pacific, the Poles.

That left the lunar bases and the orbital stations. Ours and Theirs. But they had to be supplied from Earth; the infection would come to them in rockets.

For better or worse, we had what we had always said we wanted. Ahimsa. The Age of Reason. The Kingdom of God.

And I still didn't know whether I was Judas, or the little Dutch boy with his finger in the dike.

I didn't find out until three weeks later.

We stayed on in Capetown, resting and waiting. Listening to the radio and reading newspapers kept me occupied a good part of the time. When restlessness drove me out of doors, I wandered aimlessly in the business section, or went down to the harbor and spent hours staring out past the castle and the breakwater.

But my chief occupation, the thing that obsessed me now, was the study of Aza-Kra.

He seemed very tired. His skin was turning dry and rough, more gray than blue; his eyes were blue-threaded and more opaque-looking than ever. He slept a great deal and moved little. The soy-bean paste I was able to get for him gave him insufficient nourishment; vitamins and minerals were lacking.

I asked him why he didn't make what he needed in his air machine. He said that some few of the compounds could be inhaled, and he was making those; that he had had another transmuter, for food manufacture, but that it had been taken from him; and that he would be all right; he would last until his friends came.

He didn't know when that would be; or he wouldn't tell me.

His speech was slower and his diction more slurred every day. It was obviously difficult for him to talk; but I goaded him, I nagged him, I would not let him alone. I

spent days on one topic, left it, came back to it and aske
the same questions over. I made copious notes of what h
said and the way he said it.

I wanted to learn to read the signs of his emotions; o
failing that, to catch him in a lie.

A dozen times I thought I had trapped him into a con
tradiction, and each time, wearily, patiently, he explaine
what I had misunderstood. As for his emotions, they ha
only one visible sign that I was able to discover: th
stiffening and trembling of his neck-spines.

Gestures of emotion are arbitrary. There are huma
tribes whose members never smile. There are others wh
smile when they are angry. Cf. Dodgson's Cheshire Cat.

He was doing it more and more often as the time wer
by; but what did it mean? Anger? Resentment? Annoyance
Amusement?

The riots in the United States ended on the ninth an
tenth when interfaith committees toured each city in lou
speaker trucks. Others began elsewhere.

Business was at a standstill in most larger cities. Galve
ton, Nashville, and Birmingham joined in celebratin
Hallelujah Week: dancing in the streets, bonfires day an
night, every church and every bar roaring wide open.

Russia's delegate to the United Nations, who had bee
larding his speeches with mock-sympathetic references t
the Western nations' difficulties, arose on the ninth an
delivered a furious three-hour tirade accusing the enti
non-Communist world of cowardly cryptofascistic biolog
cal warfare against the Soviet Union and the People
Republics of Europe and Asia.

The new staffs of the federal penitentiaries in Americ
in office less than a week, followed their predecessors i
mass resignations. The last official act of the wardens
Leavenworth, Terre Haute, and Alcatraz was to report th
"escape" of their entire prison populations.

Police officers in every major city were being frantical
urged to remain on duty.

Queen Elizabeth, in a memorable speech, exhorted
citizens of the empire to remain calm and meet whatev
might come with dignity, fortitude and honor.

The Scots stole the Stone of Scone again.

Rioting and looting began in Paris, Marseilles, Ba
celona, Milan, Amsterdam, Munich, Berlin.

The pope was silent.

Turkey declared war on Syria and Iraq; peace was concluded a record three hours later.

On the tenth, Warsaw Radio announced the formation of a new Polish provisional government whose first and second acts had been, respectively, to abrogate all existing treaties with the Soviet Union and border states, and to petition the UN for restoration of the 1938 boundaries.

On the eleventh, East Germany, Austria, Czechoslovakia, Hungary, Rumania, Bulgaria, Latvia, and Lithuania followed suit, with variations on the boundary question.

On the twelfth, after a brief but by no means bloodless putsch, the Spanish Republic was reestablished; the British government fell once and the French government twice; and the Vatican issued a sharp protest against the ill-treatment of priests and nuns by Spanish insurgents.

Not a shot had been fired in Indochina since the morning of the eighth.

On the thirteenth, the Karelo-Finnish S.S.R., the Estonian S.S.R., the Byelorussian S.S.R., the Ukrainian S.S.R., the Azerbaijan S.S.R., the Turkmen S.S.R., and the Uzbek S.S.R. declared their independence of the Soviet Union. A horde of men and women escaped or released from forced-labor camps, the so-called Slave Army, poured westward out of Siberia.

VI

On the fourteenth, Zebulon, Georgia (pop. 312), Murfreesboro, Tennessee (pop. 11,190), and Orange, Texas (pop. 8,470) seceded from the Union.

That might have been funny, but on the fifteenth petitions for a secession referendum were circulating in Tennessee, Arkansas, Louisiana, and South Carolina. Early returns averaged 61 percent in favor.

On the sixteenth, Texas, Oklahoma, Mississippi, Alabama, Kentucky, Virginia, Georgia, and—incongruously—Rhode Island and Minnesota added themselves to the list. Separatist fever was rising in Quebec, New Brunswick, Newfoundland and Labrador. Across the Atlantic, Catalonia, Bavaria, Moldavia, Sicily, and Cyprus declared themselves independent states.

And that might have been hysteria. But that wasn't all. Liquor stores and bars were sprouting like mushrooms in dry states. Ditto gambling halls, horse rooms, houses of prostitution, cockpits, burlesque theaters.

Moonshine whisky threatened for a few days to become the South's major industry, until standard-brand distillers cut their prices to meet the competition. Not a bottle of the new stocks of liquor carried a federal tax stamp.

Mexican citizens were walking across the border into Arizona and New Mexico, swimming into Texas. The first shipload of Chinese arrived in San Francisco on the sixteenth.

Meat prices had increased by an average of 60 percent for every day since the new control and rationing law took effect. By the sixteenth, round steak was selling for $10.80 a pound.

Resignations of public officials were no longer news; a headline in the Portland *Oregonian* for August 15th read:

WILL STAY AT DESK, SAYS GOVERNOR.

It hit me hard.

But when I thought about it, it was obvious enough; it was such an elementary thing that ordinarily you never noticed it—that all governments, not just tyrannies, but *all* governments were based on violence, as currency was based on metal. You might go for months or years without seeing a silver dollar or a policeman; but the dollar and the policeman had to be there.

The whole elaborate structure, the work of a thousand years, was coming down. The value of a dollar is established by a promise of pay; the effectiveness of a law, by a threat to punish.

Even if there were enough jailers left, how could you put a man in jail if he had ten or twenty friends who didn't want him to go?

How many people were going to pay their income taxes next year, even if there was a government left to pay them to?

And who was going to stop the landless people from spilling over into the nations that had land to spare?

Aza-Kra said, "These things are not necessary to do."

I turned around and looked at him. He had been lying motionless for more than an hour in the hammock I had rigged for him at the end of the room; I had thought he was asleep.

It was raining outside. Dim, colorless light came through the slotted window blinds and striped his body like a melted barber pole. Caught in one of the bars of light, the tips of two quivering neck-spines glowed in faint filigree against the shadow.

"All right," I said. "Explain this one away. I'd like to hear you. Tell me why we don't need governments anymore."

"The governments you have now—the governments of nations—they are not made for use. They exist to fight other nations."

"That's not true."

"It is true. Think. Of the money your government spends, in a year, how much is for war and how much for use?"

"About sixty percent for war. But that doesn't—"

"Please. This is sixty percent now, when you have only a small war. When you have a large war, how much then?"

"Ninety percent. Maybe more, but that hasn't got anything to do with it. In peace *or* wartime there are things a national government does that can't be done by anybody else. Now ask me for instance, what."

"Yes. I ask this."

"For instance, keeping an industrial country from being dragged down to coolie level by unrestricted immigration."

"You think it is better for those who have much to keep apart from those who have little and give no help?"

"In principle, no, but it isn't just that easy. What good does it do the starving Asiatics if we turn America into another piece of Asia and starve along with them?"

He looked at me unwinkingly.

"What good has it done to keep apart?"

I opened my mouth, and shut it again. Last time it had been Japan, an island chain a little smaller than California. In the next one, half the world would have been against us.

"The problem is not easy, it is very difficult. But to solve it by helping is possible. To solve it by doing nothing is not possible."

"Harbors," I said. "Shipping. Soil conservation. Communications. Flood control."

"You do not believe these things can be done if there are no nations?"

"No. We haven't got time enough to pick up all the pieces. It's a hell of a lot easier to knock things apart than to put them together again."

"Your people have done things more difficult than this. You do not believe now, but you will see it done."

After a moment I said, "We're supposed to become a member of your galactic union now. Now that you've pulled our teeth. Who's going to build the ships?"

"Those who build them now."

I said, "Governments build them now."

"No. Men build ships. Men invent ships and design ships. Government builds nothing but more government."

I put my fists in my pockets and walked over to the window. Outside, a man went hurrying by in the rain, one hand at his hat brim, the other at his chest. He didn't look around as he passed; his coffee-brown face was intent and impersonal. I watched him until he turned the corner, out of sight.

He had never heard of me, but his life would be changed by what I had done. His descendants would know my name; they would be bored by it in school, or their mothers would frighten them with it after dark. . . .

Aza-Kra said, "To talk of these things is useless. If I would lie, I would not tell you that I lie. And if I would lie about these things, I would lie well; you would not find the truth by questions. You must wait. Soon you will know."

I looked at him. "When your friends come."

"Yes," he said.

And the feathery tips of his neck-spines delicately trembled.

They came on the last day of August—fifty great rotiform ships drifting down out of space. No radar spotted them; no planes or interceptor rockets went up to meet them. They followed the terminator around, landing at dawn: thirteen in the Americas, twenty-five in Europe and Asia, five in Africa, one each in England, Scandinavia, Australia, New Zealand, New Guinea, the Philippines, Japan.

Each one was six hundred feet across, but they rested lightly on the ground. Where they landed on sloping ground, slender curved supporting members came out of the doughnut-shaped rim, as dainty as an insect's legs, and the fat lozenge of the hub lowered itself on the five fat spokes until it touched the earth.

Their doors opened.

In twenty-four days I had watched the nations of the Earth melt into shapelessness like sculptures molded of silicone putty. Armies, navies, air forces, police forces lost their cohesion first. In the beginning there were individual desertions, atoms escaping one at a time from the mass; later, when the pay failed to arrive, when there were no orders or else orders that could not be executed, men and women simply went home, orderly, without haste, in thousands.

Every useful item of equipment that could be carried or driven or flown went with them. Tractors, trucks, jeeps, bulldozers gladdened the hearts of farmers from Keokuk to Kweiyang. Bombers, small boats, even destroyers and battleships were in service as commercial transports. Quartermasters' stores were carried away piecemeal or in ton lots. Guns and ammunition rusted undisturbed.

Stock markets crashed. Banks failed. Treasuries failed. National governments broke down into states, provinces, cantons. In the United States, the president resigned his office on the eighteenth and left the White House, whose every window had been broken and whose lawn was newly landscaped with eggshells and orange rind. The vice-president resigned the next day, leaving the presidency, in theory, to the Speaker of the House; but the Speaker was at home on his Arkansas farm; Congress had adjourned on the seventeenth.

Everywhere it was the same. The new governments of Asia and Eastern Europe, of Spain and Portugal and Argentina and Iran, died stillborn.

The Moon colonies had been evacuated; work had stopped on the Mars rocket. The men on duty in the orbital stations, after an anxious week, had reached an agreement for mutual disarmament and had come down to Earth.

Seven industries out of ten had closed down. The dollar was worth half a penny, the pound sterling a little more; the ruble, the Reichsmark, the franc, the sen, the yen, the rupee were waste paper.

The great cities were nine-tenths deserted, gutted by fires, the homes of looters, rats and roaches.

Even the local governments, the states, the cantons, the

counties, the very townships, were too fragile to stand. All the arbitrary lines on the map had lost their meaning.

You could not say anymore, "Japan will—" or "India is moving toward—" It was startling to realize that; to have to think of a sprawling, amorphous, unfathomable mass of infinitely varied human beings instead of a single inclusive symbol. It made you wonder if the symbol had ever had any connection with reality at all: whether there had ever been such a thing as a nation.

Toward the end of the month, I thought I saw a flicker of hope. The problem of famine was being attacked vigorously and efficiently by the Red Cross, the Salvation Army, and thousands of local volunteer groups: they commandeered fleets of trucks, emptied warehouses with a calm disregard of legality, and distributed the food where it was most needed. It was not enough—too much food had been destroyed and wasted by looters, too much had spoiled through neglect, and too much had been destroyed in the field by wandering, half-starved bands of the homeless—but it was a beginning; it was something.

Other groups were fighting the problem of these wolf packs, with equally encouraging results. Farmers were forming themselves into mutual-defense groups, "communities of force." Two men could take any property from one man of equal strength without violence, without the penalty of pain; but not from two men, or three men.

One district warned the next when a wolf pack was on the way, and how many to expect. When the pack converged on a field or a storehouse, men in equal or greater numbers were there to stand in the way. If the district could absorb, say, ten workers, that many of the pack were offered the option of staying; the rest had to move on. Gradually, the packs thinned.

In the same way, factories were able to protect themselves from theft. By an extension of the idea, even the money problem began to seem soluble. The old currency was all but worthless, and an individual's promise to pay in kind was no better as a medium of exchange; but promissory notes obligating whole communities could and did begin to circulate. They made an unwieldy currency, their range was limited, and they depreciated rapidly. But it was something; it was a beginning.

Then the wheel-ships came.

In every case but one, they were cautious. They landed in conspicuous positions, near a city or a village, and in the dawn light, before any man had come near them, oddly shaped things came out and hurriedly unloaded boxes and bales, hundreds, thousands, a staggering array. They set up sun-reflecting beacons; then the ships rose again and disappeared, and when the first men came hesitantly out to investigate, they found nothing but the beacon, the acre of carefully stacked boxes and the signs, in the language of the country, that said:

THIS FOOD IS SENT BY THE PEOPLES OF OTHER WORLDS TO HELP YOU IN YOUR NEED. ALL MEN ARE BROTHERS.

And a brave man would lift the top of a box; inside he would see other boxes, and in them oblong pale shapes wrapped in something transparent that was not cellophane. He would unwrap one, feel it, smell it, show it around, and finally taste it; and then his eyebrows would go up.

The color and the texture were unfamiliar, but the taste was unmistakable! Tortillas and beans! (Or taro; or rice with bean sprouts; or stuffed grape leaves; or herb omelette!)

The exception was the ship that landed outside Cape-town, in an open field at the foot of Table Mountain.

Aza-Kra woke me at dawn. "They are here."

I mumbled at him and tried to turn over. He shook my shoulder again, buzzing excitedly to himself. "Please, they are here. We must hurry."

I lurched out of bed and stood swaying. "Your friends?" I said.

"Yes, yes." He was struggling into the black dress, pushing the peaked hat backward onto his head. *"Hurry."*

I splashed cold water on my face, and got into my clothes. I pulled out the top dresser drawer and looked at the two loaded automatics. I couldn't decide. I couldn't figure out any way they would do me any good, but I didn't want to leave them behind. I stood there until my legs went numb before I could make up my mind to take them anyhow, and the hell with it.

There were no taxis, of course. We walked three blocks

along the deserted streets until we saw a battered sedan nose into view in the intersection ahead, moving cautiously around the heaps of litter.

"Hold your breath!"

The car moved on out of sight. We found it around the corner, up on the sidewalk with the front fender jammed against a railing. There were two men and a woman in it, Europeans.

"Which way?"

"Left. To the mountain."

When we got to the outskirts and the buildings began to thin out, I saw it up ahead, a huge silvery-metal shelf jutting out impossibly from the slope. I began to tremble. *They'll cut me up and put me in a jar,* I thought. *Now is the time to stop, if I'm going to.*

But I kept going. Where the road veered away from the field and went curving on up the mountain the other way, I stopped and we got out. I saw dark shapes and movements under that huge gleaming bulk. We stepped over a broken fence and started across the dry, uneven clods in the half-light.

Light sprang out: a soft, pearl-gray shimmer that didn't dazzle the eye although it was aimed straight toward us, marking the way. I heard a shrill wordless buzzing, and above that an explosion of chirping, and under them both a confusion of other sounds, humming, droning, clattering. I saw a half-dozen nightmare shapes bounding forward.

Two of them were like Aza-Kra; two more were squat things with huge humped shells on top, like tortoise shells the size of a card table, with six long stump-ended legs underneath, and a tangle of eyes, tentacles, and small wriggly things peeping out in front; one, the tallest, had a long sharp-spined column of a body rising from a thick base and four startlingly human legs, and surmounted by four long whiplike tentacles and a smooth oval head; the sixth looked at first glance like an unholy cross between a grasshopper and a newt. He came in twenty-foot bounds.

They crowded around Aza-Kra, humming, chirping, droning, buzzing, clattering. Their hands and tentacles went over him, caressingly; the newt-grasshopper thing hoisted him onto its back.

They paid no attention to me, and I stayed where I was, with my hands tight and sweating on the grips of my guns.

Then I heard Aza-Kra speak, and the tallest one turned back to me.

It reeked: something like brine, something like wet fur, something rank and indescribable. It had two narrow red eyes in that smooth knob of a head. It put one of its tentacles on my shoulder, and I didn't see a mouth open anywhere, but a droning voice said, "Thank you for caring for him. Come now. We go to ship."

I pulled away instinctively, quivering, and my hands came out of my pockets. I heard a flat, echoing *crack* and a yell, and I saw a red wetness spring out across the smooth skull; I saw the thing topple and lie in the dirt, twitching.

I thought for an instant that I had done it, the shot, the yell and all. Then I heard another yell, behind me; I whirled around and heard a car grind into gear and saw it bouncing away down the road into town, lights off, a black moving shape on the dimness. I saw it veer wildly and slew into the fence at the first turn; I heard its tires popping as it went through and the muffled crash as it turned over.

Dead, I thought. But the next time I looked I saw two figures come erect beyond the overturned car and stagger toward the road. They disappeared around the turn, running.

I looked back at the others, bewildered. They weren't even looking that way; they were gathered around the body, lifting it, carrying it toward the ship.

The feeling—the black depression that had been getting stronger every day for three weeks—tightened down on me as if somebody had turned a screw. I gritted my teeth against it, and stood there wishing I were dead.

They were almost to that open hatch in the oval hub that hung under the rim when Aza-Kra detached himself from the group and walked slowly back to me. After a moment one of the others—a hump-shelled one—trundled along after him and waited a yard or two away.

"It is not your fault," said Aza-Kra. "We could have prevented it, but we were careless. We were so glad to meet that we did not take precautions. It is not your fault. Come to the ship."

The hump-shelled thing came up and squeaked something, and Aza-Kra sat on its back. The tentacles waved at me. It wheeled and started toward the hatchway. "Come," said Aza-Kra.

I followed them, too miserable to care what happened. We went down a corridor full of the sourceless pearl-gray light until a doorway suddenly appeared, somehow, and we went through that into a room where two tripeds were waiting.

Aza-Kra climbed onto a stool, and one of the tripeds began pressing two small instruments against various parts of his body; the other squirted something from a flexible canister into his mouth.

And as I stood there watching, between one breath and the next, the depression went away.

I felt like a man whose toothache has just stopped; I probed at my mind, gingerly, expecting to find that the feeling was still there, only hiding. But it wasn't. It was gone so completely that I couldn't even remember exactly what it had been like. I felt calm and relaxed—and safe.

I looked at Aza-Kra. He was breathing easily; his eyes looked clearer than they had a moment before, and it seemed to me that his skin was glossier. The feathery neck-spines hung in relaxed, graceful curves.

. . . It was all true, then. It had to be. If they had been conquerors, the automatic death of the man who had killed one of their number, just now, wouldn't have been enough. An occupying army can never be satisfied with an eye for an eye. There must be retaliation.

But they hadn't done anything; they hadn't even used the gas. They'd seen that the others in the car were running away, that the danger was over, and that ended it. The only emotions they had shown, as far as I could tell, were concern and regret—

Except that, I remembered now, I had seen two of the tripeds clearly when I turned back to look at them gathering around the body: Aza-Kra and another one. And their neck-spines had been stiff. . . .

Suddenly I knew the answer.

Aza-Kra came from a world where violence and cruelty didn't exist. To him, the Earth was a jungle—and I was one of its carnivores.

I knew, now, why I had felt the way I had for the last three weeks, and why the feeling had stopped a few minutes ago. My hostility toward him had been partly responsible for his fear, and so I had picked up an echo of it. Undirected fear is, by definition, anxiety, depression, uneasiness—the psychologists' *Angst*. It had stopped because Aza-Kra no longer had to depend on me; he was with his own people again; he was safe.

I knew the reason for my nightmares.

I knew why, time and again when I had expected Aza-Kra to be reading my mind, I had found that he wasn't. He did it only when he had to; it was too painful.

And one thing more:

I knew that when the true history of this time came to be written, I needn't worry about my place in it. My name would be there, all right, but nobody would remember it once he had shut the book.

Nobody would use my name as an insulting epithet, and nobody would carve it on the bases of any statues, either.

I wasn't the hero of the story.

It was Aza-Kra who had come down alone to a planet so deadly that no one else would risk his life on it until he had softened it up. It was Aza-Kra who had lived for nearly a month with a suspicious, irrational, combative, uncivilized flesh-eater. It was Aza-Kra who had used me, every step of the way—used my provincial loyalties and my self-interest and my prejudices.

He had done all that, weary, tortured, half-starved . . . and he'd been scared to death the whole time.

We made two stops up the coast and then moved into Algeria and the Sudan: landing, unloading, taking off again, following the dawn line. The other ships, Aza-Kra explained, would keep on circling the planet until enough food had been distributed to prevent any starvation until the next harvests. This one was going only as far as the middle of the North American continent—to drop me off. Then it was going to take Aza-Kra home.

I watched what happened after we left each place in a vision device they had. In some places there was more hesitation than in others, but in the end they always took the food: in jeep loads, by pack train, in baskets balanced on their heads.

Some of the repeaters worried me. I said, "How do you know it'll get distributed to everybody who needs it?"

I might have known the answer: "They will distribute it. No man can let his neighbor starve while he has plenty."

The famine relief was all they had come for, this time. Later, when we had got through the crisis, they would come back; and by that time, remembering the food, people would be more inclined to take them on their merits instead of shuddering because they had too many eyes or fingers. They would help us when we needed it, they would show us the way up the ladder, but we would have to do the work ourselves.

He asked me not to publish the story of Chillicothe and the month we had spent together. "Later, when it will hurt no one, you can explain. Now there is no need to make anyone ashamed; not even the officials of your government. It was not their fault; they did not make the planet as it was."

So there went even that two-bit chance at immortality.

It was still dawn when we landed on the bluff across the river from my home; sky and land and water were all the same depthless cool gray, except for the hairline of scarlet in the east. Dew was heavy on the grass, and the air had a smell that made me think of wood smoke and dry leaves.

He came out of the ship with me to say good-by.

"Will you be back?" I asked him.

He buzzed wordlessly in a way I had begun to recognize; I think it was his version of a laugh. "I think not for a very long time. I have already neglected my work too much."

"This isn't your work—opening up new planets?"

"No. It is not so common a thing, that a race becomes ready for space travel. It has not happened anywhere in the galaxy for twenty thousand of your years. I believe, and I hope, that it will not happen again for twenty thousand more. No, I am ordinarily a maker of—you have not the word, it is like porcelain, but a different material. Perhaps someday you will see a piece that I have made. It is stamped with my name."

He held out his hand and I took it. It was an awkward grip; his hand felt unpleasantly dry and smooth to me, and I suppose mine was clammy to him. We both let go as soon as we decently could.

Without turning, he walked away from me up the ramp. I said, "Aza-Kra!"

"Yes?"

"Just one more question. The galaxy's a big place. What happens if you miss just one bloodthirsty race that's ready to boil out across the stars—or if nobody has the guts to go and do to them what you did to us?"

"Now you begin to understand," he said. "That is the question the people of Mars asked us about you . . . twenty thousand years ago."

The story ends there, properly, but there's one more thing I want to say.

When Aza-Kra's ship lifted and disappeared, and I walked down to the bottom of the bluff and across the bridge into the city, I knew I was going back to a life that would be a lot different from the one I had known.

For one thing, the *Herald-Star* was all but done for when I came home: wrecked presses, half the staff gone, supplies running out. I worked hard for a little over a year trying to revive it, out of sentiment, but I knew there were more important things to be done than publishing a newspaper.

Like everybody else, I got used to the changes in the world and in the people around me: to the peaceful, unworried feel of places that had been electric with tension; to the kids—the wonderful, incredible kids; to the new kind of excitement, the excitement that isn't like the night before execution, but like the night before Christmas.

But I hadn't realized how much I had changed, myself, until something that happened a week ago.

I'd lost touch with Eli Freeman after the paper folded; I knew he had gone into pest control, but I didn't know where he was or what he was doing until he turned up one day on the wheat-and-dairy farm I help run, south of the Platte in what used to be Nebraska. He's the advance man for a fleet of spray planes working out of Omaha, aborting rabbits.

He stayed on for three days, lining up a few of the stiff-necked farmers in this area that don't believe in hormones or airplanes either; in his free time he helped with the harvest, and I saw a lot of him.

On his last night we talked late, working up from the old times to the new times and back again until there was nothing more to say. Finally, when we had both been quiet for a long time, he said something to me that is the only accolade I am likely to get, and oddly enough, the only one I want.

"You know, Bob, if it wasn't for that unique face of yours, it would be hard to believe you're the same guy I used to work for."

I said, "Hell, was I that bad?"

"Don't get shirty. You were okay. You didn't bleed the help or kick old ladies, but there just wasn't as much *to* you as there is now. I don't know," he said "You're —more human."

More human.

Yes. We all are.

Alien-Human Relations—
A Guide to Further Reading

ESPECIALLY RECOMMENDED:*

(*Editor's Note:* This listing is not intended to be exhaustive—it is, rather, a hitting of highlights, a listing of prominent landmarks. The subject is so broad, and so popular—almost every SF writer has produced *something* that would fit within its elastic boundaries—that an exhaustive listing, if it could be compiled at all, would have taken up half of this book. The intention behind the list is to guide the interested reader to further material on the subject of alien-human relations—material that we ourselves find interesting and entertaining—not to produce a heavily authoritative work of scholarship or a definitive bibliography. The listing is unabashedly arbitrary, its only criteria our own personal tastes. Omissions are the result either of oversight [there are undoubtedly many classic stories we should have listed, but simply could not bring to mind] or of prejudice—we apologize for both but cannot do much about either.)

Novels

BRIAN W. ALDISS, *Starship*
————, *The Long Afternoon of Earth**
POUL ANDERSON, *The Day after Judgement*
————, *The Earthbook of Stormgate*
————, *The Man Who Counts**
————, *The Night Face**
————, *People of the Wind*

Short Stories